**Praise for *New York Times* bestselling author
Diana Palmer**

"Diana Palmer is one of those authors whose
books are always enjoyable. She throws in
romance, suspense and a good story line."
—*The Romance Reader*

"Palmer knows how to make the sparks fly!"
—*Publishers Weekly*

"Diana Palmer is a mesmerizing storyteller
who captures the essence of what a romance
should be."
—*Affaire de Coeur*

**Praise for *New York Times* bestselling author
Maisey Yates**

"Her characters excel at defying the norms
and providing readers with…an emotional
investment."
—*RT Book Reviews* on *Claim Me, Cowboy*
(Top Pick)

"Fans of Robyn Carr and RaeAnne Thayne will
enjoy [Yates's] small-town romance."
—*Booklist* on *Part Time Cowboy*

Author of more than one hundred books, **Diana Palmer** is a multiple *New York Times* bestselling author and one of the top ten romance writers in America. She has a gift for telling even the most sensual tales with charm and humor. Diana lives with her family in Cornelia, Georgia.

www.DianaPalmer.com

Maisey Yates is a *New York Times* bestselling author of more than thirty romance novels. She has a coffee habit she has no interest in kicking and a slight Pinterest addiction. She lives with her husband and children in the Pacific Northwest. When Maisey isn't writing she can be found singing in the grocery store, shopping for shoes online and probably not doing dishes. Check out her website: maiseyyates.com.

New York Times Bestselling Author

DIANA PALMER

ENAMORED

⬥ **HARLEQUIN**® BESTSELLING AUTHOR COLLECTION

ISBN-13: 978-1-335-94243-2

Enamored

Copyright © 2019 by Harlequin Books S.A.

The publisher acknowledges the copyright holders of the individual works as follows:

Enamored
Copyright © 2014 by Diana Palmer

Claim Me, Cowboy
Copyright © 2018 by Maisey Yates

Recycling programs for this product may not exist in your area.

This edition published by arrangement with Harlequin Books S.A.

For questions and comments about the quality of this book, please contact us at CustomerService@Harlequin.com.

® and TM are trademarks of Harlequin Enterprises Limited or its corporate affiliates. Trademarks indicated with ® are registered in the United States Patent and Trademark Office, the Canadian Intellectual Property Office and in other countries.

(H) HARLEQUIN®
™ www.Harlequin.com

Printed in U.S.A.

CONTENTS

Also available from Diana Palmer

For a complete listing of books by Diana Palmer,
please visit dianapalmer.com.

ENAMORED

Diana Palmer

To my Alice with love

Prologue

The gentle face on the starched white pillow was pale and very still. The man looking down at it scowled with unfamiliar concern. For so many years, his emotions had been caged. Tender feelings were a luxury no mercenary could afford, least of all a man with the reputation of Diego Laremos.

But this woman was no stranger, and the emotions he felt when he looked at her were still confused. It had been five years since he'd seen her, yet she seemed not to have aged a day. She would be twenty-five now, he thought absently. He was forty.

He hadn't expected her to be unconscious. When the hospital had contacted him, he almost hadn't come. Melissa Sterling had betrayed him years before. He wasn't anxious to renew their painful acquaintance, but out of curiosity and a sense of duty, he'd made the trip to southern Arizona. Now he was here, and it was not a subterfuge, a trap, as it had been before. She was injured and helpless; she was alive, though he'd given her up for dead all those long years ago. The cold emptiness inside him was giving way to memories, and that he couldn't allow.

He turned, tall and dark and immaculate in his charcoal-gray suit, to stare out the window at the well-kept grounds beyond the second-floor room Melissa Sterling occupied. He had a mustache now that he hadn't sported during the turbulent days she'd shared with him. He was a little more muscular, older. But age had only emphasized his elegant good looks, made him more mature. His dark eyes slid to the bed, to the slender body of this woman, this stranger, who had trapped him into marriage and then deserted him.

Melissa was tall for a woman, although he towered above her. She had long, wavy blond hair that had once curled below her waist. That had been cut, so that now it curved around her wan oval face. Her eyes were blue-shadowed, closed, her perfect mouth almost as white as her face, her straight nose barely wrinkling now and again as it protested the air tubes taped to it. She seemed surrounded by electronic equipment, by wires that led to various monitors.

An accident, the attending physician had said over a worse-than-poor telephone conversation the day before. An airplane crash that, by some miracle, she and the pilot and several other passengers on the commuter flight from Phoenix had survived. The plane had gone down in the desert outside Tucson, and she'd been brought here to the general hospital, unconscious. The emergency room staff had found a worn, carefully folded paper in her wallet that contained the only evidence of her marital status. A marriage license, written in Spanish; the fading ink stated that she was the *esposa* of one Diego Alejandro Rodriguez Ruiz Laremos of Dos Rios, Guatemala. Was Diego her husband, the physician had persisted, and if so, would he authorize emergency surgery to save her life?

He vaguely recalled asking if she had no other relatives, but the doctor had told him that her pitifully few belongings gave no evidence of any. So Diego had left his Guatemalan farm in the hands of his hired militia and flown himself all the way from Guatemala City to Tucson.

He'd had no sleep in the past twenty-four hours. He'd been smoking himself to death and reliving a tormenting past.

The woman in the bed stirred suddenly, moaning. He turned just as her eyes opened and then closed quickly again. They were gray. Big and soft, a delicate contrast to her blond fairness; her gray eyes were the only visible evidence of Melissa's Guatemalan mother, whose betrayal had brought anguish and dishonor to the Laremos family.

His black eyes ran slowly over her pale, still features and he wondered as he watched how he and Melissa had ever come to this…

Chapter One

It was a misty rain, but Melissa Sterling didn't mind. Getting soaked was a small price to pay for a few precious minutes with Diego Laremos.

Diego's family had owned the *finca,* the giant Guatemalan farm that bordered her father's land, for four generations. And despite the fact that Melissa's late mother had been the cause of a bitter feud between the Laremos family and the Sterlings, that hadn't stopped Melissa from worshiping the son and heir to the Laremos name. Diego seemed not to mind her youthful adoration, or if he did, he was kind enough not to mock her for it.

There had been a storm the night before, and Melissa had ridden down to Mama Chavez's small house to make sure the old woman was all right, only to find that Diego, too, had been worried about his old nurse and had come to check on her. Melissa liked to visit her and listen to tales of Diego's youth and hear secret legends about the Maya.

Diego had brought some melons and fish for the old woman, whose family tree dated back to the very beginning of the Mayan empire, and now he was escorting Melissa back to her father's house.

Her dark eyes kept running over his lean, fit body, admiring the way he sat on his horse, the thick darkness of his hair under his panama hat. He wasn't an arrogant man, but he had a cold, quiet authority about him that bordered on it. He never had to raise his voice to his servants, and Melissa had only seen him in one fight. He was a dignified, self-contained man without an apparent weakness. But he was mysterious. He often disappeared for weeks at a time, and once he'd come home with scars on his cheek and a limp. Melissa had been curious, but she hadn't questioned him. Even at twenty, she was still shy with men, and especially with Diego. He'd rescued her once when she'd gotten lost in the rain forest searching for some old Mayan ruins, and she'd loved him secretly ever since.

"I suppose your grandmother and sister would die if they knew I was within a mile of you," she sighed, brushing back her long, wavy blond hair as she glanced at him with a hesitant smile that was echoed in the soft gray of her eyes.

"They bear your family no great love, that is true," he agreed. The distant mountains were a blue haze in front of them as they rode. "It is difficult for my family to forget that Edward Sterling stole my father's *novia* on the eve of their wedding and eloped with her. My father spoke of her often, with grief. My grandmother never stopped blaming your family for his grief."

"My father loved her, and she loved him," Melissa defended. "It was only an arranged marriage that your father would have had with her, anyway, not a love match. Your father was much older than my mother, and he'd been a widower for years."

"Your father is British," he said coldly. "He has never understood our way of life. Here, honor is life itself. When he stole away my father's betrothed, he dishonored my family." Diego glanced at Melissa, not adding that his father had also been counting on her late mother's inheritance to restore the family fortunes. Diego had considered his father's attitude rather mercenary, but the old man had cared about Sheila Sterling in his cool way.

Diego reined in his mount and stared at Melissa, taking in her slender body in jeans and a pink shirt unbuttoned to the swell of her breasts. She attracted him far more than he wanted to admit. He couldn't allow himself to become involved with the daughter of the woman who'd disgraced his family.

"Your father should not let you wander around in this manner," he said unexpectedly, although he softened the words with a faint smile. "You know there has been increased guerrilla activity here. It is not safe."

"I wasn't thinking," she replied.

"You never do, *chica*," he sighed, cocking his hat over one eye. "Your daydreaming will be your downfall one day. These are dangerous times."

"All times are dangerous," she said with a shy smile. "But I feel safe with you."

He raised a dark eyebrow. "And that is the most dangerous daydream of all," he mused. "But no doubt you have not yet realized it. Come; we must move on."

"In just a minute." She drew a camera from her pocket

and pointed it toward him, smiling at his grimace. "I know, not again, you're thinking. Can I help it if I can't get the right perspective on the painting of you I'm working on? I need another shot. Just one, I promise." She clicked the shutter before he could protest.

"This famous painting is taking one long time, *niña,*" he commented. "You have been hard at it for eight months, and not one glimpse have I had of it."

"I work slow," she prevaricated. In actual fact, she couldn't draw a straight line without a ruler. The photo was to add to her collection of pictures of him, to sit and sigh over in the privacy of her room. To build dreams around. Because dreams were all she was ever likely to have of Diego, and she knew it. His family would oppose any mention of having Melissa under their roof, just as they opposed Diego's friendship with her.

"When do you go off to college?" he asked unexpectedly.

She sighed as she pocketed the camera. "Pretty soon, I guess. I begged off for a year after school, just to be with Dad, but this unrest is making him more stubborn about sending me away. I don't want to go to the States. I want to stay here."

"Your father may be wise to insist," Diego murmured, although he didn't like to think about riding around his estate with no chance of being waylaid by Melissa. He'd grown used to her. To a man as worldly and experienced and cynical as Diego had become over the years, Melissa was a breath of spring air. He loved her innocence, her shy adoration. Given the chance, he was all too afraid he might be tempted to appreciate her exquisite young body, as well. She was slender, tall, with long, tanned legs, breasts that had just the right shape and a waist that was tiny, flaring to full, gently curving hips. She wasn't beautiful, but her fair complexion was exquisite in its frame of long, tangled blond hair, and her gray eyes held a kind of serenity far beyond her years. Her nose was straight, her mouth soft and pretty. In the right clothes and with the right training, she would be a unique hostess, a wife of whom a man could be justifiably proud…

That thought startled Diego. He had had no intention of thinking of Melissa in those terms. If he ever married, it would be to a Guatemalan woman of good family, not to a woman whose father had already once disgraced the name of Laremos.

"You're always at home these days," Melissa said as they rode along the valley, with the huge Atitlán volcano in the distance against the green jungle. She loved Guatemala, she loved the volcanos and the lakes and rivers, the tropical jungle, the banana and coffee plantations and the spreading valleys. She especially loved the mysterious Mayan ruins that one found so unexpectedly. She loved the markets in the small villages and the friendly warmth of the Guatemalan people whose Mayan ancestors had once ruled here.

"The *finca* demands much of my time since my father's death," he replied. "Besides, *niña,* I was getting too old for the work I used to do."

She glanced at him. "You never talked about it. What did you do?"

He smiled faintly. "Ah, that would be telling. How did your father fare with the fruit company? Were they able to recompense him for his losses during the storm?"

A tropical storm had damaged the banana plantation in which her father had a substantial interest. This year's crop had been a tremendous loss. Like Diego, though, her father had other investments—such as the cattle he and Diego raised on their adjoining properties. But as a rule, fruit was the biggest money-maker.

She shook her head. "I don't know. He doesn't share business with me. I guess he thinks I'm too dumb to understand." She smiled, her mind far away on the small book she'd found recently in her mother's trunk. "You know, Dad is so different from the way he was when my mother knew him. He's so sedate and quiet these days. Mama wrote that he was always in the thick of things when they were first married, very daring and adventurous."

"I imagine her death changed him, little one," he said absently.

"Maybe it did," she murmured. She looked at him curiously. "Apollo said that you were the best there was at your job," she added quickly. "And that someday you might tell me about it."

He said something under his breath, glaring at her. "My past is something I never expect to share with anyone. Apollo had no right to say such a thing to you."

His voice chilled her when it had that icily formal note in it. She shifted restlessly. "He's a nice man. He helped Dad round up some of the stray cattle one day when there was a storm. He must be good at his job, or you wouldn't keep him on."

"He is good at his job," he said, making a mental note to have a long talk with the African American ex-military policeman who worked for him and had been part of the band of mercenaries Diego had once belonged to. "But it does not include discussing me with you."

"Don't be mad at him, please," she asked gently. "It was my fault, not his. I'm sorry I asked. I know you're

very close about your private life, but it bothered me that
you came home that time so badly hurt." She lowered
her eyes. "I was worried."

He bit back a sharp reply. He couldn't tell her about
his past. He couldn't tell her that he'd been a professional mercenary, that his job had been the destruction
of places and sometimes people, that it had paid exceed-
ingly well, or that the only thing he had put at risk was
his life. He kept his clandestine operations very quiet at
home; only the government officials for whom he sometimes did favors knew about him. As for friends and
acquaintances, it wouldn't do for them to know how he
earned the money that kept the *finca* solvent.

He shrugged indifferently. *"No importa."* He was silent for a moment, his black eyes narrow as he glanced
at her. "You should marry," he said unexpectedly. "It
is time your father arranged for a *novio* for you, *niña*."

She wanted to suggest Diego, but that would be court-
ing disaster. She studied her slender hands on the reins.
"I can arrange my own marriage. I don't want to be
promised to some wealthy old man just for the sake of
my family fortunes."

Diego smiled at her innocence. "Oh, *niña,* the ideal-
ism of youth. By the time you reach my age, you will
have lost every trace of it. Infatuation does not last. It
is the poorest foundation for a lasting relationship, because it can exist where there are no common interests
whatsoever."

"You sound so cold," she murmured. "Don't you believe in love?"

"Love is not a word I know," he replied carelessly. "I
have no interest in it."

Melissa felt sick and shaky and frightened. She'd always assumed that Diego was a romantic like herself. But he certainly didn't sound like one. And with that attitude he probably wouldn't be prejudiced against an arranged, financially beneficial marriage. His grandmother was very traditional, and she lived with him. Melissa didn't like the thought of Diego marrying anyone else, but he was thirty-five and soon he had to think of an heir. She stared at the pommel on her saddle, idly moving the reins against it. "That's a very cynical attitude."

He looked at her with raised black eyebrows. "You and I are worlds apart, do you know that? Despite your Guatemalan upbringing and your excellent Spanish, you still think like an Anglo."

"Perhaps I've got more of my mother in me than you think," she confessed sheepishly. "She was Spanish, but she eloped with the best man at her own wedding."

"It is nothing to joke about."

She brushed back her long hair. "Don't go cold on me, Diego," she chided softly. "I didn't mean it. I'm really very traditional."

His dark eyes ran over her, and the expression in them made her heart race. "Yes. Of that I am quite certain," he said. His eyes slid up to hers again, holding them until she colored. He smiled at her expression. He liked her reactions, so virginal and flattering. "Even my grandmother approves of the very firm hand your father keeps on you. Twenty, and not one evening alone with a young man out of the sight of your father."

She avoided his piercing glance. "Not that many young men come calling. I'm not an heiress and I'm not pretty."

"Beauty is transient; character endures. You suit me as you are, *pequeña*," he said gently. "And in time the young men will come with flowers and proposals of marriage. There is no rush."

She shifted in the saddle. "That's what you think," she said miserably. "I spend my whole life alone."

"Loneliness is a fire which tempers steel," he counseled. "Benefit from it. In days to come it will give you a serenity which you will value."

She gave him a searching look. "I'll bet you haven't spent your life alone," she said.

He shrugged. "Not totally, perhaps," he said, giving away nothing. "But I like my own company from time to time. I like, too, the smell of the coffee trees, the graceful sweep of the leaves on banana trees, the sultry wind in my face, the proud Maya ruins and the towering volcanoes. These things are my heritage. Your heritage," he added with a tender smile. "One day you will look back on this as the happiest time of your life. Don't waste it."

That was possible, she mused. She almost shivered with the delight of having Diego so close beside her and the solitude of the open country around them. Yes, this was the good time, full of the richness of life and love. Never would she wish herself anywhere else.

He left her at the gate that led past the small kitchen garden to the white stucco house with its red roof. He got down from his horse and lifted her from the saddle, his lean hands firm and sure at her small waist. For one small second he held her so that her gaze was level with his, and something touched his black eyes. But it was gone abruptly, and he put her down and stepped back.

She forced herself to move away from the tangy scent of leather and tobacco that clung to his white shirt. She forced herself not to look where it was unbuttoned over a tanned olive chest feathered with black hair. She wanted so desperately to reach up and kiss his hard mouth, to hold him to her, to experience all the wonder of her first passion. But Diego saw only a young girl, not a woman.

"I will leave your mare at the stable," he promised as he mounted gracefully. "Keep close to home from now on," he added firmly. "Your father will tell you, as I already have, that it is not safe to ride alone."

"If you say so, Señor Laremos," she murmured, and curtsied impudently.

Once he would have laughed at that impish gesture. But her teasing had a sudden and unexpected effect. His blood surged in his veins, his body tautened. His black eyes went to her soft breasts and lingered there before he dragged them back to her face. *"¡Hasta luego!"* he said tersely, and wheeled his mount without another word.

Melissa stared after him with her heart in her throat. Even in her innocence, she'd recognized the hot, quick flash of desire in his eyes. She felt the look all the way to her toes and burned with an urge to run after him, to make sure she hadn't misunderstood his reaction. To have Diego look at her in that way was the culmination of every dream she'd ever had about him.

She went into the house, tingling with banked-down excitement. From now on, every day was going to be even more like a surprise package.

Estrella had outdone herself with supper. The small, plump *Ladina* woman had made steak with peppers and cheese and salsa, with seasoned rice to go with it, and cool melon for a side dish. Melissa hugged her as she sniffed the delicious aroma of the meal.

"Delicioso," she said with a grin.

"Steak is to put on a bruised eye," Estrella sniffed. "The best meat is iguana."

Melissa made a face. "I'd eat snake first," she promised.

Estrella grinned wickedly. "You did. Last night."

The younger woman's eyes widened. "That was chicken."

Estrella shook her head. "Snake." She laughed when Melissa made a threatening gesture. "No, no, no, you cannot hit me. It was your father's idea!"

"My father wouldn't do such a thing," she said.

"You do not know your father," the *Ladina* woman said with a twinkle in her eyes. "Get out now, let me work. Go and practice your piano or Señora Lopez will be incensed when she comes to hear you on Friday."

Melissa sighed. "I suppose she will, that patient soul. She never gives up on me, even when I know I'll never be able to run my cadences without slipping up on the minor keys."

"Practice!"

She nodded, then changed the subject. "Dad didn't phone, I suppose?" she asked.

"No." Estrella glanced at Melissa with one of her black eyes narrowed. "He will not like you riding with Señor Laremos."

"How did you know I was?" Melissa exclaimed. These flashes of instant knowledge still puzzled her as they had from childhood. Estrella always seemed to know things before she actually heard about them formally.

"That," the *Ladina* woman said smugly, "is my secret. Out with you. Let me cook."

Melissa went, hoping Estrella wasn't planning to share her knowledge with her father.

And apparently the *Ladina* woman didn't, but Edward Sterling knew anyway. He came back from his business trip looking preoccupied, his graying blond hair damp with rain, his elegant white suit faintly wrinkled.

"Luis Martinez saw you out riding with Diego Laremos," he said abruptly, without greeting her. Melissa sat with her hands poised over the piano in the spacious living room. "I thought we'd had this conversation already."

Melissa drew a steadying breath and put her hands in her lap. "I can't help it," she said, giving up all attempts at subterfuge. "I suppose you don't believe that."

"I believe it," he said, to her surprise. "I even understand it. But what I don't understand is why Laremos encourages you. He isn't a marrying man, Melissa, and he knows what it would do to me to see you compromised." His face hardened. "Which is what disturbs me the most. The whole Laremos family would love to see us humbled. Don't cut your leg and invite a shark to kiss it better," he added with a faint attempt at humor.

She threw up her hands. "You won't believe that Diego has no ulterior motives, will you? That he genuinely likes me?"

"I think he likes the adulation," he said sharply. He poured brandy into a snifter and sat down, crossing his long legs. "Listen, sweet, it's time you knew the truth about your hero. It's a long story, and it isn't pretty. I had hoped that you'd go away to college, and no harm done. But this hero worship has to stop. Do you have any idea what Diego Laremos did for a living until about two years ago?"

She blinked. "He traveled on business, I suppose. The Laremoses have money—"

"The Laremoses have nothing, or had nothing," he interrupted curtly. "The old man was hoping to marry Sheila and get his hands on her father's supposed mil-

lions. What Laremos didn't know was that Sheila's father
had lost everything and was hoping to get *his* hands on
the Laremoses' banana plantations. It was a comedy of
errors, and then I found your mother and that was the end
of the plotting. To this day, none of your mother's people will speak to me, and the Laremoses only do out of
politeness. And the great irony of it is that none of them
know the truth about each other's families. There never
was any money—only pipe dreams about mergers."

"Then, if the Laremoses had nothing," Melissa ventured, "why do they have so much these days?"

"Because your precious Diego had a lot of guts and
few equals with an automatic weapon," Edward Sterling
said bluntly. "He was a professional soldier."

Melissa didn't move. She didn't speak. She stared
blankly at her father. "Diego isn't hard enough to go
around killing people."

"Don't kid yourself," came the reply. "Haven't you
even realized that the men he surrounds himself with at
the Casa de Luz are his old confederates? That man they
call First Shirt, and the black ex-soldier, Apollo Blain,
and Semson and Drago…all of them are ex-mercenaries
with no country to call their own. They have no future
except here, working for their old comrade."

Melissa felt her hands trembling. She sat on them. It
was beginning to come together. The bits and pieces of
Diego's life that she'd seen and wondered about were
making sense now—a terrible kind of sense.

"I see you understand," her father said, his voice very
quiet. "You know, I don't think less of him for what he's
done. But a past like his would be rough for a woman to
take. Because of what he's done, he's a great deal less
vulnerable than an ordinary man. More than likely his

feelings are locked in irons. It will take more than an innocent, worshiping girl to unlock them, Melissa. And you aren't even in the running in his mind. He'll marry a Guatemalan woman, if he ever marries. He won't marry you. Our unfortunate connection in the past will assure that, don't you see?"

Her eyes stung with tears. Of course she did, but hearing it didn't help. She tried to smile, and the tears overflowed.

"Baby." Her father got up and pulled her gently into his arms, rocking her. "I'm sorry, but there's no future for you with Diego Laremos. It will be best if you go away, and the sooner the better."

Melissa had to agree. "You're right." She dabbed at her tears. "I didn't know. Diego never told me about his past. I suppose he was saving it for a last resort," she said, trying to bring some lightness to the moment. "Now I understand what he meant about not knowing what love was. I guess Diego couldn't afford to let himself love anyone, considering the line of work he was in."

"I don't imagine he could," her father agreed. He smoothed her hair back. "I wish your mother was still alive. She'd have known what to say."

"Oh, you're not doing too bad," Melissa told him. She wiped her eyes. "I guess I'll get over Diego one day."

"One day," Edward agreed. "But this is for the best, Melly. Your world and his would never fit together. They're too different."

She looked up. "Diego said that, too."

Edward nodded. "Then Laremos realizes it. That will be just as well. He won't put any obstacles in the way."

Melissa tried to forget that afternoon and the way Diego had held her, the way he'd looked at her. Maybe he didn't know what love was, but something inside him had reacted to her in a new and different way. And now she was going to have to leave before she could find out what he felt or if he could come to care for her.

But perhaps her father was right. If Diego felt anything, it was physical, not emotional. Desire, in its place, might be exquisite, but without love it was just a shadow. Diego's past had shocked her. A man like that—was he even capable of love?

Melissa kept her thoughts to herself. There was no sense in sharing them with her father and worrying him even more. "How did it go in Guatemala City?" she asked instead, trying to divert him.

He laughed. "Well, it's not as bad as I thought at first. Let's eat, and I'll explain it to you. If you're old enough to go to college, I suppose you're old enough to be told about the family finances."

Melissa smiled at him. It was the first time he'd offered that kind of information. In an odd way, she felt as if her father accepted the fact that she was an adult.

Chapter Two

Melissa hardly slept. She dreamed of Diego in a confusion of gunfire and harsh words, and she woke up feeling that she'd hardly closed her eyes.

She ate breakfast with her father, who announced that he had to go back into the city to finalize a contract with the fruit company.

"See that you stay home," he cautioned her as he left. "No more tête-à-têtes with Diego Laremos."

"I've got to practice piano," she said absently, and kissed his cheek as he went out the door. "You be careful, too."

He drove away, and she went into the living room where the small console piano sat, opening her practice book to the cadences. She grimaced as she began to fumble through the notes, all thumbs.

Her heart just wasn't in it, so instead she practiced a

much-simplified bit of Sibelius, letting herself go in the expression of its sweet, sad message. She was going to have to leave Guatemala, and Diego. There was no hope at all. She knew in her heart that she was never going to get over him, but it was only beginning to dawn on her that the future would be pretty bleak if she stayed. She'd wear herself out fighting his indifference, bruise her heart attempting to change his will. Why had she ever imagined that a man like Diego might come to love her? And now, knowing his background as she did, she realized that it would take a much more experienced, sophisticated woman than herself to reach such a man.

She got up from the piano, closing the lid, and sat down at her father's desk. There were sheets of white bond paper still scattered on it, along with the pencil he'd been using for his calculations. Melissa picked up the pencil and wrote several lines of breathless prose about unrequited love. Then, impulsively, she wrote a note to Diego asking him to meet her that night in the jungle so that she could show him how much she loved him until dawn came to find them...

Reading it over, she laughed at the very idea of sending such a message to the very correct, very formal Señor Diego Laremos. She crumpled it on the desk and got up, pacing restlessly. She read and went back to the piano, ate a lunch that she didn't really taste and finally decided that she'd go mad if she had to spend the rest of the afternoon just sitting around. Her father had said not to leave the house, but she couldn't bear sitting still.

She saddled her mare and, after waving to an exasperated, irritated Estrella, rode away from the house and down toward the valley. She wondered at the agitated way Estrella, with one of the vaqueros at her side, was waving, but she soon lost interest and quickened her pace. She didn't want to be called back like a delinquent child. She had to ride off some of her nervous energy.

She was galloping down the hill and across the valley when a popping sound caught her attention. Startled, her mare reared up and threw Melissa onto the hard ground.

Her shoulder and collarbone connected with some sharp rocks, and she grimaced and moaned as she tried to sit up. The mare kept going, her mane flying in the breeze, and that was when Melissa saw the approaching horseman, three armed men hot on his heels. Diego!

She couldn't believe what she was seeing. It was unreal, on this warm summer afternoon, to see such violence in the grassy meadow. So the reports about the guerrillas and the political unrest were true. Sometimes, so far away from Guatemala City, she felt out of touch with the world. But now, with armed men flying across the grassy plain, danger was alarmingly real. Her heart ran wild as she sat there, and the first touch of fear brushed along her spine. She was alone and unarmed, and the thought of what those men might do to her if Diego fell curled her hair. Why hadn't she listened to the warnings?

The popping sound came again, and she realized that the men were shooting at Diego. But he didn't look back. His attention was riveted now on Melissa, and he kept coming, his mount moving in a weaving pattern to make less of a target for the pistols of the men behind him. He circled Melissa and vaulted out of the saddle, some kind of small, chubby-looking weapon in his hands.

"Por Dios—" He dropped to his knees and fired off a volley at the approaching horsemen. The sound deafened her, bringing the taste of nausea into her throat

as she realized how desperate the situation really was. "Are you wounded?"

"No, I fell. Diego—"

"Silencio!" He fired another burst at the guerrillas, who had stopped suddenly in the middle of the valley to fire back at him. He pushed Melissa to the ground with gentle violence and aimed again, deliberately this time. He didn't want her to see it, but her life depended on whether or not he could stop his pursuers. He couldn't bear the thought of those brutal hands on her soft skin.

The firing from the other side stopped abruptly. Melissa peeked up at Diego. He didn't look like the man she knew so well. His deeply tanned face was steely, rigid, his hands incredibly steady on the small weapon.

He cursed steadily in Spanish as he surveyed his handiwork, terrible curses that shocked Melissa. She tried not to cry out in fear. The smell of gunsmoke was acrid in her nostrils, her ears were deafened by the sound of the small machine gun.

Diego turned then to sweep Melissa up in his arms, holding the automatic weapon in the hand under her knees. He got her out of the meadow with quick, long strides, his powerful body absorbing her weight as if he didn't even feel it. He darted with her into the thick jungle at the edge of the meadow and kept going. Over his shoulder she saw the horses scatter, two of the riders bent over their saddles as if in pain, the third one lying still on the ground. Diego's horse was long gone, like Melissa's.

Now that they were temporarily out of danger, relief made her body limp. She'd been shot at. She'd actually been shot at! It seemed like some impossible nightmare. Thank God Diego had seen her. She shuddered to think what might have happened if those men had come upon her and she'd been alone.

"Were you hit?" Diego asked curtly as he laid her down against a tree a good way into the undergrowth. "You're bleeding."

"I fell off," she faltered, her eyes helpless on his angry face as he bent over her. "I hit…something. Diego, those men, are we far enough away…?"

"For the moment, yes," he said shortly. "Until they get reinforcements, at least. Melissa, I told you not to go riding alone, did I not?" he demanded.

His eyes were black, and she thought she'd never really seen him before. Not the real man under the lazy good humor, the patient indulgence. This man was a stranger. The mercenary her father had told her about. The unmasked man.

"Where are your men?" she asked huskily, her body becoming rigid as his lean fingers went to the front of her blouse and started to unbutton it. "Diego, no!" she burst out in embarrassment.

He glowered at her. "The bleeding has to be stopped," he said curtly. "This is no time for outraged modesty. Lie still."

While the wind whispered through the tall trees, she fought silently, but he moved her hands aside with growing impatience and peeled the blouse away from the flimsy bra she was wearing. His black eyes made one soft foray over the transparent material covering her firm, young breasts, and then glanced at her shoulder, which was scratched and bleeding.

"We are cut off," he muttered. "I made the mistake of assuming a few rounds would frighten off a guerrilla who was scouting the area around my cattle pens.

He left, but only to come back with a dozen or so of his amigos. Apollo and the rest of my men are at the casa, trying to hold them off until Semson can get the government troops to assist them. Like a fool, I allowed myself to be cut off from the others and pursued."

"I suppose you'd have made it back except for me," she murmured quietly, her pale gray eyes apologetic as she looked up at him.

"Will you never learn to listen?" he asked coldly. He had his handkerchief at the scraped places now and was soothing away the blood. He grimaced. "This will need attention. It's a miracle that your breast escaped severe damage, *niña,* although it is badly bruised."

She flushed, averting her eyes from his scrutiny. Very likely, a woman's naked body held no mysteries for Diego, but Melissa had never been seen unclad by a man.

Diego ignored her embarrassment, spreading the handkerchief over the abrasions and refastening her blouse to hold it in place. Nothing of what he was feeling showed in his expression, but the sight of her untouched, perfect young body was making him ache unpleasantly. Until now it had been possible to think of Melissa as a child. But after tonight, he'd never be able to think of her that way again. It was going to complicate his life, he was certain of it. "We must get to higher ground, and quickly. I scattered them, but depend on it, they will be back." He helped her up. "Can you walk?"

"Of course," she said unsteadily, her eyes wide and curious as she looked at the small, bulky weapon he scooped up from the ground. He had a cartridge belt around his shoulder, over his white shirt.

"An Uzi," he told her, ignoring her fascination. "An automatic weapon of Israeli design. Thank God I listened to my old instincts and carried it with me this afternoon, or I would already be dead. I am deeply sorry that you had to see what happened, little one, but if I had not fired back at them…"

"I know that," she said. She glanced at him, then away, as he led her deeper into the jungle. "Diego, my father told me what you used to do for a living."

He stopped and turned around, his black eyes intent on hers because he needed to know her reaction to the discovery. He searched her expression, but there was no contempt, no horror, no shock. "To discourage you, I presume, from any deeper relationship with me?" he asked unexpectedly.

She blushed and lowered her gaze. "I guess I've been pretty transparent all the way around," she said bitterly. "I didn't realize everybody knew what a fool I was making of myself."

"I am thirty-five years old," he said quietly. "And women have been, forgive me, a permissible vice. Your face is expressive, Melissa, and your innocence makes you all the more vulnerable. But I would hardly call you a fool for feeling an—" he hesitated over the word "—attraction. But this is not the time to discuss it. Come, *pequeña,* we must find cover. We have little time."

It was hard going. The jungle growth of vines and underbrush was thick, and Diego had only his knife, not a machete. He was careful to leave no visible trace of the path they made, but the men following them were likely to be experienced trackers. Melissa knew she should be afraid, but being with Diego made fear impossible. She knew that he'd protect her, no matter what. And despite the danger, just being with him was sheer delight.

She watched the muscles in his lean, fit body ripple

as he moved aside the clinging vines for her. Once, his dark eyes caught hers as she was going under his arm, and they fell on her mouth with an expression that made her blood run wild through her veins. It was only a moment in time, but the flare of awareness made her clumsy and self-conscious. She remembered all too well the feel of his hard fingers on her soft skin as he'd removed the blood and bandaged the scrapes. She thought of the time ahead, because darkness would come soon. Would they stay in the jungle overnight? And would he hold her in the night, safe in his arms, against his warm body? She trembled at the delicious image, already feeling the muscles of his arms closing around her.

He paused to look at the compass in the handle of his knife, checking his bearings.

"There are ruins very near here," he murmured. "With luck, we should be able to get to them before dark." He looked up at the skies, which were darkening with the threat of a storm. "Rain clouds," he mused. "We shall more than likely be drenched before we reach cover. Your father is not at home, I assume?"

"No," she said miserably. "He'll be worried sick. And furious."

"Murderously so, I imagine," he said with an irritated sigh. "Oh, Melissa, what a situation your impulsive nature has created for us."

"I'm sorry," she said gently. "Really I am."

He shifted his head and stared down into her face with something like arrogance. "Are you? To be alone with me like this? Are you really sorry, *querida?*" he asked, and his voice was like velvet, deep and soft and tender.

Her lips parted as she tried to answer him, but she

was trembling with nervous pleasure. Her gray eyes slid over his face like loving hands.

"An unfair question," he murmured. "When I can see the answer. Come."

He turned away from her, his body rippling with desire for her. He was too hot-blooded not to feel it when he looked at her slender body, her sweet innocence like a seductive garment around her. He wanted her as he'd never wanted another woman, but to give in to his feelings would be to place himself at the mercy of her father's retribution. He was already concerned about how it would look if they were forced to bed down in the ruins. Apollo and the others would come looking for him, but the rain would wash away the tracks and slow them down, and the guerrillas would be in hot pursuit, as well. He sighed. It was going to be difficult, whichever way they went.

The rain came before they got much farther, drenching them in wet warmth. Melissa felt her hair plastered against her scalp, her clothing sticking to her like glue. Her jeans and boots were soaked, her shirt literally transparent as it dripped in the pounding rain.

Diego's black hair was like a skullcap, and his very Spanish features were more prominent now, his olive complexion and black eyes making him look faintly pagan. He had Mayan blood as well as Spanish because of the intermarriage of his Madrid-born grandparents with native Guatemalans. His high cheekbones hinted at his Indian ancestry, just as his straight nose and thin, sensual lips denoted his Spanish heritage. Watching him, Melissa wondered where he had inherited his height, because he was as tall as her British father.

"There," he said suddenly, and they came to a clearing where a Mayan temple sat like a gray sentinel in the green jungle. It was only partially standing, but at least one part of it seemed to have a roof.

Diego led her through the vined entrance, frightening away a huge snake. She shuddered, thinking of the coming darkness, but Diego was with her. He'd keep her safe.

Inside, it was musty and smelled of stone and dust, but the walls in one side of the ruin were almost intact, and there were a few timbers overhead that time hadn't completely rotted.

Melissa shivered. "We'll catch pneumonia," she whispered.

"Not in this heat, *niña*," he said with a faint smile. He moved over to a vine-covered opening in the stone wall. At least he'd be able to see the jungle from which they'd just departed. With a sigh, he stripped off his shirt and hung it over a jutting timber, stretching wearily.

Melissa watched him, her gaze caressing the darkly tanned muscles and the faint wedge of black hair that arrowed down to the belt around his lean waist. Just looking at him made her tingle, and she couldn't hide her helpless longing to touch him.

He saw her reaction, and all his good intentions melted. She looked lovely with her clothing plastered to her exquisite body, and through the wet blouse he could see the very texture of her breasts, their mauve tips firm and beautifully formed. His jaw tautened as he stared at her.

She started to lift her arms, to fold them over herself, because the way he was looking at her frightened her a little. But he turned abruptly and started out.

"I'll get some branches," he said tersely. "We'll need

something to keep us from getting filthy if we have to stay here very long."

While he was gone, Melissa stripped off her blouse and wrung it out. It didn't help much, but it did remove some of the moisture. She dabbed at her hair and pushed the strands away from her face, knowing that she must look terrible.

Diego came back minutes later with some wild-banana leaves and palm branches that he spread on the ground to make a place to sit. He was wetter than ever, because the rain was still coming down in torrents.

"Our pursuers are going to find this weather difficult to track us through," he mused as he pulled a cigarette lighter from his pocket and managed to light a small cheroot. He eased back on one elbow to smoke it, studying Melissa with intent appreciation. She'd put the blouse back on, but even though it was a little drier, her breasts were still blatantly visible through it.

"I guess they will," she murmured, answering him.

"It embarrasses you, *niña,* for me to look at you so openly?" he asked quietly.

"I don't have much experience…" She faltered, blushing.

He blew out a thick cloud of smoke while his eyes made a meal of her. It was madness to allow himself that liberty, but he couldn't seem to help himself. She was untouched, and her eyes were shyly worshipful as she looked at his body. He wanted more than anything to touch her, to undress her slowly and carefully, to show her the delight of making love. His heart began to throb as he saw images of them together on the makeshift bedding, her body receptive to his, open to his possession.

Melissa was puzzled by his behavior. He'd always

been so correct when they'd been together, but he wasn't bothering to disguise his interest in her body, and the look on his face was readable even to a novice.

"Why did you become a mercenary?" she asked, hoping to divert him.

He shrugged. "It was a question of finances. We were desperate, and my father was unable to face the degradation of seeking work after having had money all his life. I had a reckless nature, and I enjoyed the danger of combat. After I served in the army, I heard of a group that needed a small-arms expert for some 'interesting work.' I applied." He smiled in reminiscence. "It was an exciting time, but once or twice I had a close call. The others slowly drifted away to other occupations, other callings, but I continued. And then I began to slow down, and there was a mistake that almost cost me my life." He lifted the cheroot to his lips. "I had enough wealth by then not to mind settling down to a less demanding life-style. I came home."

"Do you miss it?" she asked softly, studying his handsome face.

"On occasion. There were good times. A special feeling of camaraderie with men who faced death with me."

"And women, I guess," she said hesitantly, her face more expressive than she realized.

His black eyes ran over her body like hands, slow and steady and frankly possessive. "And women," he said quietly. "Are you shocked?"

She swallowed, lowering her eyes. "I never imagined that you were a monk, Diego."

He felt himself tautening as he watched her, longed for her. The rain came harder, and she jumped as a streak of lightning burst near the temple and a shuddering thunderclap followed it.

"The lightning comes before the noise," he reminded her. "One never hears the fatal flash."

"How encouraging," she said through her teeth. "Do you have any more comforting thoughts to share?"

He smiled faintly as he put out the cheroot and laid it to one side. "Not for the moment."

He took her by the shoulders and laid her down against the palms and banana leaves, his lean hands on the buttons of her shirt once more. This time she didn't fight and she didn't protest, she simply watched him with eyes as big as saucers.

"I want to make sure the bleeding has stopped," he said softly. He pulled the edges of the blouse open and lifted the handkerchief that he'd placed over the cut. His black eyes narrowed, and he grimaced. "This may leave a scar," he said, tracing the wound with his forefinger. "A pity, on such exquisite skin."

Her breath rattled in her throat. The touch of his hand made her feel reckless. All her buried longings were coming to the surface during this unexpected interlude with him, his body above her, his chest as bare and brawny as she'd dreamed it would be.

"I have no healing balm," he said softly, searching her eyes. "But perhaps, *pequeña,* I could kiss it better…"

Even as he spoke, he bent, and Melissa moaned sharply as she felt the moist warmth of his mouth on her skin. Her hands clenched beside her, her back arched helplessly.

Startled by such a passionate reaction from a girl so virginal, he lifted his head to look at her. He was surprised, proud, when he saw the pleasure that made her cheeks burn, her eyes grow drowsy and bright, her lips part hungrily. It made him forget everything but the need to make her moan like that yet again, to see her eyes as she felt the first stirrings of passion in her untried body. The thought of her innocence and his resolve not to touch her vanished like the threat of danger.

He slid one hand under the nape of her neck to support it, his fingers spreading against her scalp as he bent again. His lips touched her tenderly, his tongue lacing against the abrasions, trailing over her silky skin. She smelled of flowers, and the scent of her went to his head. His free hand went under her back and found the catch of her bra, releasing it. He pulled the straps away from her shoulder and lifted her gently to ease the wispy material down her arms along with her blouse, leaving her bare and shivering under his quiet, experienced eyes. He hadn't meant to let it happen, but his hunger for her had burst its bonds. He couldn't hold back. He didn't want to. She was his. She belonged to him.

He stopped her impulsive movement to cover herself by shaking his head. "This between us will be a secret, something for the two of us alone to share," he whispered. His dark eyes went to her breasts, adoring them. "Such lovely young breasts," he breathed, bending toward them. "So sweet, so tempting, so exquisitely formed…"

His lips touched the hard tip of her breast, and she went rigid. His arm went under her to support her back, and his free hand edged between them, raising sweet fires as it traced over her rib cage and belly before it went up to tease at the bottom swell of her breasts and make her ache for him to touch her completely. His mouth eased down onto her breast, taking it inside, savoring its warm softness as the rain pelted down overhead and the thunder drowned out the threat of the world around them. Their drenched clothing was hardly a barrier, their bodies sliding damply against each other in the dusty semidarkness of the dry ruin.

He felt her begin to move against him with helpless longing. She wasn't experienced enough to hide her desire for him or to curb her headlong response. He delighted in the shy touch of her hands on his chest, his back, in her soft cries and moans as he moved his mouth up to hers finally and covered her soft lips, pressing them open in a kiss that defied restraint.

She arched against him, glorying in the feel of skin against wet skin, her bareness under his, the hardness of his muscles gently crushing her breasts. Her nails dug helplessly into his back while she felt the hunger in the smoke-scented warmth of his open mouth on hers, and she moaned tenderly when she felt the probing of his tongue.

He was whispering something in husky Spanish, his mouth insistent, his hands suddenly equally insistent with other fastenings, hard and swift and sure.

She started to protest, but he brushed his mouth over hers. His body was shuddering with desire, and he sat up, his eyes fiercely possessive as he began to remove the rest of her clothing.

"Shhh," he whispered when she started to speak. "Let me tell you how it will be. My body and yours," he breathed, "with the rain around us, the jungle beneath us. The sweet fusion of male and female here, in the Mayan memory. Like the first man and woman on earth, with only the jungle to hear your cries and the aching pleasure of my skin against yours, my hands holding you to me as we drown in the fulfillment of our desire for each other."

The soft deepness of his voice drugged her. Yes, she wanted that. She wanted him. She arched as his hands slid down her yielding body, his lips softly touching her in ways she'd never dreamed of. The scent of the palm leaves and the musty, damp smell of the ruins in the rain combined with the excitement of Diego's feverish lovemaking.

She watched him undress, her shyness buried in the fierce need for fulfillment, her eyes worshiping his lean, fit body as he lay down beside her. He let her look at him, taking quiet pride in his maleness. He coaxed her to touch him, to explore the hard warmth of his body while he whispered to her and kissed her and traced her skin with exquisite expertise, all restraint, all reason burned away in the fires of passion.

She gave everything he asked, yielded to him completely. At the final moment, when there was no turning back, she looked up at him with absolute trust, absorbing the sudden intrusion of his powerful body with only a small gasp of pain, lost in the tender smile of pride he gave at her courage.

"Virgin," he whispered, his eyes bright and black as they held hers. He began to move, very slowly, his body trembling with his enforced restraint. "And so we join, and you are wholly mine. *Mi mujer.* My woman."

She caught her breath at the sensations he was causing, her eyes moving and then darting away, her face surprised and loving and hungry all at the same time, her eyes full of wonder as they lifted back to his.

"Hold me," he whispered. "Hold tight, because soon you will begin to feel the whip of passion and you will need my strength. Hold fast, *querida,* hold fast to me, give me all that you are, all that you have…*adorada,*" he gasped as his movements increased with shocking effect. "Melissa *mía!*"

She couldn't even look at him. Her body was climbing to incredible heights, tautening until the muscles seemed in danger of snapping. She cried out something, but he groaned and clasped her, and all too soon she was reaching for something that had disappeared even as she sought to touch it.

She wept, frustrated and aching and not even able to explain why.

He kissed her face tenderly, his hands framing it, his eyes soft, wondering. "You did not feel it?" he whispered, making her look at him.

"It was so close," she whispered back, her eyes frantic. "I almost…oh!"

He smiled with aching tenderness, his body moving slowly, his head lifting to watch her face. "Ah, yes," he whispered. "Here. And here…gently, *querida.* Come up and kiss me, and let your body match my rhythm. Yes, *querida,* yes, like that, like—" His jaw clenched. He shouldn't be able to feel it again so quickly. He watched her face, felt her body spiraling toward fulfillment. Even as she cried out with it and whispered to him he was in his own hot, black oblivion, and this time it took forever to fall back to earth in her arms.

They lay together in the soft darkness with the rain pelting around them, sated, exquisitely fatigued, her shirt and his pulled over them for a damp blanket. He bent to kiss her lazily from time to time, his lips soft and slow, his smile gentle. For just a few minutes there was no past, no future, no threat of retribution, no piper to pay.

Melissa was shocked by what had happened, so in love with him that it had seemed the most natural thing on earth at the time to let him love her. But as her reason came back, she became afraid and apprehensive. What was he thinking, lying so quietly beside her? Was he sorry or glad, did he blame her? She started to ask him.

And then reality burst in on them in the cruelest way of all. Horses' hooves and loud voices had been drowned out by the thunder and the rain, but suddenly a small group of men was inside the ruin, and at the head of them was Melissa's father.

He stopped dead, staring at the trail of clothing and the two people, obviously lovers, so scantily covered by two shirts.

"Damn you, Laremos!" Edward Sterling burst out. "Damn you, what have you done?"

Chapter Three

Melissa knew that as long as she lived there would be the humiliation of that afternoon in her memory. Her father's outrage, Diego's taut shouldering of the blame, her own tearful shame. The men quickly left the ruins at Edward Sterling's terse insistence, but Melissa knew they'd seen enough in those brief seconds to know what had happened.

Edward Sterling followed them, giving Melissa and Diego time to get decently covered. Diego didn't speak at all. He turned his back while she dressed, and then he gestured with characteristic courtesy for her to precede him out of the entrance. He wanted to speak, to say something, but his pride was lacerated at having so far forgotten himself as to seduce the daughter of his family's worst enemy. He was appalled at his own lack of control.

Melissa went out after one hopeful glance at his rigid, set features. She didn't look at him again.

Her father was waiting outside. The rain had stopped and his men were at a respectful distance.

"It wasn't all Diego's fault," Melissa began.

"Yes, I'm aware of that," her father said coldly. "I found the poems you wrote and the note asking Laremos to meet you so that you could—how did you put it?— 'prove your love' for him."

Diego turned, his eyes suddenly icy, hellishly accusing. "You planned this," he said contemptuously. "*Dios mío,* and like a fool I walked into the trap…"

"How could I possibly plan a raid by guerrillas?" she asked, trying to reason with him.

"She certainly used it to her advantage," Edward Sterling said stiffly. "She was warned before she left the house that there was trouble at your estate, Estrella told her as she rode out of the yard, and she went in that general direction."

Melissa defended herself weakly. "I didn't hear Estrella. And the poems and the note were just daydreaming…"

"Costly daydreaming," her father replied. He stared at Diego. "No man with any sense of honor could refuse marriage in the circumstances."

"What would you know of honor?" Diego asked icily. "You, who seduced my father's woman away days before their wedding?"

Edward Sterling seemed to vibrate with bad temper. "That has nothing to do with the present situation. I won't defend my daughter's actions, but you must admit, Señor Laremos, that she couldn't have found herself in this predicament without some cooperation from you!"

It was a statement that turned Diego's blood molten,

because it was an accusation that was undeniable. He was as much to blame as Melissa. He was trapped, and he himself had sprung the lock. He couldn't even look at her. The sweet interlude that had been the culmination of all his dreams of perfection had turned to ashes. He didn't know if he could bear to go through with it, but what choice was there? Another dishonor on the family name would be too devastating to consider, especially to his grandmother and his sister.

"I will not shirk my responsibility, *señor,*" Diego said with arrogant disdain. "You may rest assured that Melissa will be taken care of."

Melissa started to speak, to refuse, but her father and Diego gave her such venomous looks that she turned away and didn't say another word.

The guerrillas had been dealt with. Apollo Blain, tall and armed to the teeth at the head of a column led by the small, wiry man Laremos called First Shirt, was waiting in the valley as the small party approached.

"The government troops are at the house, boss," Shirt said with a grin.

Apollo chuckled, his muscular arms crossed over the pommel of his saddle. "Cleaning house, if you'll forgive the pun. Glad to see you're okay, boss man. You, too, Miss Sterling."

"Thanks," Melissa said wanly.

"With your permission, I will rejoin my men," Diego said with cool formality, directing the words to Edward. "I will make the necessary arrangements for the service to take place with all due haste."

"We'll wait to hear from you, *señor,*" Edward said tersely. He motioned to his men and urged his mount into step beside Melissa's.

"I don't suppose there's any use in trying to explain?" she asked miserably, too sick to even look back toward Diego and his retreating security force.

"None at all," her father said. "I hope you love Laremos. You'll need to, now that he's well and truly hamstrung. He'll hate both of us, but I won't let you be publicly disgraced, even if it is your own damned fault."

Tears slid down her cheeks. She stared toward the distant house with a sick feeling that her life was never going to be the same again. Her hero-worshiping and daydreaming had led to the end she'd hoped for, but she hadn't wanted to trap Diego. She'd wanted him to love her, to want to marry her. She had what she thought she desired, but now it seemed that the Fates were laughing at her. She remembered a very old saying that had never made sense before: *be careful what you wish for, because you might get it.*

Weeks went by while Melissa was feted and given party after party with a stiff-necked Señora Laremos and Juana, Diego's sister, at her side. Their disapproval and frank dislike had been made known from the very beginning, but like Diego, they were making the most of a bad situation.

Diego himself hardly spoke to Melissa unless it was necessary, and when he looked at her she felt chilled to the bone. That he hated her was all too apparent. As the wedding approached, she wished with all her heart that she'd listened to her father and had never left the house that rainy day.

Her wedding gown was chosen, the Catholic church in Guatemala City was filled to capacity with friends and distant kin of both the bride's and groom's families.

Melissa was all nerves, even though Diego seemed to be as nonchalant as if he were going to a sporting event, and even less enthusiastic.

Diego spoke his vows under Father Santiago's quiet gaze with thinly veiled sarcasm and placed the ring upon Melissa's finger. He pushed back the veil and looked at her with something less than contempt, and when he kissed her it was strictly for the sake of appearances. His lips were ice-cold. Then he bowed and led her back down the aisle, his eyes as unfeeling as the carpet under their feet.

The reception was an ordeal, and there was music and dancing that seemed to go on forever before Diego announced that he and his bride must be on their way home. He'd already told Melissa there would be no honeymoon because he had too much work and not enough free time to travel. He drove her back to the casa, where he deposited her with his cold-eyed grandmother and sister. And then he packed a bag and left for an extended business trip to Europe.

Melissa missed her father and Estrella. She missed the warmth of her home. But most of all, she missed the man she'd once loved, the Diego who'd teased her and laughed with her and seemed to enjoy having her with him for company when he'd ridden around the estate. The angry, unapproachable man she'd married was a stranger.

It was almost six weeks from the day she and Diego had been together when Melissa began to feel a stirring inside, a frightening certainty that she was pregnant. She was nauseated, not just at breakfast but all the time. She hid it from Diego's grandmother and sister, although it grew more difficult all the time.

She spent her days wandering miserably around the house, wishing she had something to occupy her. She wasn't allowed to take part in any of the housework or to sit with the rest of the family, who made this apparent by simply leaving a room the moment she entered it. She ate alone, because the *señora* and the *señorita* managed to change the times of meals from day to day. She was avoided, barely tolerated, actively disliked by both women, and she didn't have the worldliness or the sophistication or the maturity to cope with the situation. She spent a great deal of time crying. And still Diego stayed away.

"Is it so impossible for you to accept me?" she asked Señora Laremos one evening as Juana left the sitting room and a stiff-backed *señora* prepared to follow her.

Señora Laremos gave her a cold, black glare from eyes so much like Diego's that Melissa shivered. "You are not welcome here. Surely you realize it?" the older woman asked. "My grandson does not want you, and neither do we. You have dishonored us yet again, like your mother before you!"

Melissa averted her face. "It wasn't my fault," she said through trembling lips. "Not completely."

"Had it not been for your father's insistence, you would have been treated like any other woman whose favors my son had enjoyed. You would have been adequately provided for—"

"How?" Melissa demanded, her illusions gone at the thought of Diego's other women, her heart broken. "With an allowance for life, a car, a mink coat?" Her chin lifted proudly. "Go ahead, *señora*. Ignore me. Nothing will change the fact that I am Diego's wife."

The older woman seemed actually to vibrate with

anger. "You impudent young cat," she snarled. "Has your family not been the cause of enough grief for mine already, without this? I despise you!"

Melissa didn't blink. She didn't flinch. "Yes, I realize that," she said with quiet pride. "God forbid that in your place I would ever be so cruel to a guest in my home. But then," she added with soft venom, "I was raised properly."

The Señora actually flushed. She went out of the room without another word, but afterward her avoidance of Melissa was total.

Melissa gave up trying to make them accept her now that she realized the futility of it. She wanted to go home to see her father, but even that was difficult to arrange in the hostile environment where she lived. She settled for the occasional phone call and had to pretend, for his sake, that everything was all right. Perhaps when Diego had time to get used to the situation, everything would be all right. That was the last hope she had—that Diego might relent. That she might be able to persuade him to give her a chance to be the wife she knew she was capable of being.

Meanwhile, the sickness went on and on, and she knew that soon she was going to have to see a doctor. She grew paler by the day. So pale, in fact, that Juana risked her grandmother's wrath to sneak into Melissa's room one night and ask how she was.

Melissa gaped at her. "I beg your pardon?" she asked tautly.

Juana grimaced, her hands folded neatly at her waist, her dark eyes oddly kind in her thin face. "You seem so pale, Melissa. I wish it were different. Diego is—" she spread her hands "—Diego. And my grandmother nurses old wounds that have been reopened by your presence here. I cannot defy her. It would break her heart if I sided with you against her."

"I understand that," Melissa said quietly, and managed a smile. "I don't blame you for being loyal to your grandmother, Juana."

Juana sighed. "Is there something, anything, I can do?"

Melissa shook her head. "But thank you."

Juana opened the door, hesitating. "My grandmother will not say so, but Diego has called. He will be home tomorrow. I thought you might like to know."

She was gone then, as quickly as she'd come. Melissa looked around the neat room she'd been given, with its dark antique furnishings. It wasn't by any means the master bedroom, and she wondered if Diego would even keep up the pretense of being married to her by sleeping in the same room. Somehow she doubted it. It would be just as well that way, because she didn't want him to know about the baby. Not until she could tell how well he was adapting to married life.

She barely slept, wondering how it would be to see him again. She overslept the next morning and for once was untroubled by nausea. She went down the hall and there he was, sitting at the head of the table. The whole family was together for breakfast for once.

Her heart jumped at just the sight of him. He was wearing a lightweight white tropical suit that suited his dark coloring, but he looked worn and tired. He glanced up as she entered the room, and she wished she hadn't worn the soft gray crepe dress. It had seemed appropriate at the time, but now she felt overdressed. Juana was wearing a simple calico skirt and a white blouse, and the *señora* had on a sedate dark dress.

Diego's eyes went from Melissa's blond hair in its neat chignon to her high-heeled shoes in one lightning-fast, not-very-interested glance. He acknowledged her with cool formality. "Señora Laremos. Are you well?"

She wanted to throw things. Nothing had changed, that was obvious. He still blamed her. Hated her. She was carrying his child, she was almost certain of it, but how could she tell him?

She went to the table and sat down gingerly, as far away from the others as she could without being too obvious. "Welcome home, *señor*," she said in a subdued tone. She hardly had any spirit left. The weeks of avoidance and cold courtesy and hostility had left their mark on her. She was pale and quiet, and something stirred in Diego as he looked at her. Then he banked down the memories. She'd trapped him. He couldn't afford to let himself forget that. First Sheila, then Melissa. The Sterlings had dealt two bitter blows to the Laremos honor. How could he even think of forgiving her?

Still, he thought, she looked unwell. Her body was thinner than he remembered, and she had a peculiar lack of interest in the world around her.

Señora Laremos also noticed these things about her unwanted houseguest but she forced herself not to bend. The girl was a curse, like her mother before her. She could never forgive Melissa for trapping Diego in such a scandalous way, so that even the servants whispered about the manner in which the two of them had been found.

"We have had our meal," the *señora* said with forced

courtesy, "but Carisa will bring something for you if you wish, Melissa."

"I don't want anything except coffee, thank you, *señora*." She reached for the silver coffeepot with a hand that trembled despite all her efforts to control it. Juana bit her lip and turned her eyes away. And Diego saw his sister's reaction with a troubled conscience. For Juana to be so affected, the weeks he'd been away must have been difficult ones. He glanced at the *señora* and wondered what Melissa had endured. His only thought had been to get away from the forced intimacy with his new wife. Now he began to wonder about the treatment she'd received from his family and was shocked to realize that it was only an echo of his own coldness.

"You are thinner," Diego said unexpectedly. "Is your appetite not good?"

She lifted dull, uninterested eyes. "It suffices, *señor*," she replied. She sipped coffee and kept her gaze on her cup. It was easier than trying to look at him.

He hated the guilt that swept over him. The situation was her fault. She'd baited a trap that he'd fallen headlong into. So why should he feel so terrible? But he did. The laughing, shy young woman who'd adored him no longer lived in the same body with this quiet, unnaturally pale woman who wouldn't look at him.

"Perhaps you would like to lie down, Melissa," the *señora* said uneasily. "You do seem pale."

Melissa didn't argue. It was obvious that she wasn't welcome here, either, even if she had been invited to join the family. "As you wish, *señora*," she said, her tone emotionless. She got up without looking at anyone and went down the long, carpeted hall to her room.

Diego began to brood. He hardly heard what his

grandmother said about the running of the estate in his absence. His mind was still on Melissa.

"How long has she been like this, *abuela?*" he asked unexpectedly. "Has she no interest in the house at all?"

Juana started to speak, but the *señora* silenced her. "She has been made welcome, despite the circumstances of your marriage," the *señora* said with dignity. "She prefers her own company."

"Excuse me," Juana said suddenly, and she left the table, her face rigid with distaste as she went out the door.

Diego finished his coffee and went to Melissa's room. But once outside it, he hesitated. Things were already strained. He didn't really want to make it any harder for her. He withdrew his hand from the doorknob and, with a faint sigh, went back the way he'd come. There would be time later to talk to her.

But business interceded. He was either on his way out or getting ready to leave every time Melissa saw him. He didn't come near her except to inquire after her health and to nod now and again. Melissa began to stay in her room all the time, eating her food on trays that Carisa brought and staring out the window. She wondered if her mind might be affected by her enforced solitude, but nothing really seemed to matter anymore. She had no emotion left in her. Even her pregnancy seemed quite unreal, although she knew it was only a matter of time before she was going to have to see the doctor.

It was storming the night Diego finally came to see her. He'd just come in from the cattle, and he looked weary. In dark slacks and an unbuttoned white shirt, he looked very Spanish and dangerously attractive, his black hair damp from the first sprinkling of rain.

"Will you not make even the effort to associate with the rest of us?" he asked without preamble. "My grandmother feels that your dislike for us is growing out of proportion."

"Your grandmother hates me," she said without inflection, her eyes on the darkness outside the window. "Just as you do."

Diego's face hardened. "After all that has happened, did you expect to find me a willing husband?"

She sighed, staring at her hands in her lap. "I don't know what I expected. I was living on dreams. Now they've all come true, and I've learned that reality is more than castles in the air. What we think we want isn't necessarily what we need. I should have gone to America. I should never have...I should have stopped you."

He felt blinding anger. "Stopped me?" he echoed, his deep voice ringing in the silence of her room. "When it was your damnable scheming that led to our present circumstances?"

She lifted her face to his. "And your loss of control," she said quietly, faint accusation in her voice. "You didn't have to make love to me. I didn't force you."

His temper exploded. He didn't want to think about that. He lapsed into clipped, furious Spanish as he expressed things he couldn't manage in English.

"All right," she said, rising unsteadily to her feet. "All right, it was all my fault—all of it. I planned to trap you and I did, and now both of us are paying for my mistakes." Her pale eyes pleaded with his unyielding ones. "I can't even express my sorrow or beg you enough to forgive me. But, Diego, there's no hope of divorce. We have to make the best of it."

"Do we?" he asked, lifting his chin.

She moved closer to him in one last desperate effort to reach him. Her soft eyes searched his. She looked young and very seductive, and Diego felt himself caving in when she was close enough that he could smell the sweet perfume of her body and feel her warmth. All the memories stirred suddenly, weakening him.

She sensed that he was vulnerable somehow. It gave her the courage to do what she did next. She raised her hands and rested them on his chest, against the cool skin and the soft feathering of hair over the hard muscles. He flinched, and she sighed softly as she looked up at him.

"Diego, we're married," she whispered, trying not to tremble. "Can't we…can't we forget the past and start again…tonight?"

His jaw went taut, his body stiffened. No, he told himself, he wouldn't allow her to make him vulnerable a second time. He had to gird himself against any future assaults like this.

He caught her shoulders and pushed her away from him, his face severe, his eyes cold and unwelcoming. "The very touch of you disgusts me, Señora Laremos," he said with icy fastidiousness. "I would rather sleep alone for the rest of my days than to share my bed with you. You repulse me."

The lack of heat in the words made them all the more damning. She looked at him with the eyes of a bludgeoned deer. Disgust. Repulse. She couldn't bear any more. His grandmother and sister like hostile soldiers living with her, then Diego's cold company, and now this. It was too much. She was bearing his child, and he wouldn't want it, because she disgusted him. Tears stung her eyes. Her hand went to her mouth.

"I can't bear it," she whimpered. Her face contorted

and she ran out the door, which he'd left open, down the hall, her hair streaming behind her. She felt rather than saw the women of the house gaping at her from the living room as she ran wildly toward the front door with Diego only a few steps behind her.

The house was one story, but there was a long drop off the porch because of the slope on which the house had been built. The stone steps stretched out before her, but she was blinded by tears and lost her footing in the driving rain. She didn't even feel the wetness or the pain as she shot headfirst into the darkness and the first impact rocked her. Somewhere a man's voice was yelling hoarsely, but she was mercifully beyond hearing it.

She came to in the hospital, surrounded by white-coated figures bending over her.

The resident physician was American, a blond-haired, blue-eyed young man with a pleasant smile. "There you are," he said gently when she stirred and opened her eyes. "Minor concussion and a close call for your baby, but I think you'll survive."

"I'm pregnant?" she asked drowsily.

"About two and a half months," he agreed. "Is it a pleasant surprise?"

"I wish it were so." She sighed. "Please don't tell my husband. He'll be worried enough as it is," she added, deliberately misleading the young man. She didn't want Diego to know about the baby.

"I'm sorry, but I told him there was a good chance you might lose it," he said apologetically. "You were in bad shape when they brought you in, *señora*. It's a miracle that you didn't lose the baby, and I'd still like to run some tests just to make sure."

She bit her lower lip and suddenly burst into tears. It

all came out then, the forced marriage, his family's hatred of her, his own hatred of her. "I don't want him to know that I'm still pregnant," she pleaded. "Oh, please, you mustn't tell him, you mustn't! I can't stay here and let my baby be born in such hostility. They'll take him away from me and I'll never see him again. You don't know how they hate me and my family!"

He sighed heavily. "You must see that I can't lie about it."

"I'm not asking you to," she said. "If I can leave in the morning, and if you'll just not talk to him, I can tell him that there isn't going to be a baby."

"I can't lie to him," the doctor repeated.

She took a slow, steadying breath. She was in pain now, and the bruises were beginning to nag her. "Then can you just not talk to him?"

"I might manage to be unavailable," he said. "But if he asks me, I'll tell him the truth. I must."

"Isn't a patient's confession sacred or something?" she asked with a faint trace of humor.

"That's so, but lying is something else again. I'm too honest anyway," he said gently. "He'd see right through me."

She lay back and touched her aching head. "It's all right," she murmured. "It doesn't matter."

He hesitated for a minute. Then he bent to examine her head and she gave in to the pain. Minutes later he gave her something for it and left her to be transported to a private room and admitted for observation overnight.

She wondered if Diego would come to see her, but she was half-asleep when she saw him standing at the foot of the bed. His face was in the shadows, so she couldn't see it. But his voice was curiously husky.

"How are you?" he asked.

"They say I'll get over it," she replied, turning her head away from him. Tears rolled down her cheeks. At least she still had the baby, but she couldn't tell him. She didn't dare. She closed her eyes.

He stuck his hands deep in his pockets and looked at her, a horrible sadness in his eyes, a sadness she didn't see. "I…am sorry about the baby," he said stiffly. "One of the nurses said that your doctor mentioned the fall had done a great deal of damage." He shifted restlessly. "The possibility of a child had simply not occurred to me," he added slowly.

As if he'd been home enough to notice, she thought miserably. "Well, you needn't worry about it anymore," she said huskily. "God forbid that you should be any more trapped than you already were. You'd have hated being tied to me by a baby."

His spine stiffened. He seemed to see her then as she was, an unhappy child who'd half worshiped him, and he wondered at the guilt he felt. That annoyed him. "Grandmother had to be tranquilized when she knew," he said curtly, averting his eyes. "*Dios mío,* you might have told me, Melissa!"

"I didn't know," she lied dully. Her poor bruised face moved restlessly against the cool pillow. "And it doesn't matter now. Nothing matters anymore." She sighed wearily. "I'm so tired. Please leave me in peace, Diego." She turned her face away. "I only want to sleep."

He stared down at her without speaking. She'd trapped him and he blamed her for it, but he was sorry about the baby, because he was responsible. He grimaced at her paleness, at the bruising on her face. She'd changed so drastically, he thought. She'd aged years.

His eyes narrowed. Well, hadn't she brought it on herself? She'd wanted to marry him, but she hadn't considered his feelings. She'd forced them into this marriage, and divorce wasn't possible. He still blamed her for that, and forgiveness was going to come hard. But for a time she had to be looked after. Well, tomorrow he'd work something out. He might send her to Barbados, where he owned land, to recover. He didn't know if he could bear having to see the evidence of his cruelty every day, because the loss of the child weighed heavily on his conscience. He hadn't even realized that he wanted a child until now, when it was too late.

He didn't sleep, wondering what to do. But when he went to see her, she'd already solved the problem. She was gone…

As past and present merged, Diego watched Melissa's eyes open suddenly and look up at him. It might have been five years ago. The pain was in those soft gray eyes, the bitter memories. She looked at him and shuddered. The eyes that once had worshiped him were filled with icy hatred. Melissa seemed no happier to see him than he was to see her. The past was still between them.

Chapter Four

Melissa blinked, moving her head jerkily so she could see him. Her gaze focused on his face, and then she shivered and closed her eyes. He pulled himself erect and turned to go and get a nurse. As he left the room, his last thought was that her expression had been that of a woman awakening not from, but into, a nightmare.

When Melissa's eyes opened again, there was a shadowy form before her in crisp white, checking her over professionally with something uncomfortably cold and metallic.

"Good," a masculine voice murmured. "Very good. She's coming around. I think we can dispense with some of this paraphernalia, Miss Jackson," he told a white-clad woman beside him, and proceeded to give unintelligible orders.

Melissa tried to move her hand. "Pl-please." Her voice sounded thick and alien. "I have...to go home."

"Not just yet, I'm afraid," he said kindly, smiling.

She licked her lips. They felt so very dry. "Matthew," she whispered. "My little boy. At a neighbor's. They won't know..."

The doctor hesitated. "You just rest, Mrs. Laremos. You've had a bad night of it—"

"Don't...call me that!" she shuddered, closing her eyes. "I'm Melissa Sterling."

The doctor wanted to add that her husband was just outside the door, but the look on her face took the words out of his mouth. He said something to the nurse and quickly went back out into the hall.

Diego was pacing, and smoking like a furnace. He'd shed his jacket on one of the colorful seats in the nearby waiting room. His white silk shirt was open at the throat and his tie was lying neatly on his folded jacket. His rolled-up sleeves were in dramatic contrast to his very olive skin. His black eyes cut around to the doctor.

"How is she?" he asked without preamble.

"Still a bit concussed." The doctor leaned against the wall, his arms folded. He was almost as tall as Diego, but a good ten years younger. "There's a problem." He hesitated, because he knew from what Diego had told him that he and Melissa had been apart many years. He didn't know if the child was her husband's or someone else's, and situations like this could get uncomfortable. He cleared his throat. "Your wife is worried about her son. He's apparently staying at a neighbor's house."

Diego felt himself go rigid. A child. His heart seemed to stop beating, and for one wild moment he enjoyed the unbounded thought that it was his child. And then he remembered that Melissa had lost his child and that it was impossible for her to have conceived again before she'd left the *finca*. They had only slept together the one time.

That meant that Melissa had slept with another man. That she had become pregnant by another man. That the child was not his. He hated her in that instant with all his heart. Perhaps she was justified in her revenge. To be fair, he'd made her life hell during their brief marriage. And now she'd had her revenge. She'd hurt him in the most basic way of all.

He had to fight not to turn on his heel and walk away. But common sense prevailed. The child wasn't responsible for its circumstances. It would be alone and probably frightened. He couldn't ignore it. "If you can find out where he is, I will see about him," he said stiffly. "Will Melissa be all right?"

"I think so. She's through the worst of it. There was a good deal of internal bleeding. We've taken care of that. There was a badly torn ligament in her leg that will heal in a month or so. And we had to remove an ovary, but the other one was undamaged. Children are still possible."

Diego didn't look at the doctor. His eyes were on the door to Melissa's room. "The child. Do you know how old he is?"

"No. Does it matter?"

Diego shook himself. What he was thinking wasn't remotely possible. She'd lost the child he'd given her. She'd been taken to the hospital after a severe fall, and the doctor had told him there was little hope of saving it. It wasn't possible that they'd both lied. Of course not.

"I'll try to find the child's whereabouts," the doctor told Diego. "Meanwhile, you can't do much good here. By tomorrow she should be more lucid. You can see her then."

Diego wanted to tell him that if she was lucid Melissa wouldn't want to see him at all. But he only shrugged and nodded his dark head.

He left a telephone number at the nurse's station and went back to his hotel, glad to be out of Tucson's sweltering midsummer heat and in the comfort of his elegant air-conditioned room. A local joke had it that when a desperado from nearby Yuma had died and gone to hell, he'd sent back home for blankets. Diego was inclined to believe it, although the tropical heat of his native Guatemala was equally trying for Americans who settled there.

He much preferred the rain forest to the desert. Even if it was a humid heat, there was always the promise of rain. He wondered if it ever rained here. Presumably it did, eventually.

His mind wandered back to Melissa in that hospital bed and the look on her face when she'd seen him. She'd hidden well. He'd tried every particle of influence and money he'd possessed to find her, but without any success. She'd covered her tracks well, and how could he blame her? His treatment of her had been cruel, and she hadn't been much more than a child hero-worshiping him.

But Diego thought about the baby with bridled fury. They were still married, despite her unfaithfulness, and there was no question of divorce. Melissa, who was also Catholic, would have been no more amenable to that solution than he. But it was going to be unbearable, seeing that child and knowing that he was the very proof of Melissa's revenge for Diego's treatment of her.

The sudden buzz of the telephone diverted him. It

was the doctor, who'd obtained the name and address of the neighbor who was caring for Melissa's son. Diego scribbled the information on a pad beside the phone, grateful for the diversion.

An hour later he was ushered into the cozy living room of Henrietta Grady's house, just down the street from the address the hospital had for Melissa's home.

Diego sat sipping coffee, listening to Mrs. Grady talk about Melissa and Matthew and their long acquaintance. She wasn't shy about enumerating Melissa's virtues. "Such a sweet girl," she said. "And Matthew's never any trouble. I don't have children of my own, you see, and Melissa and Matthew have rather adopted me."

"I'm certain your friendship has been important to Melissa," he replied, not wanting to go into any detail about their marriage. "The boy…"

"Here he is now. Hello, my baby."

Diego stopped short at the sight of the clean little boy who walked sleepily into the room in his pajamas. "All clean, Granny Grady," he said, running to her. He perched on her lap, his bare toes wiggling, eyeing the tall, dark man curiously. "Who are you?" he asked.

Diego stared at him with icy anger. Whoever Melissa's lover had been, he obviously had a little Latin blood. The boy's hair was light brown, but his skin was olive and his eyes were dark brown velvet. He was captivating, his arms around Mrs. Grady's neck, his lean, dark face full of laughter. And he looked to be just about four years old. Which meant that Melissa's fidelity had lasted scant weeks or months before she'd turned to another man.

Mrs. Grady lifted the child and cuddled him while Matthew waited for the man to answer his question.

"I'm Matthew," he told Diego, his voice uninhibited

and unaccented. "My mommy went away. Are you my papa?"

Diego wasn't sure he could speak. He stared at the little boy with faint hostility. "I am your mama's husband," he said curtly, aware of Matthew's uncertainty and Mrs. Grady's surprise.

Diego ignored the looks. "Your mama is going to be all right. She is a little hurt, but not much. She will come home soon."

"Where will Matt go?" the boy asked gently.

Diego sighed heavily. He hadn't realized how much Melissa's incapacity would affect his life. She was his responsibility until she was well again, and so was this child. It was a matter of honor, and although his had taken some hard blows in years past, it was still as much a part of him as his pride. He lifted his chin. "You and your mama will stay with me," he said stiffly, and the lack of welcome in his voice made the little boy cling even closer to Mrs. Grady. "But in the meantime, I think it would be as well if you stay here." He turned to Mrs. Grady. "This can be arranged? I will need to spend a great deal of time at the hospital until I can bring Melissa home, and it seems less than sensible to uproot him any more than necessary."

"Of course it can be arranged," Mrs. Grady said without argument. "If there's anything else I can do to help, please let me know."

"I will give you the number of the phone in my hotel room and at the hospital, should you need to contact me." He pulled a checkbook from the immaculate gray suit jacket. "No arguments, please," he said when she looked hesitant about accepting money. "If you had not been available, Melissa would certainly have had to hire a sitter for him. I must insist that you let me pay you."

Mrs. Grady gave in gracefully, grateful for his thoughtfulness. "I would have done it for nothing," she said.

He smiled and wrote out a check. "Yes. I sensed that."

"Is Matt going to live with you and Mama?" Matthew asked in a quiet, subdued tone, sadness in his huge dark eyes.

Diego lifted his chin. "Yes," Diego said formally. "For the time being."

"My mommy will miss me if she's hurt. I can kiss her better. Can't I go see her?"

It was oddly touching to see those great dark eyes filled with tears. Diego had schooled himself over the years to never betray emotion. But he still felt it, even at such an unwelcome time.

Mrs. Grady had put the boy down to pour more coffee, and Diego studied him gravely. "There is a doctor who is taking very good care of your mother. Soon you may see her. I promise."

The small face lifted warily toward him. "I love Mama," he said. "She takes me places and buys me ice cream. And she lets me sleep with her when I get scared."

Diego's face became, if anything, more reserved than before, Mrs. Grady noticed. A flash of darkness in his eyes made her more nervous than before. How could Melissa have been married to such a cold man, a man who seemed unaffected even by his own son's tears? "How about a cartoon movie before bedtime?" Mrs. Grady asked Matthew, and quickly put on a Winnie the Pooh video for him to watch. The boy sprawled in an armchair, clapping his hands as the credits began to roll.

"Gracias," Diego said as he got gracefully to his feet. "I will tell Melissa of your kindness to her son."

Mrs. Grady tried not to choke. "Excuse me, *señor,* but Matthew is surely your son, too?"

The look in his eyes made her regret ever asking the question. She moved quickly past him to the door, making a flurry of small talk while her cheeks burned with her own forwardness.

"I hope everything goes well with Melissa," she said, flustered.

"Yes. So do I." Diego glanced back at Matthew, who was watching television. His dark eyes were quiet and faintly bitter. He didn't want Melissa's child. He wasn't sure he even wanted Melissa. He'd come out of duty and honor, but those were the only things keeping him from taking the first flight home to Guatemala. He felt betrayed all over again, and he didn't know how he was going to bear having to look at that child every day until Melissa was well enough to leave him.

He went back to the hospital, pausing outside Melissa's room while he convinced himself that upsetting her at this point would be unwise. He couldn't do that to an injured woman, despite his outrage. After a moment he knocked carelessly and walked in, tall and elegant and faintly arrogant, controlling his expression so that he seemed utterly unconcerned.

Which was quite a feat, considering that inside he felt as if part of him had died over the past five years. Melissa couldn't possibly know how it had been for him when she'd first vanished from the hospital, or how his guilt had haunted him. Despite his misgivings, he'd searched for her, and if he'd found her he'd have made sure that their marriage worked. For the sake of his family's honor, he'd have made her think that he was supremely contented. And after they'd had other children, perhaps they'd have found some measure of happiness. But that was all supposition, and now he was here and the future had to be faced.

The one thing he was certain of was that he could never trust her again. Affection might be possible after he got used to the situation, but love wasn't a word he knew. He'd come close to that with Melissa before she'd forced him into an unwanted marriage. But she'd nipped that soft feeling in the bud, and he'd steeled himself in the years since to be invulnerable to a woman's lies. Nothing she did could touch him anymore. But how was he going to hide his contempt and fury from her when Matthew would remind him of it every day they had to be together?

Chapter Five

Melissa watched Diego come in the door, and it was like stepping back into a past she didn't even want to remember. She was drowsy from the painkillers, but nothing could numb her reaction to her first sight of her husband in five years.

She seemed to stop breathing as her gray eyes slid drowsily over his tall elegance. Diego. So many dreams ago, she'd loved him. So many lonely years ago, she'd longed for him. But the memory of his cold indifference and his family's hatred had killed something vulnerable in her. She'd grown up. No longer was she the adoring woman-child who'd hung on his every word. Because of Matthew, she had to conceal from Diego the attraction she still felt for him. She was helpless and Diego was wealthy and powerful. She couldn't risk letting him know the truth about the little boy, because she knew all too well that Diego would toss her aside without regret. He'd already done that once.

Even now she could recall the disgust in his face when he'd pushed her away from him that last night she'd spent under his roof.

Her eyes opened again and he was closer, his face as unreadable as ever. He was older, but just as masculine and attractive. The cologne he used drifted down to her, making her fingers curl. She remembered the clean scent of him, the delicious touch of his hard mouth on her own. The mustache was unfamiliar, very black and thick, like the wavy, neatly trimmed hair above his dark face. He was older, yes, even a little more muscular. But he was still Diego.

"Melissa." He made her name a song. It was the pronunciation, she imagined, the faint accent, that gave it a foreign sound.

She lowered her eyes to his jacket. "Diego."

"How are you feeling?"

He sounded as awkward as she felt. She wondered how they'd found him, why they'd contacted him. She was still disoriented. Her slender hand touched her forehead as she struggled to remember. "There was a plane crash," she whispered, grimacing as she felt again the horrible stillness of the engine, the sudden whining as they'd descended, her own screaming.

"You must try not to think of it now." He stood over her, his hands deep in his pockets.

Then, suddenly, she remembered. "Matthew! Oh, no. Matthew!"

"¡Cuidado!" he said gently, pressing her back into the pillows. "Your son is doing very well. I have been to see him."

There was a flicker of movement in her eyelids that she prayed he wouldn't see and become curious about. She stared at him, waiting. Waiting. But he made no comment about the child. Nothing.

His back straightened. "I have asked Mrs. Grady to keep him until you are well enough to be released."

She wished she felt more capable of coping. "That was kind of you," she said.

He turned to her again, his head to one side as he studied her. He decided not to pull any punches. "You will not be able to work for six weeks. And Mrs. Grady seemed to feel that you are in desperate financial straits."

Her eyes closed as a wave of nausea swept over her. "I had pneumonia, back in the spring," she said. "I got behind with the bills…"

"Are you listening to me, Señora Laremos?" he asked pointedly, emphasizing the married name he knew she hated. "You are not able to work. Until you are, you and the child will come home with me."

Her eyes opened then. "No!"

"It is decided," he said carelessly.

She went rigid under the sheet. "I won't go to Guatemala, Diego," she said with unexpected spirit. In the old days, she had never fought him. "Not under any circumstances."

He stared at her, his expression faintly puzzled. So the memories bothered her, as well, did they? He lifted his chin, staring down his straight nose at her. "Chicago, not Guatemala," he replied quietly. "Retirement has begun to bore me." He shrugged. "I hardly need the money, but Apollo Blain has offered me a consultant's position, and I already have an apartment in Chicago. I was spending a few weeks at the *finca* before beginning work when the hospital authorities called me about you."

Apollo. That name was familiar. She remembered the mercenaries with whom Diego had once associated himself. "He was in trouble with the law."

"No longer. J.D. Brettman defended him and won his case. Apollo has his own business now, and most of the others work for him. He is the last bachelor in the group. The others are married, even Shirt."

She swallowed. "Shirt is married?"

"To a wiry little widow. Unbelievable, is it not? I flew to Texas three years ago for the wedding."

She couldn't look at him. She knew somehow that he'd never told his comrades about his own marriage. He'd hated Melissa and the very thought of being tied to her. Hadn't he said so often enough?

"I'm very happy for them," she said tautly. "How nice to know that some people look upon marriage as a happy ending, not as certain death."

His gaze narrowed, his dark eyes wary on her face. "Looking into the past will accomplish nothing," he said finally. "We must both put it aside. I cannot desert you at such a time, and Mrs. Grady is hardly able to undertake your nursing as well as your son's welfare."

She didn't miss the emphasis he put on the reference to Matthew. He had to believe she'd betrayed him, and she had no choice but to let him think it. She couldn't fight him in her present condition.

Her gray eyes held his. "And you are?"

"It is a matter of honor," he said stiffly.

"Yes, of course. Honor," she said wearily, wincing as she moved and felt a twinge of pain. "I hope I can teach

Matthew that honor and pride aren't quite as important as compassion and love."

The reference to her own lack of honor made his temper flare. "Who was his father, Melissa?" he asked cuttingly, his eyes hard. He hadn't meant to ask that, the words had exploded from him in quiet fury. "Whose child is he?"

She turned her head back to his. "He's my child," she said with an indignant glare. Gone were the days when she'd bowed down to him. Gone were the old adulation and the pedestal she'd put him on. She was worlds more mature now, and her skin wasn't thin anymore. "When you pushed me away, you gave up any rights you had to dictate to me. His parentage is none of your business. You didn't want me, but maybe someone else did."

He glared, but he didn't fire back at her. How could he? She'd hit on his own weakness. He'd never gotten over the guilt he'd felt, both for the loss of control that had given her a weapon to force him into marriage and for causing her miscarriage.

He stared out the window. "We cannot change what was," he said again.

Melissa hated the emotions that soft, Spanish-accented voice aroused in her, and she hated the hunger she felt for his love. But she could never let him know.

She stared at her thin hands. "Why did they contact you?"

He went back to the bed, his eyes quiet, unreadable. "You had our marriage license in your purse."

"Oh."

"It amazes me that you would carry it with you," he continued. "You hated me when you left Guatemala."

"No less than you hated me, Diego," she replied wearily.

His heart leaped at the sound of his name on her lips. She'd whispered it that rainy afternoon in the mountains, then moaned it, then screamed it. His fist clenched deep in his pocket as the memories came back, unbidden.

"It seemed so, did it not?" he replied. He turned away irritably. "Nevertheless, I did try to find you," he added stiffly. "But to no avail."

She stared at the sheet over her. "I didn't think you'd look for me," she said. "I didn't think you'd mind that I was gone, since I'd lost the child," she added, forcing out the lie, "and that was the only thing you would have valued in our marriage."

He averted his head. He didn't tell her the whole truth about the devastation her disappearance had caused him. He was uncertain of his ability to talk about it, even now, without revealing his emotions. "You were my wife," he said carelessly, glancing her way with eyes as black as night. "You were my responsibility."

"Yes," she agreed. "Only that. Just an unwelcome duty." She grimaced, fighting the pain because her shot was slowly wearing off. Her soft gray eyes searched his face. "You never wanted me, except in one way. And after we were married, not even that way."

That wasn't true. She couldn't know how he'd fought to stay out of her bedroom for fear of creating an addiction that he would never be cured of. She was in his blood even now, and as he looked at her he ached for her. But he'd forced himself to keep his distance. His remoteness, his cutting remarks, had all been part of his effort to keep her out of his heart. He'd come closer to knowing love with her than with any of the women in his past, but something in him had held back. He'd lived alone all his life, he'd been free. Loving was a kind of prison, a bond. He hadn't wanted that. Even marriage hadn't changed his mind. Not at first.

"Freedom was to me a kind of religion," he said absently. "I had never foreseen that I might one day be forced to relinquish it." He shifted restlessly. "Marriage was never a state I coveted."

"Yes, I learned that," she replied. She grimaced as she shifted against the pillow. "What did they...do to me? They won't tell me anything."

"They operated to stop some internal bleeding." He stood over her, his head at a faintly arrogant angle. "There is a torn ligament in your leg which will make you uncomfortable until it heals, and some minor bruises and abrasions. And they had to remove one of your ovaries, but the physician said that you can still bear a child."

Her face colored. "I don't want another child."

He stared down at her with faint distaste. "No doubt the one your lover left you with is adequate, is he not, *señora?*" he shot back.

She wanted to hit him. Her eyes flashed wildly and her breath caught. "Oh, God, I hate you," she breathed huskily, and her face contorted with new pain.

He ignored the outburst. "Do you need something else for the discomfort?" he asked unexpectedly.

She wanted to deny it, but she couldn't. "It... hurts." She touched her abdomen.

"I will see the nurse on my way out. I must get more clothes for Matthew."

She felt drained. "I'd forgotten. My apartment. There are clothes in the tall chest of drawers for him."

"The key?" he asked.

"In my purse." She didn't really want Diego in her apartment. There were no visible traces of anything, but he might find something she'd overlooked. But what choice did she have? Matthew had to be her first consideration.

He brought it to her, took the key she extended, then replaced the pitiful vinyl purse in her locker. The sight of her clothing was equally depressing. She had nothing. His dark eyes closed. It hurt to see her so destitute when she was entitled to his own wealth. Diego knew that Melissa's father had gone bankrupt just before his death.

The apartment she shared with Matthew was as dismal as the clothing he'd seen in her locker at the hospital. The landlady had eyed him with suspicion and curiosity until he'd produced his checkbook and asked how much his *wife* owed her. That had shaken the woman considerably, and there had been no more questions or snide remarks from her.

Diego searched through the apartment until he found a small vinyl bag, which he packed with enough clothing to get Matthew through the next few days. But he knew already that he was going to have to do some shopping. The child's few things looked as if they'd been obtained at rummage sales. Probably they had, he thought bitterly, because Melissa had so little. His fault. Even that was his fault.

He looked in another chest of drawers for more gowns and underthings for Melissa, and stopped as he lifted a gown and found a small photograph tucked there. He took it out carefully. It was one that Melissa had taken of him years before. He'd been astride one of his stallions, wearing a panama hat and dark trousers with a white shirt unbuttoned over his bronzed chest with its faint feathering of black hair. He'd been smiling at her as he'd leaned over the neck of the horse to stroke its waving mane. On the back of it was written: Diego, Near Atitlán. There was no date, but the photo was worn and wrinkled, as if she'd carried it with her for a long time. And he remembered to the day when she'd taken it— the day before they'd taken refuge in the Mayan ruins.

He slowly put it back under the gown and found something else. A small book in which were tucked flowers and bits of paper and a thin silver bookmark. He recognized some of the mementos. The flowers he'd given her from time to time or picked for her when they'd walked across the fields together. The bits of paper were from things he'd scribbled for her, Spanish words that she'd been trying to master. The bookmark was one he'd given her for her eighteenth birthday. He frowned. Why should she have kept them all these years?

He put them back, folded the gown gently over them and left the drawer as he'd found it, forcing himself not to consider the implications of those revealing mementos. After all, she might have kept them to remind her more of his cruelty than of any feeling she had had for him.

He went shopping the next morning. He knew Melissa's size, but he'd had to call Mrs. Grady to ask for Matthew's. It disturbed him to buy clothes for another man's child, but he found himself in the toy department afterward. Before he could talk himself out of it he'd filled a bag with playthings for the child, chiding himself mentally for doing something so ridiculous.

But Matthew's face when he put the packages on the sofa in Mrs. Grady's apartment was a revelation. Diego smiled helplessly at the child's unbridled delight as he took out building blocks and electronic games and a small remote-controlled robot.

"He's had so little, poor thing," Mrs. Grady sighed,

smiling as she watched the boy go feverishly from one toy to another, finally settling down with a small computerized teddy bear that talked. "Not Melly's fault, of course. Money was tight. But it's nice to see him with a few new things."

"Sí." Diego watched the little boy and felt a sudden icy blast of regret for the child he'd caused Melissa to lose. He remembered with painful clarity what he'd said to her the night she'd run out into the rain and pitched down the steps in the wet darkness. *Dios,* would he never forget? He turned away. "I must go. Melissa needed some new gowns. I am taking them to the hospital for her."

"How is she?"

"Much better, *gracias.* The doctor says I may take her home in a few more days." He looked down at the heavy-set woman. "Matthew will be going with us to Chicago. I know he will miss you, and Melissa and I are grateful for the care you have taken of him."

"It was my pleasure," she assured him.

"Thank you for my toys, mister," Matthew said, suddenly underfoot. His big dark eyes were happy. He lifted his arms to Diego to be picked up; he was used to easy affection from the adults around him. But the tall man went rigid and looked unapproachable. Matthew stepped back, the happiness in his eyes fading to wary uncertainty. He shifted and ran back to his toys without trying again.

Diego hated the emotions sifting through his pride, the strongest of which was self-contempt. How could he treat a child so coldly—it wasn't Matthew's fault, after all. But years of conditioning had made it impossible for him to bend. He turned to the door, avoiding

Mrs. Grady's disapproving glance, made his goodbyes and left quickly.

Back at the hospital, while Diego went to get himself a cup of coffee, Melissa had a nurse help her into one of the three pastel gowns Diego had brought. She was delighted with the pink one. It had a low bodice and plenty of lace, and she thought how happy it would have made her years ago to have Diego buy her anything. But he'd done this out of pity, she knew, not out of love.

She thanked him when he came back. "You shouldn't have spent so much…" She faltered, because she knew the gowns were silk, not a cheap fabric.

He only shrugged. "You will be wearing gowns for a time," he said, as if that explained his generous impulse. He sat down in the armchair in the corner with a foam cup of coffee, which he proceeded to sip. "I bought a few things for your son," he added reluctantly. He crossed his long legs. "And a toy or so." He caught the look in her eyes. "He went from one to the other like a bee in search of the best nectar," he mused with stiff amusement.

Melissa almost cried. She'd wanted to give the child so many things, but there hadn't been any money for luxuries.

"Thank you for doing that for him," Melissa said quietly. "I didn't expect that you'd do anything for him under the circumstances, much less buy him expensive toys." Her eyes fell from his cold gaze. "I haven't been able to give him very much. There's never been any money for toys."

She was propped up in bed now, and her hair had been washed. It was a pale blond, curling softly toward her face, onto her flushed cheeks. She was lovely, he thought, watching her. There was a new maturity about her, and the curves he remembered were much more womanly now. His eyes dropped to the low bodice of the new gown he'd bought her, and they narrowed on the visible swell of her pink breasts.

She colored more and started to pull up the sheet, but his lean, dark hand prevented her.

"There is no need for that, Melissa," he said quietly. "You certainly do not expect me to make suggestive remarks to you under the circumstances?"

She shifted. "No. Of course not." She sighed. "I didn't expect you to buy me new gowns," she said, hoping to divert him. She didn't like the way it affected her when he looked at her that way. "Couldn't you find mine?" And as she asked the question, she remembered suddenly and with anguish what she'd hidden under those gowns. Had he seen—

He turned away so that she couldn't see his expression. "One glance in the drawer was enough to convince me that they were unsuitable, without disturbing them," he said with practiced carelessness. "Do you not like the new ones?"

"They're very nice," she said inadequately. Silk, when she could barely afford cotton. Of course she liked them, but why had he been so extravagant?

"Has it been like this since you came to America?" he asked, glancing at her. "Have you been so hard-pressed for money?"

She didn't like the question. She stared at her folded hands. "Money isn't everything," she said.

"The lack of it can be," he replied. He straightened, his eyes narrow and thoughtful. "The child's father— could he not help you financially?"

She gritted her teeth. This was going to be intolerable. She lifted her cold gaze to his. "No, he couldn't be bothered," she said tersely. "And you needn't look so self-righteous and accusing, Diego. I don't believe for a minute that you've spent the last five years without a woman."

He didn't answer her. His expression was distant, impassive. "Has Matthew seen his father?" he persisted.

She didn't answer him. She didn't dare. "I realize that you must resent Matthew, but I do hope you don't intend taking out your grievances on him," she said.

He glared at her. "As if I could treat a child so."

"I was little more than a child," she reminded him. "You and your venomous family had no qualms about treating me in just such a way."

"Yes," he admitted, as graciously as he could. He put his hands in his pockets and studied her. "My grandmother very nearly had a breakdown when you vanished. She told me then how you had been treated. It was something of a shock. I had not considered that she might feel justified in taking her vengeance out on you. I should have realized how she'd react, but I was feeling trapped and not too fond of you when I left the Casa de Luz."

Before Melissa could respond to his unexpected confession, the door opened and a nurse's aide came in with a dinner tray. She smiled at Diego and put a tray in front of Melissa. Oh, well, Melissa thought as she was propped up and her food containers were opened for her, she could argue with him later. He didn't seem inclined to leave her anytime soon.

"You eat so little," he remarked when she only picked at her food.

She glanced at him. He sat gracefully in an upholstered armchair beside the window, his long legs crossed.

He looked very Latin like that, and as immaculate as ever. She had to drag her eyes away before her expression told him how attractive she still found him.

"I'm not very hungry."

"Could you not eat a thick steak smothered in mushrooms and onions, *chiquita?*" he murmured, his black eyes twinkling gently for the first time since she'd opened her eyes and seen him in her room. "And fried potatoes and thick bread?"

"Stop," she groaned.

He smiled. "As I thought, it is the food that does not appeal. When you are released I will see to it that you have proper meals."

"I have a job," she began.

"Which you cannot do until you are completely well again," he reminded her. "I will speak to your employer."

She sighed. "It won't help. They can't afford to hold the position open for six weeks."

"Is there someone who can replace you?"

She thought of her young, eager assistant. "Oh, yes."

"Then there should be no problem."

She glared at him over the last sip of milk. "I won't let you take me over," she said. "I'm grateful for your help, but I want no part of marriage ever again."

"I want it no more than you do, Melissa," he said carelessly, with forced indifference. "But for the time being, neither of us has any choice. As for divorce—" he shrugged "—that is not possible. But perhaps a separation or some other arrangement can be made when you are well. Naturally I will provide for you and the child."

"You will like hell," she said, shocking him not only with her unfamiliar language but with the very adult and formidable anger in her gray eyes. "This isn't Guatemala. In America women have equal rights with men. We aren't property, and I'm perfectly capable of providing for Matthew and myself."

His dark eyebrows lifted. "Indeed?" he asked lightly. "And this is why I found you living in abject poverty with a child who wears secondhand clothing and had not one new toy in his possession?"

She wanted to climb out of bed and hit him over the head with her tray. Her eyes told him so. "I won't live with you."

He shrugged. "Then what will you do, *niña?*" he asked.

She thought about that for a minute and fought back tears of helpless rage. She lay back on the pillows with a heavy sigh. "I don't know," she said honestly.

"It will only be a temporary arrangement," he reminded her. "Just until you are well again. You might like Chicago," he added. "There is a lake and a beach, and many things for a small boy to explore."

She made a face. "Matt and I will catch pneumonia and die if we have to spend a winter there," she said shortly. "Neither of us has ever been out of southern Arizona in the past f—" she corrected herself quickly "—three years."

He didn't notice the slip. He was studying her slender body under the sheets. She thought that he'd spent the past five years womanizing. Little did she know that the memory of her had destroyed any transient desire he might have felt for any other woman. Even now his dreams were filled with her, obsessed with her. So much love in Melissa, but he'd managed to kill it all. Once, he'd been sure she wanted to love him, but now he couldn't really blame her for her reticence. And his own feelings had been in turmoil ever since he'd learned about the child.

"It is spring," he murmured. "By winter, much could happen."

"I won't live in Guatemala, Diego," she repeated. "And not with your grandmother and sister under any circumstances."

He ran a restless hand through his hair. "My grandmother lives in Barbados with her sister," he said. "She still grieves for the great-grandchild she might have had if not for our intolerable coldness to you. My sister is married and lives in Mexico City."

"Did they know you were coming here?" she asked casually, though she didn't feel casual about it. The *señora* had been cruel, and so, despite her reluctance to side with her grandmother, had Juana.

"I telephoned them both last night. They wish you well. Perhaps one day there may be the opportunity for them to ask your pardon for the treatment you received."

"Juana tried to be kind," she said. She traced a thread on the sheet. "Your grandmother did not. I suppose I can understand how she felt, but it didn't make it any easier for me to stay there."

"And you blame me for leaving you at her mercy, *¿Es verdad?*"

"Yes, as a matter of fact, I do," she replied, looking up. "You never allowed me to explain. You automatically convicted me on circumstantial evidence and set out to make me pay for what you thought I did. And I paid," she added icily. "I paid in ways I won't even tell you."

"But you had your revenge, did you not?" he returned with an equally cold laugh. "You took a lover and had his child."

She forced a smile to her pale lips. "You're so good at getting at the truth, Diego," she said mildly. "I'm in awe of your ability to read minds."

"A pity I had no such ability when you left the hospital without even being discharged and vanished," he replied. "There was a military coup the same day you left, and there were several deaths."

As he spoke she saw the flash of emotion in his black eyes. She hadn't noticed before how haunted he looked. There was a deep, dark coldness about him, and there were new lines in his lean face. He looked his age for once, and the old lazy indifference she remembered seemed gone forever. This remote, polite man was nothing like the man she'd known in Guatemala. He'd changed drastically.

Then what he had said began to penetrate her tired mind. She frowned. "Several deaths?" she asked suddenly.

He laughed bitterly. "During the time the coup was accomplished there were a few isolated fatalities, and one of the bodies could not be identified." His eyes went cold at the memory. "It was a young girl with blond hair."

"You thought it was me?" she exclaimed.

He took a slow, deep breath. It was a minute before he could answer her. "Yes, I thought…it was you."

Chapter Six

Diego's quiet confirmation took Melissa's breath away. She knew about the coup, of course. It was impossible not to know. But at the time her only thought had been of escape. She hadn't considered that depriving Diego of knowledge of her whereabouts might lead to the supposition that she was dead. She'd only been concerned about hiding her pregnancy from him.

"I find it very hard to believe you were concerned."

"Concerned!" He turned around, and the look in his black eyes was the old one she remembered from her teens, the one that could make even the meanest of his men back away. His eyes were like black steel in his hard face. "Shall I tell you what that young woman looked like, *niña*?"

She couldn't meet his eyes. "I can imagine how she looked," she said. "But you'll never make me believe it mattered to you. I expect you were more angry than relieved to discover that it wasn't me. How did you discover it?" she added.

"Your father told me," he said, moving restlessly to the window. "By that time you had successfully made it into the United States, and all my contacts were unable to track you down."

She wanted to ask a lot more questions, but this wasn't the time. She had other concerns. The main one was how she was going to manage living with him until she was fully recovered. And more importantly, how she was going to protect Matthew from him.

"I don't want to go with you, Diego," she said honestly. "I will, because I've no other choice. But you needn't expect me to worship the ground you walk on the way I used to. I've stopped dreaming in the past five years."

"And I have barely begun," he replied, his voice deep and soft. His gaze went over her slowly. "Perhaps it is as well that we meet again like this. Now you are old enough to deal with the man and not the illusion." He got to his feet with the easy grace Melissa remembered from the past. "I will return later. I must check on Matthew."

She turned under the sheet to keep her restless hands busy. "Tell him I love him and miss him very much, and that I'll be home soon, will you?"

"Of course." He hesitated, feeling awkward. "The child misses you, too." He smiled faintly. "He said if he could be allowed to visit you he would kiss the hurts better."

Tears sprang to her eyes and suddenly she felt terribly alone. She dabbed at the tears with the sheet, but Diego drew out a spotless white handkerchief and wiped them away. The handkerchief smelled of the cologne he favored and brought back vivid memories of him. Her eyes lifted, and she gazed at him. For one long instant, time rolled away and she was a girl with the man she loved more than her own life.

"Enamorada," he breathed huskily, his black eyes unblinking, smoldering. "If you knew how empty the years have been—"

The sudden opening of the door was like a gunshot. Melissa glanced that way as a smiling nurse's aide came into the room to check her vital signs. Diego smiled at the woman, his expression only slightly strained, and left with a brief comment about the time. Melissa clutched his handkerchief tightly in her hand, wanting nothing more than the luxury of tears. She was in pain and help-less, and she was much too vulnerable with Diego. She didn't dare let him see how she felt or make one slip that would give away Matthew's parentage. She had to bank down her hidden desire and hide it from him—now more than ever.

She was grateful Diego had left, because the look in his black eyes when he'd held that handkerchief to her eyes had brought back the most painful kind of mem-ories. He still wanted her, if that look was anything to go by, even though he didn't love or trust her. Perhaps that might have been enough for her, but it wouldn't be for Matthew. Matthew deserved a father, not a reluctant guardian. It would be hardest for him, because of Diego's resentment. But telling Diego the truth could cost her the child, and at a time when she wasn't capable of fight-ing for him. She'd have to bide her time. Meanwhile, at least she could be temporarily free of financial terrors. And that was something.

* * *

Several days later, Melissa was released from the hospital and Diego took her to the hotel where he was staying. He had chartered a plane to take Melissa to Chicago the next day, a luxury she was reluctantly grateful for.

She pleaded to let her come along when he went to Mrs. Grady's to pick up Matthew, but he wouldn't allow it. She was too weak, he insisted. So he went to get the boy and Melissa lay smoldering quietly in one of the big double beds in the exquisite hotel suite, uncomfortable and angry.

It only took a few minutes. The door was unlocked and Matthew ran toward her like a little tornado, crying and laughing as he threw himself onto her chest and held her, mumbling and muttering through his tears.

"Oh, my baby," she cooed, smiling as she smoothed his brown hair and sighed over him. It was difficult to reach out because her stitches still pulled, but she didn't complain. She had her baby back.

Diego, watching them, glared at the sight of her blond head bent over that dark one. He was jealous of the boy, and more especially of the boy's father. He hated the very thought of Melissa's body in another man's arms, another man's bed. He hated the thought of the child she'd borne her lover.

Melissa laughed as Matt lifted his electronic bear and made it talk for her.

"Isn't he nice?" Matt asked, all eyes. "My… Your… Mr. Man bought him for me."

"Diego," she prompted.

"Diego," Matthew parroted. He glanced at the tall man who'd been so quiet and distant all the way to the hotel. Matt wasn't sure if he liked Diego or not, but he was certain that the tall man didn't like him. It was going to be very hard living with a man who made him feel so unwelcome.

Melissa touched the pale little cheek. "You need sunshine, my son," she murmured. "You've spent too much time indoors."

Diego put down the cases and lit a small cheroot, pausing to open the curtains before dropping into an easy chair to smoke it at the table beside the window. "I have engaged a sitter for Matthew, since I will be away from the apartment a good deal when we get to Chicago," he told Melissa. "Perhaps the sitter will take him to the park or the beach."

Melissa felt the hair on the back of her neck bristle. Here she'd been the very model of a protective, caring mother, making sure Matt was always supervised, and now Diego came along and thought he could shift responsibility onto a total stranger about whom she knew nothing.

She clasped Matt's waist tightly. "No," she said firmly. "If he goes anywhere, it will be with me."

Diego's eyebrows lifted. She was overly protective of the child, that was obvious. Mrs. Grady had intimated something of the sort; now he could see that the older woman had been right. Something would have to be done about that, he decided. It wasn't healthy for a mother to be so sheltering. A boy who clung to his mother's apron could hardly grow into a strong man.

He crossed his legs and smoked his cheroot while his narrowed eyes surveyed woman and child. "Will you condemn him to four walls and your own company?"

She sat up, wincing as she piled pillows behind her.

"I'll be able to get up and around in no time," she protested.

"Oh, yes," he agreed blandly, watching her struggle. "Already you can sit up by yourself."

She gave him her best glare. "I can walk, too."

"Not without falling over," he murmured, watching the cheroot with a faint smile as he recalled her last attempt to use her damaged leg.

"I'll hold you up, Mama," Matt assured her. "I'm very strong."

"Yes, I know you are, my darling," she said, her voice soft and loving. The man sitting in the chair felt an explosive anger that she cared so much for another man's child.

"What would you like for dinner?" he asked suddenly, getting up. "I can get room service to bring a tray."

"Steak and a salad for me, please," she said.

"Matt wants a fish." The little boy looked up, nervous and unsure, clinging to his mother's arm.

"They may not have fish, Matt," Melissa began.

"They have it," Diego said stiffly. "I had fish last night."

"Coffee for me, and milk for Matt," she said, turning away from the coldness of Diego's face as he looked at her son.

He nodded, a bare inclination of his head, and went to telephone.

"Mr. Man doesn't like Matt," Matthew said with a sad little sigh. "Doesn't he have any children?"

Melissa wanted to cry, but she knew that wouldn't solve anything. She only hoped Diego didn't hear the little boy as she shushed him and shook her head.

Diego didn't turn or flinch, but he heard, all right. It

made the situation all the more difficult. He hadn't realized how perceptive children were.

Dinner was served from a pushcart by a white-coated waiter, and Matthew took his to the far side of the table, as if he wanted a buffer between himself and the tall man who didn't like him. Diego sat beside Melissa, and she tried not to smell the exotic cologne he wore or notice the strength of his powerful, slender body next to hers. He was the handsomest man she'd ever seen, and as he cut his steak she had to fight not to slide her fingers over the dark, lean hand holding the knife.

Diego finished first and went to the lobby on the pretext of getting Melissa something to read. In fact he wanted to get away from the boy's sad little face, with its big, haunting black eyes. He hated his own reactions because they were hurting that innocent little child who, under different circumstances, might have been his own.

He went to the lounge and had a whiskey sour, ignoring the blatant overtures of a slinky blonde who obviously found him more than attractive. He finished his drink and his cheroot and went back upstairs, taking a magazine for Melissa and a coloring book and crayons for Matt.

Melissa had Matt curled up beside her on the couch, and they both tensed the minute he walked in. His chin lifted.

"I brought a coloring book for the boy," he said hesitantly.

Matt didn't move. He looked up, waiting, without any expression on his face.

Diego took the book and the crayons and offered them to him, but still Matt didn't make a move.

"Don't you want the book, Matt?" Melissa asked softly.

"No. He doesn't like Matt," Matt said simply, lowering his eyes.

Diego frowned, torn between pain and his desire for vengeance. The child touched him in ways he had never dreamed of. He saw himself in the little boy, alone and frightened and sad. His own childhood had been an unhappy one, because his father had never truly loved his mother. His mother had known it, and suffered for it. She had died young, and his father had become even more withdrawn. Then, when his father had met the lovely Sheila, the older man's attitude had changed for the better. But the change had been short-lived—and that loss of hope Diego owed to Melissa's family, because his father had died loving Sheila Sterling, loving her with a hopeless passion that he was never able to indulge. The loss had warped him and Diego had seen what loving a woman could do to a man, and he had learned from it. Allowing a woman close enough to love was all too dangerous.

But the boy…it was hardly his fault. How could he blame Matt for Melissa's failings?

He put the coloring book and the crayons gently on the table by the sofa and handed Melissa the women's magazine he'd bought for her. Then he went back to his chair and sat smoking his cheroot, glancing through a sheaf of papers in a file.

"I'm going to read, Matt," Melissa said gently, nudging him to stand up. "You might as well try out your crayons. Do you remember how to color?"

Matt glanced at the man, who was oblivious to them

both, and then at the crayons and coloring book. "It's all right?" he asked his mother worriedly.

"It's all right," she assured him.

He sighed and got down on the floor, sprawling with crayons everywhere, and began to color one of his favorite cartoon characters.

Diego looked up then and smiled faintly. Melissa, watching him, was surprised by his patience. She'd forgotten how gentle he could be. But then it had been a long time since she and Diego had been friends.

They had an early night. Melissa almost spoke when Diego insisted that Matt pick up his crayons and put them away neatly. But she didn't take the child's side, because she knew Diego was right. Often she was less firm with Matt than she should be because she was usually so tired from her job.

She helped Matt into his pajamas and then looked quickly at Diego, because there were two double beds. She didn't want to be close to her estranged husband, but she didn't know how to say it in front of Matt.

Diego stole her thunder neatly by suggesting that the boy bunk down with her. It was only for the one night, because there were four bedrooms in the Chicago apartment. Matt would have his own room. Yes, Melissa thought, and that's when the trouble would really start, because she and Matt had been forced to share a room. She could only afford a tiny efficiency apartment with a sofa that folded out to make a bed. Matt wasn't used to being alone at night, and she wondered how they were going to cope.

But she didn't want to borrow trouble. She was tired and nervous and apprehensive, and there was worse to come. She closed her eyes and went to sleep. And she didn't dream.

The next morning, they left for Chicago. Despite the comfort of the chartered Lear jet, Melissa was still sore and uncomfortable. She had her medicine, and the attending physician at the hospital had referred her to a doctor in Chicago in case she had any complications. If only she could sit back and enjoy the flight the way Matthew was, she thought, watching his animated young face as he peered out the window and asked a hundred questions about airplanes and Chicago. Diego unbent enough to answer a few of them, although he did it with faint reluctance. But Matt seemed determined now to win him over, and Diego wasn't all that distant this morning.

Back in the old days in Guatemala, Melissa had never thought about the kind of father Diego would make. In her world of daydreams, romance had been her only concern, not the day-to-day life that a man and a woman had to concern themselves with after the wildness of infatuation wore off. Now, watching her son with his father, she realized that Diego really liked children. He was patient with Matthew, treating each new question as if it were of the utmost importance. He hadn't completely gotten over the shock of the child, she knew, and there was some reserve in him when he was with this boy he thought was another man's son. But he was polite to the child, and once or twice he actually seemed amused by Matt's excitement.

He was the soul of courtesy, but Melissa couldn't help thinking he'd much rather be traveling alone. Nevertheless, he carried her off the plane and to a waiting limousine for the trip to the Lincoln Park apartment he maintained, and she had to grind her teeth to keep from reaching up and kissing his hard, very masculine mouth as he held her. She hoped he didn't see how powerfully his nearness affected her. She was still vulnerable, even after all the years apart, but she didn't dare let him see it. She couldn't let him destroy her pride again as he had once before.

The apartment was a penthouse that overlooked the park and the shoreline, with the city skyline like a gray silhouette on the rainy horizon. Melissa was put to bed at once in one of the guest bedrooms and told to rest while Matthew explored the apartment and Diego introduced Melissa to Mrs. Albright, who was to do the babysitting as well as the cooking and cleaning. Apollo had recommended the pleasant, heavyset woman, and she'd been taking care of the apartment for Diego for over a year now.

Mrs. Albright was middle-aged and graying, with a sweet face and a personality to match. She took Melissa coffee and cake in bed and set about making her as comfortable as possible, insisting that she stay in bed to recuperate from the long flight. Then she took Matt off to the kitchen to spoil him with tiny homemade cream cakes and milk while she listened to his happy chatter about the flight from Tucson.

Once the boy and Melissa were settled, Diego picked up the phone and punched in a number.

Melissa heard him, but she couldn't make out many of the words. It sounded as though he were speaking to Apollo, and in fact he was, because Apollo showed up at the apartment an hour later with a slender, petite black woman.

Diego introduced the tall, muscular black man in the

gray suit. "This is Apollo Blain. Perhaps you remember him." Apollo smiled and nodded, and Melissa smiled back. "And this is Joyce Latham, Apollo's secretary."

"Temporarily," Apollo said with a curt nod in Joyce's direction.

"That's right, temporarily," Joyce said in a lilting West Indian accent, glaring up at the tall man. "Just until the very second I can find anybody brave enough to take my place."

Apollo glowered down at her. "Amen, sister," he bit off. "And with any luck I'll get somebody who can re-member a damned telephone number long enough to dial it and who can file my clients alphabetically so I can find the files!"

"And maybe I'll get a boss who can read!" Joyce shot back.

"Enough!" Diego laughed, getting between them. "Melissa has survived one disaster. She doesn't need to be thrust into a new one, *por favor*."

Apollo grinned sheepishly. "Sorry. I got carried away." He shot a speaking glance at Joyce.

"Me, too," she muttered, shifting so that she was a little away from him. Her features weren't pretty, but her eyes were lovely, as deep and black as a bottomless pool, and her coffee-with-cream complexion was blem-ishless. She had a nice figure, probably, but the floppy uninspired blue dress she was wearing hid that very well.

"It's nice to meet you," Melissa told the woman, smil-ing. "I remember Apollo from years ago, of course. How long have you worked for him?"

"Two weeks too long," Joyce muttered.

"That's right, two weeks and one day too long," Apollo added. "Dutch and J.D. are coming over later, and Shirt says he and his missus are going to fly up to see you next week. It'll be like a reunion."

"I remember our last reunion," Diego said, smiling faintly. "We were evicted from the suite we occupied at three in the morning."

"And one of us was arrested," Apollo said smugly.

"That so?" Joyce asked him. "How long did they keep you in jail?"

He glared. "Not me. Diego."

"Diego?" Melissa stared at him in disbelief. The cool, careless man she knew wasn't hotheaded enough to land himself in jail. But perhaps she didn't really know him at all.

"He took exception to some remarks about his Latin heritage," Apollo explained with a glance at Diego, whose expression gave nothing away. "The gentleman making the remarks was very big and very mean, and to make a long story short, Diego assisted the gentleman into the hotel swimming pool through a plate-glass window."

"It was a long time ago." Diego turned as Matthew came running into the room.

"You have to come see my drawing, Mama," the boy said urgently, tugging at his mother's hand. "I drew a puppy dog and a bee! Come look!"

"*Momento,* Matthew," Diego said firmly, holding the boy still. He introduced the visitors, who smiled down warmly at the child. "You can show your drawings to Mama in a moment, when our visitors have gone, all right, little one?"

"All right." Matthew sighed. He smiled at his mama and went shyly past the visitors and back to his crayons.

Apollo said, "He's a mirror image of you…" The

last word trailed away under the black fury of Diego's eyes. He cleared his throat. "Well, we'd better get back to work. We'll be over with the others tonight. But we won't stay long. We don't want to wear out the missus, and don't lay on food. Just drinks. Okay?"

"And we'll come in separate cars next time," Joyce grumbled, darting a glance at the black man. "His idea of city driving is to aim the car and close his eyes."

"I could drive if you could stop putting your hands over your eyes and making those noises," he shot back.

"I was trying to say my prayers!"

"See you later," Apollo told Melissa and Diego. He took Joyce by the arm and half led, half dragged her out of the apartment.

"Don't they make a sweet couple?" Melissa murmured dryly when they'd gone. "I wonder if they both carry life insurance…?"

Diego smiled faintly at the mischief in her eyes. "An interesting observation, Señora Laremos. Now, if there is nothing I can do for you, you can praise your son's art while I get back to work."

Her pale gray eyes searched his face, looking for revelations, but there were none in that stony countenance. "It offended you that Apollo mentioned a resemblance."

"The boy's father obviously had some *Ladino* blood," he countered without expression. He put his hands in his pockets, and his black eyes narrowed. "You will not divulge your lover's identity, even now?"

"Why should it matter to you?" she asked. "I had the impression when I left Guatemala that it would be too soon if you never saw me again."

"I tried to talk to you at the time. You would not listen, so I assumed that my feelings would have no effect on you."

"Do you have any feelings?" she asked suddenly. "My father said once that if you did it would take dynamite to get to them."

He stood watching her, his slightly wavy black hair thick and clean where it shone in the light, his eyes watchful. "Considering the line of work I was in, Melissa, is that so surprising? I could not afford the luxury of giving in to my emotions. It has been both a protection and a curse in later years. Perhaps if I had not been so reticent with you the past five years would not have been wasted."

Her pulse jumped, but she kept her expression calm so he wouldn't see how his words affected her. "I understood," she replied. "Even though I was young, I wasn't stupid."

"Had you no idea what would happen when you led me into that sweet trap, Melissa?" he asked with a bitter laugh.

"It wasn't a trap," she said doggedly. "I'd written a lot of silly love poems and scribbled some brazen note to you that I meant to destroy. I'd never have had the nerve to send it to you." She colored faintly at the memory. "I tried to tell you, and my father, that it was a mistake, but neither of you would listen." Her fingers toyed with the hem of her pink blouse. "I loved you," she said under her breath. Her eyes were closed, and she missed the expression that washed over his face. "I loved you more than my own life, and Dad was on the verge of sending me away to college. I knew that I'd never see you again. Every second I had with you was precious, and that's why I gave in. It wasn't planned, and it wasn't meant to be a trap." She laughed coldly. "The irony of it all is that I was stupid enough to believe that you might come to love me if we lived together. But you left me with your family and went away, and when you came back and I tried so desperately to catch your attention—" She couldn't go on. The memory of his contemptuous rejection was too vivid. She averted her eyes. "I knew then that I'd been living in a daydream. I had what I wanted, but through force, not through choice. Leaving was the first intelligent decision I made."

He felt as if she'd hit him with a rock. "Are you telling me that you didn't have marriage in mind?"

"Of course I had marriage in mind, but I never meant you to be forced into it!" she burst out, tears threatening in her eyes. "I loved you. I was twenty and there'd never been another man, and you were my world, Diego!"

His tall, elegant body tautened. He'd never let himself think about it, about what had motivated her. Perhaps, deep inside, he'd known all along how she felt but hadn't been able to face it. He drew a thin cheroot from his pocket and lit it absently. "I went to see your father after he confirmed that you were still alive. He told me nothing, except that you despised me and that you never wanted to see me again." He lifted his gaze and stared at her. "I was determined to hear that for myself, of course, so I kept searching. But to no avail."

"I used my maiden name when I applied for United States citizenship," she explained, "and I lived in big cities. After I was settled, I contacted my father and begged him not to let you know where I was. Later, when the attorney called and told me about my father's death, I grieved. But I didn't have enough money to go to the funeral. Even then, I pleaded with the lawyer not to reveal my whereabouts. I didn't really think you'd come looking for me when you knew I'd—" she forced out the lie "—lost the baby, but I had to be sure."

"You were my responsibility," he said stiffly. "You still are. Our religion does not permit divorce."

"My memory doesn't permit reconciliation," she said shortly. "I'll stay here until I'm able to work again, but that's all. I'm responsible for myself and my son. You have no place in my life, or in my heart, anymore."

He fought back the surge of misery her statement engendered. "And Matthew?"

She pushed back her hair. "Matthew doesn't concern you. He thinks you hate him, and he's probably right. The sooner I get him away from here the better."

He turned gracefully, staring hard at her. "Did you expect that I could accept him so easily? He is the very proof that your emotions were not involved when we were together. If you had loved me, Melissa, there could never have been another man. Never!"

And that was the crux of the entire problem, she thought. He didn't realize that he was stating a fact. If he'd trusted her, he'd have known that she loved him too much to take a lover. But he didn't trust her. He didn't know her. He'd never made the effort to know her in any way except the physical.

She lay back on the pillows, exhausted. "I can't fight, Diego. I'm too tired."

He nodded. "I know. You need rest. We can talk when you are more fit."

"I hope you didn't expect me to fall in line like the little slave I used to be around you," she said, lifting cold eyes to his.

"I like very much the way you are now, *niña*," he said

slowly, his accent even more pronounced than usual. His dark eyes smoldered as he drew them over her body. "A woman with fire in her veins is a more interesting proposition than a worshipful child."

"You won't start any fires with me, *señor*," she said haughtily.

"*¿Es verdad?*" He moved slowly to the bed and, leaning one long arm across her, stared into her eyes from scant inches away. "Be careful before you sling out challenges, my own," he said in the deep, soft voice she remembered so well whispering Spanish love words in the silence of the Mayan ruins. "I might take you up on them." He bent closer, and she could almost feel the hard warmth of his mouth against her parted lips, faintly smoky, teasing her mouth with the promise of the kisses she'd once starved for.

She made a sound deep in her throat, a tormented little sob, and turned her face against the pillow, closing her eyes tight. "No," she whispered. "Oh, don't!"

She felt his breath against her lips. Then, abruptly, he pushed away, shaking the bed, and stood up. He turned away to light another cheroot. "There is no need for such virginal terror," he said stiffly as he began to smoke it. "Your virtue is safe with me. I meant only to tease. I lost my taste for you the day I learned just how thirsty you were for vengeance."

She was grateful for his anger. It had spared her the humiliation of begging for his kisses. Because she wasn't looking at his face, she didn't realize that her rejection had bruised his ego and convinced him that she no longer wanted his kisses.

He got control over his scattered emotions. "The

man who replaced me in your affections—Matthew's father—where is he now, Melissa?"

Her eyes closed. She prayed for deliverance, and it came in the form of Matthew, who came running in to see why Mama hadn't come to look at his drawings. Melissa got up very slowly and allowed Matt to lead her into his bedroom, her steps hesitant and without confidence. She didn't look at Diego.

That night, Mrs. Albright bathed Matthew and put him to bed so that Diego and Melissa would be free to greet their guests. Melissa's leg still made walking difficult, as did the incision where her ovary had been removed. She managed to bathe and dress alone, but she was breathless when Diego came to carry her into the living room.

He stopped in the doorway, fascinated by the picture she made in the pale blue silky dress that emphasized her wavy blond hair, gray eyes and creamy complexion. She'd lost weight, but she still had such a lovely figure that even her slenderness didn't detract from it.

Diego was wearing a dark suit, and his white shirt emphasized his very Latin complexion and his black hair and eyes. It was so sweet just to look at him, to be with him. Melissa hadn't realized how empty the years without him had been, but now the impact of his company was fierce.

She had barely a minute to savor it before the doorbell rang and the guests came in. Apollo and Joyce were together, if reluctantly, and Melissa mused that since the black man hated his secretary so much it was odd that he'd bring her along on a social call. Behind them was a slender blond man with the masculine perfection of a movie star and a mountain of a man with dark, wavy hair.

Diego introduced the blond man. "Eric 'Dutch' van Meer. And this—" he smiled toward the big man "—is Archer, better known as J.D. Brettman. Gentlemen, my wife, Melissa."

They smiled and said all the right things, but Melissa could tell that they were surprised that Diego had never mentioned her. They apologized for not bringing their wives, Danielle and Gabby, but their children had given each other a virus and they were at home nursing them. Melissa would be introduced to them at a later time.

Melissa smiled back. "I'll look forward to that," she said politely. These men made her oddly nervous because she didn't know them as she knew Apollo. They formed into a group and began talking about work, and Melissa felt very isolated from her husband as he spoke with his old comrades. She could see the real affection he felt for them. What a pity that he had none to give her. But what should she have expected under the circumstances? Diego was responsible for her, as he'd said. He was only her caretaker until she was well again, and she'd better remember that. There might be the occasional flare-up of the old attraction, but she couldn't allow herself to dream of a reconciliation. It was dangerous to dream—dreams could become a painful reality.

Joyce had eased away from the others to sit beside Melissa on the huge corner sofa. "I feel as out of place as a green bean in a gourmet ice-cream shop," she mumbled.

Melissa laughed in spite of herself. "So do I, so let's stick together," she whispered.

Joyce straightened the skirt of her beige dress. Her

long hair was a little unkempt, and she slumped. Melissa thought what a shame it was that the woman didn't take care with her appearance. With a little work, she could be a knockout.

"How did you wind up working for Apollo?" Melissa asked.

The other woman smiled ruefully. "I was new to the city—I moved here from Miami—and I signed up with a temporary agency." She glanced at Apollo with more warmth than she seemed to realize. "They sent me to him and he tried to send me right back, but the agency was shorthanded, so he was stuck with me."

"He doesn't seem to mind too much," Melissa murmured dryly. "After all, most bosses don't take their secretaries along on social engagements."

Joyce sighed. "Oh, that. He thought you might feel uncomfortable around all these men. Since the wives couldn't come, here I am." She grinned. "I'm kind of glad that I was invited, you know. I'm not exactly flooded with social invitations."

"I know what you mean," Melissa said, smiling. "Thanks for coming."

As Apollo had promised, they didn't stay long. But as the men said their goodbyes and left, J.D. Brettman shot an openly curious glance in Melissa's direction.

Later, when the guests had gone, Melissa asked Diego about it as he removed his jacket and tie and loosened the top buttons of his shirt.

"Why was Mr. Brettman so curious about me?" she asked gently.

He poured himself a brandy, offered her one and was refused, and dropped gracefully into the armchair across from her. "He knew there was a woman somewhere in my life," he said simply. "There was a rumor to the effect that I had hurt one very badly." He shrugged. "Servants talk, you see. It was known that you fell and were rushed to the hospital." As he lifted the brandy to his lips, his eyes had a sad, faraway look. "I imagine it was said that I pushed you."

"But you didn't!"

His dark eyes caught hers. "Did I not?" His chin lifted, and he looked very Latin, very attractive. "It was because of me that you ran into the night. I was responsible."

She lowered her gaze. "I'm sorry that people thought that about you. I was too desperate at the time to think how it might look to outsiders."

"No importa," he said finally. "It was a long time ago, after all."

"I need to check on Matthew. Mrs. Albright left with the others." She started to stand, but the torn ligament was still tricky and painful, like the incision. She stood very still to catch her breath and laughed self-consciously. "I guess I'm not quite up to the hundred-yard dash."

He got up lazily and put his snifter down. His arms went under her, lifting her with ridiculous ease. "You are still weak," he murmured as he walked down the long hall. "It will take time for you to heal properly."

She had to fight not to lay her cheek against his shoulder, drinking in the scent of his cologne, savoring the warmth of his body and its lean strength as he carried her. "I like your old comrades," she remarked quietly.

"They like you." He carried her through the open door to Matthew's room and let her slide gently to her feet. The little boy was sleeping, his long lashes black against his olive skin, his dark hair disheveled on the white pillow. Diego stared down at him quietly.

Melissa saw the look on his face and almost blurted out the truth. It took every ounce of willpower in her to keep still.

"There is so little of you in him," he said, his voice deep and softly accented. "Except for his hair, which has traces of your fairness in it." He turned, his eyes challenging. "His father was *Ladino*, Melissa?"

She went beet red. She tried to speak, but the words wouldn't come.

"You loved me, you said," he persisted. His eyes narrowed. "If that was so, then how could you give yourself, even to avenge the wounds I caused you?"

She knew she was barely breathing. She felt and looked hunted.

"What was his name?" he asked, moving closer so that he towered over her, warming her, drowning her in the exquisite scent of the cologne he wore.

Her lips parted. "I… You don't need to know," she whispered.

He framed her face with his dark, lean hands, holding her eyes up to his. "Where did you meet him?"

She swallowed. His black eyes filled the world. In the dim light from Matthew's lamp, he seemed huge, dangerous. "Diego…"

"Yes," he breathed, bending to her soft mouth. "Yes, say it like that, *querida*. Say my name, breathe it into my mouth…"

He brushed her lips apart with the soft drugging pressure of his own, teasing, cherishing. Her nervous hands lingered at his hard waist, lost in the warmth of his body under the silky white shirt. She hadn't meant to give in so easily, but the old attraction was every bit as overwhelming as it had been years ago. She was powerless to stop what was happening.

And he knew it. He sighed gently against her mouth, tilting her head at a more accommodating angle. Then the gentleness left him. She felt his mouth growing harder, more insistent. He whispered something in Spanish, and his hands slid into her hair, dragging her mouth closer under his. He groaned and she moved against him, her body trembling with the need to be close to him, to hold him. Her arms slid around him, and suddenly his arms were around her, molding her body to his with a pressure that was painful heaven.

She gasped under his demanding mouth and he stopped at once. He lifted his head, and his eyes were fierce and dark, his breathing as quick as hers.

"I hurt you?" he asked roughly. And then he seemed to come to his senses. He released her slowly, moving away. He turned his eyes briefly to the still-sleeping child. "I must ask your pardon for that," he said stiffly. "It was not intended."

She dropped her gaze to the opening of his white shirt, where dark olive skin and black hair peeked out. "It's all right," she said hesitantly, but she couldn't look up any farther than his chin.

He shifted restlessly, his body aching for the warm softness of hers, his mind burning with confused emotions. He raised her head. "Perhaps it would be wise for you to go to bed."

She wasn't about to argue. "No, I... You don't need to carry me," she protested when he moved toward her. "I can manage. I need to start exercising my leg. But thanks anyway."

He nodded, standing aside to let her leave. His dark eyes followed her hungrily, but when she was out of sight they turned to the sleeping child. His face was so like Melissa's, he thought quietly. But the boy's Spanish heritage was evident. He wondered if Melissa still loved the boy's father or thought about him.

The bitterness he felt drove him from the child's room and into his study. And not until he had worked himself into exhaustion did he fall into his bed to sleep.

Chapter Seven

The atmosphere at breakfast was strained. Melissa had hardly slept, remembering with painful clarity her headlong response to Diego's ardor. If only she could have kept up the front, convinced him that she wasn't attracted to him anymore. She'd almost accomplished that, and then he'd come too close and her aching heart had given in.

She felt his eyes on her as she tried to eat scrambled eggs and bacon. Matthew, too, was unusually silent. He was much more careful of his behavior at the table than he'd ever been when he and Melissa had lived by themselves. Probably, she thought sadly, because he felt the tension and was reacting to it.

"You are quiet this morning, Señora Laremos," Diego said gently, his black eyes slow and steady on her pale face as she toyed with her toast. "Did you not sleep well?"

He was taunting her, but she was too weary to play the game. "No," she confessed, meeting his searching gaze squarely. "In fact, I hardly slept at all, if you want the truth."

He traced the rim of his coffee cup with a finger, and his gaze held hers. "Nor did I, to be equally frank," he said quietly. "I have been alone for many years, Melissa, despite the opinion you seem to have of me as a philandering playboy."

She lifted her coffee cup to her lips for something to do. "You were never lacking in companionship in the old days."

"Before I married you, surely," he agreed. "But marriage is a sacred vow, *niña*."

"I'm not a girl," she retorted.

His chiseled lips tugged into a reluctant smile. "Ah, but you were, that long-ago summer," he recalled, his eyes softening with the memory. "Girlish and sweet and bright with the joy of life. And then, so soon, you became a sad, worn ghost who haunted my house even when you were not in it."

"I should have gone to college in America," she replied, glancing at a quiet but curious Matthew. "There was never any hope for me where you were concerned. But I was too young and foolish to realize that a sophisticated man could never care for an inexperienced, backward child."

"It was the circumstance of our marriage which turned me against you, Melissa," he said tersely. "And but for that circumstance, we might have come together naturally, with a foundation of affection and comradeship to base our marriage on."

"I would never have been able to settle for crumbs, Diego," she said simply. "Affection wouldn't have been enough."

"You seemed to feel that desire was enough, at the time," he reminded her.

Wary of Matt's sudden interest, she smiled at the child and sent him off to watch his cartoons with his breakfast only half eaten.

"He's little, but he hears very well," she told Diego curtly, her gray eyes accusing. "Arguments upset him."

"Was I arguing?" he asked with lifted eyebrows.

She finished her coffee and put the cup down. "Won't you be late for work?"

"By all means let me relieve you of my company, since you seem to find it so disturbing," he said softly. He removed a drop of coffee from his mustache with his napkin and got to his feet. *"Adiós."*

She looked up as he started to the front door, mingled emotions tearing at her.

Diego paused at the door, glaring toward Matthew, who'd just turned the television up very loud. He said something to the boy, who cut down the volume and glared accusingly at the tall man.

"If you disturb the other tenants, little one, we will all be evicted," Diego told him. "And forced to live on the street."

"Then Matt can go home with Mama," the child said stubbornly, "and go away from you."

Diego smiled faintly at that show of belligerence. Even at such a young age, the boy had spirit. It wouldn't do to break it, despite the fact that he was another man's

child. Matt had promise. He was intelligent and he didn't
back down. Despite himself, Diego was warming to the
little boy.

Impulsively he went to the television and went down
on one knee in front of the dark-eyed child. Melissa,
surprised, watched from the doorway.

"On the weekend, we might go to the zoo," Diego
told the boy with pursed lips and a calculating look in
his black eyes. "Of course, if you really would rather
leave me, little one, I can go to see the lions and tigers
alone—"

Matt blinked, his eyes widening. "Lions and tigers?"

Diego nodded. "And elephants and giraffes and
bears."

Matt moved a little closer to Diego. "And could I have
cotton candy? Billy's dad took him to the zoo and he got
cotton candy and ice cream."

Diego smiled gently. "We might manage that, as
well."

"Tomorrow?"

"A few days past that," Diego told him. "I have a great
deal to do during the week, and you have to take care of
your Mama until she gets well."

Matt nodded. "I can read her a story."

Melissa almost giggled, because Matt's stories were
like no one else's, a tangle of fairy-tale characters and
cartoon characters from television in unlikely situations.

"Then if you will be good, *niño,* on Saturday you and
I will go see the animals."

Matt looked at Melissa and then at Diego again,
frowning. "Can't Mama come?"

"Mama cannot walk so much," Diego explained pa-
tiently. "But you and I can, *si?*"

Matt shifted. He was still nervous with the man, but he wanted very much to go to the zoo. *"Sí,"* he echoed.

Diego smiled. "It is a deal, then." He got to his feet. "No more loud cartoons," he cautioned, shaking his finger at the boy.

Matt smiled back hesitantly. "All right."

Diego glanced at Melissa, who was standing in the doorway in her pink silk gown and her long white chenille housecoat, with no makeup and her soft blond hair curling around her pale face. Even like that, she was lovely. He noticed the faint surprise in her gray eyes, mingled with something like…hope.

His black eyes held hers until she flushed, and her gaze dropped. He laughed softly. "Do I make you shy, *querida?*" he asked under his breath. "A mature woman like you?"

She shifted. "Of course not." She flushed even more, looking anywhere but at him.

He opened the front door, his glance going from the child back to her. "Stay in bed," he said. "The sooner the leg is better, the sooner we can begin to do things as a family."

"It's too soon," she began.

"No. It is five years too late." His eyes flashed at her. "But you are my responsibility, and so is Matt. We have to come to terms."

"I've told you I can get a job—"

"No!"

She started to say something, but he held up a hand and his eyes cut her off.

"¡Cuidado!" he said softly. "You said yourself that arguing is not healthy for the child. *¡Hasta luego!*"

He was gone before she could say another word.

It was a hectic morning. Diego had hardly gotten to the office before he and Dutch had to go out to give a demonstration to some new clients. When they got back, voices were raised behind the closed office door. Diego hesitated, listening to Joyce and Apollo in the middle of a fiery argument over some filing.

Dutch came down the hall behind him, a lighted cigarette in his hand, looking as suave as ever. He glanced at Diego with a rueful smile.

"Somehow combat was a little easier to adjust to than that," he said, indicating the clamor behind the closed office door. "I think I'll smoke my cigarette out here until they get it settled or kill each other."

Diego lit a cheroot and puffed away. "Perhaps someday they will marry and settle their differences."

"They'd better settle them first," Dutch remarked. "I've found that marriage doesn't resolve conflicts. In fact, it intensifies them."

Diego sighed. "Yes, I suppose it does." His dark eyes narrowed thoughtfully. Last night seemed more and more like a dream as the din grew. Would he and Melissa become like that arguing couple in the office? Matthew was their unresolved conflict, and despite his growing interest in the child, he still couldn't bear the thought of the man who'd fathered him.

"Deep thoughts?" Dutch asked quietly.

The other man nodded. "Marriage is not something I ever coveted. Melissa and I were caught in a—how do you say?—compromising situation. Our marriage was a matter of honor, not choice."

"She seems to care about you," the other man ventured. "And the boy—"

"The boy is not mine," Diego said harshly, his black eyes meeting the equally dark ones of the other man.

"My God." Dutch stared at him.

"She left me after I cost her our child," Diego said, his eyes dark and bitter with the memories. "Perhaps she sought consolation, or perhaps she did it for revenge. Whatever the reason, the child is an obstacle I cannot overcome." His eyes fell to the cheroot in his hand. "It has made things difficult."

Dutch was silent for a long moment. "You're very sure that she lost your child?"

That was when Diego first began to doubt what he'd been told five years ago. When Dutch put it into words, he planted a seed. Diego stared back at him with knitted brows.

"There was a doctor at the hospital," he told Dutch. "I tried later to find him, but he had gone to South America to practice. The nurse said Melissa was badly hurt in the fall, and Melissa herself told me the child was dead."

"You got drunk at our last reunion," Dutch recalled. "And I put you to bed. You talked a lot. I know all about Melissa."

Diego averted his eyes. "Do you?" he asked stiffly.

"And you can take the poker out of your back," Dutch said. "You and I go back a long way. We don't have many secrets from each other. Things were strained between you and her. Isn't it possible that she might have hidden her pregnancy from you for fear that you'd try to take the boy from her?"

Diego stared at him, half-blind with shock. "Melissa would not do such a thing," he said shortly. "It is not her nature to lie. Even now, she has no heart for subterfuge."

Dutch shrugged. "You could be wrong."

"Not in this. Besides, the years are wrong," he said heavily. "Matthew is not yet four."

"I see."

Diego took another draw on his cheroot. Inside the office, the voices got louder, then stopped when the telephone rang. "I had my own suspicions at first, you know," he confessed. "But I soon forgot them."

"You might take a look at his birth certificate, all the same," Dutch suggested. "Just to be sure."

Diego smiled and said something polite. In the back of his mind there were new doubts. He wasn't certain about anything anymore, least of all his feelings for Melissa and his stubborn certainty that he knew her. He was beginning to think that he'd never known her at all. He'd wanted her, but he'd never made any effort to get to know her as a person.

When Diego came home, Matthew was sprawled on the bed and Melissa was reading to him. He paused in the doorway to watch them for a few seconds, his eyes growing tender as they traced the graceful lines of Melissa's body and then went to Matt, becoming puzzled and disturbed as he really looked at the child for the first time.

Yes, it could be so. Matthew could be his child. He had to admit it now. The boy had his coloring, his eyes. Matt had his nose and chin, but he had the shape of his mother's eyes, and his hair was only a little darker than hers. Except that the years were wrong—Matt would have to be over four years old if he was truly Diego's son. Melissa had said that he was just past three. But Diego knew so little about children of any age, and there was always the possibility that she hadn't told the exact truth.

Little things she'd said, slips she'd made, could reveal a monumental deception.

She didn't lie as a rule, but this was an extraordinary situation. After all, she'd had more than enough reason to want to pay him back for his cruelty. And was she the kind of woman who could go from him to another man so easily? Had she? Or had she only been afraid, as Dutch had hinted—afraid of losing her son to his real father? She might think Diego capable of taking Matt away from her and turning her out of their lives. His jaw tautened as he remembered his treatment of her and exactly why she had good reason to see him that way. If he didn't know Melissa, then she certainly didn't know him. He'd never let her close enough to know him. What if he did let her come close? He turned away from the door, tempted for the first time to think of pulling down the barriers he'd built between them. He was alone, and so was she. Was there any hope for them now?

Melissa hobbled to the supper table with Matt's help. She looked worried, and Diego wondered what had upset her.

He didn't have to wait long. Halfway through the first course, she got up enough nerve to ask him a question that had plagued her all day.

"Do you think I might get a job when the doctor gives me the all-clear?" Melissa asked cautiously.

He put down his coffee cup and stared at her. "You have a job already, do you not?" he asked, nodding toward a contented Matthew, who was obviously enjoying his chicken dish.

"Of course, and I love looking after him and having time to spend with him for a change," she confessed. "But…" She sighed heavily. "I feel as if I'm not pulling my weight," she said finally. "It doesn't seem fair to make you support us."

He looked, and was, surprised at the remark. He leaned back in his chair, looking very Latin and faintly arrogant. "Melissa, you surely remember that I was a wealthy man in Guatemala. I work because I enjoy it, not because I need to. I have more than enough in Swiss banks to support all of us into old age and beyond."

"I didn't realize that." She toyed with her fork. "Still, I don't like feeling obligated to you."

His eyes flashed. "I am your husband. It is my duty, my obligation, my responsibility, to take care of you."

"And that's an archaic attitude," Melissa muttered, her own temper roused. "In the modern world, married people are partners."

"José's mama and papa used to fight all the time," Matthew observed with a wary glance at his mother. "And José's papa went away."

Diego drew in a sharp breath. *"Niñito,"* he said gently, "your mama and I will inevitably disagree from time to time. Married people do, *comprende?"*

Matthew moved a dumpling around on his plate with his fork. *"Yo no sé,"* he murmured miserably, but in perfect Spanish.

Diego frowned. He got up gracefully to kneel beside Matthew's chair. *"¿Hablas español?"* he asked gently, using the familiar tense.

"Sí," Matthew said, and burst into half a dozen incomplete fears and worries in that language before Diego interrupted him by placing a long finger over his small mouth. His voice, when he spoke, was more tender than Melissa had ever heard it.

"Niño," he said, his deep voice soothing, "we are a

family. It will not be easy for any of us, but if we try, we can learn to get along with each other. Would it not please you, little one, to have time to spend with Mama, and a nice place to live, and toys to play with?"

Matt looked worried. "You don't like Matt," he mumbled.

Diego took a slow breath and ran his hand gently over the small head. "I have been alone for a long time," he said hesitantly. "I have had no one to show me how to be a father. It must be taught, you see, and only a small boy can teach it."

"Oh," Matt said, nodding his head. He shifted restlessly, and his dark eyes met Diego's. "Well...I guess I could." His brows knitted. "And we can go to the zoo and to the park and see baseball games and things?"

Diego nodded. "That, too."

"You don't have a little boy?"

Diego hated the lump in his throat. It was as if the years of feeling nothing at all had caught up with him at last. He felt as if a butterfly's wings had touched his heart and brought it to life for the first time. He looked at the small face, so much like his own, and was surprised at the hunger he felt to be this child's father, his real father. The loneliness was suddenly unbearable. "No," he said huskily. "I have...no little boy."

Melissa felt tears running hot down her shocked face. It was more than she'd dared hope for that Diego might be able to accept Matt, to want him, even though he believed he was another man's child. It was the first step in a new direction for all of them.

"I guess so," Matthew said with the simple acceptance of childhood. "And Mama and I would live with you?"

"*Sí.*"

"I always wanted a papa of my own," Matthew confessed. "Mama said my own papa was a very brave man. He went away, but Mama used to say he might come back."

That broke the spell. Diego's face tautened as it turned to Melissa, his black eyes accusing, all the tenderness gone out of him at once as he considered that his whole line of thought might have been a fabrication, created out of his own loneliness and need and guilt.

"Did she?" he asked tersely.

Melissa fought for control, dabbing at the tears. "Matt, wouldn't you like to go and play with your bear?"

"Okay." He jumped down from his chair with a shy grin at Diego and ran off to his room. Except for the first night, he'd given them no trouble about sleeping alone. He seemed to enjoy having a room of his very own.

Diego's face was without a trace of emotion when he turned to her. "His father is still alive?" he said tersely.

She dropped her eyes to the table while her heartbeat shook her. "Yes."

"Where is he?"

She shook her head, unable to speak, to tell any more lies.

He took an angry breath. "Until you can trust me, how can we have a marriage?"

She looked up. "And that works both ways. You never trusted me. How can you expect me to trust you, Diego?"

"I was not aware that he spoke such excellent Spanish," he remarked after a minute, lessening the tension.

"It seemed to come naturally to him," she said. "It isn't bad for a child to be bilingual, especially in Tucson, where so many people speak Spanish anyway. Most of his friends did."

He leaned back in his chair, his dark eyes sliding carelessly over Melissa's body. "You grow more lovely with each passing day," he said unexpectedly.

She flushed. "I didn't think you ever looked at me long enough to form an opinion."

He lit a cheroot, puffing on it quietly. "Things are not so simple anymore, are they? The boy is insecure."

"I'm sorry I argued with you," she said sadly. "I made everything worse."

"No. You and I are both responsible for that." He shrugged. "It is not easy, is it, *pequeña,* to forget the past we share?"

"Guatemala seems very far away sometimes, though." She leaned back. "What about the *finca,* Diego?"

"I have given that more thought than you realize, Melissa," he replied. He studied his cheroot. "It is growing more dangerous by the day to try to hold the estate, to provide adequate protection for my workers. I loathe the very thought of giving it up, but it is becoming too much of a financial risk. Now that I have you and the boy to consider, I have decided that I may well have to sell it."

"But your family has lived there for three generations," she protested. "It's your heritage."

"*Niña,* it is a spread of land," he said gently. "A bit of stone and soil. Many lives have been sacrificed for it over the years, and more will be asked. I begin to think the sacrifices are too many." He leaned forward suddenly, his black eyes narrow. "Suppose I asked you to come with me to Guatemala, to bring Matthew, to raise him there."

Her breathing stopped for an instant. She faltered, trying to reconcile herself to the fear his words had fostered.

He nodded, reading her apprehension. "You see? You

could no more risk the boy's life than I could." He sat
back again. "It is much more sensible to lease or sell it
than to take the risk of trying to live there. I like Chicago, *niña*. Do you?"

"Why, yes," she said slowly. "I suppose I do. I don't
know about the winter…"

"We can spend the winter down in the Caribbean and
come back in the spring. Apollo is thinking of expanding
the company, Blain Security Consultants, to include an-
titerrorism classes in that part of the world." He smiled.
"I can combine business with pleasure."

"You haven't told me about the kind of work you do,"
she reminded him. She wanted to know. This was one
of the few times he'd ever let down his guard and talked
to her, sharing another part of his life. It was flattering
and pleasant.

"I teach tactics," he said. He put out the cheroot.
"Dutch and I share the duties, and I also teach defensive
driving to the chauffeurs of the very rich." He looked up
at her. "You remember that I raced cars for a few years."

"My father mentioned it once," she said. Her eyes ran
over his dark face. "You can't live without a challenge,
can you? Without some kind of risk?"

"I have grown used to surges of adrenaline over the
years," he mused, smiling. "Perhaps I have become ad-
dicted." He shrugged. "It is unlikely that I will make you
a rich widow in the near future, Señora Laremos," he
added mockingly, thinking bitterly of the boy's father.

"Money was never one of my addictions," she said
with quiet pride. She got to her feet slowly. "But think
what you like. Your opinion doesn't matter a lot to me
these days, *señor.*"

"Yet it did once," he said softly, rising to catch her

gently by the waist and hold her in front of him. "There was a time when you loved me, Melissa."

"Love can die, like dreams." She sighed wistfully, watching the quick rise and fall of his chest. "It was a long time ago, and I was very young."

"You are still very young, *querida*," he said, his voice deep and very quiet. "How did you manage, alone and pregnant, in a strange place?"

"I had friends," she said hesitantly. "And a good job, working as an assistant buyer for a department store's clothing department. Then I got pneumonia and everything fell apart."

"Yet you have managed enough time with Matthew to teach him values and pride and honor in his heritage."

She smiled. "I wanted him to be a whole person," she said. She looked up, searching the dark eyes so close to hers. "You blame me, don't you? For betraying you…"

Her humility hurt him. It made him feel guilty for the things he'd said to her. He sighed wearily. "Was it not I who betrayed you?" he breathed, and bent to her mouth.

He'd never kissed her in quite that way before. She felt the soft pressure of his mouth with wonder as he cherished it, savored it in a silence ablaze with shared pleasure.

"But, Matthew…" she whispered.

"Kiss me, *querida*," he whispered, and his mouth covered hers again as he drew her against his lean, hard body and his lips grew quietly insistent.

She felt the need in him. Her legs trembled against his. Her mouth followed where his led, lost in its warm, bristly pressure. She put her arms around him and moved closer until she felt him stiffen, until she felt the sudden urgency of his body and heard him groan.

"No," he whispered roughly, pushing her away. His eyes glittered. His breathing was quick and unsteady. "No half measures. I want all of you or nothing. And it is too soon, is it not?"

She wanted to say no, but of course it was too soon, and not just physically. There were too many wounds, too many questions. She lowered her eyes to his chest. "I won't stop you," she said, shocking herself as well as the man standing so still in front of her. "I won't say no."

His fingers contracted, but only for an instant. "It has been a long time," he said in a deep, soft voice. "I do not think that I could be gentle with you the first time, despite the tenderness I feel for you." He shuddered almost imperceptibly. "My possession of you would be violent, and I could not bear to hurt you. It is not wise to let this continue." He let her go and moved away, with his back to her, while he lit another cheroot.

She watched him with curious eyes. Her body trembled with frustration, her leg ached. But she wanted nothing more in life than his body over hers in the sweet darkness.

"I want you," she whispered achingly.

He turned, his black eyes steady and hot. "No less than I want you, I assure you," he said tersely. "But first there must be a lowering of all the barriers. Tell me about Matthew's father, Melissa."

She wanted to. She needed to. But she couldn't tell him. He had to come to the realization himself, he had to believe in her innocence without having proof. "I can't," she moaned.

"Then know this: I have had enough of subterfuge and pretense. Until you tell me the truth, I swear that I will never touch you again."

She exhaled unsteadily. He was placing her in an intolerable position. She couldn't tell him the truth. She didn't trust him enough, and obviously he didn't trust her enough. If he loved her, he'd trust her enough to know that Matthew was his. But that had always been the problem—she loved too much and he loved too little. He was hot-blooded, and he desired her. But desire was a poor foundation for marriage. It wouldn't be enough.

Diego watched the expressions pass over her face. When he saw her teeth clench, he knew that he'd lost the round. She wasn't going to tell him. She was afraid. Well, there was still one other way to get at the truth. As Dutch had mentioned, there would surely be a birth certificate for Matthew. He would write to the Arizona Bureau of Vital Statistics and obtain a copy of it. That would give Diego the truth about Matt's age and his parentage. Diego had to know, once and for all, who Matthew's father was. Until he did, there was no hope of a future for him and Matthew and Melissa.

"It is late," he said without giving her a chance to say anything else. "You had better get some sleep."

Melissa hesitated, but only for an instant. It was disappointing. She felt they'd been so close to an understanding. She nodded, turning toward her room without another word.

It was like sitting on top of a bomb for the next few days. Melissa was more aware of Diego than ever before, but he was polite and courteous and not much more. The nights grew longer and longer.

But if she was frustrated, her son wasn't. Diego seemed to have a new shadow, because Matthew followed him everywhere when he wasn't working. Rather than resenting it, Diego seemed to love it. He indulged the child as never before, noticed him, played with him. His efforts were hesitant at first because he'd never spent much time around children. But as time wore on he learned to play, and the child became a necessary part of his day, of his life.

They went to the zoo that weekend, leaving Melissa with the television and a new videocassette of an adventure movie for company. They stayed until almost dark, and when they came back Matthew seemed a different boy. Oddly enough, Diego was different, too. There was an expression on his face and in his black eyes that Melissa didn't understand.

"We saw a cobra!" Matt told Melissa, his young face alive with excitement. "And a giraffe, and a lion, and a monkey! And I had cotton candy, and I rode a train, and a puppy dog chased me!" He giggled gleefully.

"And Papa is worn to a nub," Diego moaned, dropping wearily onto the sofa beside Melissa with a weary grin. "*Dios mío,* I almost bought a motorcycle just to keep up with him!"

"I wore Papa out," Matt chuckled, "didn't I, Papa?"

Melissa glanced from one of them to the other, curiosity evident in her gray eyes.

"Matthew's papa isn't coming back," Diego told her. He lit a cheroot with steady hands, his black eyes daring her to challenge the statement. "So I'm going to be his papa and take care of him. And he will be my son."

"I always wanted a papa of my own," Matthew told Melissa. He leaned his chin on the arm of the sofa and stared at her. "Since my papa's gone away, I want Diego."

Melissa drew a slow breath, barely breathing as all the things she'd told Matt about his father came back with vivid clarity. She prayed that he hadn't mentioned any of them to Diego. Especially the photograph…why in heaven's name had she shown Matt that photo!

But Diego looked innocent, and Matthew was obviously unruffled, so there couldn't have been any shared secrets. No. Of course not. She was worrying over nothing.

"Did you have a good time?"

Matt grinned. "We had a really good time, and tomorrow we're going to church."

Melissa hoped she wouldn't pass out. It wouldn't be good to shock the child. But her eyes looked like saucers as they slid to Diego's face.

"A child should be raised in the church," he said tersely. "When you are able, you may come with us."

"I'm not arguing," she said absently.

"Good, because it would avail you nothing. Matt, suppose you watch television while I organize something for us to eat? Do you want a fish?"

"Yes, please," the child said with a happy laugh, and ran to turn on cartoons.

"And you, *querida?*" he asked Melissa, letting his dark eyes slide over her gray slacks and low-cut cream sweater with soft desire.

"I'd like a chef's salad," she murmured. "There's a fish dinner in the freezer that Matt can have, and the salad's already made. I prepared it while you were gone. There's a steak I can grill for you…"

"I can do it." He got up, stretching lazily, and her eyes moved over him with helpless longing, loving the powerful lines of his tall body.

"I need to move around, though," she murmured. She got up and stood for a minute before she started to walk. The limp was still pronounced, but it didn't hurt half as bad to move as it had only a week ago. She laughed at her own progress.

"How easily the young heal," Diego remarked with a smile.

"I'm not that young, Diego," she said.

He moved close to her, taking her by the waist to lazily draw her body to him, holding her gently. "You are when you laugh, *querida*," he said, smiling. "What memories you bring back of happy times we shared in Guatemala."

The smile faded. "Were there any?" she asked sadly.

He searched her soft gray eyes. "Do you not remember how it was with us, before we married? The comradeship we had, the ease of being together?"

"I was a child and you were an adult." She dropped her eyes. "I was bristling with hero worship and buried in dreams."

"And then we took refuge in a Mayan ruin." He was whispering so that Matt, who was engrossed in a television program, wouldn't hear. "And we became lovers, with the rain blowing around us and the threat of danger everywhere. Your body under my body, *Melissa mía,* your cries in my mouth as I kissed you…"

She moved away too fast and almost fell, her face beet red and her heart beating double time. "I—" She had to try again because her voice squeaked. "I'll just fix the salad dressing, Diego."

He watched her go with a faint, secretive smile. Behind him, Matt was laughing at a cartoon, and Diego glanced his way with an expression that he was glad Melissa couldn't see. Matt had told him about the photograph of his father while they'd been looking at a poster that showed banana trees.

Those funny-looking trees, Matt exclaimed, were in the photo his Mama had of his papa. And his papa was wearing a big hat and riding a horse.

Diego had leaned against a wall for support, and he didn't remember what he'd mumbled when Matt had kept on talking. But even though he'd sent for the birth certificate, it was no longer necessary. There couldn't be another photo like the one Matt described, and it was with amused fury that he realized the man he'd been jealous of was himself.

He was Matt's father. Matt was the child Melissa had sworn she'd lost. It even made sense that she'd hidden her pregnancy from him. She'd probably been afraid that he didn't care enough about her to let her stay after the child was born. More than likely she'd thought that Diego would take her baby from her and send her away. She'd run to keep that from happening.

She was still running. She hadn't told him the truth about Matt because she didn't trust him enough. Perhaps she didn't love him enough anymore, either. He was going to have to work on that. But at least he knew the truth, and that was everything. He looked at his son with fierce pride and knew that, whatever happened, he couldn't give up Matt. He couldn't give up Melissa, either, but he was going to have to prove that to her first.

After supper, Diego and Matthew sprawled on the carpet in front of the television. Melissa's eyes softened at the two of them, so alike, so dark and delightfully Latin, laughing and wrestling in front of the television. Diego was in his stocking feet, his shirt unbuttoned in front, his hair disheveled, his eyes laughing at his son. He looked up with the laughter still in his face and saw Melissa watching him. For an instant, something flared in his eyes and left them darkly disturbing. She flushed and looked away, and she heard him laugh. Then Matthew attacked him again and the spell was broken. But it left Melissa shaken and hungry. Diego was accepting Matt, and that should have satisfied her. But it didn't. She wanted Diego to love her. When, she wondered bitterly, had she ever wanted anything else? But it seemed as impossible now as it had in the past. He wanted her, but perhaps he had nothing left to offer.

Diego was involved with work for the next few weeks. The atmosphere at the apartment was much less strained. Matt played with Diego, and the two of them were becoming inseparable. And Diego looked at Melissa with lazy indulgence and began to tease her gently now and again. But the tension between them was growing, and her nervousness with him didn't help. She couldn't understand his suddenly changed attitude toward Matt and herself. Because she couldn't figure out the reason behind his turnaround, she didn't trust it.

When the time came for her final checkup, Diego took time off from work to take her to the doctor.

She was pronounced cured and released from the doctor's care. He told her to progress slowly with her rapidly healing leg but said she was fit to work again.

When she told Diego that and started hinting at wanting to get a job, he felt uneasy. She'd run away from him once, and he was no longer able to hide his growing affection for the boy. What if she knew that he suspected the truth? Would she take Matt and run again, fearing that Diego might be trying to steal him away from her? His blood ran cold at the prospect, but he wasn't confident enough to put the question to her. He might force her hand if he wasn't careful. The thing was, how was he going to keep her?

He worried the question all the way back to the apartment, reserved and remote as he pondered. He went back to work immediately after dropping her off at the apartment. He didn't even speak as he went out the door. His withdrawal worried Melissa.

"You need some diversion, Mrs. Laremos," Mrs. Albright chided as she fixed lunch for them. "Staying around this apartment all the time just isn't healthy."

"You know, I do believe you're right," Melissa agreed with a sigh. "I think I'll call Joyce and take her out to lunch tomorrow. I might even get a job."

"Your husband won't like that, if you don't mind my saying so, ma'am," Mrs. Albright murmured as she shredded carrots for a salad.

"I'm afraid he won't," Melissa said. "But that isn't going to stop me."

She dropped a kiss on Matthew's dark head as he sat engrossed in a children's program on the educational network and went into Diego's study to use the phone.

It was bad luck that she couldn't remember the name of Apollo's company. Diego surely had it written down somewhere. She didn't like going into his desk, but this was important. She opened the middle drawer and found a black book of numbers. But underneath it was an open envelope that caught her attention.

With a quick glance toward the door and a pounding heart, she drew it out and looked at it. The return address was the Arizona Bureau of Vital Statistics. Her cold, nervous hands fumbled it open, and she drew out what she'd been afraid she'd find—a copy of Matthew's birth certificate. Under father, Diego's full name and address were neatly typed.

She sighed, fighting back tears. So he knew. But he hadn't said anything. He'd questioned her and promised her that he wouldn't come near her again until she told him the truth about Matthew. Why? Did it matter so much to his pride? Or was he just buying time to gain Matthew's affection before he forced Melissa out of their lives? Perhaps despite what he'd said about Guatemala he meant to take Matthew there and leave Melissa behind. His lack of ardor since he and Matt had gone to the zoo, his lack of attention to her, made her more uncertain than ever. And today, his remoteness when the doctor had said she could work. Was he thinking about throwing her out now that she no longer needed his support?

She was frightened, and her first thought was to pack a case and get Matthew far away, as fast as possible. But that would be irrational. She had to stop and think. She had to be logical, not make a spur-of-the-moment decision that she might come to regret.

She put the birth certificate back into the envelope and replaced it carefully, facedown under the black book, and closed the drawer. She didn't dare get a number out of it now because Diego would know that she'd been into his desk drawer.

Then she remembered that Mrs. Albright would surely have his number. She went into the kitchen and asked the woman.

"Oh, certainly, Mrs. Laremos," she smiled. "It's listed under Blain Security Consultants, Incorporated, in the telephone directory." She eyed Melissa curiously. "Are you all right? You seem very pale."

"I'm fine." Melissa forced a smile. "It's just a little

hard to get around. The ligament is healed, but my leg is stiff. They wanted me to have physical therapy, but I settled for home exercises instead. I'm sure it will limber up once I start them."

"My sister had a bad back, and the doctor put her on exercises," Mrs. Albright remarked. "They helped a great deal. I'm sure you'll do fine, ma'am."

"Yes. So am I. Thank you."

She went into the living room and looked up the number, dialing it with shaky hands.

Joyce's musical voice answered after the second ring. "Blain Security Consultants. How may we help you?"

"You can come out to lunch with me tomorrow and help me save my sanity," Melissa said dryly. "It's Melissa, Diego's wife."

"Yes, I recognized your voice, Melissa," Joyce said with a laugh. "And I'd be delighted to go to lunch with you. Shall I pick you up at your apartment about 11:30? If my boss will let me—"

Apollo's deep, angry voice sounded from a distance. "Since when do I deny you a lunch hour, Miss Latham? By all means, if that's Melissa, you can take her to lunch. Stop making me out to be an ogre."

"I'd never do such a thing, Mr. Blain," Joyce assured him stiffly. "It would be an insult to the ogre."

There was a muttered curse, and a door slammed. Joyce sighed and Melissa hid a giggle.

"See you tomorrow," Joyce whispered. "I'd better get to work or I may wind up out the window on my head."

"It sounds that way, yes. Have a nice day."

"You, too!"

That evening, Diego came home late. He was just in time to kiss Matthew good-night. Melissa, watching them from the doorway, saw the affection and pride in his dark face as he looked at his son. How long had he known? Perhaps he'd suspected it from the beginning. She sighed, thinking how transparent she'd always been to him. She was so green, how could he help but know that she couldn't sleep with anyone except him? Probably he even knew how deeply she loved him. His cruelty in the past, his rejection, even his indifference, didn't seem to affect her feelings. She wondered where she was going to get the strength to leave him. But if he was thinking about taking Matthew away from her, she wouldn't have any choice. He'd never made any secret of his opinion about love. He didn't believe in it. She had no reason to suspect that his feelings had changed over the years.

He loved Matthew, if he loved anyone. Melissa was a complication he didn't really seem to want. When he stood up and moved to the door, Melissa hid her eyes from him. She didn't want him to see the worry in them.

"Joyce said you're taking her out to lunch tomorrow," he remarked after she'd called another good-night to Matthew and closed his bedroom door.

"Yes. I thought I might try getting out of the apartment a little bit," she said. "It's...lonely here."

He stopped at her bedroom door, his eyes dark and quiet. "It will not always be like this," he said. "When time permits, now that you are able to get around, we will find some things that we can do as a family."

She smiled wistfully. "You don't need to feel obligated to include me."

He frowned. "Why?"

She'd forgotten how clever he was. She averted her eyes. "Well, boys like to be with men sometimes without women along, don't they?"

He eyed her curiously. He'd expected her to say more than that. He felt irritable at his own disappointment. What had he expected? She'd held out so long now that he didn't really expect her to give in. He was giving way slowly to a black depression. He'd left her alone, hoping she'd come to him and tell him the truth, and she hadn't. Suppose he'd misjudged her feelings? What if she didn't care? What if she left him, now that she didn't need him to take care of her?

He barely remembered that she'd asked him a question. "I suppose it is good for Matthew to spend some time with just me," he answered her wearily. His face mirrored his fatigue. There were new, harsh lines on it. He studied her slowly for a moment before he turned away. "I have had a long day. If you don't mind, Señora Laremos, I prefer sleep to conversation."

"Of course. Good night," she said, surprised by his tone as well as by the way he looked.

He nodded and went down the hall. She watched him, her eyes wistful and soft and full of regret. Love wasn't the sweet thing the movies made of it, she thought bitterly. It was painful and long-suffering for all its sweetness. He wanted Matthew, but did he want her? She wondered what she was going to do.

She turned away and went into her own bedroom, looking at herself in the mirror. She looked thinner and older, and there were new lines in her face. Did Diego ever think about the past, she wondered, about the times the two of them had gone riding in the Guatemalan valleys and talked about a distant future? She thought of it often, of the way Diego had once been.

She opened her chest of drawers and pulled out the snapshot she'd taken of Diego the day before her father had found them in the hills. Her fingers touched the face lightly and she sighed. How long ago it all seemed, how futile. She'd loved him, and pain was the only true memory she had. If only, she thought, he'd loved her a little in return. But perhaps he really wasn't capable of it. She tucked the photo away and closed the drawers. Dreams were no substitute for reality.

Chapter Eight

The restaurant that Joyce and Melissa went to was small and featured French cuisine. Melissa picked her way through a delicious chicken-and-broccoli crepe and a fresh melon while Joyce frowned over her elaborate beef dish.

"You're very quiet for someone who wanted to talk," Joyce remarked fifteen minutes into the exquisite meal, her dark eyes quietly scrutinizing Melissa's face.

Melissa sighed. "I've got a problem."

Joyce smiled. "Who hasn't?"

"Yes. Well, mine is about to make me pack a bag and leave Chicago."

Joyce put down her fork. "In that case, I'm all ears."

Melissa picked up her coffee cup and sipped the sweet, dark liquid. "Matthew is Diego's son," she said.

"The son I told him I lost before I ran away from him five years ago."

"That's a problem?" Joyce asked blankly.

"I didn't think he knew. He didn't seem to like Matt at first, but now they're inseparable. I thought that maybe he was beginning to accept Matt even though he thought he was another man's son. But yesterday I found a copy of Matthew's birth certificate in his desk drawer."

"If he knows, everything will be all right, won't it?" Joyce asked her.

"That's just it," Melissa said miserably. "It was important to me that he'd believe Matt was his son, without proof, that he'd believe I could never have betrayed him. But now I'll never be sure. And lately Diego acts as if he doesn't want me around. I even think I know why. He knows that Matt is his, and he hates me for letting him think I lost his child."

Joyce blinked. "Come again?"

"That's really a long story." Melissa smiled and stared into her coffee. "I thought I was justified at the time not to tell him or get in touch with him. The way he used to feel about me, I was sure he'd try to take Matt away."

"Maybe he would have," the other woman said gently. "You can't blame yourself too much. You must have had good reasons."

Melissa lifted tortured eyes. "Did I? Oh, there's been fault on both sides, you know. But now that he knows Matt is his, he has to be thinking about all the time he's missed with his son. He has to blame me for that, even though I had provocation. And now I'm afraid that he may be trying to win Matt away from me. He may take him away!"

"That is pure hysteria," Joyce said firmly. "Get hold

of yourself, girl! You can't run away this time. You've got to stay and fight for your son. Come to think of it," she added, "you might try fighting for your husband, as well. He married you. He had to care about you."

Melissa grimaced as she fingered her cup. "Diego didn't really want to marry me. We were found in a compromising situation, which he thought I planned, and he was forced to marry me. He and his family made me feel like a leper, and when I discovered that I was pregnant, I couldn't bear the thought of bringing up my child in such an atmosphere of hatred. So I let him think I lost the baby and I ran away."

"There's no chance that he loves you?"

She smiled wistfully. "Diego was a mercenary for even longer than the rest of the group. He told me once that he didn't believe in love, that it was a luxury he couldn't afford. He wants me. But that's all."

Joyce studied her friend's sad expression. "You and I are unlucky in love," she said finally. "I work for a man who hates me and you live with a man who doesn't love you."

"You hate Apollo, too," Melissa pointed out.

Joyce smiled, her eyes wistful. "Do I?"

"Oh." Melissa put the cup down. "I see."

"I give him the response he expects to keep him from seeing how I really feel. Look at me," she moaned. "He's a handsome, rich, successful man. Why would he want someone as plain and unattractive as I am? I wish I were as pretty as you are."

"Me? Pretty?" Melissa was honestly astounded.

Joyce glowered at her. "Do you love Diego?"

It was a hard question to answer honestly, but in the

end she had to. "I always have," she confessed. "I suppose I always will."

"Then why don't you stop running away from him and start running toward him?" Joyce suggested. "Running hasn't made you very happy, has it?"

"It's made me pretty miserable. But how can I stay with a man who doesn't want me?"

"You could make him want you." She reached out and touched Melissa's hand. "Is he worth fighting for?"

"Oh, yes!"

"Then do it. Stop letting the past create barriers."

Melissa frowned slightly. "I don't know very much about how to vamp a man."

Joyce shrugged. "Neither do I. So what? We can learn together."

This was sounding more delightful by the minute. Melissa was nervous, but she knew that Diego wanted her, and the knowledge gave her hope. "I suppose we could give it a try. If things don't work out—"

"Trust me. They'll work out."

"Then if I have to do it, so do you." Melissa pursed her lips. "Did you know that I was an assistant buyer for a clothing store? I have a passable eye for fashion, and I know what looks good on people. Suppose we go shopping together. I'll show you what to buy to make you stand out."

Joyce raised her eyebrows. "Why?"

"Because with very little work you could be a knock-out. Think of it, Apollo on his knees at your desk, sighing with adoration," she coaxed.

Joyce grimaced. "The only way he'd be on his knees at my desk would be if I kicked him in the stomach."

"Pessimist! You're the one giving the pep talk. Suppose we both listen to you and try to practice what you preach?"

The other woman sighed. "Well, what have we got to lose, after all?"

"Not much, from where I'm sitting. How about Saturday morning? You can take me to the right department stores, and I'll make suggestions."

"I do have a little in my savings account," Joyce murmured. She smiled. "All right. We'll do it."

"Great!" Melissa started on her dessert. "Amazing how good this food tastes all of a sudden. I think I feel better already."

"So do I. But if Apollo throws me out the window, you're in a lot of trouble."

"He won't. Eat up."

Melissa's head was full of ideas. Joyce had inspired her. She hadn't really tried to catch Diego's eye since they'd been back together. Even in the old days she'd never quite lived up to her potential. She wasn't any more experienced now, but she was well-traveled and she'd learned a lot from listening to other women talk and watching them in action as they attracted men. She was going to turn the tables on her reluctant husband and see if she couldn't make him like captivity. Whether or not the attempt failed, she had to try. Joyce was right. Running away had only complicated things. This time, she had to stand and fight.

While she was out, she'd bought a memory card game for Matthew, and when Diego came home that night she was sprawled on the carpet with her son. She made a pretty picture in a clinging beige sleeveless blouse and tight jeans. Diego paused in the doorway, and when she saw him she rolled onto her side, striking a frankly seductive pose.

"Good evening, Señor Laremos," she murmured. "Matthew has a new game."

"I can remember where the apple is," Matthew enthused, jumping up to hug his father and babble excitedly about the game and how he'd already beaten Mama once.

"He has a quick mind," Diego remarked as he studied the large pile of matched cards on Matthew's side of the playing area and the small one on Melissa's.

"Very quick," she agreed, laughing at Matthew's smug little face. "And he's modest, too."

"I know everything," Matthew said with innocent certainty. "Will you play with us, Papa?"

"After dinner, *niño*," the tall man agreed. "I must change, and there is a phone call I have to make."

"Okay!" Matthew went back to turning over cards.

"Only two," Melissa cautioned. "It's cheating if you keep peeking under all of them."

"Yes, Mama."

She took her turn, aware that Diego's eyes were on the deep V of her blouse, under which she was wearing nothing at all.

She sat up again, glancing at him. "Is something wrong, *señor?*"

"Of course not. Excuse me." He turned, frowning, and went off toward his bedroom. Melissa smiled secretively as she watched Matthew match two oranges.

Dinner was noisy because Mrs. Albright had taken Matthew down to the lobby to meet her daughter and grandson, who were just back from a Mexican trip, and the daughter had given Matt a small wooden toy, a ball on a string that had to be bounced into the cup it was at-

tached to. Matt was overjoyed with both his new friend
and his toy.

"Ah," Diego smiled. "Yes, these are very common
in my part of the world, and your mother's," he added
with a smile at Melissa. "Are they not, *querida?* I can
remember playing with one as a child myself."

"Where we lived there were no toy stores," she told
Matthew. "We lived far back in the country, near a vol-
cano, and there were ancient Mayan ruins all around."
She colored a little, remembering one particular ruin.
She looked at Diego and found the same memory in his
dark eyes as they searched hers.

"Sí," he said gently. "The ruins were...potent."

Her lips parted. "Five years," she said, her eyes more
eloquent than she knew. "And sometimes it seems like
days."

"Not for me," he said abruptly, drawing his eyes back
to his coffee cup. "It has not been easy, living through
the black time that came afterward."

Matthew was trying to play with his toy, but Melissa took it and put it firmly beside his plate, indicating that he should eat his food first. He grimaced and
picked up his fork.

"Did you never think of contacting me?" he asked unexpectedly, and his eyes narrowed. It disturbed him more
and more, thinking about all he'd missed. Understanding the reason for Melissa's actions didn't make the lack
of contact with his child any easier to bear. He'd missed
so much of the boy's life, all the things that most fathers
experienced and cherished in memory. Matt's first word,
his first step, the early days when parents and children
became bonded. He'd had none of that.

Melissa sighed sadly, remembering when Matthew

had been born and how desperately she'd wanted Diego. But he hadn't wanted her. He'd made it so plain after their marriage, and even after her fall down the steps he'd been unapproachable. "I thought about it once," she said quietly, wondering if he was going to accuse her of denying him his rights. She wouldn't have had a reply. "But you'd made it clear that I had no place in your life, Diego, that you only married me to spare your family more disgrace."

He studied his cup. "You never considered that I might have had a change of heart, Melissa? That I might have regretted, bitterly, my treatment of you?"

"No," she said honestly. Her pale eyes searched his dark ones. "I didn't want to play on your guilt. It was better that I took care of myself." She dropped her gaze to the table. "And Matt."

"It must have been difficult when he was born," he probed, trying to draw her out.

She smiled faintly, remembering. "Something went wrong," she murmured. "They had to do a cesarean section."

He caught his breath. "My God. And you had no one to turn to."

She looked at Matthew warmly. "I managed very well. I had neighbors who were kind, and the company I worked for was very understanding. My boss made sure my insurance paid all my bills, and he even gave me an advance on my salary so that we had enough to eat."

His fingers contracted around the cup almost hard enough to break it. It didn't bear thinking about. Melissa must have been in severe pain, alone and with an infant to be responsible for. His eyes closed. It hurt him terribly to think that if he'd been kinder to her he could have shared that difficulty with her. He could have been there when she'd needed someone, been there to take care of her. His anguish at being denied all those years with Matt seemed a small thing by comparison.

"It wasn't so bad, Diego," she said softly, because there was pain in his face. "Really it wasn't. And he was the sweetest baby—"

Diego got up abruptly. "I have phone calls to make. Please excuse me."

Melissa watched him, aching for him. His stiff back said it all. She realized then that it wasn't so much her predicament as missing the birth of his son that had hurt him. She felt guilty about that, too, but there was nothing to be done about it now.

Diego went into the study and closed the door, leaning heavily back against it. He couldn't stand the anguish of knowing what she'd suffered because of him. If only he could talk to her. Bare his heart. Tell her what he really felt, how much she and the boy meant to him. He wondered sometimes if he was still capable of real emotion. His past had been so violent, and tenderness had no place in it. He was only now learning that he was capable of it, with his child and even with Melissa, who more and more was becoming the one beautiful thing in his life. The longer they stayed together, the harder it became for him to hide his increasing hunger for her. Not that it was completely physical now, as it had been in the very beginning in Guatemala. No. It was becoming so much more. But he was uncertain of her. She changed before his eyes, first resentful, then shy and remote, and now she seemed oddly affectionate and teasing.

That, of course, could be simply a kind of repayment, for his having taken care of her and Matt and given them a home when she'd needed time to heal. Was that it? Was it gratitude, or was it something more? He couldn't tell.

But perhaps it was too soon. She didn't trust him enough to tell him about Matthew. When she did, there might be time for such confessions.

Melissa went back into the living room with Matthew and spread the memory cards out on the floor. They were into the second round before Diego came in again. He'd taken off his jacket and tie and rolled up the sleeves of his white shirt. It was unbuttoned in front, and Melissa's eyes went helplessly to the hair-covered expanse of brown muscle.

He noticed her glance and delighted in her response to him. No woman had ever made him feel as masculine and proud as Melissa. Her soft eyes had a light in them when she looked at him that made his body sing with pleasure. Desire was the one thing he was certain of. She couldn't begin to hide it from his experienced eyes.

"Play with us, Papa!" Matthew called, inviting the tall man down onto the carpet with them.

"We'll make room for you," Melissa said, smiling softly. She moved toward Matthew, making a space beside her where she was lying on her stomach and lifting cards.

"Perhaps for a moment or two," Diego agreed. He took off his shoes and slid alongside Melissa, the warm, cologne-scented length of his body almost touching hers. "How does one play this game?"

They explained it to him and watched him turn over two cards that matched. Matthew laughed and Melissa groaned as he pulled them near him and made a neat stack.

He smiled at Melissa with a wicked twinkle in his

black eyes. "I was watching from the doorway," he confessed. "Although not so much the cards as—" his gaze went to her derriere, so nicely outlined in the tight jeans "—other things."

She flushed, but her gaze didn't falter. "Lecher," she accused in a whisper, teasing.

That surprised and delighted him. His gaze dropped to her smiling mouth, and he bent suddenly and brushed his lips over hers in a whisper of pressure.

Matthew laughed joyfully. "Bobby's mama and daddy used to kiss like that, only Bobby said his mama used to kiss his daddy all the time."

Diego chuckled. "Your mama is not up to kissing me, *niño*. She is weak from her accident."

Melissa glanced at him mischievously. "Matt, will you go to the kitchen and bring me a cold soft drink, please? And be careful not to open it, okay?"

"Okay!" He jumped up and ran from the room.

Melissa smiled at Diego wickedly. "So I'm too weak to kiss you, am I, *señor?*" she murmured with soft bravado, enjoying the dark, glittering pleasure she read in his faintly shocked eyes.

She rolled over, pushing him gently onto the carpet. He chuckled with open delight as she bent over him and kissed him with a fervor that dragged a reluctant groan from his lips before his arms reached up and gathered her against him.

"Too weak, am I?" Melissa breathed into his hard mouth.

His hand contracted in her soft, wavy blond hair, and the bristly pressure of his mouth grew rough as he turned her gently and eased her down onto the carpet. She could feel the fierce thunder of his heartbeat against her breasts as her arms curled around his neck and she sighed into his hungry mouth. Her blood sang at the sweet contact. He lifted his head abruptly, and she saw the savage desire in the black eyes that stared unblinking into hers.

"*¡Cuidado!*" he murmured. "You tempt fate."

"Not fate," she whispered unsteadily. "Only you, *señor.*" Her hand slid under his shirt, against his body, her fingers spearing into the dark hair that covered his warm muscles. He stiffened, and she sighed contentedly. "Well, if you don't want to be assaulted, keep your shirt buttoned."

He laughed, thrown completely off balance by the way she was acting with him. "*Dios,* what has become of my shy little jungle orchid?"

"She grew up." Her soft eyes searched his. "You don't mind…?"

He pressed her hand against his chest. "No," he said quietly. "Do what you please, little one. So long as you do not mind the inevitable consequence of such actions as this. You understand?"

"I understand," she whispered, her eyes warm with secrets.

As she spoke, she drew one of Diego's hands to her body and sat up gracefully. Holding his eyes, she pressed his palm against her blouse where there was no fabric to conceal the hard thrust of her body.

His breath sighed out as his hand caressed her. "Is this premeditated?" he asked roughly.

"Oh, yes," she confessed, leaning her head against his shoulder because his touch was so sweet. "Diego—"

He drew his hand away. "No. Not here."

She looked up at him. "Not interested?" she asked bravely.

His jaw clenched. "Sweet idiot," he breathed. "If I held you against me now, my interest would be all too apparent. But this is not the game we need to be playing at the moment."

She cleared her throat, aware of where they were. "Yes. Of course." She smiled, avoiding his eyes, and turned over again as Matt came rushing back into the room with her soft drink. She opened it after thanking the laughing little boy. Then sighing, she turned back to the game.

Diego lounged nearby, watching but not participating. The look in his dark eyes was soft and dangerous, and he hardly glanced away from Melissa for the rest of the evening. But his attitude was both curious and remote. He seemed to suspect her motives for this new ardor, and she lost her nerve because of it, withdrawing into her shell again. There were times when Diego seemed very much a stranger.

Matthew was put to bed eventually. Melissa kept her expression hidden from Diego but felt her knees knocking every time he came close. She wished she knew if her forwardness had offended him, but she was too shy to ask him. While he was bidding Matthew good-night, she called her own good-night and went into her room. She locked it for the first time since she'd come to the apartment, and only breathed again when she heard his footsteps going down the hall. To her secret chagrin, the steps didn't even hesitate at her door.

On Saturday, Melissa and Joyce spent the entire day buying clothes and having their hair done. The colors she pointed Joyce toward were flamboyant and colorful, bringing attention to her lovely figure and making the most of her exquisite complexion.

"These are sexy clothes," Joyce said, her misgivings evident as she tried on a dress with a halter top that clung like ivy to her slender body. The color was a swirl of reds and yellows and oranges and whites, and it suited her beautifully. "I'll never be able to pull this off."

"Of course you will," Melissa assured her. "All you really need is a little self-confidence. The clothes will give you that and improve your posture, too. You'll feel slinky, so you'll walk like a cat. Try it and see."

Joyce laughed nervously, but when she got a look at herself in one of the exclusive boutique's full-length mirrors, she blinked and drew in her breath. It was as if she suddenly felt reborn. She began to walk, hesitantly at first, then with more and more poise, until she was moving like the graceful West Indian woman she was.

"Yes!" Melissa laughed, clapping her hands. "Yes, that's exactly what I expected. You have a natural grace of carriage, but you've been hiding it in drab, loose clothing. You have a beautiful figure. Show it off!"

Joyce could hardly believe what she was seeing. She tried on another outfit and a turban, and seemed astonished by the elegant creature who looked out of the mirror at her.

"That can't be me," she murmured.

"But it is." Melissa grinned. "Come on. You've got the clothes. Now let's get the rest of the image."

She took Joyce to a hairstylist who did her hair in a fashionable cut that took years off her age and gave her even more poise, drawing her long hair back into an elegant bun with wisps around her small ears. She looked suddenly like a painting, all smooth lines and graceful curves.

"Just one more thing," Melissa murmured, and took her friend to the cosmetics department.

Joyce was given a complete make-over, with an expert cosmetician to show her which colors of powder to have mixed especially for her and which lipsticks and eye shadows and blushers to set off her creamy, blemishless complexion.

"That is not me," Joyce assured her image when the woman was finished and smiling contentedly at her handiwork.

"Poor Apollo," Melissa said with a faint smile. "Poor, poor man. He's done for."

Joyce's heart was in her big eyes. "Is he really?"

"I would say so," Melissa assured her. "Now. Let's get my wardrobe completed and then we'll get to work on the menu for a dinner party Monday night. But you can't wear any of your new clothes or makeup until then," she cautioned. "It has to be a real surprise."

Joyce grinned back at her. "Okay. I can hardly wait!"

"That makes two of us!"

Melissa still had a little money in her own bank account, which she'd had Diego move to Chicago from Tucson. She drew on that to buy some new things of her own. She had her own hair styled, as well, and opted for the makeup job. She tingled with anticipation and fear. Diego wasn't the same easygoing man she'd known in Guatemala. He was much more mature, and his experience intimidated her. If only she could get her nerve back. She had to, because he seemed determined not to make the first move.

By the time she and Joyce finished and went back to the apartment, it was almost dark and Melissa was limping a little.

"You've overdone it," Joyce moaned. "Oh, I hope all this hasn't caused a setback!"

"I'm just sore," Melissa assured her. "And it was fun! Wait until next week, and then the fireworks begin. Don't you dare go near the office like that."

"I wouldn't dream of shocking Apollo into a nervous breakdown," the other woman promised. "I'll go home and practice slinking. Melissa, I can never thank you enough."

Melissa only smiled. "What are friends for? You gave me the pep talk. The least I could do was help you out a little. You look great, by the way. Really pretty."

Joyce beamed. "I hope that wild man at the office thinks so."

"You mark my words, he will. Good night."

"Good night."

Melissa let herself into the apartment. Mrs. Albright had the evening off, and it was a shock to find Diego and their son in the kitchen with spicy smells wafting up from the stove.

Diego was wearing Mrs. Albright's long white apron over his slacks and sports shirt, and little Matthew was busily tearing up lettuce to make a salad.

"What are you doing?" Melissa burst out after she'd deposited her packages on the living-room sofa.

"Making dinner, *querida*," Diego said with a smile. "Our son is preparing a heart-of-lettuce salad, and I am making chili and enchiladas. Did you and Joyce have a good time?"

"A wonderful time. My goodness, can't I help?"

"Of course. Set the table, if you please. And do not disturb the cooks," he added with a wicked glance.

She laughed softly, moving to his side. She reached up

impulsively and brushed a kiss against his hard cheek. "You're a darling. Can I have the van Meers and the Brettmans and Apollo and Joyce to dinner Monday night?"

Diego caught his breath at her closeness and the unexpected kiss. "Little one, you can have the boy's club wrestling team over if this change in you is permanent."

"Have I changed?" she mused, her pale gray eyes searching his as she clung to his arm and smiled, encouraged by his smile and the softness in his dark eyes.

"More than you realize, perhaps. The leg, it is not painful?"

"A little stiff, that's all."

"Papa, something is burning," Matthew pointed out.

Diego jerked his attention back to the heavy iron skillet he was using, and he began to stir the beef quickly. "The cook had better return to the chili, *amada,* or we will all starve. Dessert must wait, for the moment," he added in a tone that made her toes curl.

"As you wish, *señor.*" She laughed softly, moving away reluctantly to put the dishes and silverware on the table.

It was the best meal she could remember in a long time, and dinner brought with it memories of Guatemala and its spicy cuisine. She and Diego talked, but of work and shopping trips and how much Diego had enjoyed the trip to the zoo with Matthew, who enthused about seeing a real lion. For the first time, there were no arguments.

When the little boy was put to bed, Melissa curled up on the sofa to watch a movie on cable while Diego apologetically did paperwork.

"This is new to me," he murmured as he scribbled notes. "But I find that I like the involvement in Apollo's company, as well as the challenge of helping business-men learn to combat terrorism."

"I suppose it's all very hush-hush," she ventured.

"Assuredly so." He chuckled. "Or what would be the purpose in having such a business to teach survival tac-tics, hmm?"

She pushed her hair away from her face. "Diego… how do you think Apollo really feels about Joyce?"

He looked up. "No, no," he cautioned, waving a lean finger at her with an indulgent smile. "Such conversa-tions are privileged. I will not share Apollo's secrets with you."

She colored softly. "Fair enough. I won't tell you Joyce's."

"You look just as you did at sixteen," he said softly, watching her, "when I refused to take you to the bull ring with me. You remember, *querida?* You would not speak to me for days afterward."

"I'd have gone to a snake charmer's cell to be with you in those days," she confessed quietly. "I adored you."

"I knew that. It was why I was so careful to keep you at arm's length. I succeeded particularly well, in fact, until we were cut off by a band of guerrillas and forced to hide out in a Mayan ruin. And then I lost my head and satisfied a hunger that had been gnawing at me for a long, long time."

"And paid the price," she added quietly.

He sighed. "You paid more than I did. I never meant to hurt you. It was difficult knowing that my own lack of control had led me to that precipice and pushed me over. I should never have accused you of trapping me."

"But there was so much animosity in our pasts," she said. "And you didn't love me."

His dark eyes narrowed. "I told you once that my emotions were deeply buried."

"Yes. I remember. You needn't worry, Diego," she said wearily. "I know you don't have anything to offer me, and I'm not asking for anything. Only for a roof over my head and the chance to raise my son without having to go on welfare." Her pale eyes searched his hard face. "But I'll gladly get a job and pull my weight. I want you to know that."

He glared at her. "Have I asked for such a sacrifice?"

"Well, you aren't getting any other benefits, are you?" she muttered. "All I'm giving you is two more mouths to feed and memories of the past that must be bitter and uncomfortable."

He got up, holding his paperwork in one clenched fist. He stared at her angrily. "You build walls, when I seek only to remove barriers. We still have a long way to go, *querida*. But before we can make a start, you have to learn to trust me."

"Trust is difficult," she retorted, glaring at him. "And you betrayed me once."

"Yes. Did you not betray me with Matthew's father?"

She started to speak and couldn't. She turned and left the room, her new resolve forgotten in the heat of anger. They seemed to grow further apart every day, and she couldn't get through to Diego, no matter how hard she tried.

Perhaps the dinner party would open a few doors. Meanwhile, she'd bide her time and pray. He had to care a little about her. If not, why would the past even matter to him? The thought gave her some hope, at least.

Chapter Nine

The one consolation Melissa had after a sleepless night was the equally bloodshot look of Diego's eyes. Apparently their difference of opinion the night before had troubled him as much as it had her. And until the argument, things had been going so well. Was Diego right? Was she building walls?

She dressed for church and helped Matthew into the handsome blue suit that Diego had insisted they buy him. She didn't knock on the door of Diego's room as they went into the living room. He was already there, dressed in a very becoming beige suit.

He turned, his dark eyes sweeping over the pale rose dress she wore, which emphasized the soft curves of her body. In the weeks of her recovery, her thinness had left her. She looked much healthier now, and her body was exquisitely appealing. He almost ground his teeth at the effect just gazing at her had on him.

"You look lovely," he said absently.

"I'd look lovelier if I got more sleep," she returned. "We argue so much lately, Diego."

He sighed, moving close to her. Matthew took advantage of their distraction to turn on an educational children's program and laugh with delight at some rhymes.

"And at a time when we should have laid the ghosts to rest, *si?*" he asked. His lean hands rested gently on her shoulders, caressing her skin through the soft fabric. His black eyes searched hers restlessly. "A little trust, *niña,* is all that we need."

She smiled wistfully. "And what neither of us seem to have."

He bent to brush his mouth softly over her lips. "Let it come naturally," he whispered. "There is still time, is there not?"

Tears stung her eyes at the tenderness in his deep voice. She lifted her arms and twined them around his neck, her fingers caressing the thick hair at the back of his head. "I hope so," she whispered achingly. "For Matthew's sake."

"For his—and not for ours?" he asked quietly. "We lead separate lives, and that cannot continue."

"I know." She leaned her forehead against his firm chin and closed her eyes. "You never really wanted me. I suppose I should be grateful that you came when I went down in the crash. I never expected you to take care of Matt and me."

He touched her hair absently. "How could I leave you like that?" he asked.

"I thought you would when you knew about Matt," she confessed.

He tilted her chin and looked into her eyes. His were solemn, unreadable. "Melissa, I have been alone all my life, except for family. Every day I lived as if death were at the door. I never meant to become involved with you. But I wanted you, little one," he whispered huskily. "Wanted you obsessively, until you were all I breathed. It was my own loss of control, my guilt, which drove us apart. I could not bear to be vulnerable. But I was." He shrugged. "That was what sent me from the casa. It was the reason I lied the night you ran out into the rain and had to be taken to the hospital. Repulse me?" He laughed bitterly. "If only you knew. Even now, I tremble like a boy when you touch me…"

Her heart jerked at his admission, because she could feel the soft tremor that ran through his lean body. But after all, it was only desire. And she wanted, needed, so much more.

"Would desire be enough, though?" she asked sadly, watching him.

He touched her soft cheek. "Melissa, we enjoy the same things. We like the same people. We even agree on politics. We both love the child." He smiled. "More important, we have known each other for oh, so long, *niña*. You know me to the soles of my feet, faults and all. Is that not a better basis for marriage than the desire you seem to think is our only common ground?"

"You might fall in love with someone—" she began.

He touched her mouth with a lean forefinger. "Why not tempt me into falling in love with you, *querida?*" he murmured. "These new clothes and the way you play lately have more effect than you realize." He bent toward her.

She met his lips without restraint, smiling against their warmth. "Could you?"

"Could I what?" he whispered.

"Fall in love with me?"

He chuckled. "Why not tempt me and see?"

She felt a surge of pure joy at the sweetness of the way he was looking at her, but before she could answer him, Matt wormed his way between them and wanted to know if they were ever going to leave to go to church.

They went to lunch after mass and then to a movie that Matt wanted to see. For the rest of the day, there was a new comradeship in the way Diego reacted to her. There were no more accusations or arguments. They played with Matt and cooked supper together for the second night in a row. And that night, when Matt was tucked up and Melissa said good-night to Diego, it was with real reluctance that she went to her room.

"Momento, niña," he called, and joined her at her door. Without another word, he drew her gently against him and bent to kiss her with aching tenderness. "Sleep well."

She touched his mouth with hers. "You...too." Her eyes asked a question she was too shy to put into words, but he shook his head.

"Not just yet, my own," he breathed. His black eyes searched hers. "Only when all the barriers are down will we take that last, sweet step together. For now it is enough that we begin to leave the past behind. Is it tomorrow night that our guests are expected?"

The sudden change of subject was rather like jet lag, she thought amusedly, but she adjusted to it. "Yes. Mrs.

Albright and I will no doubt spend the day in the kitchen, but I've already called Gabby and Danielle and Joyce, and they've accepted. I'm looking forward to actually meeting the other wives, although we've talked on the phone quite a lot. I like them."

"I like you," he said unexpectedly, and smiled. "Dream of me," he whispered, brushing his mouth against hers one last time. Then he was gone, quietly striding down the hall to his study.

Melissa went into her room, but not to sleep. She did dream of him, though.

The next day was hectic. That evening, Melissa dressed nervously in one of her new dresses. It was a sweet confection in tones of pink, mauve and lavender with a wrapped bodice and a full skirt and cap sleeves. It took five years off her age and made her look even more blond and fair than she was.

She was trying to fasten a bracelet when she came out of her bedroom. Diego was in the living room, sipping brandy. He watched her approach with a familiar darkness in his eyes, an old softness that brought back so many memories.

"Allow me," he said, putting the brandy snifter down to fasten the bracelet for her. He didn't release her arm when he finished. He frowned, staring at the bracelet.

She knew immediately why he was staring. The bracelet was a tiny strand of white gold with inlaid emeralds, an expensive bit of nothing that Diego had given her when she'd graduated from high school. She colored delicately, and his eyes lifted to hers.

"So long ago I gave you this, *querida*," he said softly. He lifted her wrist to his lips and kissed it. His mustache tickled her delicate skin. "It still means something to you—is that why you kept it all these years, even when you hated me?" he probed.

She closed her eyes at the sight of the raven-black head bent over her hand. "I was never able to hate you, though," she said with a bitter laugh. Tears burned her eyes. "I tried, but you haunted me. You always have."

He drew in a steadying breath as his black head lifted and his eyes searched hers. "As you haunted me," he breathed roughly. "And now, *niña?* Do you still care for me, a little, despite the past?" he added, hoping against hope for mere crumbs.

"You needn't pretend that you don't know how I feel about you," she said, her chin trembling under her set lips. "You're like an addiction that I can't quite cure. I gave you everything I had to give, and still it wasn't enough…!" Tears slipped from her eyes.

"Melissa, don't!" He caught her to him in one smooth, graceful motion, his lean hand pressing her face into his dark dinner jacket. "Don't cry, little one, I can't bear it."

"You hate me!"

His fingers contracted in her hair and his eyes closed. "No! *Dios mío, amada,* how could I hate you?" His cheek moved roughly against hers as he sought her mouth and found it suddenly with his in the silence of the room. He kissed her with undisguised hunger, his hands gentle at her back, smoothing her body into his, caressing her. "Part of me died when you left. You took the very color from my life and left me with nothing but guilt and grief."

She hardly heard him. His mouth was insistent and she needed him, wanted him. She was reaching up to hold him when the doorbell sounded loudly in the silence.

He drew his head back reluctantly, and the arms that held her had a faint tremor. "No more deceptions," he said softly. "We must be honest with each other now. Tonight, when the others leave, we have to talk."

She touched his mouth, tracing the thick black mustache. "Can you bear total honesty, Diego?" she asked huskily.

"Perhaps you underestimate me."

"Didn't I always?" she sighed.

He heard voices out in the hall and released Melissa to take her hand and lead her toward the group. "When our guests leave, there will be all the time in the world to talk. Matthew has gone to bed, but you might check on him while I pass around drinks to our visitors. Mrs. Albright mentioned that his stomach was slightly uneasy."

"I'll go now." Melissa felt his fingers curl around hers with a thrill of pleasure and gazed up at him. She found his dark eyes smiling down into hers. It had been a long time since they'd been close like this, and lately it had been difficult even to talk to him. She returned the pressure of his hand as they joined a shell-shocked Apollo and a smug Joyce. The West Indian woman didn't even look like Joyce. She was wearing one of the dresses she and Melissa had found while they'd been shopping. It was a cinnamon-and-rust chiffon that clung lovingly to her slender figure, with a soft cowl neckline. Her feet were in strappy high heels. Her hair was pulled back with wisps at her ears, and she was wearing the makeup she'd bought at the boutique. She was a knockout, and Apollo's eyes were registering that fact with reluctance and pure malice.

"Now what did I tell you?" Melissa asked, gesturing at Joyce's dress. "You're just lovely!"

"Indeed she is." Diego lifted her hand to his lips and smiled at her while Apollo shifted uncomfortably and muttered good evening to his host and hostess.

"I'm just going to look in on Matthew. I'll be right back," Melissa promised, excusing herself.

The little boy was oddly quiet, his eyes drowsy. Melissa pushed back his dark hair and smiled at him.

"Feel okay?" she asked.

"My tummy doesn't," he said. "It hurts."

"Where does it hurt, baby?" she asked gently, and he indicated the middle of his stomach. She asked as many more questions as she could manage and decided it was probably either a virus or something he'd eaten. Still, it could be appendicitis. If it was, it would get worse very quickly, she imagined. She'd have to keep a careful eye on him.

"Try to sleep," she said, her voice soft and loving. "If you don't feel better by morning, we'll see the doctor, all right?"

"I don't want to see the doctor," Matthew said mutinously. "Doctors stick needles in people."

"Not all the time. And you want to get better, don't you? Papa mentioned that we might go to the zoo again next weekend," she whispered conspiratorially. "Wouldn't you like that?"

"Oh, yes," he said. "There are bears at the zoo."

"Then we'll have to get you better. Try to get some sleep, and maybe you'll feel better in the morning."

"All right, Mama."

"I'm just down the hall, and I'll leave your door open a crack. If you need me, call, okay?" She kissed his forehead and paused to smile at him before leaving. But she was almost sure it was a stomach virus. Mrs. Albright's grandson had come down with it just after Matthew had been downstairs to visit him again two days before. It was just a twenty-four-hour bug, but it could make a little boy pretty miserable all the same.

She wiped the frown off her face when she got into the living room. Gabby and J.D. Brettman had arrived by now, and Diego put a snifter of brandy into Melissa's hand and drew her to his side while they talked about Chicago and the business. His arm was possessive, and she delighted in the feel of it, in the feel of him, so close. Her love for him had grown by leaps and bounds in the past few weeks. She wondered if she could even exist apart from him now. Minutes later, Eric van Meer and his wife, a rather plain brunette with glasses and a lovely smile, joined the group. Melissa was surprised; she'd expected Dutch to show up with some beautiful socialite. But as she got to know Danielle, his interest in her was apparent. Dani was unique. So was Gabby.

"Let's let the girls talk fashion for a while. I've got something I need to kick over with you three before we eat," Apollo said suddenly, smiling at the wives and pointedly ignoring Joyce as he moved the men to the other side of the room.

"Just like men," Gabby sighed with a wistful glance at her enormous husband's back. "We're only afterthoughts."

"Someday I'll strangle him," Joyce was muttering to herself. "Someday I'll kick him out the window suspended by the telephone cord and I'll grin while I cut it."

"Now, now." Danielle chuckled. "That isn't a wholesome mental attitude."

Joyce's eyes were even blacker than usual. "I hate him!" she said venomously. "That's wholesome."

Gabby grinned. "He's running scared, haven't you noticed?" she whispered to Joyce. "He's as nervous as a schoolboy. You intimidate him. He comes from share-croppers down South, and your parents are well-to-do. In a different way, J.D. was much the same before we married. He seemed to hate me, and nothing I did suited him. He fought to the bitter end. Apollo is even less marriage-minded than Dutch, and Dani could write you a book on reluctant husbands. Dutch hated women!"

"He thought he did," Dani corrected with a loving glance at her handsome husband. "But perhaps all they really need is the incentive to become husbands and fathers."

Melissa nodded. "Diego is very good with Matthew, and I never even knew that he liked children in the old days in Guatemala."

"It must have been exciting, growing up in Central America," Gabby remarked.

Melissa's eyes were soft with memories. "It was exciting living next door to Diego Laremos," she corrected. "He was my whole world."

Gabby's eyes narrowed as she studied the blonde woman. "And yet the two of you were apart for a long time."

Melissa nodded. "It was a reluctant marriage. I left because I thought he didn't want me anymore, and now we're trying to pick up the pieces. It isn't easy," she confided.

"He's a good man," Gabby said, her green eyes quiet and friendly. "He saved my life in Guatemala when J.D. and I were there trying to rescue J.D.'s sister. Under fire he's one of the coolest characters I've ever seen. So are J.D. and Apollo."

"I suppose it's the way they had to live," Joyce remarked. Her eyes slid across the room to Apollo, and for one instant, everything she felt for the man was in her expression.

Apollo chose that moment to let his attention be diverted, and he looked at the West Indian woman. The air fairly sizzled with electricity, and Joyce's breath caught audibly before she lowered her eyes and clenched her hands in her lap.

"Excuse me, ma'am," Mrs. Albright said from the doorway in time to save Joyce from any ill-timed comments. "But dinner is served."

"Thank you, Mrs. Albright." Melissa smiled and went to Diego's side, amazed at how easy it was to slip her hand into the bend of his elbow and draw him with her. "Dinner, darling," she said softly.

His arm tautened under her gentle touch. "In all the time we have been together," he remarked as they went toward the elegant dining room, "I cannot remember hearing you say that word."

"You say it all the time," she reminded him with a pert smile. "Or the Spanish equivalent, at least, don't you?"

He shrugged. "It seems to come naturally." He pressed her hand against his sleeve, and the look he bent on her was full of affection.

She nuzzled his shoulder with her head, loving the new sense of intimacy she felt with him.

Behind them, the other husbands and wives exchanged expressive smiles. Bringing up the rear, Joyce was touching Apollo's sleeve as if it had thorns on it, and Apollo was as stiff as a man with a poker up his back.

"Relax, will you?" Apollo muttered at Joyce.

"You're a fine one to talk, iron man."

He turned and gazed down at her. They searched each other's eyes in a silence gone wild with new longings, with shared hunger.

"God, don't look at me like that," he breathed roughly. "Not here."

Her lips parted on a shaky breath. "Why not?"

He moved toward her and then abruptly moved away, jerking her along with him into the dining room. He was almost frighteningly stern.

It was a nice dinner, but the guests—two of them at least—kept the air sizzling with tension. When they'd eaten and were enjoying after-dinner coffee from a tray in the living room, the tension got even worse.

"You're standing on my foot," Joyce said suddenly, bristling at Apollo.

"With feet that size, how is that you can even feel it?" he shot back.

"That's it. That's it! You big overstuffed facsimile of a Chicago big shot, who do you think you're talking to?"

"A small overstuffed chili pepper with delusions of beauty," he retorted, his eyes blazing.

Joyce tried to speak but couldn't. She grabbed her purse and, with a terse, tear-threatening good-night to the others, ran for the door.

"Damn it!" Apollo went after her out the door, slamming it behind him, while the others paused to exchange conspiratorial smiles and then continue their conversation.

When Apollo eventually came back into the apartment to say good-night, he was alone. He looked drawn and a little red on one cheek, but his friends were too kind to remark on it. He left with a rather oblivious

smile, and the others said their good-nights shortly there-
after and left, too.

The door closed, and Melissa let Diego lead her back
into the living room, where there was still half a pot of
hot coffee.

"We can drink another cup together," he said, "while
Mrs. Albright clears away the dishes."

She poured and watched him add cream to his coffee,
her eyes soft and loving. "It went well, don't you think?"

He lifted an eyebrow and smiled. "Apollo and Joyce,
you mean? I expect he has met his match there. Properly attired, she has excellent carriage and a unique kind
of beauty."

"I thought so, too." She laughed. "I think she hit him.
Did you notice his cheek?"

"I was also noticing the very vivid lipstick on his
mouth," he mused with a soft chuckle. He leaned back
in his chair with a sigh. "Poor man. He'll be married
before he knows it."

She balanced her cup and saucer on her lap. "Is that
how you think of marriage? As something to cause a
man to be pitied?"

"Oh, yes, at one time I felt exactly that way," he admitted. He lit a cheroot and blew out a cloud of smoke.
"I even told you so."

"I remember." She smiled into her coffee as she
sipped it. "I was young enough and naive enough to
think I could make you like it."

"Had I given you the chance, perhaps you might
have," he said. His dark eyes narrowed. "I cannot remember even once in my life thinking of children and
a home when I was escorting a woman, do you know?
Even with you, it was your delectable body I wanted the

most, not any idea of permanence. And then I lost my head and found myself bound to you in the most permanent way of all. I hated you and your father for that."

"As I found out," she said miserably.

"It was only when you lost the baby that I came to my senses, as odd as that may sound," he continued, watching her face. "It was then that I realized how much I had thrown away. I had some idea of my grandmother's resentment of you when I left you at the casa and took myself away from your influence. Perhaps I even hoped that my family's coldness would make you leave me." He dropped his dark eyes to his shoes. "I had lived alone so long, free to do as I wanted, to travel as I pleased. But the weeks grew endless without you, and always there was the memory of that afternoon in the rain on our bed of leaves." He sighed heavily. "I came home hoping to drive you away before I capitulated. And then you came to me, and because I was so hungry for you, I told you that you repulsed me. And I pushed you away." His eyes closed briefly.

She felt a stirring of compassion for what he'd gone through, even though her own path hadn't been an easy one.

"When you left, how did you manage?" he asked.

"By sheer force of will, at first." She sighed. "I had to go through a lot of red tape to get to stay in the United States, and when Matthew came along, it got rough. I made a good salary, but it took a lot of money to keep him in clothes and to provide for a babysitter. Without Mrs. Grady, I really don't know what I'd have done."

His chin lifted, and he studied her through narrow dark eyes. "Did you never wonder about me?"

"At first I wondered. I was afraid that you'd try to

find me." She twisted her wedding band on her finger. "Then, after I got over that, I wondered if you were with some other woman, having a good time without me."

He scowled. "You thought me a shallow man, *niña*."

Her thin shoulders lifted, then fell. "You said yourself that you didn't love me or need me, that I was a nuisance you'd been saddled with. What else was I to think, Diego? That you were pining away for love of me?"

He took a draw from his cheroot and quietly put it out with slow, deliberate movements of his hand. "When I began selling my services abroad for a living, it was to help my family out of a financial bind," he began. "Because your mother had run away with your father, taking her dowry from us, the family fortunes suffered and we were in desperate need. After a while I began to enjoy the excitement of what I did, and the risk. Eventually the reason I began was lost in the need for adventure and the love of freedom and danger. I suppose I fed on adrenaline."

"There's something your family never knew about my mother's dowry, Diego," Melissa said. "She didn't have one."

He scowled. "What is this? My father said—"

"Your father didn't know. My grandfather was in financial straits himself. He was hoping for a merger between his fruit company and your family's banana plantations to help him get his head above water." She smiled ironically. "There was never any dowry. That was one reason she ran away with my father, because she felt guilty that her father was trying to use her in a dishonest way to make money. My father's father died soon afterward, and my father inherited his fortune. That's where our money came from, not from my mother's dowry."

"Dios mío," he breathed, putting his face in his hands. "*Dios,* and my family blamed your father all those years for our financial problems."

"He thought it best not to tell you," she said. "The wounds were deep enough, and your father said some harsh things to him after he and my mother were married. I suppose he rubbed salt in the wounds, because my father never forgave him."

"You make me ashamed, Melissa," he said finally, lifting his dark head. "I seem to have given you nothing but heartache."

"I wasn't blameless," she said. "The poems and the note I wrote so impulsively were genuine, you know. All I lacked was the courage to send them to you. I knew even then that a sophisticated man would never want an unworldly girl like me. I wasn't even pretty," she said wistfully.

"But you were exquisite," he said. He looked and sounded astonished at her denial of her own beauty. "A tea rose in bud, untouched by sophistication and cynicism. I adored you. And once I tasted your sweetness, *amada,* I was intoxicated."

"Yes, I noticed that." She sighed bitterly.

"I fought against marriage, that is true," he admitted. "I fought against your influence, and to some extent I won. But even as you ran from my bedroom that last night at the casa, I knew that I had lost. I was going after you, to tell you that I had meant none of what I said. I was going to ask you to try to make our marriage work, Melissa. And I would have tried. At least I was fond of you, and I wanted you. There was more than enough to build a marriage on." He didn't add how that feeling had grown over the years until now the very force of it almost winded him when he looked at her. He couldn't tell her everything just yet.

She searched his dark, unblinking eyes. "I was too young, though," she said. "I would have wanted things you couldn't have given me. You were my idol, not a flesh-and-blood man. You were larger than life, and how can a mere mortal woman live up to such a paragon? Oh, no, *señor.* I prefer you as you are now. Flesh and blood and sometimes a little flawed. I can deal with a man who is as human as I am."

He began to smile, and the warmth of his lips was echoed in his quiet, possessive gaze. "Can you, *enamorada?*" he asked. "Then come here and show me."

Her heart skipped with pure delight. "On the couch?" she asked, her eyebrows raised. "With the door wide open and Mrs. Albright in the kitchen?"

He chuckled softly. "You see the way you affect my brain, Melissa. It seems to stop working when I am in the same room with you."

"All finished, except for the coffee things," Mrs. Albright said cheerfully as she came into the room.

"Leave the coffee things until tomorrow," Diego said, smiling at her. "You have done quite enough, and your check this week will reflect our appreciation. Now go home and enjoy your own family. *¡Buenas noches!*"

"Thank you, *señor,* and *buenas noches* to you, too. Ma'am." She nodded to Melissa, got her coat from the closet and let herself out of the apartment.

Diego's eyes darkened as they slid over Melissa with an expression in them that could have melted ice. "Now," he said softly. "Come here to me, little one."

She got up, her heartbeat shaking her, and moved toward him. Diego caught her around the waist and pulled her down into his lap with her blond head in the crook of his arm and his black eyes searing down into hers.

"No more barriers," he breathed as he lowered his head, drowning her in his expensive cologne and the faint tobacco scent of his mouth. "No more subterfuge, no more games. We are husband and wife, and now we become one mind, one heart, one body...*amada!*"

His mouth moved hungrily on hers and she clung to him warmly, delighting in his possessive hold, in the need she could sense as well as feel. He was going to possess her, but she was no longer a twenty-year-old girl with stars in her eyes. She was a woman, and fully awakened to her own wants and needs.

She bit his lower lip, watching to see his expression. He chuckled softly, arrogance in every line of his dark face.

"So," he breathed. "You are old enough now for passion, is that what you are telling me with this provocative caress? Then beware, *querida,* because in this way my knowledge is far superior to yours."

Her breath quickened. "Show me," she whispered, curling her fingers into the thick hair at the nape of his neck. "Teach me."

"It will not be as tender as it was the first time, *amada,*" he said roughly, and something dark kindled in his eyes. "It will be a savage loving."

"Savage is how I feel about you, *señor,*" she whispered, lifting her mouth to tease his. "Savage and sweet and oh, so hungry!"

He allowed the caress and repeated it against her starving mouth. "Then taste me, *querida,*" he whispered as he opened her lips with his and his arms contracted. "And let us feast on passion."

She moaned, because the pleasure was feverish. He bruised her against him, and she felt his hand low on her hips, gathering them against the fierce tautness of his body. She began to tremble. She'd lived on dreams of him for years, but now there was the remembered delight of his mouth, of his body. He wanted her, and she wanted him so much it was agonizing. She clung, a tiny cry whispering into his mouth as she gave in completely, loving him beyond bearing.

He rose gracefully, lifting her easily as he got up. He lifted his head only a breath away, holding her eyes as he walked down the hall with her, his gaze possessive, explosively sweet.

"No quarter, *enamorada*," he whispered huskily. "This night, I will show no mercy. I will fulfill you and you will complete me. I will love you as I never dreamed of loving a woman in the darkness."

She trembled at the emotion in his deep, softly accented voice. "You don't believe in love," she whispered shakily.

His dark eyes held her wide gray ones. "Do I not, Melissa? Wait and see what I feel. By morning you may have learned a great deal more about me than you think you know."

She buried her face in his throat and pressed closer, shuddering with the need to give him her heart along with her body.

"*Querida...*" he breathed. His arms tightened bruisingly.

At the same time, a childish voice cried out in the darkness, and that sound was followed by the unmistakable sound of someone's dinner making a return appearance.

Chapter Ten

Matthew was sick twice. Melissa mopped up after him with the ease of long practice and changed his clothes and his sheets after bathing him gently with soap and warm water.

He cried, his young pride shattered by his loss of control. "I'm sorry," he wailed.

"For what, baby?" she said gently, kissing his forehead. "Darling, we all get sick from time to time. Mrs. Albright's grandson had this virus, and I'm sure that's where you caught it, but you'll be much better in the morning. I'm going to get you some cracked ice so that you don't get dehydrated, and perhaps Papa will sit with you until I get back."

"Of course," Diego said, catching Melissa's hand to kiss it gently as she went past him. "Make a pot of coffee for us, *amada*."

"You don't need to sit up, too," she said. "I can do it."

His dark eyes searched hers. "This is what being a father is all about, is it not? Sharing the bad times as well as the good? What kind of man would I be to go merrily to my bed and leave you to care for a sick little boy?"

She could barely breathe. He was incredible. She touched his mouth with her forefinger. "I adore you," she breathed, and left before she gave way to tears.

When she came back, with the coffee dripping and its delicious aroma filling the kitchen, she was armed with a cup of cracked ice and a spoon. Diego was talking to Matthew in a low voice. It was only when Melissa was in the room that she recognized the story he was telling the boy. It was *Beauty and the Beast,* one of her own favorites.

"And they lived happily ever after?" Matthew asked, looking pale but temporarily keeping everything down.

"Happiness is not an automatic thing in the real world, *mi hijo,*" Diego said as Melissa perched on the side of the bed and spooned a tiny bit of cracked ice into Matthew's mouth. "It is rather a matter of compromise, communication and tolerance. Is this not so, Señora Laremos?"

She smiled at him. He was lounging in the chair beside the bed with his shirt unbuttoned and his sleeves rolled up, looking very Latin and deliciously masculine with the shirt and slacks outlining every powerful muscle in his body.

"Yes. It is so," she agreed absently, but her eyes were saying other things.

He chuckled deeply, and the message in his own eyes was more than physical.

She gave Matthew the ice and took heart when it stayed in his stomach. In a little while he dozed off, and

Melissa pushed the disheveled dark hair away from his forehead and adored him with her eyes.

"A fine young man," Diego said softly. "He has character, even at so early an age. You have done well."

She glanced at him with a smile. "He was all I had of—" She bit her tongue, because she had almost said "of you."

But he knew. He smiled, his eyes lazily caressing her. "I have waited a long time for you to tell me. Do you not think that this is the proper time, *querida?* On a night when we meant to love each other in the privacy of my bedroom and remove all the barriers that separate us? Here, where the fruit of our need for each other sleeps so peacefully in the security of our love for him?"

She drew in a steadying breath. "Did you know all the time?" she asked.

"No," he said honestly, and smiled. "I was insanely jealous of Matt's mythical father. It made me unkind to him at first, and to you. But as I grew to know him, and you, I began to have my suspicions. That was why I sent for his birth certificate."

"Yes, I saw it accidentally in your desk," she confessed, and noted the surprise in his face.

"But before I saw it," he continued softly, "Matthew described to me a photograph of his father that you had shown him." He smiled at her flush. "Yes, *niña.* The same photograph I had seen in your drawer under your gowns, and never told you. So many keepsakes. They gave me the only hope I had that you still had a little affection for me."

She laughed. "I was afraid you'd seen them." She shook her head. "I cared so much. And I was afraid, I've always been afraid, that you might want Matt more than you wanted me." She lowered her eyes. "You said that love wasn't a word you knew. But Matt was your son," she whispered, admitting it at last, "and you'd have wanted him."

"Him, and not you?" he asked softly. He leaned forward, watching her. "Melissa, I have not been kind to you. We married for the worst of reasons, and even when I found you again I was still fighting for my freedom. But now..." He smiled tenderly. "*Amada,* I awaken each morning with the thought that I will see you over the breakfast table. At night I sleep soundly, knowing that you are only a few yards away from me. My day begins and ends with you. And in these past weeks, you have come to mean a great deal to me. I care very much for my son. But, Melissa, you mean more to me than anything on earth. Even more than Matthew."

She gnawed her lower lip while tears threatened. She took a slow, shuddering breath. "I wanted to tell you before I left Guatemala that I hadn't lost the baby. But I couldn't let him be born and raised in such an atmosphere of hatred." She looked down at the carpet. "He was all I had left of you, and I wanted him desperately. So I came to America, gave birth to him and raised him." Her eyes found his. "But there was never a day, or a night, or one single second, when you weren't in my thoughts and in my heart. I never stopped loving you. I never will."

"Amada," he breathed.

"Matthew is your son," she said simply, smiling through tears. "I'm sorry I didn't trust you enough to tell you."

"I'm sorry I made it so difficult." He leaned forward and took her hand in his, kissing the palm softly, hungrily. "We made a beautiful child together," he said, lifting his dark eyes to hers. "He combines the best of both of us."

"And we can look into his face and see generations of Sterlings and Laremoses staring back at us," she agreed. Her soft eyes held his. "Oh, Diego, what a waste the past years have been!"

He stood up, drawing her into his arms. He held her and rocked her, his voice soft at her ear, whispering endearments in Spanish while she cried away the bitterness and the loneliness and the pain.

"Now, at last, we can begin again," he said. "We can have a life together, a future together."

"I never dreamed it would happen." She wiped at her eyes. "I almost ran away again. But then Joyce reminded me that I'd done that before and solved nothing. So I stayed to fight for you."

He laughed delightedly. "So you did, in ways I never expected. I had married a child in Guatemala. I hardly expected the woman I found in Tucson."

"I couldn't believe it when I saw you there," she said. "I'd dreamed of you so much, wanted you so badly, and then there you were. But I thought you hated me, so I didn't dare let you see how I felt. And there was Matt."

"Why did you not tell me the truth at the beginning?" he asked quietly.

"Because I couldn't be sure that you wouldn't take him away from me." She sighed. "And because I wanted you to trust me, to realize all by yourself that I'd loved you far too much to betray you with another man."

"To my shame, I believed that at first," he confessed. "And blamed myself for being so cruel to you that I made you hate me enough to run away."

"I never hated you," she said, loving his face with her eyes. "I never could. I understood, even then. And it was my own fault. The note, the poems, and I gave in without even a fight..."

"The fault was mine as well, for letting my desire for you outweigh my responsibility to protect you." He sighed heavily. "So much tragedy, my own, because we abandoned ourselves to pleasure. At the time, consequences were the last thought we had, no?"

"Our particular consequence, though, is adorable, don't you think, *esposo mío?*" she smiled at their sleeping son.

He followed her glance. *"Muy adorable."* His eyes caressed her. "Like his oh-so-beautiful *madrecita*."

Touched by the tenderness in his deep voice, she reached up and kissed him, savoring the warm hunger of his embrace. Matthew stirred, and she sat back down beside him, watching his eyes open sleepily.

"Feeling better?" she asked gently.

"I'm hungry," he groaned.

"Nothing else to eat just yet, young man," she said, smiling. "You have to make sure your tummy's settled. But how about some more cracked ice?"

"Yes, please," he mumbled.

Diego got up and took the cup and the spoon from her. "I could use some coffee, *querida,*" he suggested.

"So could I. I'll get it."

She left him there after watching the tender way he fed ice to Matthew, the wonder of fatherhood and the pride of it written all over his dark face. Melissa had never felt so happy in all her life. As she left the room she heard his voice, softly accented, exquisitely loving, telling the little boy at last that he was his real papa. Tears welled up in her eyes as she left them, and she smiled secretly through them, bursting with joy.

It was a long night, but the two of them stayed with the little boy. Melissa curled up on the foot of his bed finally to catch a catnap, and Diego slept sprawled in the chair. Mrs. Albright found them like that the next morning and smiled from the doorway. But Matthew was nowhere in sight.

Frowning, she went toward the kitchen, where there was a strange smell...

"Matthew!" she gasped at the doorway.

"I'm hungry," Matthew muttered, "and Mama and Papa won't wake up."

He was standing in his pajamas at the stove, barefoot, cooking himself two eggs. Unfortunately, he had the heat on high and several pieces of eggshell in the pan, and the result was a smelly black mess.

Mrs. Albright got it all cleared away and picked him up to carry him back to bed. "I'll get your breakfast, my lamb. Why were you hungry?"

"My supper came back up again," he explained.

Mrs. Albright nodded wisely. "Stomach bug."

"A very bad bug," he agreed. "Papa is my real papa, you know, he said so, and we're going to live with him forever. Can I have some eggs?"

"Yes, lamb, in just a minute," she promised with a laugh as they went into the bedroom.

"Matthew?" Melissa mumbled as she looked up and saw Mrs. Albright bringing Matthew into the room.

Diego blinked and yawned as Mrs. Albright put the boy back in bed. "Where did you find him?" he asked, his face unshaven and his eyes bleary.

"In the kitchen cooking his breakfast," Mrs. Albright

chuckled, registering their openly horrified expressions. "It's all right now. I've taken care of everything. I'll get him some scrambled eggs and toast if you think it's safe. I'd bet that it is, if my opinion is wanted. He looks fit to me."

"You should have seen him last night," Melissa said with a drowsy smile. "But if he thinks he's hungry, he can have some eggs."

"You two go and get some sleep," Mrs. Albright said firmly. "Matthew's fine, and I'll look out for him. I'll even call the office for you, *señor,* if you like, and tell them where you are."

"That would be most kind of you." He yawned, taking Melissa by the hand. "Come along, Señora Laremos, while I can stand up long enough to guide us to bed."

"¡Buenas noches!" Matthew grinned.

"¡Buenos días!" Melissa corrected with a laugh. "And eat only a little breakfast, okay?" She threw him a kiss. "Good night, baby chick."

She followed Diego into his bedroom and got into the bed while he locked the door. She hardly felt him removing her dress and hose and shoes and slip. Seconds later, she was asleep.

Sunshine streamed lazily through the windows when she stretched under the covers, frowning as she discovered that she didn't have a stitch of clothing on her body.

Diego came into the bedroom from the bathroom with a towel around his lean hips and his hair still damp.

"Awake at last," he murmured dryly. He reached down and jerked the covers off, his dark eyes appreciative of every soft, pink inch of her body as he looked at her openly for the first time in five years. The impact of it was in his eyes, his face. "*Dios mío,* what a beautiful sight," he breathed, smiling at her shy blush.

As he spoke, he unfastened his towel and threw it carelessly on the floor. "Now," he breathed, easing down beside her. "This is where we meant to begin last night, is it not, *querida?*"

She knew it was incredible to be shy with him, but it had been five years. She lowered her eyes to his mouth and looped her arms around his neck and shifted to accommodate the warm weight of his muscular body. She shivered, savoring the abrasive pleasure of his chest hair against her soft breasts, the hardness of his long legs tangling intimately with hers.

Tremors of pleasure wound through her. "Sweet," she whispered shakily, drawing him closer. Her mouth nipped at his, pleaded, danced with it. "It's so sweet, feeling you like this."

"An adequate word for something so wondrous," he whispered, smiling against her eager mouth. He touched her, watching her eyes dilate and her body stiffen. "There, *querida?*" he asked sensuously. "Softly, like this?" He did it again, and she shuddered deliciously and arched. A sensual banquet, after years of starvation.

"You…beast," she chided. Her nails dug into his shoulders as she watched the face above hers grow dark with passion, his eyes glittering as he bent to her body.

"A feast fit for a starving man," he whispered as his lips traced her soft curves, lingering to tease and nip at the firm thrust of her breasts, at her rib cage, her flat belly. And all the while he talked to her, described what he felt and what he was doing and what he was going to do.

She moved under the exploration of his hands, her

eyes growing darker and wilder as he kindled the flames of passion. Once she looked directly into his eyes as he moved down, and she saw the naked hunger in them as his body penetrated hers for the first time in more than five years.

She cried, a keening, husky, breathless little sound that was echoed in her wide eyes and the stiffening of her welcoming body. She cried in passion and in pain, because at first there was the least discomfort.

"Ah, it has been a long time, has it not?" he whispered softly, delighting in the pleasure he read in her face. "Relax, my own." His body stilled, giving hers time to adjust to him, to admit him without discomfort. "Relax. Yes, *querida,* yes, yes…" His eyes closed as he felt the sudden ease of his passage, and his teeth ground together at an unexpected crest of fierce pleasure. He shuddered. "Exquisite," he groaned, opening his eyes to look at her as he moved again, his weight resting on his forearms. "Exquisite, this…with you…this sharing." His eyes closed helplessly as his movements became suddenly harsh and sharp. "Forgive me…!"

But she was with him every step of the way, her fit young body matching his passion, equaling it. She adjusted her body to the needs of his, and held him and watched him and gloried in his fulfillment just before she found her own and cried out against his shoulder in anguished completion.

He shuddered over her, his taut body relaxing slowly, damp, his arms faintly tremulous. She bit his shoulder and laughed breathlessly, feeling for the first time like a whole woman, like a wife.

"Now try to be unfaithful to me," she dared him, whispering the challenge into his ear. "Just try and I'll wear you down until you can hardly crawl away from my bed!"

He nipped her shoulder, laughing softly. "As if I could have touched another woman after you," he whispered. "*Querida,* I took my marriage vows as seriously as you took yours. Guilt and anguish over losing you made it impossible for me to sleep with anyone else." He lifted his damp head and searched her drowsy, shocked eyes. "*Amada,* I love you," he said softly. He brushed her mouth with his. "I do not want anyone else. Not since that first time with you, when I knew that your soul had joined with mine so completely that part of me died when you left."

She hid her face against him, weeping with joy and pain and pleasure. "I'm sorry."

"It is I who am sorry. But our pain is behind us, and now our pleasure begins. This is only the start, this sweet sharing of our bodies. We will share our lives, Melissa. Our sorrow and our joy. Laughter and tears. For this is what makes a marriage."

She reached up and kissed his dark cheek. "I love you so much."

"As I love you." He twined a strand of her long blond hair around his forefinger. His eyes searched hers. He bent, and his mouth opened hers. Seconds later she pulled him down to her again, and he groaned as the flare of passion burned brightly again, sending them down into a fiery oblivion that surpassed even the last one.

Mrs. Albright was putting supper on the table when they reappeared, freshly showered and rested and sharing glances that held a new depth of belonging.

Matthew was still in his room. They ate supper alone

and then went to see him, delighting in the strength of their attachment to each other, delighting in their son.

"Tomorrow I will bring you a surprise when I come home from work. What would you like?" Diego asked his son.

"Only you, Papa," the little boy laughed, reaching up to be held and hugged fiercely.

"In that case, I shall bring you a battleship, complete with crew," his Papa chuckled with a delighted glance toward Melissa, who smiled and leaned against him adoringly.

Diego went to work reluctantly the next morning to find Apollo like a cat with a bad leg and Joyce as cold as if she'd spent two days in a refrigerator.

"How's Matthew?" Apollo asked when Diego entered the office.

"He's much better, thanks, but his mama and I are still trying to catch up on our sleep," Diego laughed, and told him about Matthew's attempt to make breakfast.

Joyce laughed. "I hope your fire insurance is paid up."

Apollo stared at her with unconcealed hunger. "Don't you have something to do?" he asked curtly.

"Of course, but I have to work for you instead," she said with a sweet smile. She was wearing another one of the new outfits, and she looked very pretty in a red-and-orange print that showed off her figure to its best advantage. Apollo could hardly keep his eyes off her, which made for a long and confusing workday.

When Diego went home that afternoon, Apollo was at the end of his rope. He glared at Joyce and she glared back until they both had to look away or die from the electricity in their joined gaze.

"You look nice," he said irritably.

"Thank you," she said with equal curtness.

He drew in an angry breath. "Oh, hell, we can't go on like this," he muttered, going around the desk after her. He caught her by the arms and pulled her against him, his mind registering that she barely came up to his shoulder and that she made him feel violently masculine. "Look, it's impossible to treat each other this way after what happened at the Laremoses two nights ago. I'm going crazy. Just looking at you makes my body ache."

She drew in a steadying breath, because he was affecting her, too. "What do you want to do about it?" she asked, certain that he was thinking along serious lines and wondering how she was going to bear it if he wasn't.

He tilted her mouth up to his and kissed her, long and hard and hungrily. She moaned, stepping closer, pushing against him. His arms swallowed her and he groaned.

"I won't hurt you," he promised huskily, his black eyes holding hers. "I swear to God, I won't. I'll take a long time…"

She could barely make her mind work. "What?"

"I'll get you a better apartment, in the same building as mine," he went on. "We'll spend almost every night together, and if things work out, maybe you can move in with me eventually."

She blinked. "You…want me to be your mistress?"

He scowled. "What's this mistress business? This is America. People live together all the time—"

"I come from a good home and *we* don't live together," she said proudly. "We get married and have babies and behave like a family! My mother would shoot you stone-cold dead if she thought you were trying to seduce me!"

"Who is your mama, the Lone Ranger?" he chided.

"Listen, honey, I can have any woman I want. I don't have to go hungry just because my little virgin secretary has too many hang-ups to—oof!"

Joyce surveyed her handiwork detachedly, registering the extremely odd look on Apollo's face as he bent over the stomach she'd put her knee into. He was an interesting shade of purple, and it served him right.

"I quit, by the way," Joyce said with a smile he couldn't see. She turned, cleaned out her desk drawer efficiently and picked up her purse. There wasn't much to get together. She felt a twinge of regret because she loved the stupid man. But perhaps this was best, because she wasn't going to be any man's kept woman, modern social fad or not.

"Goodbye, boss," she said as she headed for the door. "I hope you have better luck with your next secretary."

"She can't…be worse…than you!" he bit off, still doubled over.

"You sweet man," she said pleasantly as she paused in the doorway. "It's been a joy working for you. I do hope you'll give me a good reference."

"I wouldn't refer you to hell!"

"Good, because I don't want to go anyplace where I'd be likely to run into you!" She slammed the door and walked away. By the time she was in the elevator going down, the numbness had worn off and she realized that she'd burned her bridges. There were tears welling up in her eyes before she got out of the building.

She wound up at Melissa's apartment, crying in great gulps. Diego took one look at her and poured her a drink, then left the women alone in the living room and went off to play the memory game with his son.

"Tell me all about it," Melissa said gently when Joyce managed to stop crying.

"He wants me to be his mistress," she wailed, and buried her face in the tissue Melissa had given her.

"Oh, you poor thing." Melissa curled her feet under her on the sofa. "What did you tell him, as if I didn't know?"

"It wasn't so much what I told him as what I did," Joyce confessed. She grinned sheepishly. "I kicked him in the stomach."

"Oops."

"Well, he deserved it. Bragging about how many women he could get if he wanted them, laughing at me for being chaste." Joyce lifted her chin pugnaciously. "My mother would die if she heard him say such a thing. She has a very religious background, and I was raised strictly and in the church."

"So was I, so don't apologize," Melissa said softly. "Let me tell you, I learned the hard way that it's best to save intimacy for marriage. I'm a dinosaur, I suppose. Where I grew up, the family had its own special place. No member of the family ever did anything to besmirch the family name. Now honor is just a word, but at what cost?"

"You really are a dinosaur," Joyce sighed.

"Purely prehistoric," Melissa agreed. "What are you going to do, my friend?"

"What most dinosaurs do, I guess. I'm going to become extinct, at least as far as Apollo Blain is concerned. I resigned before I left." Her eyes misted again. "I'll never see him again."

"I wouldn't bet on it. Stay for supper and then we'll see what we can do about helping you get another job."

"You're very kind," Joyce said, "but I think it might be best if I go back to Miami. Or even home to my mother." She shrugged. "I don't think I'll be able to fit into this sophisticated world. I might as well go back where I belong."

"I'll have no one to talk to or shop with," Melissa moaned. "You can't! Listen, we'll dig a Burmese tiger trap outside Apollo's office door..."

"You're a nice friend," Joyce said, smiling. "But it really won't do. We'll have to think of something he can't gnaw through."

"Let's have supper. Then we'll talk."

Joyce shook her head. "I can't eat. I want to go home and have a good cry and call my mother. I'll talk to you tomorrow, all right? Meanwhile, thank you for being my friend."

"Thank you for being mine. If you get too depressed, call me. Okay?"

Joyce got up, smiling. "Okay."

Melissa walked her to the door and let her out. Then she leaned back against it, sighing.

Diego came into the hall with his eyebrows raised. "Trouble?"

"She quit. After she kicked your boss in the stomach," she explained. "I think he's probably going to be in a very bad mood for the rest of the week, although I'm only guessing," she added, grinning.

He moved toward her, propping his arms at either side of her head. He smiled. "Things are heating up," he remarked.

"And not only for Joyce and Apollo," she whispered, tempting him until he bent to her mouth and kissed her softly.

She nibbled his lower lip, smiling. "Come here," she breathed, reaching around his waist to draw his weight down on hers.

He obliged her, and she could tell by his breathing as well as by the tautness of his body and his fierce heartbeat that he felt as great a need for her as she felt for him. She opened her mouth to the fierce pressure of his.

"Papa!"

Diego lifted his head reluctantly. "In a moment, *mi hijo,*" he called back. "Your mother and I are discussing plans," he murmured, brushing another kiss against Melissa's eager mouth.

"What kind of plans, Papa, for a trip to the zoo?" Matthew persisted.

"Not exactly. I will be back in a moment, all right?"

There was a long sigh. "All right."

Diego shifted his hips and smiled at Melissa's helpless response. "I think an early night is in order," he breathed. "To make up for our lack of sleep last night," he added.

"I couldn't possibly agree more," she murmured as his mouth came down again. It grew harder and more insistent by the second, but the sound of Mrs. Albright's voice calling them into the dining room broke the spell.

"I long for that ancient Mayan ruin where we first knew each other," Diego whispered as he stood up and let her go.

"With armed guerrillas hunting us, spiders crawling around, snakes slithering by and lightning striking all around," she recalled. She shook her head. "I'll take Chicago any day, Diego!"

He chuckled. "I can hardly argue with that. Let us eat, then we will discuss this trip to the zoo that our son seems determined to make."

* * *

There was a new temporary secretary at work for the rest of the week, but Apollo didn't give her a hard time. In fact, he looked haggard and weary and miserable.

"Perhaps you need a vacation, amigo," Diego said.

"It wouldn't hurt," Dutch nodded, propped gracefully against Apollo's desk with a lighted cigarette in one lean hand.

Apollo glowered at them. "Where would I go?"

Diego studied his fingernails. "You could go to Ferris Street," he remarked. "I understand the weather there is quite nice."

Ferris Street was where Joyce's apartment was, and Apollo glowered furiously at the older man.

"You could park your car there and just relax," Dutch seconded, pursing his lips. His blond hair looked almost silver in the light. "You could read a book or take along one of those little television sets and watch soap operas with nobody to bother you."

"Ferris Street is the end of the world," Apollo said. "You don't take a vacation sitting in your damned car on a side street in Chicago! What's the matter with you people?"

"You could entice women to sit in your car with you," Dutch said. "Ferris Street could be romantic with the right companion. You were a counterterrorist. You know how to appropriate people."

"This is true," Diego agreed. "He appropriated us for several missions, at times when we preferred not to go."

"Right on," Dutch said. He studied Apollo curiously. "I was like you once. I hated women with a hell of lot more reason than you've got. But in the end I discovered that living with a woman is a hell of a lot more interesting than being shot at."

"I asked her to live with me, for your information, Mr. Social Adviser," Apollo muttered. "She kicked me in the gut!"

"What about marriage?" Dutch persisted.

"I don't want to get married," Apollo said.

"Then it is as well that she resigned," Diego said easily. "She can find another man to marry and give her children—"

"Shut up, damn you!" Apollo looked shaken. He wiped the sweat off his forehead. "Oh, God, I've got to get out of here. You guys have things to do, don't you? I'm going for a walk!"

He started out the door.

"You might walk along Ferris Street," Dutch called after him. "I hear flowers are blooming all over the place."

"You might even see a familiar face," Diego added with a grin.

Apollo threw them a fiercely angry gesture and slammed the door behind him.

Dutch got off the desk and moved toward the door with Diego. "He'll come around," the blond man mused. "I did."

"We all come to it," Diego said. He smiled at the younger man. "Bring Dani to supper Saturday. And bring the children. Matthew would enjoy playing with your eldest."

Dutch eyed him. "Everything's okay now, I gather?"

Diego sighed. "My friend, if happiness came in grains of sand, I would be living on a vast desert. I have the world."

"I figured Matthew was yours," Dutch said unexpectedly. "Melissa didn't strike me as the philandering kind."

"As in the old days, you see deeply," Diego replied. He smiled at his friend. "And your Dani, she is content to stay with the children instead of working?"

"Until they're in school, yes. After that, I keep hearing these plans for a really unique used bookstore." Dutch grinned. "Whatever she wants. I come first, you know. I always have and I always will. It's enough to make a man downright flexible."

Diego thought about that all the way home. Yes, it did. So if Melissa wanted to work when Matthew started school, why not? He told her so that night as she lay contentedly in his arms watching the city lights play on the ceiling of the darkened room. She smiled and rolled over and kissed him. And very soon afterward, he was glad he'd made the remark.

Chapter Eleven

There were bells ringing. Melissa put her head under the pillow, but still they kept on. She groaned, reaching out toward the telephone and fumbled it under the pillow and against her ear.

"Hello?" she mumbled.

"Melissa? Is Diego awake?" Apollo asked.

She murmured something and put the receiver against Diego's ear. It fell off and she put it back, shaking his brown shoulder to make him aware of it.

"Hello," he said drowsily. "Who is it?"

There was a pause. All at once he sat straight up in bed, knocking off the pillow and stripping back the covers. "You what?"

Melissa lifted her head, because the note in Diego's voice sounded urgent and shocked. "What is it?" she whispered.

"You what?" Diego repeated. He launched into a wild mixture of Spanish and laughter, then reverted to English. "I wouldn't have believed it. When?"

"What is it?" Melissa demanded, punching Diego.

He put his hand over the receiver. "Apollo and Joyce are being married two days from now. They want us to stand up with them."

Melissa laughed delightedly and clapped her hands. "We'll all come," she said. "There'll be photographers and we'll bring the press!"

"Yes, we'll be delighted," Diego was telling Apollo. "Melissa sends her love to Joyce. We'll see you there. Yes. Congratulations! *¡Hasta luego!*"

"Married!" Melissa sighed, sending an amused, joyful glance at her husband. "And he swore he never would."

"He shouldn't have." Diego grinned. He picked up the phone again and dialed. "I have to tell Dutch," he explained. "I'll tell you later about how we suggested Apollo should take his vacation in his car on Ferris Street."

Melissa giggled, because she had a pretty good idea what kind of vacation they'd had in mind…

Two days later, a smiling justice of the peace married Apollo and Joyce in a simple but beautiful ceremony while Melissa, Diego, the Brettmans and the van Meers, Gabby's mother and First Shirt, Semson and Drago all stood watching. It was the first time the entire group had been together in three years.

Apollo, in a dark business suit, and Joyce, in a white linen suit, clasped hands and repeated their vows with exquisite joy on their faces. They smiled at each other with wonder and a kind of shyness that touched Melissa's heart. Clinging to her husband's hand, she felt as if all of them shared in that marriage ceremony. It was like a rededication of what they all felt for their spouses, a renewal of hope for the future.

Afterward, all of them gathered at a local restaurant for the reception, and Apollo noticed for the first time the number of photographers who were enjoying hors d'oeuvres and coffee and soft drinks.

He frowned. "I don't mean to sound curious," he murmured to Diego and Dutch, "but there sure are a lot of cameras here."

"Evidence," Dutch said.

"In case you got cold feet," Diego explained, "we were going to blackmail you by sending photographs to all the news media showing that your courage had deserted you at the altar."

"You guys," Apollo muttered.

Joyce leaned against his shoulder and reached up to kiss his lean cheek warmly. "I helped pay for the photographers," she confessed. "Well, I had to have an ace in the hole, you know."

He just smiled, too much in love and too happy to argue.

Melissa and Diego left early, holding hands as they wished the happy couple the best, promised to have them over for dinner after the honeymoon and said goodbye to the rest of the gang.

Melissa sighed. "It was a nice wedding."

"As nice as our own?" he asked.

"Ours was a beautiful affair, but it lacked heart," she reminded him. "It was a reluctant marriage."

"Suppose we do it again?" he asked, studying her soft face. "Suppose we have a priest marry us all over again, so that we can repeat our vows and mean them this time?"

"My husband," she said softly, "each day with you is a rededication of our marriage and a reaffirmation of what we feel for each other. The words are meaningless without the day-to-day proving of them. And we have that."

His dark eyes smiled at her. "Yes, *querida,*" he agreed quietly. "We have that in abundance."

She clung to his hand. "Diego, I had a letter yesterday. I didn't show it to you, but I think you expected it all the same."

He frowned. "Who was it from?"

"From your grandmother. There was a note from your sister enclosed with it."

He sighed. "A happy message, I hope?" he asked. He wasn't certain that his family had relented, even though they'd promised him they had.

She smiled at him, reading his uneasiness in his face. "An apology for the past and a message of friendship in the future. They want us to come and visit them in Barbados and bring Matthew. Your grandmother wants to meet her great-grandson."

"And do you want to go?" he asked.

She curled her fingers into his. "You said we might go down to the Caribbean for the summer, didn't you?" she asked. "And combine business with pleasure? I'd like to make my peace with your people. I think you'd like that, too."

"I would. But there is so much to forgive, *querida,*" he said softly, his dark face quiet and still. "Can you find that generosity in your heart?"

"I love you," she said, and the words were sweet and heady in his ears. "I'd do anything for you. Forgiveness is a small thing to ask for the happiness you've given me."

"And you have no regrets?" he persisted.

She nuzzled her cheek against his jacket. "Don't be absurd. I regret all those years we spent apart. But now we have something rare and beautiful. I'm grateful for miracles, because our marriage is certainly one."

He looked down at her bright head against his arm and felt that miracle right to his toes. He brought her hand to his lips and kissed it warmly. "Suppose we get Matthew and take him on a picnic?" he suggested. "He can feed the ducks and we can sit and plan that trip to Barbados."

Melissa pressed closer against Diego, all the nightmares of the past lost in the sunshine of the present. "I'd like that," she said. She watched the sky, thinking about how many times in the past she'd looked up and wondered if Diego was watching it as she was and thinking of her. Her eyes lifted to his smiling face. She laughed. The sound startled a small group of pigeons on the sidewalk, and they flew up in a cacophony of feathery music. Like the last of her doubts, they vanished into the trees and left not a trace of themselves in sight.

* * * * *

Also by Maisey Yates

HQN Books

Harlequin Desire

For more books by Maisey Yates,
visit www.maiseyyates.com.

CLAIM ME, COWBOY

Maisey Yates

For Jackie Ashenden, my conflict guru
and dear friend. Without you my books
would take a heck of a lot longer to write,
and my life would be a heck of a lot more boring.
Thank you for everything. Always.

November 1, 2017
LOOKING FOR A WIFE—

Wealthy bachelor, 34, looking for a wife. Never married, no children. Needs a partner who can attend business and social events around the world. Must be willing to move to Copper Ridge, Oregon. Perks include: travel, an allowance, residence in several multimillion-dollar homes.

November 5, 2017
LOOKING FOR AN UNSUITABLE WIFE—

Wealthy bachelor, 34, irritated, looking for a woman to pretend to be my fiancée in order to teach my meddling father a lesson. Need a partner who is rough around the edges. Must be willing to come to Copper Ridge, Oregon, for at least thirty days. Generous compensation provided.

Chapter One

"No. You do not need to *send pics*."

Joshua Grayson looked out the window of his office and did not feel the kind of calm he ought to feel.

He'd moved back to Copper Ridge six months ago from Seattle, happily trading in a man-made, rectangular skyline for the natural curve of the mountains.

Not the best thing for a man who worked at an architecture company to feel, perhaps. But he spent his working hours dealing in design, in business. Numbers. Black, white and the bottom line. There was something about looking out at the mountains that restarted him.

That, and getting on the back of a horse. Riding from one end of the property to the other. The wind blocking out every other sound except hoofbeats on the earth.

Right now, he doubted anything would decrease the tension he was feeling from dealing with the fallout of his father's ridiculous ad. Another attempt by the old man to make Joshua live the life his father wanted him to.

The only kind of life his father considered successful: a wife, children.

He couldn't understand why Joshua didn't want the same.

No. That kind of life was for another man, one with another past and another future. It was not for Joshua. And that was why he was going to teach his father a lesson.

But not with Brindy, who wanted to send him selfies with "no filter."

The sound she made in response to his refusal was so petulant he almost laughed.

"But your ad said…"

"That," he said, "was not my ad. Goodbye."

He wasn't responsible for the ad in a national paper asking for a wife, till death do them part. But an unsuitable, temporary wife? Yes. That had been his ad.

He was done with his father's machinations. No matter how well-meaning they were. He was tired of tripping over daughters of "old friends" at family gatherings. Tired of dodging women who had been set on him like hounds at a fox hunt.

He was going to win the game. Once and for all. And the woman he hoped would be his trump card was on her way.

His first respondent to his counter ad—Danielle Kelly—was twenty-two, which suited his purposes nicely. His dad would think she was too young, and frankly, Joshua also thought she was too young. He didn't get off on that kind of thing.

He understood why some men did. A tight body was hot. But in his experience, the younger the woman, the less in touch with her sensuality she was and he didn't have the patience for that.

He didn't have the patience for this either, but here he was. The sooner he got this farce over with, the sooner he could go back to his real life.

The doorbell rang and he stood up behind his desk. She was here. And she was—he checked his watch—late.

A half smile curved his lips.

Perfect.

He took the stairs two at a time. He was impatient to meet his temporary bride. Impatient to get this plan started so it could end.

He strode across the entryway and jerked the door open. And froze.

The woman standing on his porch was small. And young, just as he'd expected, but... She wore no makeup, which made her look like a damned teenager. Her features were fine and pointed; her dark brown hair hung lank beneath a ragged beanie that looked like it was in the process of unraveling while it sat on her head.

He didn't bother to linger over the rest of the details—her threadbare sweater with too-long sleeves, her tragic skinny jeans—because he was stopped, immobilized really, by the tiny bundle in her arms.

A baby.

His prospective bride had come with a baby.

Well, hell.

She really hoped he wasn't a serial killer. Well, *hoped* was an anemic word for what she was feeling. Particularly considering the possibility was a valid concern.

What idiot put an ad in the paper looking for a temporary wife?

Though, she supposed the bigger question was: What idiot responded to an ad in the paper looking for a temporary wife?

This idiot, apparently.

It took Danielle a moment to realize she was staring directly at the center of a broad, muscular male chest. She had to raise her head slightly to see his face. He was just so…tall. And handsome.

And she was confused.

She hadn't imagined that a man who put an ad in the paper for a fake fiancée might be attractive. Another anemic word. *Attractive.* This man wasn't simply *attractive*…

He was… Well, he was unreal.

Broad shouldered, muscular, with stubble on his square jaw adding a roughness to features that might have otherwise been considered pretty.

"Please don't tell me you're Danielle Kelly," he said, crossing his arms over that previously noted broad chest.

"I am. Were you expecting someone else? Of course, I suppose you could be. I bet I'm not the only person who responded to your ad, strange though it was. The mention of compensation was pretty tempting. Although, I might point out that in the future maybe you should space your appointments further apart."

"You have a baby," he said, stating the obvious.

Danielle looked down at the bundle in her arms. "Yes."

"You didn't mention that in our email correspondence."

"Of course not. I thought it would make it too easy for you to turn me away."

He laughed, somewhat reluctantly, a muscle in his jaw twitching. "Well, you're right about that."

"But now I'm here. And I don't have the gas money to get back home. Also, you said you wanted unsuitable." She spread one arm wide, keeping Riley clutched firmly in her other arm. "I would say that I'm pretty unsuitable."

She could imagine the picture she made. Her hideous, patchwork car parked in the background. Maroon with lighter patches of red and a door that was green, since it had been replaced after some accident that had happened before the car had come into her possession. Then there was her. In all her faded glory. She was hungry, and she knew she'd lost a lot of weight over the past few weeks, which had taken her frame from slim to downright pointy. The circles under her eyes were so dark she almost looked like she'd been punched.

She considered the baby a perfect accessory. She had that new baby tiredness they never told you about when they talked about the miracle of life.

She curled her toes inside her boots, one of them going through a hole at the end of her sock. She frowned. "Anyway, I figured I presented a pretty poor picture of a fiancée for a businessman such as yourself. Don't you agree?"

The corners of his lips tightened further. "The baby."

"Yes?"

"You expect it to live here?"

She made an exasperated noise. "No. I expect him to live in the car while I party it up in your fancy-pants house."

"A baby wasn't part of the deal."

"What do you care? Your email said it's only through

Christmas. Can you imagine telling your father that you've elected to marry Portland hipster trash and she comes with a baby? I mean, it's going to be incredibly awkward, but ultimately kind of funny."

"Come in," he said, his expression no less taciturn as he stood to the side and allowed her entry into his magnificent home.

She clutched Riley even more tightly to her chest as she wandered inside, looking up at the high ceiling, the incredible floor-to-ceiling windows that offered an unparalleled mountain view. As cities went, Portland was all right. The air was pretty clean, and once you got away from the high-rise buildings, you could see past the iron and steel to the nature beyond.

But this view… This was something else entirely.

She looked down at the floor, taking a surprised step to the side when she realized she was standing on glass. And that underneath the glass was a small, slow-moving stream. Startlingly clear, rocks visible beneath the surface of the water. Also, fish.

She looked up to see him staring at her. "My sister's work," he said. "She's the hottest new architect on the scene. Incredible, considering she's only in her early twenties. And a woman, breaking serious barriers in the industry."

"That sounds like an excerpt from a magazine article."

He laughed. "It might be. Since I write the press releases about Faith. That's what I do. PR for our firm, which has expanded recently. Not just design, but construction. And as you can see, Faith's work is highly specialized, and it's extremely coveted."

A small prickle of…something worked its way under

her skin. She couldn't imagine being so successful at such a young age. Of course, Joshua and his sister must have come from money. You couldn't build something like this if you hadn't.

Danielle was in her early twenties and didn't even have a checking account, much less a successful business.

All of that had to change. It had to change for Riley. He was why she was here, after all.

Truly, nothing else could have spurred her to answer the ad. She had lived in poverty all of her life. But Riley deserved better. He deserved stability. And he certainly didn't deserve to wind up in foster care just because she couldn't get herself together.

"So," she said, cautiously stepping off the glass tile. "Tell me more about this situation. And exactly what you expect."

She wanted him to lay it all out. Wanted to hear the terms and conditions he hadn't shared over email. She was prepared to walk away if it was something she couldn't handle. And if he wasn't willing to take no for an answer? Well, she had a knife in her boot.

"My father placed an ad in a national paper saying I was looking for a wife. You can imagine my surprise when I began getting responses before I had ever seen the ad. My father is well-meaning, Ms. Kelly, and he's willing to do anything to make his children's lives better. However, what he perceives as perfection can only come one way. He doesn't think all of this can possibly make me happy." Joshua looked up, seeming to indicate the beautiful house and view around them. "He's wrong. However, he won't take no for an answer, and I want to teach him a lesson."

"By making him think he won?"

"Kind of. That's where you come in. As I said, he can only see things from his perspective. From his point of view, a wife will stay at home and massage my feet while I work to bring in income. He wants someone traditional. Someone soft and biddable." He looked her over. "I imagine you are none of those things."

"Yeah. Not so much." The life she had lived didn't leave room for that kind of softness.

"And you are right. He isn't going to love that you come with a baby. In fact, he'll probably think you're a gold digger."

"I am a gold digger," she said. "If you weren't offering money, I wouldn't be here. I need money, Mr. Grayson, not a fiancé."

"Call me Joshua," he said. "Come with me."

She followed him as he walked through the entryway, through the living area—which looked like something out of a magazine that she had flipped through at the doctor's office once—and into the kitchen.

The kitchen made her jaw drop. Everything was so shiny. Stainless steel surrounded by touches of wood. A strange clash of modern and rustic that seemed to work.

Danielle had never been in a place where so much work had gone into the details. Before Riley, when she had still been living with her mother, the home decor had included plastic flowers shoved into some kind of strange green Styrofoam and a rug in the kitchen that was actually a towel laid across a spot in the linoleum that had been worn through.

"You will live here for the duration of our arrangement. You will attend family gatherings and work events with me."

"Aren't you worried about me being unsuitable for your work arrangements too?"

"Not really. People who do business with us are fascinated by the nontraditional. As I mentioned earlier, my sister, Faith, is something of a pioneer in her field."

"Great," Danielle said, giving him a thumbs-up. "I'm glad to be a nontraditional asset to you."

"Whether or not you're happy with it isn't really my concern. I mean, I'm paying you, so you don't need to be happy."

She frowned. "Well, I don't want to be unhappy. That's the other thing. We have to discuss…terms and stuff. I don't know what all you think you're going to get out of me, but I'm not here to have sex with you. I'm just here to pose as your fiancée. Like the ad said."

The expression on his face was so disdainful it was almost funny. Almost. It didn't quite ascend to funny because it punched her in the ego. "I think I can control myself, Ms. Kelly."

"If I can call you Joshua, then you can call me Danielle," she said.

"Noted."

The way he said it made her think he wasn't necessarily going to comply with her wishes just because she had made them known. He was difficult. No wonder he didn't have an actual woman hanging around willing to marry him. She should have known there was something wrong with him. Because he was rich and kind of disgustingly handsome. His father shouldn't have had to put an ad in the paper to find Joshua a woman.

He should be able to snap his fingers and have them come running.

That sent another shiver of disquiet over her. Yeah,

maybe she should listen to those shivers… But the compensation. She needed the compensation.

"What am I going to do…with the rest of my time?"

"Stay here," he said, as though that were the most obvious thing in the world. As though the idea of her rotting away up here in his mansion wasn't weird at all. "And you have that baby. I assume it takes up a lot of your time?"

"He. Riley. And yes, he does take up a lot of time. He's a baby. That's kind of their thing." He didn't respond to that. "You know. Helpless, requiring every single one of their physical and emotional needs to be met by another person. Clearly you don't know."

Something in his face hardened. "No."

"Well, this place is big enough you shouldn't have to ever find out."

"I keep strange hours," he said. "I have to work with offices overseas, and I need to be available to speak to them on the phone, which means I only sleep for a couple of hours at a time. I also spend a lot of time outdoors."

Looking at him, that last statement actually made sense. Yes, he had the bearing of an uptight businessman, but he was wearing a T-shirt and jeans. He was also the kind of physically fit that didn't look like it had come from a gym, not that she was an expert on men or their physiques.

"What's the catch?" she asked.

Nothing in life came this easy—she knew that for certain. She was waiting for the other shoe to drop. Waiting for him to lead her down to the dungeon and show her where he kept his torture pit.

"There is no catch. This is what happens when a man

with a perverse sense of humor and too much money decides to teach his father a lesson."

"So basically I live in this beautiful house, I wear your ring, I meet your family, I behave abominably and then I get paid?"

"That is the agreement, Ms. Kelly."

"What if I steal your silverware?"

He chuckled. "Then I still win. If you take off in the dead of night, you don't get your money, and I have the benefit of saying to my father that because of his ad I ended up with a con woman and then got my heart broken."

He really had thought of everything. She supposed there was a reason he was successful.

"So do we... Is this happening?"

"There will be papers for you to sign, but yes. It is." Any uncertainty he'd seemed to feel because of Riley was gone now.

He reached into the pocket of his jeans and pulled out a small, velvet box. He opened it, revealing a diamond ring so beautiful, so big, it bordered on obscene.

This was the moment. This was the moment when he would say he actually needed her to spend the day wandering around dressed as a teddy bear or something.

But that moment didn't come either. Instead, he took the ring out of the box and held it out to her. "Give me your hand."

She complied. She complied before she gave her body permission to. She didn't know what she expected. For him to get down on one knee? For him to slide the ring onto her fourth finger? He did neither. Instead, he dropped the gem into her palm.

She curled her fingers around it, an electric shock

moving through her system as she realized she was probably holding more money in her hand right now than she could ever hope to earn over the course of her lifetime.

Well, no, that wasn't true. Because she was about to earn enough money over the next month to take care of herself and Riley forever. To make sure she got permanent custody of him.

Her life had been so hard, a constant series of moves and increasingly unsavory *uncles* her mother brought in and out of their lives. Hunger, cold, fear, uncertainty…

She wasn't going to let Riley suffer the same fate. No, she was going to make sure her half brother was protected. This agreement, even if Joshua did ultimately want her to walk around dressed like a sexy teddy bear, was a small price to pay for Riley's future.

"Yes," she said, testing the weight of the ring. "It is."

Chapter Two

As Joshua followed Danielle down the hall, he regretted not having a live-in housekeeper. An elderly British woman would come in handy at a time like this. She
would probably find Danielle and her baby to be absolutely delightful. He, on the other hand, did not.

No, on the contrary, he felt invaded. Which was stupid. Because he had signed on for this. Though, he had
signed on for it only after he had seen his father's ad.
After he had decided the old man needed to be taught a
lesson once and for all about meddling in Joshua's life.

It didn't matter that his father had a soft heart or that
he was coming from a good place. No, what mattered
was the fact that Joshua was tired of being hounded
every holiday, every time he went to dinner with his
parents, about the possibility of him starting a family.

It wasn't going to happen.

At one time, he'd thought that would be his future. Had been looking forward to it. But the people who said it was better to have loved and lost than never to have loved at all clearly hadn't *caused* the loss.

He was happy enough now to be alone. And when he didn't want to be alone, he called a woman, had her come spend a few hours in his bed—or in the back of his truck, he wasn't particular. Love was not on his agenda.

"This is a big house," she said.

Danielle sounded vaguely judgmental, which seemed wrong, all things considered. Sure, he was the guy who had paid a woman to pose as his temporary fiancée. And sure, he was the man who lived in a house that had more square footage than he generally walked through in a day, but she was the one who had responded to an ad placed by a complete stranger looking for a temporary fiancée. So, all things considered, he didn't feel like she had a lot of room to judge.

"Yes, it is."

"Why? I mean, you live here alone, right?"

"Because size matters," he said, ignoring the shifting, whimpering sound of the baby in her arms.

"Right," she said, her tone dry. "I've lived in apartment buildings that were smaller than this."

He stopped walking, then he turned to face her. "Am I supposed to feel something about that? Feel sorry for you? Feel bad about the fact that I live in a big house? Because trust me, I started humbly enough. I choose to live differently than my parents. Because I can. Because I earned it."

"Oh, I see. In that case, I suppose I earned my dire straits."

"I don't know your life, Danielle. More important,

I don't want to know it." He realized that was the first time he had used her first name. He didn't much care.

"Great. Same goes. Except I'm going to be living in your house, so I'm going to definitely…infer some things about your life. And that might give rise to conversations like this one. And if you're going to be assuming things about me, then you should be prepared for me to respond in kind."

"I don't have to do any such thing. As far as I'm concerned, I'm the employer, you're the employee. That means if I want to talk to you about the emotional scars of my childhood, you had better lie back on my couch and listen. Conversely, if I do not want to hear about any of the scars of yours, I don't have to. All I have to do is throw money at you until you stop talking."

"Wow. It's seriously the job offer I've been waiting for my entire life. Talking I'm pretty good at. And I don't do a great job of shutting up. That means I would be getting money thrown at me for a long, long time."

"Don't test me, Ms. Kelly," he said, reverting back to her last name, because he really didn't want to know about her childhood or what brought her here. Didn't want to wonder about her past. Didn't want to wonder about her adulthood either. Who the father of her baby was. What kind of situation she was in. It wasn't his business, and he didn't care.

"Don't test me, Ms. Kelly," she said, in what he assumed was supposed to be a facsimile of his voice.

"Really?" he asked.

"What? You can't honestly expect to operate at this level of extreme douchiness and not get called to the carpet on it."

"I expect that I can do whatever I want, since I'm paying you to be here."

"You don't want me to dress up as a teddy bear and vacuum, do you?"

"What?"

She shifted her weight, moving the baby over to one hip and spreading the other arm wide. "Hey, man, some people are into that. They like stuffed animals. Or rather, they like people dressed as stuffed animals."

"I don't."

"That's a relief."

"I like women," he said. "Dressed as women. Or rather, undressed, generally."

"I'm not judging. Your dad put an ad in the paper for some reason. Clearly he really wants you to be married."

"Yes. Well, he doesn't understand that not everybody needs to live the life that he does. He was happy with a family and a farmhouse. But none of the rest of us feel that way, and there's nothing wrong with that."

"So none of you are married?"

"One of us is. The only brother that actually wanted a farmhouse too." He paused in front of the door at the end of the hall. He was glad he had decided to set this room aside for the woman who answered the ad. He hadn't known she would come with a baby in tow, but the fact that she had meant he really, really wanted her out of earshot.

"Is this it?" she asked.

"Yes," he said, pushing the door open.

When she looked inside the bedroom, her jaw dropped, and Joshua couldn't deny that he took a small amount of satisfaction in her reaction. She looked... Well, she looked amazed. Like somebody standing in front of a great work of art. Except it was just a bedroom. Rather a grand one, he had to admit, down to the details.

There was a large bed fashioned out of natural, twisted pieces of wood with polished support beams that ran from floor to ceiling and retained the natural shape they'd had in the woods but glowed from the stain that had been applied to them. The bed made the whole room look like a magical forest. A little bit fanciful for him. His own bedroom had been left more Spartan. But, clearly, Danielle was enchanted.

And he shouldn't care.

"I've definitely lived in apartments that were smaller than this room," she said, wrapping both arms around the baby and turning in a circle. "This is… Is that a loft? Like a reading loft?" She was gazing up at the mezzanine designed to look as though it was nestled in the tree branches.

"I don't know." He figured it was probably more of a sex loft. But then, if he slept in a room with a loft, obviously he would have sex in it. That was what creative surfaces were for, in his opinion.

"It reminds me of something we had when I was in first grade." A crease appeared between her eyebrows. "I mean, not me as in at our house, but in my first-grade classroom at school. The teacher really loved books. And she liked for us all to read. So we were able to lie around the classroom anywhere we wanted with a book and—" She abruptly stopped talking, as though she realized exactly what she was doing. "Never mind. You think it's boring. Anyway, I'm going to use it for a reading loft."

"Dress like a teddy bear in it, for all I care," he responded.

"That's your thing, not mine."

"Do you have any bags in the car that I can get for you?"

She looked genuinely stunned. "You don't have to get anything for me."

It struck him that she thought he was being nice. He didn't consider the offer particularly nice. It was just what his father had drilled into him from the time he was a boy. If there was a woman and she had a heavy thing to transport, you were no kind of man if you didn't offer to do the transporting.

"I don't mind."

"It's just one bag," she said.

That shocked him. She was a woman. A woman with a baby. He was pretty sure most mothers traveled with enough luggage to fill a caravan. "Just one bag." He had to confirm that.

"Yes," she returned. "Baggage is another thing entirely. But in terms of bags, yeah, we travel light."

"Let me get it." He turned and walked out of the room, frustrated when he heard her footsteps behind him. "I said I would get it."

"You don't need to," she said, following him persistently down the stairs and out toward the front door.

"My car is locked," she added, and he ignored her as he continued to walk across the driveway to the maroon monstrosity parked there.

He shot her a sideways glance, then looked down at the car door. It hung a little bit crooked, and he lifted up on it hard enough to push it straight, then he jerked it open. "Not well."

"You're the worst," she said, scowling.

He reached into the back seat and saw one threadbare duffel bag, which had to be the bag she was talking about. The fabric strap was dingy, and he had a feeling it used to be powder blue. The zipper was broken and there were four safety pins holding the end of the bulging bag together. All in all, it looked completely impractical.

"Empty all the contents out of this tonight. In the morning, I'm going to use it to fuel a bonfire."

"It's the only bag I have."

"I'll buy you a new one."

"It better be in addition to the fee that I'm getting," she said, her expression stubborn. "I mean it. If I incur a loss because of you, you better cover it."

"You have my word that if anything needs to be purchased in order for you to fit in with your surroundings, or in order for me to avoid contracting scabies, it will be bankrolled by me."

"I don't have scabies," she said, looking fierce.

"I didn't say you did. I implied that your gym bag might."

"Well," she said, her cheeks turning red, "it doesn't. It's clean. I'm clean."

He heaved the bag over his shoulder and led the way back to the house, Danielle trailing behind him like an angry wood nymph. That was what she reminded him of, he decided. All pointed angles and spiky intensity. And a supernaturally wicked glare that he could feel boring into the center of his back. Right between his shoulder blades.

This was not a woman who intimidated easily, if at all.

He supposed that was signal enough that he should make an attempt to handle her with care. Not because she needed it, but because clearly nobody had ever made the attempt before. But he didn't know how. And he was paying her an awful lot to put up with him as he was.

And she had brought a baby into his house.

"You're going to need some supplies," he said, frowning. Because he abruptly realized what it meant that she had brought a baby into his house. The bedroom he had installed her in was only meant for one. And there was no way—barring the unlikely reality that she was related to Mary Poppins in some way—that her ratty old bag contained the supplies required to keep both a baby and herself in the kind of comfort that normal human beings expected.

"What kind of supplies?"

He moved quickly through the house, and she scurried behind him, attempting to match his steps. They walked back into the bedroom and he flung the bag on the ground.

"A bed for the baby. Beyond that, I don't know what they require."

She shot him a deadly glare, then bent down and unzipped the bag, pulling out a bottle and a can of formula. She tossed both onto the bed, then reached back into the bag and grabbed a blanket. She spread it out on the floor, then set the baby in the center of it.

Then she straightened, spreading her arms wide and slapping her hands back down on her thighs. "Well, this is more than we've had for a long time. And yeah, I guess it would be nice to have nursery stuff. But I've never had it. Riley and I have been doing just fine on our own." She looked down, picking at some dirt beneath her fingernail. "Or I guess we haven't been *fine*. If we had, I wouldn't have responded to your ad. But I don't need more than what I have. Not now. Once you pay me? Well, I'm going to buy a house. I'm going to change things for us. But until then, it doesn't matter."

He frowned. "What about Riley's father? Surely he should be paying you some kind of support."

"Right. Like I have any idea who he is." He must have made some kind of facial expression that seemed judgmental, because her face colored and her eyebrows lowered. "I mean, I don't know how to get in touch with him. It's not like he left contact details. And I sincerely doubt he left his real name."

"I'll call our office assistant, Poppy. She'll probably know what you need." Technically, Poppy was his brother Isaiah's assistant, but she often handled whatever Joshua or Faith needed, as well. Poppy would arrange it so that various supplies were overnighted to the house.

"Seriously. Don't do anything… You don't need to do anything."

"I'm supposed to convince my parents that I'm marrying you," he said, his tone hard. "I don't think they're going to believe I'm allowing my fiancée to live out of one duffel bag. No. Everything will have to be outfitted so that it looks legitimate. Consider it a bonus to your salary."

She tilted her chin upward, her eyes glittering. "Okay, I will."

He had halfway expected her to argue, but he wasn't sure why. She was here for her own material gain. Why would she reduce it? "Good." He nodded once. "You probably won't see much of me. I'll be working a lot. We are going to have dinner with my parents in a couple of days. Until then, the house and the property are yours to explore. This is your house too. For the time being."

He wasn't being particularly generous. It was just

that he didn't want to answer questions, or deal with her being tentative about where she might and might not be allowed to go. He just wanted to install her and the baby in this room and forget about them until he needed them as convenient props.

"Really?" Her natural suspicion was shining through again.

"I'm a very busy man, Ms. Kelly," he said. "I'm not going to be babysitting. Either the child or you."

And with that, he turned and left her alone.

Chapter Three

Danielle had slept fitfully last night. And, of course, she hadn't actually left her room once she had been put there. But early the next morning there had been a delivery. And the signature they had asked for was hers. And then the packages had started to come in, like a Christmas parade without the wrapping.

Teams of men carried the boxes up the stairs. They had assembled a crib, a chair, and then unpacked various baby accoutrements that Danielle hadn't even known existed. How could she? She certainly hadn't expected to end up caring for a baby.

When her mother had breezed back into her life alone and pregnant—after Danielle had experienced just two carefree years where she had her own space and wasn't caring for anyone—Danielle had put all of her focus into caring for the other woman. Into arranging state health insurance so the prenatal care and hospital bill for the delivery wouldn't deter her mother from actually taking care of herself and the baby.

And then, when her mother had abandoned Danielle and Riley…that was when Danielle had realized her brother was likely going to be her responsibility. She had involved Child Services not long after that.

There had been two choices. Either Riley could go into foster care or Danielle could take some appropriate parenting classes and become a temporary guardian.

So she had.

But she had been struggling to keep their heads above water, and it was too close to the way she had grown up. She wanted more than that for Riley. Wanted more than that for both of them. Now it wasn't just her. It was him. And a part-time job as a cashier had never been all that lucrative. But with Riley to take care of, and her mother completely out of the picture, staying afloat on a cashier's pay was impossible.

She had done her best trading babysitting time with a woman in her building who also had a baby and nobody else to depend on. But inevitably there were schedule clashes, and after missing a few too many shifts, Danielle had lost her job.

Which was when she had gotten her first warning from Child Services.

Well, she had a job now.

And, apparently, a full nursery.

Joshua was refreshingly nowhere to be seen, which made dealing with her new circumstances much easier. Without him looming over her, being in his house felt a lot like being in the world's fanciest vacation rental. At least, the fanciest vacation rental she could imagine.

She had a baby monitor in her pocket, one that would allow her to hear when Riley woke up. A baby monitor that provided her with more freedom than she'd had since Riley had been born. But, she supposed, in her old apartment a monitor would have been a moot point considering there wasn't anywhere she could go and not hear the baby cry.

But in this massive house, having Riley take his nap in the bedroom—in the new crib, his first crib—would have meant she couldn't have also run down to the kitchen to grab snacks. But she had the baby monitor. A baby monitor that vibrated. Which meant she could also listen to music.

She had the same ancient MP3 player her mother had given her for her sixteenth birthday years ago, but Danielle had learned early to hold on to everything she had, because she didn't know when something else would come along. And in the case of frills like her MP3 player, nothing else had ever come along.

Of course, that meant her music was as old as her technology. But really, music hadn't been as good since she was sixteen anyway.

She shook her hips slightly, walking through the kitchen, singing about how what didn't kill her would only make her stronger. Digging through cabinets, she came up with a package of Pop-Tarts. *Pop-Tarts!*

Her mother had never bought those. They were too expensive. And while Danielle had definitely indulged herself when she had moved out, that hadn't lasted. Because they were too expensive.

Joshua had strawberry. And some kind of mixed berry with bright blue frosting. She decided she would eat one of each to ascertain which was best.

Then she decided to eat one more of each. She hadn't realized how hungry she was. She had a feeling the hunger wasn't a new development. She had a feeling she had been hungry for days. Weeks even.

Suddenly, sitting on the plush couch in his living area, shoving toaster pastries into her mouth, she felt a whole lot like crying in relief. Because she and Riley were warm; they were safe. And there was hope. Finally, an end point in sight to the long, slow grind of poverty she had existed in for her entire life.

It seemed too good to be true, really. That she had managed to jump ahead in her life like this. That she was really managing to get herself out of that hole without prostituting herself.

Okay, so some people might argue this agreement with Joshua *was* prostituting herself, a little bit. But it wasn't like she was going to have sex with him.

She nearly choked on her Pop-Tart at the thought. And she lingered a little too long on what it might be like to get close to a man like Joshua. To any man, really. The way her mother had behaved all of her life had put Danielle off men. Or, more specifically, she supposed it was the way men had behaved toward Danielle's mother that had put her off.

As far as Danielle could tell, relationships were a whole lot of exposing yourself to pain, deciding you were going to depend on somebody and then having that person leave you high and dry.

No, thank you.

But she supposed she could see how somebody might lose their mind enough to take that risk. Especially when the person responsible for the mind loss had eyes that were blue like Joshua's. She leaned back against the couch, her hand falling slack, the Pop-Tart dangling from her fingertips.

Yesterday there had been the faint shadow of golden stubble across that strong face and jaw, his eyes glittering with irritation. Which she supposed shouldn't be a bonus, shouldn't be appealing. Except his irritation made her want to rise to the unspoken challenge. To try to turn that spark into something else. Turn that irritation into something more...

"Are you eating my Pop-Tarts?"

The voice cut through the music and she jumped, flinging the toaster pastry into the air. She ripped her headphones out of her ears and turned around to see Joshua, his arms crossed over his broad chest, his eyebrows flat on his forehead, his expression unreadable.

"You said whatever was in your house was mine to use," she squeaked. "And a warning would've been good. You just about made me jump out of my skin. Which was maybe your plan all along. If you wanted to make me into a skin suit."

"That's ridiculous. I would not fit into your skin."

She swallowed hard, her throat dry. "Well, it's a figure of speech, isn't it?"

"Is it?" he asked.

"Yes. Everybody knows what that means. It means that I think you might be a serial killer."

"You don't really think I'm a serial killer, or you wouldn't be here."

"I am pretty desperate." She lifted her hand and licked off a remnant of jam. "I mean, obviously."

"There are no Pop-Tarts left," he said, his tone filled with annoyance.

"You said I could have whatever I wanted. I wanted Pop-Tarts."

"You ate all of them."

"Why do you even have Pop-Tarts?" She stood up, crossing her arms, mimicking his stance. "You don't look like a man who eats Pop-Tarts."

"I like them. I like to eat them after I work outside."

"You work outside?"

"Yes," he said. "I have horses."

Suddenly, all of her annoyance fell away. Like it had been melted by magic. *Equine* magic. "You have horses?" She tried to keep the awe out of her voice, but it was nearly impossible.

"Yes," he said.

"Can I… Can I see them?"

"If you want to."

She had checked the range on the baby monitor, so depending on how far away from the house the horses were, she could go while Riley was napping.

"Could we see the house from the barn? Or wherever you keep them?"

"Yeah," he said, "it's just right across the driveway."

"Can I see them *now*?"

"I don't know. You ate my Pop-Tarts. Actually, more egregious than eating my Pop-Tarts, you threw the last half of one on the ground."

"Sorry about your Pop-Tarts. But I'm sure that a man who can have an entire nursery outfitted in less than twenty-four hours can certainly acquire Pop-Tarts at a moment's notice."

"Or I could just go to the store."

She had a hard time picturing a man like Joshua Grayson walking through the grocery store. In fact, the image almost made her laugh. He was way too commanding to do something as mundane as pick up a head of lettuce and try to figure out how fresh it was. Far too…masculine to go around squeezing avocados.

"What?" he asked, his eyebrows drawing together.

"I just can't imagine you going to the grocery store. That's all."

"Well, I do. Because I like food. Food like Pop-Tarts."

"My mom would never buy those for me," she said. "They were too expensive."

He huffed out a laugh. "My mom would never buy them for me."

"This is why being an adult is cool, even when it sucks."

"Pop-Tarts whenever you want?"

She nodded. "Yep."

"That seems like a low bar."

She lifted a shoulder. "Maybe it is, but it's a tasty one."

He nodded. "Fair enough. Now, why don't we go look at the horses."

Joshua didn't know what to expect by taking Danielle outside to see the horses. He had been irritated that she had eaten his preferred afternoon snack, and then, perversely, even more irritated that she had questioned the fact that it was his preferred afternoon snack. Irritated that he was put in the position of explaining to someone what he did with his time and what he put into his body.

He didn't like explaining himself.

But then she saw the horses. And all his irritation faded as he took in the look on her face. She was filled with…wonder. Absolute wonder over this thing he took for granted.

The fact that he owned horses at all, that he had felt compelled to acquire some once he had moved into this place, was a source of consternation. He had hated doing farm chores when he was a kid. Hadn't been able to get away from home and to the city fast enough. But in recent years, those feelings had started to change. And he'd found himself seeking out roots. Seeking home.

For better or worse, this was home. Not just the misty Oregon coast, not just the town of Copper Ridge. But a ranch. Horses. A morning spent riding until the sun rose over the mountains, washing everything in a pale gold.

Yeah, that was home.

He could tell this ranch he loved was something beyond a temporary home for Danielle, who was looking at the horses and the barn like they were magical things.

She wasn't wearing her beanie today. Her dark brown hair hung limply around her face. She was pale, her chin pointed, her nose slightly pointed, as well. She was elfin, and he wasn't tempted to call her beautiful, but there was something captivating about her. Something fascinating. Watching her with the large animals was somehow just as entertaining as watching football and he couldn't quite figure out why.

"You didn't grow up around horses?"

"No," she said, taking a timid step toward the paddock. "I grew up in Portland."

He nodded. "Right."

"Always in apartments," she said. Then she frowned. "I think one time we had a house. I can't really remember it. We moved a lot. But sometimes when we lived with my mom's boyfriends, we had nicer places. It had its perks."

"What did?"

"My mom being a codependent hussy," she said, her voice toneless so it was impossible to say whether or not she was teasing.

"Right." He had grown up in one house. His family had never moved. His parents were still in that same farmhouse, the one his family had owned for a couple of generations. He had moved away to go to college and then to start the business, but that was different. He had always known he could come back here. He'd always had roots.

"Will you go back to Portland when you're finished here?" he asked.

"I don't know," she said, blinking rapidly. "I've never really had a choice before. Of where I wanted to live."

It struck him then that she was awfully young. And that he didn't know quite *how* young. "You're twenty-two?"

"Yes," she said, sounding almost defensive. "So I haven't really had a chance to think about what all I want to do and, like, be. When I grow up and stuff."

"Right," he said.

He'd been aimless for a while, but before he'd graduated high school, he'd decided he couldn't deal with a life of ranching in Copper Ridge. He had decided to get out of town. He had wanted more. He had wanted bigger. He'd gone to school for marketing because he was good at selling ideas. Products. He wasn't necessarily the one who created them, or the one who dreamed them up, but he was the one who made sure a consumer would see them and realize that product was what their life had been missing up until that point.

He was the one who took the straw and made it into gold.

He had always enjoyed his job, but it would have been especially satisfying if he'd been able to start his career by building a business with his brother and sister. To be able to market Faith's extraordinary talent to the world, as he did now. But he wasn't sure that he'd started out with a passion for what he did so much as a passion for wealth and success, and that had meant leaving behind his sister and brother too, at first. But his career had certainly grown into a passion. And he'd learned that he was the practical piece. The part that everybody needed.

A lot of people had ideas, but less than half of them had the follow-through to complete what they started. And less than half of *those* people knew how to get to the consumer. That was where he came in.

He'd had his first corporate internship at the age of twenty. He couldn't imagine being aimless at twenty-two.

But then, Danielle had a baby and he couldn't imagine having a baby at that age either.

A hollow pang struck him in the chest.

He didn't like thinking of babies at all.

"You're judging me," she said, taking a step back from the paddock.

"No, I'm not. Also, you can get closer. You can pet them."

Her head whipped around to look at the horses, then back to him, her eyes round and almost comically hopeful. "I can?"

"Of course you can. They don't bite. Well, they *might* bite, just don't stick your fingers in their mouths."

"I don't know," she said, stuffing her hands in her pockets. Except he could tell she really wanted to. She was just afraid.

"Danielle," he said, earning himself a shocked look when he used her name. "Pet the horses."

She tugged her hand out of her pocket again, then took a tentative step forward, reaching out, then drawing her hand back just as quickly.

He couldn't stand it. Between her not knowing what she wanted to be when she grew up and watching her struggle with touching a horse, he just couldn't deal with it. He stepped forward, wrapped his fingers around her wrist and drew her closer to the paddock. "It's fine," he said.

A moment after he said the words, his body registered what he had done. More than that, it registered the fact that she was very warm. That her skin was smooth.

And that she was way, way too thin.

A strange combination of feelings tightened his whole body. Compassion tightened his heart; lust tightened his groin.

He gritted his teeth. "Come on," he said.

He noticed the color rise in her face, and he wondered if she was angry, or if she was feeling the same flash of awareness rocking through him. He supposed it didn't matter either way. "Come on," he said, drawing her hand closer to the opening of the paddock. "There you go, hold your hand flat like that."

She complied, and he released his hold on her, taking a step back. He did his best to ignore the fact that he could still feel the impression of her skin against his palm.

One of his horses—a gray mare named Blue—walked up to the bars and pressed her nose against Danielle's outstretched hand. Danielle made a sharp, shocked sound, drew her hand back, then giggled. "Her whiskers are soft."

"Yeah," he said, a smile tugging at his lips. "And she is about as gentle as they come, so you don't have to be afraid of her."

"I'm not afraid of anything," Danielle said, sticking her hand back in, letting the horse sniff her.

He didn't believe that she wasn't afraid of anything. She was definitely tough. But she was brittle. Like one of those people who might withstand a beating, but if something ever hit a fragile spot, she would shatter entirely.

"Would you like to go riding sometime?" he asked.

She drew her hand back again, her expression… Well, he couldn't quite read it. There was a softness to it, but also an edge of fear and suspicion.

"I don't know. Why?"

"You seem to like the horses."

"I do. But I don't know how to ride."

"I can teach you."

"I don't know. I have to watch Riley." She began to withdraw, both from him and from the paddock.

"I'm going to hire somebody to help watch Riley," he said, making that decision right as the words exited his mouth.

There was that look again. Suspicion. "Why?"

"In case I need you for something that isn't baby friendly. Which will probably happen. We have over a month ahead of us with you living with me, and one never knows what kinds of situations we might run into. I wasn't expecting you to come with a baby, and while

I agree that it will definitely help make the case that you're not suitable for me, I also think we'll need to be able to go out without him."

She looked very hesitant about that idea. And he could understand why. She clung to that baby like he was a life preserver. Like if she let go of him, she might sink and be in over her head completely.

"And I would get to ride the horses?" she asked, her eyes narrowed, full of suspicion still.

"I said so."

"Sure. But that doesn't mean a lot to me, Mr. Grayson," she said. "I don't accept people at their word. I like legal documents."

"Well, I'm not going to draw up a legal document about giving you horse-riding lessons. So you're going to have to trust me."

"You want me to trust the sketchy rich dude who put an ad in the paper looking for a fake wife?"

"He's the devil you made the deal with, Ms. Kelly. I would say it's in your best interest to trust him."

"We shake on it at least."

She stuck her hand out, and he could see she was completely sincere. So he stuck his out in kind, wrapping his fingers around hers, marveling at her delicate bone structure. Feeling guilty now about getting angry over her eating his Pop-Tarts. The woman needed him to hire a gourmet chef too. Needed him to make sure she was getting three meals a day. He wondered how long it had been since she'd eaten regularly. She certainly didn't have the look of a woman who had recently given birth. There was no extra weight on her to speak of. He wondered how she had survived something so taxing as labor and delivery. But those were questions he was not going to ask. They weren't his business.

And he shouldn't even be curious about them.

"All right," she said. "You can hire somebody. And I'll learn to ride horses."

"You're a tough negotiator," he said, releasing his hold on her hand.

"Maybe I should go into business."

He tried to imagine this fragile, spiky creature in a boardroom, and it nearly made him laugh. "If you want to," he said, instead of laughing. Because he had a feeling she might attack him if he made fun of her. And another feeling that if Danielle attacked, she would likely go straight for the eyes. Or the balls.

He was attached to both of those things, and he liked them attached to him.

"I should go back to the house. Riley might wake up soon. Plus, I'm not entirely sure if I trust the new baby monitor. I mean, it's probably fine. But I'm going to have to get used to it before I really depend on it."

"I understand," he said, even though he didn't.

He turned and walked with her back toward the house. He kept his eyes on her small, determined frame. On the way, she stuffed her hands in her pockets and hunched her shoulders forward. As though she were trying to look intimidating. Trying to keep from looking at her surroundings in case her surroundings looked back.

And then he reminded himself that none of this mattered. She was just a means to an end, even if she was a slightly more multifaceted means than he had thought she might be.

It didn't matter how many facets she had. Danielle Kelly needed to fulfill only one objective. She had to be introduced to his parents and be found completely wanting.

He looked back at her, at her determined walk and her posture that seemed to radiate with *I'll cut you*.

Yeah. He had a feeling she would fulfill that objective just fine.

Chapter Four

Danielle was still feeling wobbly after her interaction with Joshua down at the barn. She had touched a horse. And she had touched *him*. She hadn't counted on doing either of those things today. And he had told her they were going to have dinner together tonight and he was going to give her a crash course on the Grayson family. She wasn't entirely sure she felt ready for that either.

She had gone through all her clothes, looking for something suitable for having dinner with a billionaire. She didn't have anything. Obviously.

She snorted, feeling like an idiot for thinking she could find something relatively appropriate in that bag of hers. A bag he thought had scabies.

She turned her snort into a growl.

Then, rebelliously, she pulled out the same pair of faded pants she had been wearing yesterday.

He had probably never dealt with a woman who wore the same thing twice. Let alone the same thing two days in a row. Perversely, she kind of enjoyed that. Hey, she was here to be unsuitable. Might as well start now.

She looked in the mirror, grabbed one stringy end of her hair and blew out a disgusted breath. She shouldn't care how her hair looked.

But he was just so good-looking. It made her feel like a small, brown mouse standing next to him. It wasn't fair, really. That he had the resources to buy himself nice clothes and that he just naturally looked great.

She sighed, picking Riley up from his crib and sticking him in the little carrier she would put him in for dinner. He was awake and looking around, so she wanted to be in his vicinity, rather than leaving him upstairs alone. He wasn't a fussy baby. Really, he hardly ever cried.

But considering how often his mother had left him alone in those early days of his life, before Danielle had realized she couldn't count on her mother to take good care of him, she was reluctant to leave him by himself unless he was sleeping.

Then she paused, going back over to her bag to get the little red, dog-eared dictionary inside. She bent down, still holding on to Riley, and retrieved it. Then she quickly looked up scabies.

"I knew it," she said derisively, throwing the dictionary back into her bag.

She walked down the stairs and into the dining room, setting Riley in his seat on the chair next to hers. Joshua was already sitting at the table, looking as though he had been waiting for them. Which, she had a feeling, he was doing just to be annoying and superior.

"My bag can't have scabies," she said by way of greeting.

"Oh really?"

"Yes. I looked it up. Scabies are mites that burrow into your skin. Not into a duffel bag."

"They have to come from somewhere."

"Well, they're not coming from my bag. They're more likely to come from your horses, or something."

"You like my horses," he said, his tone dry. "Anyway, we're about to have dinner. So maybe we shouldn't be discussing skin mites?"

"You're the one who brought up scabies. The first time."

"I had pretty much dropped the subject."

"Easy enough for you to do, since it wasn't your hygiene being maligned."

"Sure." He stood up from his position at the table. "I'm just going to go get dinner, since you're here. I had it warming."

"Did you cook?"

He left the room without answering and returned a moment later holding two plates full of hot food. Her stomach growled intensely. She didn't even care what was on the plates. As far as she was concerned, it was gourmet. It was warm and obviously not from a can or a frozen pizza box. Plus, she was sitting at a real dining table and not on a patio set that had been shoved into her tiny living room.

The meal looked surprisingly healthy, considering she had discovered his affinity for Pop-Tarts earlier. And it was accompanied by a particularly nice-looking rice. "What is this?"

"Chicken and risotto," he said.

"What's risotto?"

"Creamy rice," he said. "At least, that's the simple explanation."

Thankfully, he wasn't looking at her like she was an alien for not knowing about risotto. But then she remembered he had spoken of having simple roots. So maybe he was used to dealing with people who didn't have as sophisticated a palate as he had.

She wrinkled her nose, then picked up her fork and took a tentative bite. It was good. So good. And before she knew it, she had cleared out her portion. Her cheeks heated when she realized he had barely taken two bites.

"There's plenty more in the kitchen," he said. Then he took her plate from in front of her and went back into the kitchen. She was stunned, and all she could do was sit there and wait until he returned a moment later with the entire pot of risotto, another portion already on her plate.

"Eat as much as you want," he said, setting everything in front of her.

Well, she wasn't going to argue with that suggestion. She polished off the chicken, then went back for thirds of the risotto. Eventually, she got around to eating the salad.

"I thought we were going to talk about my responsibilities for being your fiancée and stuff," she said after she realized he had been sitting there staring at her for the past ten minutes.

"I thought you should have a chance to eat a meal first."

"Well," she said, taking another bite, "that's unexpectedly kind of you."

"You seem…hungry."

That was the most loaded statement of the century. She was so hungry. For so many things. Food was kind of the least of it. "It's just been a really crazy few months."

"How old is the baby? Riley. How old is Riley?"

For the first time, because of that correction, she became aware of the fact that he seemed reluctant to call Riley by name. Actually, Joshua seemed pretty reluctant to deal with Riley in general.

Riley was unperturbed. Sitting in that reclined seat, his muddy blue eyes staring up at the ceiling. He lifted his fist, putting it in his mouth and gumming it idly.

That was one good thing she could say about their whole situation. Riley was so young that he was largely unperturbed by all of it. He had gone along more or less unaffected by their mother's mistakes. At least, Danielle hoped so. She really did.

"He's almost four months old," she said. She felt a soft smile touch her lips. Yes, taking care of her half brother was hard. None of it was easy. But he had given her a new kind of purpose. Had given her a kind of the drive she'd been missing before.

Before Riley, she had been somewhat content to just enjoy living life on her own terms. To enjoy not cleaning up her mother's messes. Instead, working at the grocery store, going out with friends after work for coffee or burritos at the twenty-four-hour Mexican restaurant.

Her life had been simple, and it had been carefree. Something she hadn't been afforded all the years she'd lived with her mother, dealing with her mother's various heartbreaks, schemes to try to better their circumstances and intense emotional lows.

So many years when Danielle should have been a child but instead was expected to be the parent. If her mother passed out in the bathroom after having too much to drink, it was up to Danielle to take care of her. To put a pillow underneath her mother's head, then make herself a piece of toast for dinner and get her homework done.

In contrast, taking care of only herself had seemed simple. And in truth, she had resented Riley at first, resented the idea that she would have to take care of another person again. But taking care of a baby was different. He wasn't a victim of his own bad choices. No, he was a victim of circumstances. He hadn't had a chance to make a single choice for himself yet.

To Danielle, Riley was the child she'd once been.

Except she hadn't had anyone to step in and take care of her when her mother failed. But Riley did. That realization had filled Danielle with passion. Drive.

And along with that dedication came a fierce, unexpected love like she had never felt before toward another human being. She would do anything for him. Give anything for him.

"And you've been alone with him all this time?"

She didn't know why she was so reluctant to let Joshua know that Riley wasn't her son. She supposed it was partly because, for all intents and purposes, he was her son. She intended to adopt him officially as soon as she had the means to do so. As soon as everything in her life was in order enough that Child Services would respond to her favorably.

The other part was that as long as people thought Riley was hers, they would be less likely to suggest she make a different decision about his welfare. Joshua Grayson had a coldness to him. He seemed to have a family who loved and supported him, but instead of finding it endearing, he got angry about it. He was using her to get back at his dad for doing something that, in her opinion, seemed mostly innocuous. And yes, she was benefiting from his pettiness, so she couldn't exactly judge.

Still, she had a feeling that if he knew Riley wasn't her son, he would suggest she do the "responsible" thing and allow him to be raised by a two-parent family, or whatever. She just didn't even want to have that discussion with him. Or with anybody. She had too many things against her already.

She didn't want to fight about this too.

"Mostly," she said carefully, treading the line between the truth and a lie. "Since he was about three weeks old. And I thought… I thought I could do it. I'd been self-sufficient for a long time. But then I realized there are a lot of logistical problems when you can't just leave your apartment whenever you want. It's harder to get to work. And I couldn't afford childcare. There wasn't any space at the places that had subsidized rates. So I was trading childcare with a neighbor, but sometimes our schedules conflicted. Anyway, it was just difficult. You can imagine why responding to your ad seemed like the best possible solution."

"I already told you, I'm not judging you for taking me up on an offer I made."

"I guess I'm just explaining that under other circumstances I probably wouldn't have sought you out. But things have been hard. I lost my job because I wasn't flexible enough and I had missed too many shifts because babysitting for Riley fell through."

"Well," he said, a strange expression crossing his face, "your problems should be minimized soon. You should be independently wealthy enough to at least afford childcare."

Not only that, she would actually be able to make

decisions about her life. About what she wanted. When Joshua had asked her earlier today about whether or not she would go back to Portland, it had been the first time she had truly realized she could make decisions about where she wanted to live, rather than just parking herself somewhere because she happened to be there already.

It would be the first time in her life she could make proactive decisions rather than just reacting to her situation.

"Right. So I guess we should talk about your family," she said, determined to move the conversation back in the right direction. She didn't need to talk about herself. They didn't need to get to know each other. She just needed to do this thing, to trick his family, lie… whatever he needed her to do. So she and Riley could start their new life.

"I already told you my younger sister is an architectural genius. My older brother Isaiah is the financial brain. And I do the public relations and marketing. We have another brother named Devlin, and he runs a small ranching operation in town. He's married, no kids. Then there are my parents."

"The reason we find ourselves in this situation," she said, folding her hands and leaning forward. Then she cast a glance at the pot of risotto and decided to grab the spoon and serve herself another helping while they were talking.

"Yes. Well, not my mother so much. Sure, she wrings her hands and looks at me sadly and says she wishes I would get married. My father is the one who…actively meddles."

"That surprises me. I mean, given what I know about fathers. Which is entirely based on TV. I don't have one."

He lifted a brow.

"Well," she continued, "sure, I guess I do. But I never met him. I mean, I don't even know his name."

She realized that her history was shockingly close to the story she had given about Riley. Which was a true one. It just wasn't about Danielle. It was about her mother. And the fact that her mother repeated the same cycle over and over again. The fact that she never seemed to change. And never would.

"That must've been hard," he said. "I'm sorry."

"Don't apologize. I bet he was a jerk. I mean, circumstances would lead you to believe that he must be, right?"

"Yeah, it's probably a pretty safe assumption."

"Well, anyway, this isn't about my lack of a paternal figure. This is about the overbearing presence of yours."

He laughed. "My mother is old-fashioned—so is my father. My brother Devlin is a little bit too, but he's also something of a rebel. He has tattoos and things. He's a likely ally for you, especially since he got married a few months ago and is feeling soft about love and all of that. My brother Isaiah isn't going to like you. My sister, Faith, will try. Basically, if you cuss, chew with your mouth open, put your elbows on the table and in general act like a feral cat, my family will likely find you unsuitable. Also, if you could maybe repeatedly bring up the fact that you're really looking forward to spending my money, and that you had another man's baby four months ago, that would be great."

She squinted. "I think the fact that I have a four-month-old baby in tow will be reminder enough."

The idea of going into his family's farmhouse and behaving like a nightmare didn't sit as well with her as it had when the plan had been fully abstract. But now he had given names to the family members. Now she had been here for a while. And now it was all starting to feel a little bit real.

"It won't hurt. Though, he's pretty quiet. It might help if he screamed."

She laughed. "Oh, I don't know about that. I have a feeling your mom and sister might just want to hold him. That will be the real problem. Not having everyone hate me. That'll be easy enough. It'll be keeping everyone from loving him."

That comment struck her square in the chest, made her realize just what they were playing at here. She was going to be lying to these people. And yes, the idea was to alienate them, but they were going to think she might be their daughter-in-law, sister-in-law…that Riley would be their grandson or nephew.

But it would be a lie.

That's the point, you moron. And who cares? They're strangers. Riley is your life. He's your responsibility. And you'll never see these people again.

"We won't let them hold the baby," he said, his expression hard, as if he'd suddenly realized she wasn't completely wrong about his mother and sister and it bothered him.

She wished she could understand why he felt so strongly about putting a stop to his father playing matchmaker. As someone whose parents were ambivalent about her existence, his disregard for his family's well wishes was hard to comprehend.

"Okay," she said. "Fine by me. And you just want me to…be my charming self?"

"Obviously we'll have to come up with a story about

our relationship. We don't have to make up how we met. We can say we met through the ad."

"The ad your father placed, not the ad you placed."

"Naturally."

She looked at Joshua then, at the broad expanse of table between them. Two people who looked less like a couple probably didn't exist on the face of the planet. Honestly, two strangers standing across the street from each other probably looked more like a happily engaged unit than they did.

She frowned. "This is very unconvincing."

"What is? Be specific."

She rolled her eyes at his impatience. "Us."

She stood up and walked toward him, sitting down in the chair right next to him. She looked at him for a moment, at the sharp curve of his jaw, the enticing shape of his lips. He was an attractive man. That was an understatement. He was also so uptight she was pretty sure he had a stick up his behind.

"Look, you want your family to think you've lost your mind, to think you have hooked up with a totally unsuitable woman, right?"

"That is the game."

"Then you have to look like you've lost your mind over me. Unfortunately, Joshua, you look very much in your right mind. In fact, a man of sounder mind may not exist. You are…responsible. You literally look like The Man."

"Which man?"

"Like, The Man. Like, fight the power. *You're* the power. Nobody's going to believe you're with me. At least, not if you don't seem a little bit…looser."

A slight smile tipped up those lips she had been thinking about only a moment before. His blue eyes warmed, and she felt an answering warmth spread low in her belly. "So what you're saying is we need to look like we have more of a connection?"

Her throat went dry. "It's just a suggestion."

He leaned forward, his gaze intent on hers. "An essential one, I think." Then he reached up and she jerked backward, nearly toppling off the side of her chair. "It looks like I'm not the only one who's wound a bit tight."

"I'm not," she said, taking a deep breath, trying to get her jittery body to calm itself down.

She wasn't used to men. She wasn't used to men touching her. Yes, intermittently she and her mother had lived with some of her mother's boyfriends, but none of them had ever been inappropriate with her. And she had never been close enough to even give any of them hugs.

And she really, really wasn't used to men who were so beautiful it was almost physically painful to look directly at them.

"You're right. We have to do a better job of looking like a couple. And that would include you not scampering under the furniture when I get close to you."

She sat up straight and folded her hands in her lap. "I did not scamper," she muttered.

"You were perilously close to a scamper."

"Was not," she grumbled, and then her breath caught in her throat as his warm palm made contact with her cheek.

He slid his thumb down the curve of her face to that dent just beneath her lips, his eyes never leaving hers. She felt…stunned and warm. No, hot. So very hot. Like there was a furnace inside that had been turned up the moment his hand touched her bare skin.

She supposed she was meant to be flirtatious. To play the part of the moneygrubbing tart with loose morals he needed her to be, that his family would expect her to be. But right now, she was shocked into immobility.

She took a deep breath, fighting for composure. But his thumb migrated from the somewhat reasonable point just below her mouth to her lip and her composure dissolved completely. His touch felt…shockingly intimate and filthy somehow. Not in a bad way, just in a way she'd never experienced before.

For some reason she would never be able to articulate—not even to herself—she darted her tongue out and touched the tip to his thumb. She tasted salt, skin and a promise that arrowed downward to the most private part of her body, leaving her feeling breathless. Leaving her feeling new somehow.

As if a wholly unexpected and previously unknown part of herself had been uncovered, awoken. She wanted to do exactly what he had accused her of doing earlier. She wanted to turn away. Wanted to scurry beneath the furniture or off into the night. Somewhere safe. Somewhere less confrontational.

But he was still looking at her. And those blue eyes were like chains, lashing her to the seat, holding her in place. And his thumb, pressed against her lip, felt heavy. Much too heavy for her to push against. For her to fight.

And when it came right down to it, she didn't even want to.

Something expanded in her chest, spreading low, opening up a yawning chasm in her stomach. Deepening her need, her want. Her desire for things she hadn't known she could desire until now.

Until he had made a promise with his touch that she hadn't known she wanted fulfilled.

She was just about to come back to herself, to pull away. And then he closed the distance between them.

His lips were warm and firm. The kiss was nothing like she had imagined it might be. She had always thought a kiss must reach inside and steal your brain. Transform you. She had always imagined a kiss to be powerful, considering the way her mother acted.

When her mother was under the influence of love— at least, that was what her mother had called it; Danielle had always known it was lust—she acted like someone entirely apart from herself.

Yes, Danielle had always known a kiss could be powerful. But what she hadn't counted on was that she might feel wholly like *herself* when a man fused his lips to hers. That she would be so perfectly aware of where she was, of what she was doing.

Of the pressure of his lips against hers, the warmth of his hand as he cradled her face, the hard, tightening knot of desire in her stomach that told her how insufficient the kiss was.

The desire that told her just how much more she wanted. Just how much more there could be.

He was kissing her well, this near stranger, and she never wanted it to end.

Instinctively, she angled her head slightly, parting her lips, allowing him to slide his tongue against hers. It was unexpectedly slick, unexpectedly arousing. Unexpectedly everything she wanted.

That was the other thing that surprised her. Because not only had she imagined a woman might lose herself entirely when a man kissed her, she had also imagined she would be immune. Because she knew better. She knew the cost. But she was sitting here, allowing him to kiss her and kiss her and kiss her. She was Danielle Kelly, and she was submitting herself to this sensual assault with almost shocking abandon.

Her hands were still folded in her lap, almost primly, but her mouth was parted wide, gratefully receiving every stroke of his tongue, slow and languorous against her own. Sexy. Deliciously affecting.

He moved his hands then, sliding them around the back of her neck, down between her shoulder blades, along the line of her spine until his hands spanned her waist. She arched, wishing she could press her body against his. Wishing she could do something to close the distance between them. Because he was still sitting in his chair and she in hers.

He pulled away, and she followed him, leaning into him with an almost humiliating desperation, wanting to taste him again. To be kissed again. By Joshua Grayson, the man she was committing an insane kind of fraud with. The man who had hired her to play the part of his pretend fiancée.

"That will do," he said, lifting his hand and squeezing her chin gently, those blue eyes glinting with a sharpness that cut straight to her soul. "Yes, Ms. Kelly, that will do quite nicely."

Then he released his hold on her completely, settling back in his seat, his attention returning to his dinner plate.

A slash of heat bled across Danielle's cheekbones. He hadn't felt anything at all. He had been proving a point. Just practicing the ruse they would be performing for his family tomorrow night. The kiss hadn't changed anything for him at all. Hadn't been more than the simple meeting of mouths.

It had been her first kiss. It had been everything.

And right then she got her first taste of just how badly a man could make a woman feel. Of how—when wounded—feminine pride could be a treacherous and testy thing.

She rose from her seat and rounded to stand behind his. Then, without fully pausing to think about what she might be doing, she placed her hands on his shoulders, leaned forward and slid her hands beneath the collar of his shirt and down his chest.

Her palms made contact with his hot skin, with hard muscle, and she had to bite her lip to keep from groaning out loud. She had to plant her feet firmly on the wood floor to keep herself from running away, from jerking her hands back like a child burned on a hot oven.

She'd never touched a man like this before. It was shocking just how arousing she found it, this little form of revenge, this little rebellion against his blasé response to the earthquake he had caused in her body.

She leaned her head forward, nearly pressing her lips against his ear. Then her teeth scraped his earlobe.

"Yes," she whispered. "I think it's quite convincing."

She straightened again, slowly running her fingernails over his skin as she did. She didn't know where this confidence had come from. Where the know-how and seemingly deep, feminine instinct had come from that allowed her to toy with him. But there it was.

She was officially playing the part of a saucy minx. Considering that was what he had hired her for, her flirtation was a good thing. But her heart thundered harder than a drum as she walked back to Riley, picked up his carrier and flipped her hair as she turned to face Joshua.

"I think I'm going to bed. I had best prepare myself to meet your family."

"You'll be wearing something different tomorrow," he said, his tone firm.

"Why?" She looked down at her ragged sweatshirt and skinny jeans. "That doesn't make any sense. You wanted me to look unsuitable. I might as well go in this."

"No, you brought up a very good point. You have to look unsuitable, but this situation also has to be believable. Plus, I think a gold digger would demand a new wardrobe, don't you?" One corner of his lips quirked upward, and she had a feeling he was punishing her for her little display a moment ago.

If only she could work out quite where the trap was.

"I don't know," she said, her voice stiff.

"But, Ms. Kelly, you told me yourself that you *are* a gold digger. That's why you're here, after all. For my gold."

"I suppose so," she said, keeping her words deliberately hard. "But I want actual gold, not clothes. So this is another thing that's going to be on you."

Those blue eyes glinted, and right then she got an idea of just how dangerous he was to her. "Consider it done."

And if there was one thing she had learned so far about Joshua Grayson, it was that if he said something would be done, it would be.

Chapter Five

Joshua wasn't going to try to turn Danielle into a sophisticate overnight. He was also avoiding thinking about the way it had felt to kiss her soft lips. Was avoiding remembering the way her hands had felt sliding down his chest.

He needed to make sure the two of them looked like a couple, that much was true. But he wouldn't allow himself to be distracted by her. There were a million reasons not to touch Danielle Kelly—unless they were playing a couple. Yes, there would have to be some touching, but he was not going to take advantage of her.

First of all, she was at his financial mercy. Second of all, she was the kind of woman who came with entanglements. And he didn't want any entanglements.

He wasn't the type to have trouble with self-control. If it wasn't a good time to seek out a physical relationship, he didn't. It wasn't a good time now, which meant he would defer any kind of sexual gratification until the end of his association with Danielle.

That should be fine.

He should be able to consider any number of women who he had on-again, off-again associations with, choose one and get in touch with her after Danielle left. His mind and body should be set on that.

Sadly, all he could think of was last night's kiss and the shocking heat that had come with it.

And then Danielle came down the stairs wearing the simple black dress he'd had delivered for her.

His thoughts about not transforming her into a sophisticated woman overnight held true. Her long, straight brown hair still hung limp down to her waist, and she had no makeup on to speak of except pale pink gloss on her lips.

But the simple cut of the dress suited her slender figure and displayed small, perky breasts that had been hidden beneath her baggy, threadbare sweaters.

She was holding on to the handle of the baby's car seat with both hands, lugging it down the stairs. For one moment, he was afraid she might topple over. He moved forward quickly, grabbing the handle and taking the seat from her.

When he looked down at the sleeping child, a strange tightness invaded his chest. "It wouldn't be good for you or for Riley if you fell and broke your neck trying to carry something that's too heavy for you," he said, his tone harder than he'd intended it to be.

Danielle scowled. "Well, offer assistance earlier next time. I had to get down the stairs somehow. Anyway, I've been navigating stairs like this with the baby since he was born. I lived in an apartment. On the third floor."

"I imagine he's heavier now than he used to be."

"An expert on child development?" She arched one dark brow as she posed the question.

He gritted his teeth. "Hardly."

She stepped away from the stairs, and the two of them walked toward the door. Just because he wanted to make it clear that he was in charge of the evening, he placed his hand low on her back, right at the dip where her spine curved, right above what the dress revealed to be a magnificent backside.

He had touched her there to get to her, but he had not anticipated the touch getting to him.

He ushered her out quickly, then handed the car seat to her, allowing her to snap it into the base—the one he'd had installed in his car when all of the nursery accoutrements had been delivered—then sat waiting for her to get in.

As they started to pull out of the driveway, she wrapped her arms around herself, rubbing her hands over her bare skin. "Do you think you could turn the heater on?"

He frowned. "Why didn't you bring a jacket?"

"I don't have one? All I have are my sweaters. And I don't think either of them would go with the dress. Would kind of ruin the effect."

He put the brakes on, slipped out of his own jacket and handed it to her. She just looked at him like he was offering her a live gopher. "Take it," he said.

She frowned but reached out, taking the jacket and slipping it on. "Thank you," she said, her voice sounding hollow.

They drove to his parents' house in silence, the only sounds coming from the baby sitting in the back seat.

A sobering reminder of the evening that was about to unfold. He was going to present a surprise fiancée and a surprise baby to his parents, and suddenly, he didn't look at this plan in quite the same way as he had before.

He was throwing Danielle into the deep end. Throwing Riley into the deep end.

Joshua gritted his teeth, tightening his hold on the steering wheel. Finally, the interminable drive through town was over. He turned left off a winding road and onto a dirt drive that led back to the familiar, humble farmhouse his parents still called home.

That some part of his heart still called home too.

He looked over at Danielle, who had gone pale. "It's fine," he said.

Danielle looked down at the ring on her finger, then back up at him. "I guess it's showtime."

Danielle felt warm all over, no longer in need of Joshua's jacket, and conflicted down to the brand-new shoes Joshua had ordered for her.

But it wasn't the dress, or the shoes, that had her feeling warm. It was the jacket. Well, obviously a jacket was supposed to make her warm, but this was different. Joshua had realized she was cold. And it had mattered to him.

He had given her his own jacket so she could keep warm.

It was too big, the sleeves went well past the edges of her fingertips, and it smelled like him. From the moment she had slipped it on, she had been fighting the urge to bury her nose in the fabric and lose herself in the sharp, masculine smell that reminded her of his skin. Skin she had tasted last night.

Standing on the front step of this modest farmhouse that she could hardly believe Joshua had ever lived in, wearing his coat, with him holding Riley's car seat, it was too easy to believe this actually was some kind of "meet the parents" date.

In effect, she supposed it was. She was even wearing his jacket. His jacket that was still warm from his body and smelled—

Danielle was still ruminating about the scent of Joshua's jacket when the door opened. A blonde woman with graying hair and blue eyes that looked remarkably like her son's gave them a warm smile.

"Joshua," she said, glancing sideways at Danielle and clearly doing her best not to look completely shocked, "I didn't expect you so early. And I didn't know you were bringing a guest." Her eyes fell to the carrier in Joshua's hand. "Two guests."

"I thought it would be a good surprise."

"What would be?"

A man who could only be Joshua's father came to the door behind the woman. He was tall, with dark hair and eyes. He looked nice too. They both did. There was a warmth to them, a kindness, that didn't seem to be present in their son.

But then Danielle felt the warmth of the jacket again, and she had to revise that thought. Joshua might not exude kindness, but it was definitely there, buried. And for the life of her, she couldn't figure out why he hid it.

She was prickly and difficult, but at least she had an excuse. Her family was the worst. As far as she could tell, his family was guilty of caring too much. And she just couldn't feel that sorry for a rich dude whose parents loved him and were involved in his life more than he wanted them to be.

"Who is this?" Joshua's father asked.

"Danielle, this is my mom and dad, Todd and Nancy Grayson. Mom, Dad, this is Danielle Kelly," Joshua said smoothly. "And I have you to thank for meeting her, Dad."

His father's eyebrows shot upward. "Do you?"

"Yes," Joshua said. "She responded to your ad. Mom, Dad, Danielle is my fiancée."

They were ushered into the house quickly after that announcement, and there were a lot of exclamations. The house was already full. A young woman sat in the corner holding hands with a large, tattooed man who was built like a brick house and was clearly related to Joshua somehow. There was another man, as tall as Joshua, with slightly darker hair and the same blue eyes but who didn't carry himself quite as stiffly. His build was somewhere in between Joshua and the tattooed man, muscular but not a beast.

"My brother Devlin," Joshua said, indicating the tattooed man before putting his arm around Danielle's waist as they moved deeper into the room, "and his wife, Mia. And this is my brother Isaiah. I'm surprised his capable assistant, Poppy, isn't somewhere nearby."

"Isaiah, did you want a beer or whiskey?" A petite woman appeared from the kitchen area, her curly, dark hair swept back into a bun, a few stray pieces bouncing around her pretty face. She was impeccable. From that elegant updo down to the soles of her tiny, high-heeled feet. She was wearing a high-waisted skirt that flared out at the hips and fell down past her knees, along with a plain, fitted top.

"Is that his…girlfriend?" Danielle asked.

Poppy laughed. "Absolutely not," she said, her tone clipped. "I'm his assistant."

Danielle thought it strange that an assistant would be at a family gathering but didn't say anything.

"She's more than an assistant," Nancy Grayson said. "She's part of the family. She's been with them since they started the business."

Danielle had not been filled in on the details of his family's relationships because she only needed to know how to alienate them, not how to endear herself to them.

The front door opened again and this time it was a younger blonde woman whose eyes also matched Joshua's who walked in. "Sorry I'm late," she said, "I got caught up working on a project."

This had to be his sister, Faith. The architect he talked about with such pride and fondness. A woman who was Danielle's age and yet so much more successful they might be completely different species.

"This is Joshua's fiancée," Todd Grayson said. "He's engaged."

"Shut the front door," Faith said. "Are you really?"

"Yes," Joshua said, the lie rolling easily off his tongue.

Danielle bit back a comment about his PR skills. She was supposed to be hard to deal with, but they weren't supposed to call attention to the fact this was a ruse.

"That's great?" Faith took a step forward and hugged her brother, then leaned in to grab hold of Danielle, as well.

"Is nobody going to ask about the baby?" Isaiah asked.

"Obviously *you* are," Devlin said.

"Well, it's kind of the eight-hundred-pound gorilla in the room. Or the ten-pound infant."

"It's my baby," Danielle said, feeling color mount in her cheeks.

She noticed a slight shift in Joshua's father's expression. Which was the general idea. To make him suspicious of her. To make him think he had gone and caught his son a gold digger.

"Well, that's…" She could see Joshua's mother searching for words. "It's definitely unexpected." She looked apologetically at Danielle the moment the words left her mouth. "It's just that Joshua hasn't shown much interest in marriage or family."

Danielle had a feeling that was an understatement. If Joshua was willing to go to such lengths to get his father out of his business, then he must be about as anti-marriage as you could get.

"Well," Joshua said, "Danielle and I met because of Dad."

His mother's blue gaze sharpened. "How?"

His father looked guilty. "Well, I thought he could use a little help," he said finally.

"What kind of help?"

"It's not good for a man to be alone, especially not our boys," he said insistently.

"Some of us like to be alone," Isaiah pointed out.

"You wouldn't feel that way if you didn't have a woman who cooked for you and ran your errands," his father responded, looking pointedly at Poppy.

"She's an employee," Isaiah said.

Poppy looked more irritated and distressed by Isaiah's comment than she did by the Grayson family patriarch's statement. But she didn't say anything.

"You were right," Joshua said. "I just needed to find the right woman. You placed that ad, listing all of my assets, and the right woman responded."

This was so ridiculous. Danielle felt her face heating. The assets Joshua's father had listed were his bank account, and there was no way in the world that wasn't exactly what everyone in his family was thinking.

She knew this was her chance to confirm her gold-digging motives. But right then, Riley started to cry.

"Oh," she said, feeling flustered. "Just let me... I need to..."

She fumbled around with the new diaper bag, digging around for a bottle, and then went over to the car seat, taking the baby out of it.

"Let me help," Joshua's mother said.

She was being so kind. Danielle felt terrible.

But before Danielle could protest, the other woman was taking Riley from her arms. Riley wiggled and fussed, but then she efficiently plucked the bottle from Danielle's hand and stuck it right in his mouth. He quieted immediately.

"What a good baby," she said. "Does he usually go to strangers?"

Danielle honestly didn't know. "Other than a neighbor whose known him since he was born, I'm the only one who takes care of him," she said.

"Don't you have any family?"

Danielle shook her head, feeling every inch the curiosity she undoubtedly was. Every single eye in the room was trained on her, and she knew they were all waiting for her to make a mistake. She was *supposed* to make a mistake, dammit. That was what Joshua was paying her to do.

"I don't have any family," she said decisively. "It's just been me and Riley from the beginning."

"It must be nice to have some help now," Faith said, not unkindly, but definitely probing.

"It is," Danielle said. "I mean, it's really hard taking care of a baby by yourself. And I didn't make enough money to…well, anything. So meeting Joshua has been great. Because he's so…helpful."

A timer went off in the other room and Joshua's mother blinked. "Oh, I have to get dinner." She turned to her son. "Since you're so helpful, Joshua." And before Danielle could protest, before Joshua could protest, Nancy dumped Riley right into his arms.

He looked like he'd been handed a bomb. And frankly, Danielle felt a little bit like a bomb might detonate at any moment. It had not escaped her notice that Joshua had never touched Riley. Yes, he had carried his car seat, but he had never voluntarily touched the baby. Which, now that she thought about it, must have been purposeful. But then, not everybody liked babies. She had never been particularly drawn to them before Riley. Maybe Joshua felt the same way.

She could tell by his awkward posture, and the way Riley's small frame was engulfed by Joshua's large, muscular one, that any contact with babies was not something he was used to.

She imagined Joshua's reaction would go a long way in proving how unsuitable she was. Maybe not in the way he had hoped, but it definitely made his point.

He took a seat on the couch, still holding on to Riley, still clearly committed to the farce.

"So you met through an ad," Isaiah said, his voice full of disbelief. "An ad that Dad put in the paper."

Everyone's head swiveled, and they looked at Todd. "I did what any concerned father would do for his son."

Devlin snorted. "Thank God I found a wife on my own."

"You found a wife by pilfering from my friendship pool," Faith said, her tone disapproving. "Isaiah and Joshua have too much class to go picking out women that young."

"Actually," Danielle said, deciding this was the perfect opportunity to highlight another of the many ways in which she was unsuitable, "I'm only twenty-two."

Joshua's father looked at him, his gaze sharp. "Really?"

"Really," Danielle said.

"That's unexpected," Todd said to his son.

"That's what's so great about how we met," Joshua said. "Had I looked for a life partner on my own, I probably would have chosen somebody with a completely different set of circumstances. Had you asked me only a few short weeks ago, I would have said I didn't want children. And now look at me."

Everybody *was* looking at him, and it was clear he was extremely uncomfortable. Danielle wasn't entirely sure he was making the point he hoped to make, but he did make a pretty amusing picture. "I also would have chosen somebody closer to my age. But the great thing about Danielle is that she is so mature. I think it's because she's a mother. And yes, it happened for her in non-ideal circumstances, but her ability to rise above her situation and solve her problems—namely by responding to the ad—is one of the many things I find attractive about her."

She wanted to kick him in the shin. He was being

a complete jerk, and he was making her sound like a total flake... But that was the whole idea. And, honestly, given the information Joshua had about her life...he undoubtedly thought she *was* a flake. It was stupid, and it wasn't fair. One of the many things she had learned about people since becoming the sole caregiver for Riley was that even though everyone had sex, a woman was an immediate pariah the minute she bore the evidence of that sex.

All that mattered to the hypocrites was that Danielle appeared to be a scarlet woman, therefore she was one.

Never mind that in reality she was a virgin.

Which was not a word she needed to be thinking while sitting in the Grayson family living room.

Her cheeks felt hot, like they were being stung by bees.

"Fate is a funny thing," Danielle said, edging closer to Joshua. She took Riley out of his arms, and from the way Joshua surrendered the baby, she could tell he was more than ready to hand him over.

The rest of the evening passed in a blur of awkward moments and stilted conversation. It was clear to her that his family was wonderful and warm, but that they were also seriously questioning Joshua's decision making. Todd Grayson looked as if he was going to be physically assaulted by his wife.

Basically, everything was going according to Joshua's plan.

But Danielle couldn't feel happy about it. She couldn't feel triumphant. It just felt awful.

Finally, it was time to go, and Danielle was ready to scurry out the door and keep on scurrying away from the entire Grayson family—Joshua included.

She was gathering her things, and Joshua was talking to one of his brothers, when Faith approached.

"We haven't gotten a chance to talk yet," she said.

"I guess not," Danielle said, feeling instantly wary. She had a feeling that being approached by Joshua's younger sister like this wouldn't end well.

"I'm sure he's told you all about me," Faith said, and Danielle had a feeling that statement was a test.

"Of course he has." She sounded defensive, even though there was no reason for her to feel defensive, except that she kind of did anyway.

"Great. So here's the thing. I don't know exactly what's going on here, but my brother is not a 'marriage and babies' kind of guy. My brother dates a seemingly endless stream of models, all of whom are about half a foot taller than you without their ridiculous high heels on. Also, he likes blondes."

Danielle felt her face heating again as the other woman appraised her and found her lacking. "Right. Well. Maybe I'm a really great conversationalist. Although, it could be the fact that I don't have a gag reflex."

She watched the other woman's cheeks turn bright pink and felt somewhat satisfied. Unsophisticated, virginal Danielle had made the clearly much more sophisticated Faith Grayson blush.

"Right. Well, if you're leading him around by his… *you know*…so you can get into his wallet, I'm not going to allow that. There's a reason he's avoided commitment all this time. And I'm not going to let you hurt him. He's been hurt enough," she said.

Danielle could only wonder what that meant, because Joshua seemed bulletproof.

"I'm not going to break up with him," Danielle said.

"Why would I do that? I'd rather stay in his house than in a homeless shelter."

She wanted to punch her own face. And she was warring with the fact that Faith had rightly guessed that she was using Joshua for his money—though not in the way his sister assumed. And Danielle needed Faith to think the worst. But it also hurt to have her assume something so negative based on Danielle's circumstances. Based on her appearance.

People had been looking at Danielle and judging her as low-class white trash for so long—not exactly incorrectly—that it was a sore spot.

"We're a close family," Faith said. "And we look out for each other. Just remember that."

"Well, your brother loves me."

"If that's true," Faith said, "then I hope you're very happy together. I actually do hope it's true. But the problem is, I'm not sure I believe it."

"Why?" Danielle was bristling, and there was no reason on earth why she should be. She shouldn't be upset about this. She shouldn't be taking it personally. But she was.

Faith Grayson had taken one look at Danielle and judged her. Pegged her for exactly the kind of person she was, really—a low-class nobody who needed the kind of money and security a man like Joshua could provide. Danielle had burned her pride to the ground to take part in this charade. Poking at the embers of that pride was stupid. But she felt compelled to do it anyway.

"Is it because I'm some kind of skank he would never normally sully himself with?"

"Mostly, it's because I know my brother. And I know

he never intended to be in any kind of serious relationship again."

Again.

That word rattled around inside of Danielle. It implied
he had been in a serious relationship before. He hadn't
mentioned that. He'd just said he didn't want his father
meddling. Didn't want marriage. He hadn't said it was
because he'd tried before.

She blinked.

Faith took that momentary hesitation and ran with
it. "So you don't know that much about him. You don't
actually know anything about him, do you? You just
know he's rich."

"And he's hot," Danielle said.

She wasn't going to back down. Not now. But she
would have a few very grumpy words with Joshua once
they left.

He hadn't prepared her for this. She looked like an
idiot. As she gathered her things, she realized looking
like an idiot was his objective. She could look bad in a
great many ways, after all. The fact that they might be
an unsuitable couple because she didn't know anything
about him would be one way to accomplish that.

When she and Joshua finally stepped outside, heading back to the car amid a thunderous farewell from the
family, Danielle felt like she could breathe for the first
time in at least two hours. She hadn't realized it, but
being inside that house—all warm and cozy and filled
with the kind of love she had only ever seen in movies—
had made her throat and lungs and chest, and even her
fingers, feel tight.

They got into the car, and Danielle folded her arms
tightly, leaning her head against the cold passenger-side

window, her breath fanning out across the glass, leaving mist behind. She didn't bother fighting the urge to trace a heart in it.

"Feeling that in character?" Joshua asked, his tone dry, as he put the car in Reverse and began to pull out of the driveway.

She stuck her tongue out and scribbled over the heart. "Not particularly. I don't understand. Now that I've met them, I understand even less. Your sister grilled me the minute she got a chance to talk to me alone. Your father is worried about the situation. Your mother is trying to be supportive in spite of the fact that we are clearly the worst couple of all time. And you're doing this why, Joshua? I don't understand."

She hadn't meant to call him out in quite that way. After all, what did she care about his motivations? He was paying her. The fact that he was a rich, eccentric idiot kind of worked in her favor. But tonight had felt wrong. And while she was more into survival than into the nuances of right and wrong, the ruse was getting to her.

"I explained to you already," he said, his tone so hard it elicited a small, plaintive cry from Riley in the back.

"Don't wake up the baby," she snapped.

"We really are a convincing couple," he responded.

"Not to your sister. Who told me we didn't make any sense together because you had never shown any interest in falling in love *again*."

It was dark in the car, so she felt rather than saw the tension creep up his spine. It was in the way he shifted in his seat, how his fists rolled forward as he twisted his hands on the steering wheel.

"Well," he said, "that's the thing. They all know. Because family like mine doesn't leave well enough alone. They want to know about all your injuries, all your scars, and then they obsess over the idea that they might be able to heal them. And they don't listen when you tell them healing is not necessary."

"Right," she said, blowing out an exasperated breath. "Here's the thing. I'm just a dumb bimbo you picked up through a newspaper ad who needed your money. So I don't understand all this coded nonsense. Just tell me what's going on. Especially if I'm going to spend more nights trying to alienate your family—who are basically a childhood sitcom fantasy of what a family should be."

"I've done it before, Danielle. Love. It's not worth it. Not considering how badly it hurts when it ends. But even more, it's not worth it when you consider how badly you can hurt the other person."

His words fell flat in the car, and she didn't know how to respond to them. "I don't…"

"Details aren't important. You've been hurt before, haven't you?"

He turned the car off the main road and headed up the long drive to his house. She took a deep breath. "Yes."

"By Riley's father?"

She shifted uncomfortably. "Not exactly."

"You didn't love him?"

"No," she said. "I didn't love him. But my mother kind of did a number on me. I do understand that love hurts. I also understand that a supportive family is not necessarily guaranteed."

"Yeah," Joshua said, "supportive family is great." He put the car in Park and killed the engine before getting out and stalking toward the house.

Danielle frowned, then unbuckled quickly, getting out

of the car and pushing the sleeves of Joshua's jacket back so she could get Riley's car seat out of the base. Then she headed up the stairs and into the house after him.

"And yet you are trying to hurt yours. So excuse me if I'm not making all the connections."

"I'm not trying to hurt my family," he said, turning around, pushing his hand through his blond hair. His blue eyes glittered, his jaw suddenly looking sharper, his cheekbones more hollow. "What I want is for them to leave well enough alone. My father doesn't understand. He thinks all I need is to find somebody to love again and I'm going to be fixed. But there is no fixing this. There's no fixing me. I don't want it. And yeah, maybe this scheme is over the top, but don't you think putting an ad in the paper looking for a wife for your son is over the top too? I'm not giving him back anything he didn't dish out."

"Maybe you could talk to him."

"You think I haven't talked to him? You think this was my first resort? You're wrong about that. I tried reasonable discourse, but you can't reason with an unreasonable man."

"Yeah," Danielle said, picking at the edge of her thumbnail. "He seemed like a real monster. What with the clear devotion to your mother, the fact that he raised all of you, that he supported you well enough that you could live in that house all your life and then go off to become more successful than he was."

She set the car seat down on the couch and unbuckled it, lifting Riley into her arms and heading toward the stairs.

"We didn't have anything when I was growing up," he said, his tone flat and strange.

Danielle swallowed hard, lifting her hand to cradle Riley's soft head. "I'm sorry. But unless you were homeless or were left alone while one of your parents went to work all day—and I mean *alone*, not with siblings—then we might have different definitions of nothing."

"Fine," he said. "We weren't that poor. But we didn't have anything extra, and there was definitely nothing to do around here but get into trouble when you didn't have money."

She blinked. "What kind of trouble?"

"The usual kind. Go out to the woods, get messed up, have sex."

"Last I checked, condoms and drugs cost money." She held on to Riley a little bit tighter. "Pretty sure you could have bought a movie ticket."

He lifted his shoulder. "Look, we pooled our money. We did what we did. Didn't worry about the future, didn't worry about anything."

"What changed?" Because obviously something had. He hadn't stayed here. He hadn't stayed aimless.

"One day I looked up and realized this was all I would ever have unless I changed something. Let me tell you, that's pretty sobering. A future of farming, barely making it, barely scraping by? That's what my dad had. And I hated it. I drank in the woods every night with my friends to avoid that reality. I didn't want to have my dad's life. So I made some changes. Not really soon enough to improve my grades or get myself a full scholarship, but I ended up moving to Seattle and getting myself an entry-level job with a PR firm."

"You just moved? You didn't know anybody?"

"No. I didn't know anyone. But I met people. And, it turned out, I was good at meeting people. Which was interesting because you don't meet very many new people in a small town that you've lived in your entire life. But in Seattle, no one knew me. No one knew who my father was, and no one had expectations for me. I was judged entirely on my own merit, and I could completely rewrite who I was. Not just some small-town deadbeat, but a young, bright kid who had a future in front of him."

The way he told that story, the very idea of it, was tantalizing to Danielle. The idea of starting over. Having a clean slate. Of course, with a baby in tow, a change like that would be much more difficult. But her association with Joshua would allow her to make it happen.

It was…shocking to realize he'd had to start over once. Incredibly encouraging, even though she was feeling annoyed with him at the moment.

She leaned forward and absently pressed a kiss to Riley's head. "That must've been incredible. And scary."

"The only scary thing was the idea of going back to where I came from without changing anything. So I didn't allow that to happen. I worked harder than everybody else. I set goals and I met them. And then I met Shannon."

Something ugly twisted inside of Danielle's stomach the moment he said the other woman's name. For the life of her she couldn't figure out why. She felt…curious. But in a desperate way. Like she needed to know everything about this other person. This person who had once shared Joshua's life. This person who had undoubtedly made him the man standing in front of her. If she didn't know about this woman, then she would never understand him.

"What, then? Who was Shannon?" Her desperation was evident in her words, and she didn't bother hiding it.

"She was my girlfriend. For four years, while I was

getting established in Seattle. We lived together. I was going to ask her to marry me."

He looked away from her then, something in his blue eyes turning distant. "Then she found out she was pregnant, and I figured I could skip the elaborate proposal and move straight to the wedding."

She knew him well enough to know this story wasn't headed toward a happy ending. He didn't have a wife. He didn't have a child. In fact, she was willing to bet he'd never had a child. Based on the way he interacted with Riley. Or rather, the very practiced way he avoided interacting with Riley.

"That didn't happen," she said, because she didn't know what else to say, and part of her wanted to spare him having to tell the rest of the story. But, also, part of her needed to know.

"She wanted to plan the wedding. She wanted to wait until after the baby was born. You know, wedding dress sizes and stuff like that. So I agreed. She miscarried late, Danielle. Almost five months. It was…the most physically harrowing thing I've ever watched anyone go through. But the recovery was worse. And I didn't know what to do. So I went back to work. We had a nice apartment, we had a view of the city, and if I worked, she didn't have to. I could support her, I could buy her things. I could do my best to make her happy, keep her focused on the wedding."

He had moved so quickly through the devastating, painful revelation of his lost baby that she barely had time to process it. But she also realized he had to tell the story this way. There was no point lingering on the details. It was simple fact. He had been with a woman he loved very much. He had intended to marry her, had been expecting a child with her. And they had lost the baby.

She held on a little bit more tightly to Riley.

"She kept getting worse. Emotionally. She moved into a different bedroom, then she didn't get out of bed. She had a lot of pain. At first, I didn't question it, because it seemed reasonable that she'd need pain medication after what she went through. But then she kept taking it. And I wondered if that was okay. We had a fight about it. She said it wasn't right for me to question her pain—physical or otherwise—when all I did was work. And you know… I thought she was probably right. So I let it go. For a year, I let it go. And then I found out the situation with the prescription drugs was worse than I realized. But when I confronted Shannon, she just got angry."

It was so strange for Danielle to imagine what he was telling her. This whole other life he'd had. In a city where he had lived with a woman and loved her. Where he had dreamed of having a family. Of having a child. Where he had buried himself in work to avoid dealing with the pain of loss, while the woman he loved lost herself in a different way.

The tale seemed so far removed from the man he was now. From this place, from that hard set to his jaw, that sharp glitter in his eye, the way he held his shoulders straight. She couldn't imagine this man feeling at a loss. Feeling helpless.

"She got involved with another man, someone I worked with. Maybe it started before she left me, but I'm not entirely sure. All I know is she wasn't sleeping with me at the time, so even if she was with him before she moved out, it hardly felt like cheating. And anyway, the affair wasn't really the important part. That guy was into recreational drug use. It's how he functioned. And he made it all available to her."

"That's…that's awful, Joshua. I know how bad that stuff can be. I've seen it."

He shook his head. "Do you have any idea what it's like? To have somebody come into your life who's beautiful, happy, and to watch her leave your life as something else entirely. Broken, an addict. I ruined her."

Danielle took a step back, feeling as though she had been struck by the impact of his words. "No, you didn't. It was drugs. It was…"

"I wasn't there for her. I didn't know how to be. I didn't like hard things, Danielle. I never did. I didn't want to stay in Copper Ridge and work the land—I didn't want to deal with a lifetime of scraping by, because it was too hard."

"Right. You're so lazy that you moved to Seattle and started from scratch and worked your way to the highest ranks of the company? I don't buy that."

"There's reward in that kind of work, though. And you don't have to deal with your life when it gets bad. You just go work more. And you can tell yourself it's fine because you're making more money. Because you're making your life easier, life for the other person easier, even while you let them sit on the couch slowly dying, waiting for you to help them. I convinced myself that what I was doing was important. It was the worst kind of narcissism, Danielle, and I'm not going to excuse it."

"But that was… It was a unique circumstance. And you're different. And…it's not like every future relationship…"

"And here's the problem. You don't know me. You don't even like me and yet you're trying to fix this. You're trying to convince me I should give relationships another try. It's your first instinct, and you don't even actually care. My father can't stop any more than you could stop yourself just now. So I did this." He gestured between the two of them. "I did this because he escalated it all the way to putting an ad in the paper. Because he won't listen to me. Because he knows my ex is a junkie somewhere living on the damned street, and that I feel responsible for that, and still he wants me to live his life. This life here, where he's never made a single mistake or let anyone down."

Danielle had no idea what to say to that. She imagined that his dad had made mistakes. But what did she know? She only knew about absentee fathers and mothers who treated their children like afterthoughts.

Her arms were starting to ache. Her chest ached too. All of her ached.

"I'm going to take Riley up to bed," she said, turning and heading up the stairs.

She didn't look back, but she could hear the heavy footfalls behind her, and she knew he was following her. Even if she didn't quite understand why.

She walked into her bedroom, and she left the door open. She crossed the space and set Riley down in the crib. He shifted for a moment, stretching his arms up above his head and kicking his feet out. But he didn't wake up. She was sweaty from having his warm little body pressed against her chest, but she was grateful for that feeling now. Thinking about Joshua and his loss made her feel especially grateful.

Joshua was standing in the doorway, looking at her. "Did you still want to argue with me?"

She shook her head. "I never wanted to argue with you."

She went to walk past him, but his big body blocked her path. She took a step toward him, and he refused to move, his blue eyes looking straight into hers.

"You seemed like you wanted to argue," he responded.

"No," she said, reaching up to press her hand against him, to push him out of the way. "I just wanted an explanation."

The moment her hand made contact with his shoulder, something raced through her. Something electric. Thrilling. Something that reached back to that feeling, that tightening low in her stomach when he'd first mentioned Shannon.

The two feelings were connected.

Jealousy. That was what she felt. Attraction. That was what this was.

She looked up, his chin in her line of sight. She saw a dusting of golden whiskers, and they looked prickly. His chin looked strong. The two things in combination—the strength and the prickliness—made her want to reach out and touch him, to test both of those hypotheses and see if either was true.

Touching him was craziness. She knew it was. So she curled her fingers into a fist and lowered her hand back down to her side.

"Tell me," he said, his voice rough. "After going through what you did, being pregnant. Being abandoned… You don't want to jump right back into relationships, do you?"

He didn't know the situation. And he didn't know it because she had purposefully kept it from him. Still, because of the circumstances surrounding Riley's birth, because of the way her mother had always conducted relationships with men, because of the way they had always ended, Danielle wanted to avoid romantic entanglements.

So she could find an honest answer in there somewhere.

"I don't want to jump into anything," she said, keeping her voice even. "But there's a difference between being cautious and saying never."

"Is there?"

He had dipped his head slightly, and he seemed to loom over her, to fill her vision, to fill her senses. When she breathed in, the air was scented with him. When she felt warm, the warmth was from his body.

Her lips suddenly felt dry, and she licked them. Then became more aware of them than she'd ever been in her entire life. They felt…obvious. Needy.

She was afraid she knew exactly what they were needy for.

His mouth. His kiss.

The taste of him. The feel of him.

She wondered if he was thinking of their kiss too. Of course, for him, a kiss was probably a commonplace event.

For her, it had been singular.

"You can't honestly say you want to spend the rest of your life alone?"

"I'm only alone when I want to be," he said, his voice husky. "There's a big difference between wanting to share your life with somebody and wanting to share your bed sometimes." He tilted his head to the side. "Tell me. Have you shared your bed with anyone since you were with him?"

She shook her head, words, explanations, getting

stuck in her throat. But before she knew it, she couldn't speak anyway, because he had closed the distance between them and claimed her mouth with his.

Chapter Six

He was hell bound, that much was certain. After everything that had happened tonight with his family, after Shannon, his fate had been set in stone. But if it hadn't been, then this kiss would have sealed that fate, padlocked it and flung it right down into the fire.

Danielle was young, she was vulnerable and contractually she was at his mercy to a certain degree. Kissing her, wanting to do more with her, was taking being jackass to extremes.

Right now, he didn't care.

If this was hell, he was happy to hang out for a while. If only he could keep kissing her, if only he could keep tasting her.

She held still against his body for a moment before angling her head, wrapping her arms around his neck, sliding her fingers through his hair and cupping the back of his head as if she was intent on holding him against her mouth.

As if she was concerned he might break the kiss. As if he was capable of that.

Sanity and reasonable decision making had exited the building the moment he had closed the distance between them. It wasn't coming back anytime soon. Not as long as she continued to make those sweet, kittenish noises. Not as long as she continued to stroke her tongue against his—tentatively at first and then with much more boldness.

He gripped the edge of the doorjamb, backing her against the frame, pressing his body against hers. He was hard, and he knew she would feel just how much he wanted her.

He slipped his hands around her waist, then down her behind to the hem of her dress. He shoved it upward, completely void of any sort of finesse. Void of anything beyond the need and desperation screaming inside of him to be inside her. To be buried so deep he wouldn't remember anything.

Not why he knew her. Why she was here. Not what had happened at his parents' house tonight. Not the horrific, unending sadness that had happened in his beautiful high-rise apartment overlooking the city he'd thought of as his. The penthouse that should have kept him above the struggle and insulated him from hardship.

Yeah, he didn't want to think about any of it.

He didn't want to think of anything but the way Danielle tasted. How soft her skin was to the touch.

Why the hell some skinny, bedraggled urchin had suddenly managed to light a fire inside of him was beyond him.

He didn't really care about the rationale right now. No. He just wanted to be burned.

He moved his hands around, then dipped one between her legs, rubbing his thumb against the silken fabric of her panties. She gasped, arching against him, wrenching her mouth away from his and letting her head fall back against the door frame.

That was an invitation to go further. He shifted his stance, drawing his hand upward and then down beneath the waistband of her underwear. He made contact with slick, damp skin that spoke of her desire for him. He had to clench his teeth to keep from embarrassing himself then and there.

He couldn't remember the last time a woman had affected him like this, if ever. When a simple touch, the promise of release, had pushed him so close to the edge.

When so little had felt like so much.

He stroked her, centering his attention on her most sensitive place. Her eyes flew open wide as if he had discovered something completely new. As if she was discovering something completely new. And that did things to him. Things it shouldn't do. Mattered in ways it shouldn't.

Because this shouldn't matter and neither should she.

He pressed his thumb against her chin, leaned forward and captured her open mouth with his.

"I have to have you," he said, the words rough, unpracticed, definitely not the way he usually propositioned a woman.

His words seemed to shock her. Like she had made contact with a naked wire. She went stiff in his arms, and then she pulled away, her eyes wide. "What are we doing?"

She was being utterly sincere, the words unsteady, her expression one of complete surprise and even…fear.

"I'm pretty sure we were about to make love," he said, using a more gentle terminology than he normally would have because of that strange vulnerability lurking in her eyes.

She shook her head, wiggling out of his hold and moving away from the door, backing toward the crib. "We can't do that. We can't." She pressed her hand against her cheek, and she looked so much like a stereotypical distressed female from some 1950s comic that he would have laughed if she hadn't successfully made him feel like he would be the villain in that piece. "It would be… It would be wrong."

"Why exactly?"

"Because. You're paying me to be here. You're paying me to play the part of your fiancée, and if things get physical between us, then I don't understand exactly what separates me from a prostitute."

"I'm not paying you for sex," he said. "I'm paying you to pretend to be my fiancée. I want you. And that's entirely separate from what we're doing here."

She shook her head, her eyes glistening. "Not to me. I already feel horrible. Like the worst person ever, after what I did to your family. After the way we tricked them tonight. After the way we will continue to trick them. I can't add sex to this situation. I have to walk away from this, Joshua. I have to walk away and not feel like I lost myself. I can't face the idea that I might finally sort out the money, where I'm going to live, how I'll survive… and lose the only thing I've always had. Myself. I just can't."

He had never begged a woman in his life, but he realized right then that he was on the verge of begging her to agree that it would feel good enough for whatever consequences to be damned. But as he looked behind her at the crib—the crib with the woman's baby in it, for heaven's sake—he realized the argument wasn't going to work with her.

She had been badly used, and though she had never really given him details, the evidence was obvious. She was alone. She had been abandoned at her most vulnerable. For her, the deepest consequences of sex were not hypothetical.

Though, they weren't for him either. And he was a stickler for safe sex, so there was that. Still, he couldn't blame her for not trusting him. And he should want nothing more than to find a woman who was less complicated. One who didn't have all the baggage that Danielle carried.

Still, he wanted to beg.

But he didn't.

"Sex isn't that big of a deal for me," he said. "If you're not into it, that's fine."

She nodded, the gesture jerky. "Good. That's probably another reason we shouldn't."

"I'm going to start interviewing nannies tomorrow," he said, abruptly changing the subject, because if he didn't, he would haul her back into his arms and finish what he had started.

"Okay," she said, looking shell-shocked.

"You'll have a little bit more freedom then. And we can go out riding."

She blinked. "Why? I just turned you down. Why do you want to do anything for me?"

"I already told you. None of this is a trade for sex. You turning me down doesn't change my intentions."

She frowned. "I don't understand." She looked down, picking at her thumbnail. "Everything has a price. There's no reason for you to do something for me when you're not looking for something in return."

"Not everything in life is a transaction, Danielle."

"I suppose it's not when you care about somebody." She tilted her head to the side. "But nobody's ever really cared about me."

If he hadn't already felt like a jerk, then her words would have done it. Because his family did care about him. His life had been filled with people doing things for him just because they wanted to give him something. They'd had no expectation of receiving anything in return.

But after Shannon, something had changed inside of him. He wanted to hold everybody at arm's length. Explaining himself felt impossible.

He hadn't wanted to give to anyone, connect with anyone, in a long time. But for some reason, he wanted to connect with Danielle. Wanted to give to that fragile, sweet girl.

It wasn't altruistic. Not really. She had so little that it was easy to step in and do something life altering. She didn't understand the smallest gesture of kindness, which meant the smallest gesture was enough.

"Tomorrow the interview process starts. I assume you want input?"

"Do I want input over who is going to be watching my baby? Yeah. That would be good."

She reached up, absently touching her lips, then lowered her hand quickly, wiggling her fingers slightly. "Good night," she said, the words coming out in a rush.

"Good night," he said, his voice hard. He turned, closing the door resolutely behind him, because if he didn't, he couldn't be responsible for what he might do.

He was going to leave her alone. He was going to do something nice for her. As if that would do something for his tarnished soul.

Well, maybe it wouldn't. But maybe it would do something for her. And for some reason, that mattered.

Maybe that meant he wasn't too far gone, after all.

Danielle had never interviewed anyone who was going to work for her. She had interviewed for several jobs herself, but she had never been on the reverse side. It was strange and infused her with an inordinate sense of power.

Which was nice, considering she rarely felt powerful.

Certainly not the other night when Joshua had kissed her. Then she had felt weak as a kitten. Ready to lie down and give him whatever he wanted.

Except she hadn't. She had said no. She was proud of herself for that, even while she mourned the loss of whatever pleasure she might have found with him.

It wasn't about pleasure. It was about pride.

Pride and self-preservation. What she had said to him had been true. If she walked away from this situation completely broken, unable to extricate herself from him, from his life, because she had allowed herself to get tangled up in ways she hadn't anticipated, then she would never forgive herself. If she had finally made her life easier in all the ways she'd always dreamed of, only to snare herself in a trap she knew would end in pain...

She would judge herself harshly for that.

Whatever she wanted to tell herself about Joshua—he was a tool, he didn't deserve the wonderful family he had—she was starting to feel things for him. Things she really couldn't afford to feel.

That story about his girlfriend had hit her hard and deep. Hit her in a place she normally kept well protected.

Dammit.

She took a deep breath and looked over at the new nanny, Janine, who had just started today, and who was going to watch Riley while Joshua and Danielle went for a ride.

She was nervous. Unsteady about leaving Riley for the first time in a while. Necessity had meant she'd had to leave him when she was working at the grocery store. Still, this felt different. Because it wasn't necessary. It made her feel guilty. Because she was leaving him to do something for herself.

She shook her head. Her reaction was ridiculous. But she supposed it was preferable to how her mother had operated. Which was to never think about her children at all. Her neglect of Danielle hadn't come close to her disinterest in her youngest child. Danielle supposed that by the time Riley was born, her mother had been fully burned-out. Had exhausted whatever maternal instinct she'd possessed.

Danielle shook her head. Then took a deep breath and turned to face Janine. "He should nap most of the time we're gone. And even if he wakes up, he's usually really happy."

Janine smiled. "He's just a baby. I've watched a lot of babies. Not that he isn't special," she said, as though she were trying to cover up some faux pas. "I just mean, I'm confident that I can handle him."

Danielle took a deep breath and nodded. Then Joshua came into the room and the breath she had just drawn into her lungs rushed out.

He was wearing a dark blue button-down shirt and jeans, paired with a white cowboy hat that made him look like the hero in an old Western movie.

Do not get that stupid. He might be a hero, but he's not your hero.

No. Girls like her didn't get heroes. They had to be their own heroes. And that was fine. Honestly, it was.

If only she could tell her heart that. Her stupid heart, which was beating out of control.

It was far too easy to remember what it had been like to kiss him. To remember what it had felt like when his stubble-covered cheek scraped against hers. How sexy it had felt. How intoxicating it had been to touch a man like that. To experience the differences between men and women for the first time.

It was dangerous, was what it was. She had opened a door she had never intended to open, and now it was hard to close.

She shook her hands out, then balled them into fists, trying to banish the jitters that were racing through her veins.

"Are you ready?" he asked.

His eyes met hers and all she could think was how incredible it was that his eyes matched his shirt. They were a deep, perfect shade of navy.

There was something wrong with her. She had never been this stupid around a man before.

"Yes," she said, the answer coming out more as a squeak than an actual word. "I'm ready."

The corner of his mouth lifted into a lopsided grin. "You don't have to be nervous. I'll be gentle with you."

She nearly choked. "Good to know. But I'm more worried about the horse being gentle with me."

"She will be. Promise. I've never taught a girl how to ride before, but I'm pretty confident I can teach you."

His words ricocheted around inside of her, reaching the level of double entendre. Which wasn't fair. That wasn't how he'd meant it.

Or maybe it was.

He hadn't been shy about letting her know exactly what he wanted from her that night. He had put his hand between her legs. Touched her where no other man ever had. He'd made her see stars, tracked sparks over her skin.

It was understandable for her to be affected by the experience. But like he'd said, sex didn't really matter to him. It wasn't a big deal. So why he would be thinking of it now was beyond her. He had probably forgotten already. Probably that kiss had become an indistinct blur in his mind, mixed with all his other sexual encounters.

There were no other encounters for her. So there he was in her mind, and in front of her, far too sharp and far too clear.

"I'm ready," she said, the words rushed. "Totally ready."

"Great," he said. "Let's go."

Taking Danielle out riding was submitting himself to a particular kind of torture, that was for sure. But he was kind of into punishing himself…so he figured it fit his MO.

He hadn't stopped thinking about her since they had kissed—and more—in her bedroom the other night. He had done his best to throw himself into work, to avoid her, but still, he kept waking up with sweat slicked over his skin, his body hard and dreams of…her lips, her tongue, her scent…lingering in his thoughts.

Normally, the outdoors cleared his mind. Riding his horse along the length of the property was his therapy. Maneuvering her over the rolling hills, along the ridge line of the mountain, the evergreen trees rising behind them in a stately backdrop that left him feeling small within the greater context of the world. Which was something a man like him found refreshing some days.

But not today.

Today, he was obsessing. He was watching Danielle's behind as she rode her horse in front of him, the motion of the horse's gait making him think of what it would look like if the woman was riding him instead of his mare.

He couldn't understand this. Couldn't understand this obsession with her.

She wasn't the kind of sophisticated woman he tended to favor. In a lot of ways, she reminded him of the kind of girl he used to go for here in town, back when he had been a good-for-nothing teenager spending his free time drinking and getting laid out in the woods.

Back then he had liked hometown girls who wanted the same things he did. A few hours to escape, a little bit of fun.

The problem was, he already knew Danielle didn't

want that. She didn't find casual hookups fun. And he didn't have anything to offer beyond a casual hookup.

The other problem was that the feelings he had for her were not casual. If they were, then he wouldn't be obsessing. But he was.

In the couple of weeks since she had come to live with him, she had started to fill out a bit. He could get a sense of her figure, of how she would look if she were thriving rather than simply surviving. She was naturally thin, but there was something elegant about her curves.

But even more appealing than the baser things, like the perky curve of her high breasts and the subtle slope of her hips, was the stubborn set of her jaw. The straight, brittle weight of her shoulders spoke of both strength and fragility.

While there was something unbreakable about her, he worried that if a man ever were to find her weakness, she would do more than just break. She would shatter.

He shook his head. And then he forced himself to look away from her, forced himself to look at the scenery. At the mountain spread out before them, and the ocean gray and fierce behind it.

"Am I doing okay?"

Danielle's question made it impossible to ignore her, and he found himself looking at her ass again. "You haven't fallen off yet," he said, perhaps a bit unkindly.

She snorted, then looked over her shoulder, a challenging light glittering in her brown eyes. "Yet? I'm not going to fall off, Joshua Grayson. It would take a hell of a lot to unseat me."

"Says the woman who was shaking when I helped her mount up earlier."

She surprised him by releasing her hold on the reins

with one hand and waving it in the air. "Well, I'm getting the hang of it."

"You're a regular cowgirl," he said.

Suddenly, he wanted that to be true. It was the strangest thing. He wanted her to have this outlet, this freedom. Something more than a small apartment. Something more than struggle.

You're giving her that. That's what this entire bargain is for. Like she said, she's a gold digger, and you're giving her your gold.

Yes, but he wanted to give her more than that.

Just like he had told her the other day, what he wanted to give her wasn't about an exchange. He wanted her to have something for herself. Something for Riley.

Maybe it was a misguided attempt to atone for what he hadn't managed to give Shannon. What he hadn't ever been able to give the child he lost.

He swallowed hard, taking in a deep breath of the sharp pine and salt air, trying to ease the pressure in his chest.

She looked at him again, this time a dazzling smile on her lips. It took all that pressure in his chest and punched a hole right through it. He felt his lungs expand, all of him begin to expand.

He clenched his teeth, grinding them together so hard he was pretty sure his jaw was going to break. "Are you about ready to head back?"

"No. But I'm not sure I'm ever going to be ready to head back. This was… Thank you." She didn't look at him this time. But he had a feeling it was because she was a lot less comfortable with sincere connection than she was with sarcasm.

Well, that made two of them.

"You're welcome," he said, fixing his gaze on the line of trees beside them.

He maneuvered his horse around in front of hers so he could lead the way back down to the barn. They rode on in silence, but he could feel her staring holes into his back.

"Are you looking at my butt, Danielle?"

He heard a sputtering noise behind him. "No."

They rode up to the front of the barn and he dismounted, then walked over to her horse. "Liar. Do you need help?"

She frowned, her brows lowering. "Not from you. You called me a liar."

"Because you were looking at my butt and we both know it." He raised his hand up, extending it to her. "Now let me help you so you don't fall on your pretty face."

"Bah," she said, reaching out to him, her fingers brushing against his, sending an electrical current arcing between them. He chose to ignore it. Because there was no way in the whole damn world that the brush of a woman's fingertips against his should get him hot and bothered.

He grabbed hold of her and helped get her down from the horse, drawing her against him when her feet connected with the ground. And then it was over.

Pretending that this wasn't a long prelude to him kissing her again. Pretending that the last few days hadn't been foreplay. Pretending that every time either of them had thought about the kiss hadn't been easing them closer and closer to the inevitable.

She wanted him, he knew that. It was clear in the way she responded to him. She might have reservations about acting on it, and he had his own. But need was bigger than any of that right now, building between them, impossible to ignore.

He was a breath away from claiming her mouth with his when she shocked him by curving her fingers around his neck and stretching up on her toes.

Her kiss was soft, tentative. A question where his kiss would have been a command. But that made it all the sweeter. The fact that she had come to him. The fact that even though she was still conflicted about all of it, she couldn't resist any longer.

He cupped her cheek, calling on all his restraint—what little there was—to allow her to lead this, to allow her to guide the exploration. There was something so unpracticed about that pretty mouth of hers, something untutored about the way her lips skimmed over his. About the almost sweet, soft way her tongue tested his.

What he wanted to do was take it deep. Take it hard. What he wanted to do was grab hold of her hips and press her back against the barn. Push her jeans down her thighs and get his hand back between her gorgeous legs so he could feel all that soft, slick flesh.

What he wanted was to press himself against her and slide in slowly, savoring the feel of her desire as it washed over him.

But he didn't.

And it was the damned hardest thing he had ever done. To wait. To let her lead. To let her believe she had the control here. Whatever she needed to do so she wouldn't get scared again. If he had to be patient, if he had to take it slow, he could. He would.

If it meant having her.

He had to have her. Had to exorcise the intense demon

that had taken residence inside of him, that demanded he take her. Demanded he make her his own.

His horse snickered behind them, shifting her bulk, drawing Danielle's focus back to the present and away from him. Dammit all.

"Let me get them put away," he said.

He was going to do it quickly. And then he was going to get right back to tasting her. He half expected her to run to the house as he removed the tack from the animals and got them brushed down, but she didn't. Instead, she just stood there watching him, her eyes large, her expression one of absolute indecision.

Because she knew.

She knew that if she stayed down here, he wasn't going to leave it at a kiss. He wasn't going to leave it at all.

But he went about his tasks, slowing his movements, forcing himself not to rush. Forcing himself to draw it out. For her torture as well as his. He wanted her to need it, the way that he did.

And yes, he could see she wanted to run. He could also tell she wanted him, she wanted this. She was unbearably curious, even if she was also afraid.

And he was counting on that curiosity to win out.

Finally, she cleared her throat, shifting impatiently. "Are you going to take all day to do that?"

"You have to take good care of your horses, Danielle. I know a city girl like you doesn't understand how that works."

She squinted, then took a step forward, pulling his hat off his head and depositing it on her own. "Bull. You're playing with me."

He couldn't hold back the smile. "Not yet. But I plan to."

After that, he hurried a bit. He put the horses back in their paddock, then took hold of Danielle's hand, leading her deeper into the barn, to a ladder that went up to the loft.

"Can I show you something?"

She bit her lip, hesitating. "Why do I have a feeling that it isn't the loft you're going to show me?"

"I'm going to show you the loft. It's just not all I'm going to show you."

She took a step back, worrying her lip with her teeth. He reached out, cupping the back of her head and bringing his mouth down on hers, kissing her the way he had wanted to when she initiated the kiss outside. He didn't have patience anymore. And he wasn't going to let her lead. Not now.

He cupped her face, stroking her cheeks with his thumbs. "This has nothing to do with our agreement. It has nothing to do with the contract. Nothing to do with the ad or my father or anything other than the fact that I want you. Do you understand?"

She nodded slowly. "Yes," she said, the word coming out a whisper.

Adrenaline shot through him, a strange kind of triumph that came with a kick to the gut right behind it. He wanted her. He knew he didn't deserve her. But he wasn't going to stop himself from having her in spite of that.

Then he took her hand and led her up the ladder.

Chapter Seven

Danielle's heart was pounding in her ears. It was all she could hear. The sound of her own heart beating as she climbed the rungs that led up to the loft.

It was different than she had imagined. It was clean. There was a haystack in one corner, but beyond that the floor was immaculate, every item stored and organized with precision. Which, knowing Joshua like she now did, wasn't too much of a surprise.

That made her smile, just a little. She did know him. In some ways, she felt like she knew him better than she knew anyone.

She wasn't sure what that said about her other relationships. For a while, she'd had friends, but they'd disappeared when she'd become consumed with caring for her pregnant mother and working as much as possible at the grocery store. And then no one had come back when Danielle ended up with full care of Riley.

In some ways, she didn't blame them. Life was hard enough without dealing with a friend who was juggling all of that. But just because she understood didn't mean she wasn't lonely.

She looked at Joshua, their eyes connecting. He had shared his past with her. But she was keeping something big from him. Even while she was prepared to give him her body, she was holding back secrets.

She took a breath, opening her mouth to speak, but something in his blue gaze stopped the words before they could form. Something sharp, predatory. Something that made her feel like she was the center of the world, or at least the center of his world.

It was intoxicating. She'd never experienced it before.

She wanted more, all of it. Wherever it would lead.

And that was scary. Scarier than agreeing to do something she had never done before. Because she finally understood. Understood why her mother had traded her sanity, and her self-worth, for that moment when a man looked at you like you were his everything.

Danielle had spent so long being nothing to anyone. Nothing but a burden. Now, feeling like the solution rather than the problem was powerful, heady. She knew she couldn't turn back now no matter what.

Even if sanity tried to prevail, she would shove it aside. Because she needed this. Needed this balm for all the wounds that ran so deep inside of her.

Joshua walked across the immaculate space and opened up a cabinet. There were blankets inside, thick, woolen ones with geometric designs on them. He pulled out two and spread one on the ground.

She bit her lip, fighting a rising tide of hysteria, fighting a giggle that was climbing its way up her throat.

"I know this isn't exactly a fancy hotel suite."

She forced a smile. "It works for me."

He set the other blanket down on the end of the first one, still folded, then he reached out and took her hand, drawing her to him. He curved his fingers around her wrist, lifting her arm up, then shifted his hold, lacing his fingers through hers and dipping his head, pressing his lips to her own.

Her heart was still pounding that same, steady beat, and she was certain he must be able to hear it. Must be aware of just how he was affecting her.

There were all sorts of things she should tell him. About Riley's mother. About this being her first time.

But she didn't have the words.

She had her heartbeat. The way her limbs trembled. She could let him see that her eyes were filling with tears, and no matter how fiercely she blinked, they never quite went away.

She was good at manipulating conversation. At giving answers that walked the line between fact and fiction.

Her body could only tell the truth.

She hoped he could see it. That he understood. Later, they would talk. Later, there would be honesty between them. Because he would have questions. God knew. But for now, she would let the way her fingertips trailed down his back—uncertain and tentative—the way she peppered kisses along his jaw—clumsy and broken— say everything she couldn't.

"It doesn't need to be fancy," she said, her voice sounding thick even to her own ears.

"Maybe it should be," he said, his voice rough. "But

if I was going to take you back to my bedroom, I expect I would have to wait until tonight. And I don't want to wait."

She shook her head. "It doesn't have to be fancy. It just has to be now. And it has to be you."

He drew his head back, inhaling sharply. And then he cupped her cheek and consumed her. His kiss was heat and fire, sparking against the dry, neglected things inside her and raging out of control.

She slid her hands up his arms, hanging on to his strong shoulders, using his steadiness to hold her fast even as her legs turned weak.

He lifted her up against him, then swept his arm beneath her legs, cradling her against his chest like she was a child. Then he set her down gently on the blanket, continuing to kiss her as he did so.

She was overwhelmed. Overwhelmed by the intensity of his gaze, by his focus. Overwhelmed by his closeness, his scent.

He was everywhere. His hands on her body, his face filling her vision.

She had spent the past few months caring for her half brother, pouring everything she had onto one little person she loved more than anything in the entire world. But in doing so, she had left herself empty. She had been giving continually, opening a vein and bleeding whenever necessary, and taking nothing in to refill herself.

But this… This was more than she had ever had. More than she'd ever thought she could have. Being the focus of a man's attention. Of his need.

This was a different kind of need than that of a child. Because it wasn't entirely selfish. Joshua's need gave her something in return; it compelled him to be close.

Compelled him to kiss her, to skim his hands over her body, teasing and tormenting her with the promise of a pleasure she had never experienced.

Before she could think her actions through, she was pushing her fingertips beneath the hem of his shirt, his hard, flat stomach hot to the touch. And then it didn't matter what she had done before or what she hadn't done. Didn't matter that she was a virgin and this was an entirely new experience.

Need replaced everything except being skin to skin with him. Having nothing between them.

Suddenly, the years of feeling isolated, alone, cold and separate were simply too much. She needed his body over hers, his body inside hers. Whatever happened after that, whatever happened in the end, right now she couldn't care.

Because her desire outweighed the consequences. A wild, desperate thing starving to be fed. With his touch. With his possession.

She pushed his shirt up, and he helped her shrug it over his head. Her throat dried, her mouth opening slightly as she looked at him. His shoulders were broad, his chest well-defined and muscular, pale hair spreading over those glorious muscles, down his ridged abdomen, disappearing in a thin trail beneath the waistband of his low-slung jeans.

She had never seen a man who looked like him before, not in person. And she had never been this close to a man ever. She pressed her palm against his chest, relishing his heat and his hardness beneath her touch. His heart raging out of control, matching the beat of her own.

She parted her thighs and he settled between them. She could feel the hard ridge of his arousal pressing against that place where she was wet and needy for him. She was shocked at how hard he was, even through layers of clothing.

And she lost herself in his kiss, in the way he rocked his hips against hers. This moment, this experience was like everything she had missed growing up. Misspent teenage years when she should have been making out with boys in barns and hoping she didn't get caught. In reality, her mother wouldn't have cared.

This was a reclamation. More than that, it was something completely new. Something she had never even known she could want.

Joshua was something she had never known she could want.

It shouldn't make sense, the two of them. This brilliant businessman in his thirties who owned a ranch and seemed to shun most emotional connections. And her. Poor. In her twenties. Desperately clinging to any connection she could forge because each one was so rare and special.

But somehow they seemed to make sense. Kissing each other. Touching each other. For some reason, he was the only man that made sense.

Maybe it was because he had taught her to ride a horse. Maybe it was because he was giving her and Riley a ticket out of poverty. Maybe it was because he was handsome. She had a feeling this connection transcended all those things.

As his tongue traced a trail down her neck to the collar of her T-shirt, she was okay with not knowing. She didn't need to give this connection a name. She didn't even want to.

Her breath caught as he pushed her shirt up and over

her head, then quickly dispensed with her bra using a skill not even she possessed. Her nipples tightened, and she was painfully aware of them and of the fact that she was a little lackluster in size.

If Joshua noticed, he didn't seem to mind.

Instead, he dipped his head, sucking one tightened bud between his lips. The move was so sudden, so shocking and so damned unexpected that she couldn't stop herself from arching into him, a cry on her lips.

He looked up, the smile on his face so damned cocky she should probably have been irritated. But she wasn't. She just allowed herself to get lost. In his heat. In the fire that flared between them. In the way he used his lips, his teeth and his tongue to draw a map of pleasure over her skin. All the way down to the waistband of her pants. He licked her. Just above the snap on her jeans. Another sensation so deliciously shocking she couldn't hold back the sound of pleasure on her lips.

She pressed her fist against her mouth, trying to keep herself from getting too vocal. From embarrassing herself. From revealing just how inexperienced she was. The noises she was making definitely announced the fact that these sensations were revelatory to her. And that made her feel a touch too vulnerable.

She was so used to holding people at a distance. So used to benign neglect and general apathy creating a shield around her feelings. Her secrets.

But there was no distance here.

And certainly none as he undid the button of her jeans and drew the zipper down slowly. As he pushed the rough denim down her legs, taking her panties with them.

If she had felt vulnerable a moment before, that was

nothing compared to now. She felt so fragile. So exposed. And then he reached up, pressing his hand against her leg at the inside of her knee, spreading her wide so he could look his fill.

She wanted to snap her legs together. Wanted to cover up. But she was immobilized. Completely captive to whatever might happen next. She was so desperate to find out, and at the same time desperate to escape it.

Rough fingertips drifted down the tender skin on her inner thigh, brushing perilously close to her damp, needy flesh. And then he was there. His touch in no way gentle or tentative as he pressed his hand against her, the heel of his palm putting firm pressure on her most sensitive place before he pressed his fingers down and spread her wide.

He made his intentions clear as he lowered his head, tasting her deeply. She lifted her hips, a sharp sound on her lips, one she didn't even bother to hold back. He shifted his hold, gripping her hips, holding her just wide enough for his broad shoulders to fit right there, his sensual assault merciless.

Tension knotted her stomach like a fist, tighter and tighter with each pass of his tongue. Then he pressed his thumb against her at the same time as he flicked his tongue in the same spot. She grabbed hold of him, her fingernails digging into his back.

He drew his thumb down her crease, teasing the entrance of her body. She rocked her hips with the motion, desperate for something. Feeling suddenly empty and achy and needy in ways she never had before.

He rotated his hand, pressing his middle finger deep inside of her, and she gasped at the foreign invasion. But any discomfort passed quickly as her body grew wetter beneath the ministrations of his tongue. By the time he added a second finger, it slipped in easily.

He quickened his pace, and it felt like there was an earthquake starting inside her. A low, slow pull at her core that spread outward, her limbs trembling as the pressure at her center continued to mount.

His thumb joined with his tongue as he continued to pump his fingers inside her, and it was that added pressure that finally broke her. She was shaken. Rattled completely. The magnitude of measurable aftershocks rocking her long after the primary force had passed.

He moved into a sitting position, undoing his belt and the button on his jeans. Then he stood for a moment, drawing the zipper down slowly and pushing the denim down his muscular thighs.

She had never seen a naked man in person before, and the stark, thick evidence of his arousal standing out from his body was a clear reminder that they weren't finished, no matter how wrung out and replete she felt.

Except, even though she felt satisfied, limp from the intensity of her release, she did want more. Because there was more to have. Because she wanted to be close to him. Because she wanted to give him even an ounce of the satisfaction that she had just experienced.

He knelt back down, pulling his jeans closer and taking his wallet out of his back pocket. He produced a condom packet and she gave thanks for his presence of mind. She knew better than to have unprotected sex with someone. For myriad reasons. But still, she wondered if she would have remembered if he had not.

Thank God one of them was thinking. She was too overwhelmed. Too swamped by the release that had overtaken her, and by the enormity of what was about to happen. When he positioned himself at the entrance of her body and pressed against her, she gasped in shock.

It *hurt*. Dear God it hurt. His fingers hadn't prepared her for the rest of him.

He noticed her hesitation and slowed his movements, pressing inside her inch by excruciating inch. She held on to his shoulders, closing her eyes and burying her face in his neck as he jerked his hips forward, fully seating himself inside her.

She did her best to breathe through it. But she was in a daze. Joshua was inside her, and she wasn't a virgin anymore. It felt… Well, it didn't feel like losing anything. It felt like gaining something. Gaining a whole lot.

The pain began to recede and she looked up, at his face, at the extreme concentration there, at the set of his jaw, the veins in his neck standing out.

"Are you okay?" he asked, his voice strangled.

She nodded wordlessly, then flexed her hips experimentally.

He groaned, lowering his head, pressing his forehead against hers, before kissing her. Then he began to move.

Soon, that same sweet tension began to build again in her stomach, need replacing the bone-deep satisfaction that she had only just experienced. She didn't know how it was possible to be back in that needy place only moments after feeling fulfilled.

But she was. And then she was lost in the rhythm, lost in the feeling of his thick length stroking in and out of her, all of the pain gone now, only pleasure remaining. It was so foreign, so singular and unlike anything she had ever experienced. And she loved it. Reveled in it.

But even more than her own pleasure, she reveled in watching his unraveling.

Because he had pulled her apart in a million astounding ways, and she didn't know if she could ever be reassembled. So it was only fair that he lost himself too. Only fair that she be his undoing in some way.

Sweat beaded on his brow, trickled down his back. She reveled in the feel of it beneath her fingertips. In the obvious evidence of what this did to him.

His breathing became more labored, his muscles shaking as each thrust became less gentle. As he began to pound into her. And just as he needed to go harder, go faster, so did she.

Her own pleasure wound around his, inextricably linked.

On a harsh growl he buried his face in her neck, his arms shaking as he thrust into her one last time, slamming into her, breaking a wave of pleasure over her body as he found his own release.

He tried to pull away, but she wrapped her arms around him, holding him close. Because the sooner he separated from her body, the sooner they would have to talk. And she wasn't exactly sure she wanted to talk.

But when he lifted his head, his blue eyes glinting in the dim light, she could tell that whether or not she wanted to talk, they were going to.

He rolled away from her, pushing into a sitting position. "Are you going to explain all of this to me? Or are you going to make me guess?"

"What?" She sounded overly innocent, her eyes wider than necessary.

"Danielle, I'm going to ask you a question, and I need you to answer me honestly. Were you a virgin?"

Joshua's blood was still running hot through his veins,

arousal still burning beneath the surface of his skin. And he knew the question he had just asked her was probably insane. He could explain her discomfort as pain because she hadn't taken a man to her bed since she'd given birth.

But that wasn't it. It wasn't.

The more credence he gave to his virgin theory, the more everything about her started to make sense. The way she responded to his kiss, the way she acted when he touched her.

Her reaction had been about more than simple attraction, more than pleasure. There had been wonder there. A sense of discovery.

But that meant Riley wasn't her son. And it meant she had been lying to him.

"Well, Joshua, given that this is not a New Testament kind of situation…"

He reached out, grabbing hold of her wrist and tugging her upward, drawing her toward him. "Don't lie to me."

"Why would you think that?" she asked, her words small. Admission enough as far as he was concerned.

"A lot of reasons. But I have had sex with a virgin before. More accurately, Sadie Miller and I took each other's virginity in the woods some eighteen years ago. You don't forget that. And, I grant you, there could be other reasons for the fact that it hurt you, for the fact that you were tight." A flush spread over her skin, her cheeks turning beet red. "But I don't think any of those reasons are the truth. So what's going on? Who is Riley's mother?"

A tear slid down her cheek, her expression mutinous and angry. "I am," she said, her voice trembling. "At least, I might as well be. I should be."

"You didn't give birth to Riley."

She sniffed loudly, another tear sliding down her cheek. "No. I didn't."

"Are you running from somebody? Is there something I need to know?"

"It's not like that. I'm not hiding. I didn't steal him. I have legal custody of Riley. But my situation was problematic. At least, as far as Child Services was concerned. I lost my job because of the babysitting situation and I needed money."

She suddenly looked so incredibly young, so vulnerable... And he felt like the biggest jerk on planet Earth.

She had lied to him. She had most definitely led him to believe she was in an entirely different circumstance than she was, and still, he was mostly angry at himself.

Because the picture she was painting was even more desperate than the one he had been led to believe. Because she had been a virgin and he had just roughly dispensed with that.

She had been desperate. Utterly desperate. And had taken this post with him because she hadn't seen another option. Whatever he'd thought of her before, he was forced to revise it, and there was no way that revision didn't include recasting himself as the villain.

"Whose baby is he?"

She swallowed hard, drawing her knees up to her chest, covering her nudity. "Riley is my half brother. My mother showed up at my place about a year ago pregnant and desperate. She needed someone to help her out. When she came to me, she sounded pretty determined to take care of him. She even named him. She told me she would do better for him than she had for me, because she was done with men now and all of that.

But she broke her promises. She had the baby, she met somebody else. I didn't know it at first. I didn't realize she was leaving Riley in the apartment alone sometimes while I was at work."

She took a deep, shuddering breath, then continued. "I didn't mess around when I found out. I didn't wait for her to decide to abandon him. I called Child Services. And I got temporary guardianship. My mother left. But then things started to fall apart with the work, and I didn't know how I was going to pay for the apartment... Then I saw your ad."

He swore. "You should have told me."

"Maybe. But I needed the money, Joshua. And I didn't want to do anything to jeopardize your offer. I could tell you were uncomfortable that I brought a baby with me, and now I know why. But, regardless, at the time, I didn't want to do anything that might compromise our arrangement."

He felt like the jackass he undoubtedly was. The worst part was, it shone a light on all the BS he'd put her through. Regardless of Riley's parentage, she'd been desperate and he'd taken advantage of that. Less so when he'd been keeping his hands to himself. At least then it had been feasible to pretend it was an even exchange.

But now?

Now he'd slept with her and it was impossible to keep pretending.

And frankly, he didn't want to.

He'd been wrestling with this feeling from the moment they'd gone out riding today, or maybe since they'd left his parents' house last week.

But today...when he'd looked at her, seen her smile...

noticed the way she'd gained weight after being in a place where she felt secure…

He'd wanted to give her more of that.

He'd wanted to do more good than harm. Had wanted to fix something instead of break it.

It was too late for Shannon. But he could help Danielle. He could make sure she always felt safe. That she and Riley were always protected.

The realization would have made him want to laugh if it didn't all feel too damned grim. Somehow his father's ad had brought him to this place when he'd been determined to teach the old man a lesson.

But Joshua hadn't counted on Danielle.

Hadn't counted on how she would make him feel. That she'd wake something inside him he'd thought had been asleep for good.

It wasn't just chemistry. Wasn't just sex. It was the desire to make her happy. To give her things.

To fix what was broken.

He knew the solution wouldn't come from him personally, but his money could sure as hell fix her problems. And they did have chemistry. The kind that wasn't common. It sure as hell went beyond anything he'd ever experienced before.

"The truth doesn't change anything," she said, lowering her face into her arms, her words muffled. "It doesn't."

He reached out, taking her chin between his thumb and forefinger, tilting her face back up. "It does. Even if it shouldn't. Though, maybe it's not Riley that changes it. Maybe it's just the two of us."

She shook her head. "It doesn't have to change anything."

"Danielle… I can't…"

She lurched forward, grabbing his arm, her eyes wide, her expression wild. "Joshua, please. I need this money. I can't go back to where we were. I'm being held to a harsher standard than his biological mother would be and I can't lose him."

He grabbed her chin again, steadying her face, looking into those glistening brown eyes. "Danielle, I would never let you lose him. I want to protect you. Both of you."

She tilted her head to the side, her expression growing suspicious. "You…do?"

"I've been thinking. I was thinking this earlier when we were riding, but now, knowing your whole story… I want you and Riley to stay with me."

She blinked. "What?"

"Danielle, I want you to marry me."

Chapter Eight

Danielle couldn't process any of this.

She had expected him to be angry. Had expected him to get mad because she'd lied to him.

She hadn't expected a marriage proposal.

At least, she was pretty sure that was what had just happened. "You want to…marry me? For real marry me?"

"Yes," he said, his tone hard, decisive. "You don't feel good about fooling my family—neither do I. You need money and security and, hell, I have both. We have chemistry. I want… I don't want to send you back into the world alone. You don't even know where you're going."

He wasn't wrong. And dammit his offer was tempting. They were both naked, and he was so beautiful, and she wanted to kiss him again. Touch him again. But more than that, she wanted him to hold her in his arms again.

She wanted to be close to him. Bonded to him.

She wanted—so desperately—to not be alone.

But there had to be a catch.

There was always a catch. He could say whatever he wanted about how all of this wasn't a transaction, how he had taken her riding just to take her riding. But then they'd had sex. And he'd had a condom in his wallet.

So he'd been prepared.

That made her stomach sour.

"Did you plan this?" she asked. "The horse-riding seduction?"

"No, I didn't plan it. I carry a condom because I like to be prepared to have sex. You never know. You can get mad at me for that if you want, but then, we did need one, so it seems a little hypocritical."

"Are you tricking me?" she asked, feeling desperate and panicky. "Is this a trick? Because I don't understand how it benefits you to marry me. To keep Riley and me here. You don't even like Riley, Joshua. You can't stand to be in the same room with him."

"I broke Shannon," he said, his voice hard. "I ruined her. I did that. But I won't break you. I want to fix this."

"You can't slap duct tape and a wedding band on me and call it done," she said, her voice trembling. "I'm not a leaky faucet."

"I didn't say you were. But you need something I have and I… Danielle, I need you." His voice was rough, intense. "I'm not offering you love, but I can be faithful. I was ready to be a husband years ago, that part doesn't faze me. I can take care of you. I can keep you safe. And if I send you out into the world with nothing more than money and something happens to you or Riley, I won't forgive myself. So stay with me. Marry me."

It was crazy. He was crazy.

And she was crazy for sitting there fully considering everything he was offering.

But she was imagining a life here. For her, for Riley. On Joshua's ranch, in his beautiful house.

And she knew—she absolutely knew—that what she had felt physically with him, what had just happened, was a huge reason why they were having this conversation at all.

More than the pleasure, the closeness drew her in. Actually, that was the most dangerous part of his offer. The idea that she could go through life with somebody by her side. To raise Riley with this strong man backing her up.

Something clenched tight in her chest, working its way down to her stomach. Riley. He could have a father figure. She didn't know exactly what function Joshua would play in his life. Joshua had trouble with the baby right now. But she knew Joshua was a good man, and that he would never freeze Riley out intentionally. Not when he was offering them a life together.

"What about Riley?" she asked, her throat dry. She swallowed hard. She had to know what he was thinking.

"What about him?"

"This offer extends to him too. And I mean...not just protection and support. But would you... Would you teach him things? Would your father be a grandfather to him? Would your brothers be uncles and your sister be an aunt? I understand that having a child around might be hard for you, after you lost your chance at being a father. And I understand you want to fix me, my situation.

And it's tempting, Joshua, it's very tempting. But I need to know if that support, if all of that, extends to Riley."

Joshua's face looked as though it had been cast in stone. "I'm not sure if I would be a good father, Danielle. I was going to be a father, and so I was going to figure it out—how to do that, how to be that. I suppose I can apply that same intent here. I can't guarantee that I'll be the best, but I'll try. And you're right. I have my family to back me up. And he has you."

That was it.

That was the reason she couldn't say no. Because if she walked away from Joshua now, Riley would have her. Only her. She loved him, but she was just one person. If she stayed here with Joshua, Riley would have grandparents. Aunts and uncles. Family. People who knew how to be a family. She was doing the very best she could, but her idea of family was somewhere between cold neglectful nightmare and a TV sitcom.

The Grayson family knew—Joshua knew—what it meant to be a family. If she said yes, she could give that to Riley.

She swallowed again, trying to alleviate the scratchy feeling in her throat.

"I guess… I guess I can't really say no to that." She straightened, still naked, and not even a little bit embarrassed. There were bigger things going on here than the fact that he could see her breasts. "Okay, Joshua. I'll marry you."

Chapter Nine

The biggest problem with this sudden change in plan was the fact that Joshua had deliberately set out to make his family dislike Danielle. And now he was marrying her for real.

Of course, the flaw in his original plan was that Danielle *hadn't* been roundly hated by his family. They'd distrusted the whole situation, certainly, but his family was simply too fair, too nice to hate her.

Still, guilt clutched at him, and he knew he was going to have to do something to fix this. Which was why he found himself down at the Gray Bear Construction office rather than working from home. Because he knew Faith and Isaiah would be in, and he needed to have a talk with his siblings.

The office was a newly constructed building fashioned to look like a log cabin. It was down at the edge of

town, by where Rona's diner used to be, a former greasy
spoon that had been transformed into a series of smaller,
hipper shops that were more in line with the interests of
Copper Ridge's tourists.

It was a great office space with a prime view of the
ocean, but still, Joshua typically preferred to work in
the privacy of his own home, secluded in the mountains.

Isaiah did too, which was why it was notable that his
brother was in the office today, but he'd had a meeting
of some kind, so he'd put on a decent shirt and a pair
of nice jeans and gotten himself out of his hermitage.

Faith, being the bright, sharp creature she was, always
came into the office, always dressed in some variation
of her personal uniform. Black pants and a black top—a
sweater today because of the chilly weather.

"What are you doing here?" Faith asked, her expression scrutinizing.

"I came here to talk to you," he said.

"I'll make coffee." Joshua turned and saw Poppy
standing there. Strange, he hadn't noticed. But then,
Poppy usually stayed in the background. He couldn't
remember running the business without her, but like use-
ful office supplies, you really only noticed them when
they didn't work. And Poppy always worked.

"Thanks, Poppy," Faith said.

Isaiah folded his arms over his chest and leaned back
in his chair. "What's up?"

"I'm getting married in two weeks."

Faith made a scoffing sound. "To that child you're
dating?"

"She's your age," he said. "And yes. Just like I said
I was."

"Which begs the question," Isaiah said. "Why are you telling us again?"

"Because. The first time I was lying. Dad put that ad in the paper trying to find a wife for me, and I selected Danielle in order to teach him a lesson. The joke's on me it turns out." Damn was it ever.

"Good God, Joshua. You're such a jerk," Faith said, leaning against the wall, her arms folded, mirroring Isaiah's stance. "I knew something was up, but of all the things I suspected, you tricking our mother and father was not one of them."

"What did you suspect?"

"That you were thinking with your... Well. And now I'm back to that conclusion. Because why are you marrying her?"

"I care about her. And believe me when I say she's had it rough."

"You've slept with her?" This question came from Isaiah, and there was absolutely no tact in it. But then, Isaiah himself possessed absolutely no tact. Which was why he handled money and not people.

"Yes," Joshua said.

"She must be good. But I'm not sure that's going to convince either of us you're thinking with your big brain." His brother stood up, not unfolding his arms.

"Well, you're obnoxious," Joshua returned. "The sex has nothing to do with it. I can get sex whenever I want."

Faith made a hissing sound. He tossed his younger sister a glance. "You can stop hissing and settle down," he said to her. "You were the one who brought sex into it, I'm just clarifying. You know what I went through with Shannon, what I put Shannon through. If I send Danielle and her baby back out into the world and something happens to them, I'll never forgive myself."

"Well, Joshua, that kind of implies you aren't already living in a perpetual state of self-flagellation," Faith said.

"Do you want to see if it can get worse?"

She shook her head. "No, but marrying some random woman you found through an ad seems like an extreme way to go about searching for atonement. Can't you do some Hail Marys or something?"

"If it were that simple, I would have done it a long time ago." He took a deep breath. "I'm not going to tell Mom and Dad the whole story. But I'm telling you because I need you to be nice about Danielle. However it looked when I brought her by to introduce her to the family... I threw her under the bus, and now I want to drag her back out from under it."

Isaiah shook his head. "You're a contrary son of a gun."

"Well, usually that's your function. I figured it was my turn."

The door to the office opened and in walked their business partner, Jonathan Bear, who ran the construction side of the firm. He looked around the room, clearly confused by the fact that they were all in residence. "Is there a meeting I didn't know about?"

"Joshua is getting married," Faith said, looking sullen.

"Congratulations," Jonathan said, smiling, which was unusual for the other man, who was typically pretty taciturn. "I can highly recommend it."

Jonathan had married the pastor's daughter, Hayley Thompson, in a small ceremony recently.

In the past, Jonathan had walked around like he had his own personal storm cloud overhead, and since meeting Hayley, he had most definitely changed. Maybe there was something to that whole marriage thing. Maybe Joshua's idea of atonement wasn't as outrageous as it might have initially seemed.

"There," Joshua said. "Jonathan recommends it. So you two can stop looking at me suspiciously."

Jonathan shrugged and walked through the main area and into the back, toward his office, leaving Joshua alone with his siblings.

Faith tucked her hair behind her ear. "Honestly, whatever you need, whatever you want, I'll help. But I don't want you to get hurt."

"And I appreciate that," he said. "But the thing is, you can only get hurt if there's love involved. I don't love her."

Faith looked wounded by that. "Then what's the point? I'm not trying to argue. I just don't understand."

"Love is not the be-all and end-all, Faith. Sometimes just committing to taking care of somebody else is enough. I loved Shannon, but I still didn't do the right thing for her. I'm older now. And I know what's important. I'm going to keep Danielle safe. I'm going to keep Riley safe. What's more important than that?" He shook his head. "I'm sure Shannon would have rather had that than any expression of love."

"Fine," she said. "I support you. I'm in."

"So you aren't going to be a persnickety brat?"

A small smile quirked her lips upward. "I didn't say that. I said I would support you. But as a younger sister, I feel the need to remind you that being a persnickety brat is sometimes part of my support."

He shot Isaiah a baleful look. "I suppose you're still going to be obnoxious?"

"Obviously."

Joshua smiled then. Because that was the best he was going to get from his siblings. But it was a step toward making sure Danielle felt like she had a place in the family, rather than feeling like an outsider.

And if he wanted that with an intensity that wasn't strictly normal or healthy, he would ignore that. He had never pretended to be normal or healthy. He wasn't going to start now.

Danielle was getting fluttery waiting for Joshua to come home. The anticipation was a strange feeling. It had been a long time since she'd looked forward to someone coming home. She remembered being young, when it was hard to be alone. But she hadn't exactly wished for her mother to come home, because she knew that when her mother arrived, she would be drunk. And Danielle would be tasked with managing her in some way.

That was the story of her life. Not being alone meant taking care of somebody. Being alone meant isolation, but at least she had time to herself.

But Joshua wasn't like that. Being with him didn't mean she had to manage him.

She thought of their time together in the barn, and the memory made her shiver. She had gone to bed in her own room last night, and he hadn't made any move toward her since his proposal. She had a feeling his hesitation had something to do with her inexperience.

But she was ready for him again. Ready for more.

She shook her hands out, feeling jittery. And a little scared.

It was so easy to want him. To dream about him coming home, how she would embrace him, kiss him. And

maybe even learn to cook, so she could make him dinner.
Learn to do something other than warm up Pop-Tarts.

Although, he liked Pop-Tarts, and so did she.

Maybe they should have Pop-Tarts at their wedding.
That was the kind of thing couples did. Incorporate the
cute foundations of their relationships into their wedding ceremonies.

She made a small sound that was halfway between
a whimper and a growl. She was getting loopy about
him. About a guy. Which she had promised herself she
would never do. But it was hard *not* to get loopy. He had
offered her support, a family for Riley, a house to live
in. He had become her lover, and then he had asked to
become her husband.

And in those few short moments, her entire vision for
the rest of her life had changed. It had become something so much warmer, so much more secure than she
had ever imagined it could be. She just wasn't strong
enough to reject that vision.

Honestly, she didn't know a woman who would be
strong enough. Joshua was hot. And he was nice. Well,
sometimes he was kind of a jerk, but mostly, at his core,
he was nice and he had wonderful taste in breakfast
food.

That seemed like as good a foundation for a marriage as any.

She heard the front door open and shut, and as it
slammed, her heart lurched against her breastbone.

Joshua walked in looking so intensely handsome in
a light blue button-up shirt, the sleeves pushed up his
arms, that she wanted to swoon for the first time in her
entire life.

"Do you think they can make a wedding cake out of

Pop-Tarts?" She didn't know why that was the first thing that came out of her mouth. Probably, it would have been better if she had said something about how she couldn't wait to tear his clothes off.

But no. She had led with toaster pastry.

"I don't know. But we're getting married in two weeks, so if you can stack Pop-Tarts and call them a cake, I suppose it might save time and money."

"I could probably do that. I promise that's not all I thought about today, but for some reason it's what came out of my mouth."

"How about I keep your mouth busy for a while," he said, his blue gaze getting sharp. He crossed the space between them, wrapping his arm around her waist and drawing her against him. And then he kissed her.

It was so deep, so warm, and she felt so…sheltered. Enveloped completely in his arms, in his strength. Who cared if she was lost in a fantasy right now? It would be the first time. She had never had the luxury of dreaming about men like him, or passion this intense.

It seemed right, only fair, that she have the fantasy. If only for a while. To have a moment where she actually dreamed about a wedding with cake. Where she fantasized about a man walking in the door and kissing her like this, wanting her like this.

"Is Janine here?" he asked, breaking the kiss just long enough to pose the question.

"No," she said, barely managing to answer before he slammed his lips back down on hers.

Then she found herself being lifted and carried from the entryway into the living room, deposited on the couch. And somehow, as he set her down, he managed to raise her shirt up over her head.

She stared at him, dazed, while he divested himself of his own shirt. "You're very good at this," she said. "I assume you've had a lot of practice?"

He lifted an eyebrow, his hands going to his belt buckle. "Is this a conversation you want to have?"

She felt…bemused rather than jealous. "I don't know. I'm just curious."

"I got into a lot of trouble when I was a teenager. I think I mentioned the incident with my virginity in the woods."

She nodded. "You did. And since I lost my virginity in a barn, I suppose I have to reserve judgment."

"Probably. Then I moved to Seattle. And I was even worse, because suddenly I was surrounded by women I hadn't known my whole life."

Danielle nodded gravely. "I can see how that would be an issue."

He smiled. Then finished undoing his belt, button and zipper before shoving his pants down to the floor. He stood in front of her naked, aroused and beautiful.

"Then I got myself into a long-term relationship, and it turns out I'm good at that. Well, at the being faithful part."

"That's a relief."

"In terms of promiscuity, though, my behavior has been somewhat appalling for the past five years. I have picked up a particular set of skills."

She wrinkled her nose. "I suppose that's something."

"You asked."

She straightened. "And I wanted to know."

He reached behind her back, undoing her bra, pulling it off and throwing it somewhere behind him. "Well, now you do." He pressed his hands against the back of the couch, bracketing her in. "You still want to marry me?"

"I had a very tempting proposal from the UPS man today. He asked me to sign for a package. So I guess you could say it's getting kind of serious."

"I don't think the UPS man makes you feel like this." He captured her mouth with his, and she found herself being pressed into the cushions, sliding to the side, until he'd maneuvered her so they were both lying flat on the couch.

He wrapped his fingers around her wrists, lifting them up over her head as he bent to kiss her neck, her collarbone, to draw one nipple inside his mouth.

She bucked against him, and he shifted, pushing his hand beneath her jeans, under the fabric of her panties, discovering just how wet and ready she was for him.

She rolled her hips upward, moving in time with the rhythm of his strokes, lights beginning to flash behind her eyelids, orgasm barreling down on her at an embarrassingly quick rate.

Danielle sucked in a deep breath, trying her best to hold her climax at bay. Because how embarrassing would it be to come from a kiss? A brief bit of attention to her breast and a quick stroke between the legs?

But then she opened her eyes and met his gaze. His lips curved into a wicked smile as he turned his wrist, sliding one finger deep inside as he flicked his thumb over her.

All she could do then was hold on tight and ride out the explosion. He never looked away from her, and as much as she wanted to, she couldn't look away from him.

It felt too intense, too raw and much too intimate.

But she was trapped in it, drowning in it, and there

was nothing she could do to stop it. She just had to surrender.

While she was still recovering from her orgasm, Joshua made quick work of her jeans, flinging them in the same direction her bra had gone.

Then, still looking right at her, he stroked her, over the thin fabric of her panties, the tease against her overly sensitized skin almost too much to handle.

Then he traced the edge of the fabric at the crease of her thigh, dipping one finger beneath her underwear, touching slick flesh.

He hooked his finger around the fabric, pulling her panties off and casting them aside. And here she was, just as she'd been the first time, completely open and vulnerable to him. At his mercy.

It wasn't as though she didn't want that. There was something wonderful about it. Something incredible about the way he lavished attention on her, about being his sole focus.

But she wanted more. She wanted to be… She wanted to be equal to him in some way.

He was practiced. And he had skill. He'd had a lot of lovers. Realistically, she imagined he didn't even know exactly how many.

She didn't have skill. She hadn't been tutored in the art of love by anyone. But she *wanted*.

If desire could equal skill, then she could rival any woman he'd ever been with. Because the depth of her need, the depth of her passion, reached places inside her she hadn't known existed.

She pressed her hands down on the couch cushions, launching herself into a sitting position. His eyes widened, and she reveled in the fact that she had surprised him. She reached out, resting one palm against his chest, luxuriating in the feel of all that heat, that muscle, that masculine hair that tickled her sensitive skin.

"Danielle," he said, his tone filled with warning.

She didn't care about his warnings.

She was going to marry this man. He was going to be her husband. That thought filled her with such a strange sense of elation.

He had all the power. He had the money. He had the beautiful house. What he was giving her...it bordered on charity. If she was ever going to feel like she belonged— like this place was really hers—they needed to be equals in some regard.

She had to give him something too.

And if it started here, then it started here.

She leaned in, cautiously tasting his neck, tracing a line down to his nipple. He jerked beneath her touch, his reaction satisfying her in a way that went well beyond the physical.

He was beautiful, and she reveled in the chance to explore him. To run her fingertips over each well-defined muscle. Over his abs and the hard cut inward just below his hip bone.

But she didn't stop there. No, she wasn't even remotely finished with him.

He had made her shake. He had made her tremble. He had made her lose her mind.

And she was going to return the favor.

She took a deep breath and kissed his stomach. Just one easy thing before she moved on to what she wanted, even though it scared her.

She lifted her head, meeting his gaze as she wrapped her fingers around him and squeezed. His eyes glittered like ice on fire, and he said nothing. He just sat there, his jaw held tight, his expression one of absolute concentration.

Then she looked away from his face, bringing her attention to that most masculine part of him. She was hungry for him. There was no other word for it.

She was starving for a taste.

And that hunger overtook everything else.

She flicked her tongue out and tasted him, his skin salty and hot. But the true eroticism was in his response. His head fell back, his breath hissing sharply through his teeth. And he reached out, pressing his hand to her back, spreading his fingers wide at the center of her shoulder blades.

Maybe she didn't have skill. Maybe she didn't know what she was doing. But he liked it. And that made her feel powerful. It made her feel needed.

She slid her hand down his shaft, gripping the base before taking him more deeply into her mouth. His groan sounded torn from him, wild and untamed, and she loved it.

Because Joshua was all about control. Had been from the moment she'd first met him.

That was what all this was, after all. From the ad in the paper to his marriage proposal—all of it was him trying to bend the situation to his will. To bend those around him to his will, to make them see he was right, that his way was the best way.

But right now he was losing control. He was at her mercy. Shaking. Because of her.

And even though she was the one pleasuring him, she felt an immense sense of satisfaction flood her as she continued to taste him. As she continued to make him tremble.

He needed her. He wanted her. After a lifetime of feeling like nobody wanted her at all, this was the most brilliant and beautiful thing she could ever imagine.

She'd heard her friends talk about giving guys blow jobs before. They laughed about it. Or said it was gross. Or said it was a great way to control their boyfriends.

They hadn't said what an incredible thing it was to make a big, strong alpha male sweat and shake. They hadn't said it could make you feel so desired, so beloved. Or that giving someone else pleasure was even better—in some ways—than being on the receiving end of the attention.

She swallowed more of him, and his hand jerked up to her hair, tugging her head back. "Careful," he said, his tone hard and thin.

"Why?"

"You keep doing that and I'm going to come," he said, not bothering to sugarcoat it.

"So what? When you did it for me, that's what I did."

"Yes. But you're a woman. And you can have as many orgasms as I can give you without time off in between. I don't want it to end like this."

She was about to protest, but then he pulled her forward, kissing her hard and deep, stealing not just her ability to speak, but her ability to think of words.

He left her for a moment, retrieving his wallet and the protection in it, making quick work of putting the condom on before he laid her back down on the couch.

"Wait," she said, the word husky, rough. "I want... Can I be on top?"

He drew back, arching one brow. "Since you asked so nicely."

He gripped her hips, reversing their position, bringing her to sit astride him. He was hard beneath her, and she shifted back and forth experimentally, rubbing her slick folds over him before positioning him at the entrance of her body.

She bit her lip, lowering herself onto him, taking it slow, relishing that moment of him filling her so utterly and completely.

"I don't know what I'm doing," she whispered when he was buried fully inside of her.

He reached up, brushing his fingertips over her cheek before lowering his hand to grip both her hips tightly, lift her, then impale her on his hard length again.

"Just do what feels good," he ground out, the words strained.

She rocked her hips, then lifted herself slightly before taking him inside again. She repeated the motion. Again and again. Finding the speed and rhythm that made him gasp and made her moan. Finding just the right angle, just the right pressure, to please them both.

Pleasure began to ripple through her, the now somewhat familiar pressure of impending orgasm building inside her. She rolled her hips, making contact right where she needed it. He grabbed her chin, drawing her head down to kiss her. Deep, wet.

And that was it. She was done.

Pleasure burst behind her eyes, her internal muscles gripping him tight as her orgasm rocked her.

She found herself being rolled onto her back and Joshua began to pound into her, chasing his own release with a raw ferocity that made her whole body feel like it was on fire with passion.

He was undone. Completely. Because of her.

He growled, reaching beneath her to cup her behind, drawing her hard against him, forcing her to meet his every thrust. And that was when he proved himself right. She really could come as many times as he could make her.

She lost it then, shaking and shivering as her second orgasm overtook her already sensitized body.

He lowered his head, his teeth scraping against her collarbone as he froze against her, finding his own release.

He lay against her for a moment, his face buried in her neck, and she sifted her fingers through his hair, a small smile touching her lips as ripples of lingering pleasure continued to fan out through her body.

He looked at her, then brushed his lips gently over hers. She found herself being lifted up, cradled against his chest as he carried her from the couch to the stairs.

"Time for bed," he said, the words husky and rough.

She reached up and touched his face. "Okay."

He carried her to his room, laid her down on the expansive mattress, the blanket decadent and soft beneath her bare skin.

This would be their room. A room they would share.

For some reason, that thought made tears sting her eyes. She had spent so long being alone that the idea of so much closeness was almost overwhelming. But no matter what, she wanted it.

Wanted it so badly it was like a physical hunger.

Joshua joined her on the bed and she was overwhelmed by the urge to simply fold herself into his embrace. To enjoy the closeness.

But then he was naked. And so was she. So the desire for closeness fought with her desire to play with him a little more.

He pressed his hand against her lower back, then slid it down to her butt, squeezing tight. And he smiled.

Something intense and sharp filled her chest. It was almost painful.

Happiness, she realized. She was happy.

She knew in that moment that she never really had been happy before. At least, not without an equally weighty worry to balance it. To warn her that on the other side of the happiness could easily lie tragedy.

But she wasn't thinking of tragedy now. She couldn't.

Joshua filled her vision, and he filled her brain, and for now—just for now—everything in her world felt right.

For a while, she wanted that to be the whole story.

So she blocked out every other thought, every single what-if, and she kissed him again.

When Joshua woke up, the bedroom was dark. There was a woman wrapped around him. And he wasn't entirely sure what had pulled him out of his deep slumber.

Danielle was sleeping peacefully. Her dark hair was wrapped around her face like a spiderweb, and he reached down to push it back. She flinched, pursing her lips and shifting against him, tightening her arms around his waist.

She was exhausted. Probably because he was an animal who had taken her three, maybe four times before they'd finally both fallen asleep.

He looked at her, and the hunger was immediate. Visceral. And he wondered if he was fooling himself pretending, even for a moment, that any of this was for her.

That he had any kind of higher purpose.

He wondered if he had any purpose at all beyond trying to satisfy himself with her.

And then he realized what had woken him up.

He heard a high, keening cry that barely filtered through the open bedroom door. Riley.

He looked down at Danielle, who was still fast asleep, and who would no doubt be upset that they had forgotten to bring the baby monitor into the room. Joshua had barely been able to remember his own name, much less a baby monitor.

He extricated himself from her hold, scrubbing his hand over his face. Then he walked over to his closet, grabbing a pair of jeans and pulling them on with nothing underneath.

He had no idea what in the hell to do with the baby. But Danielle was exhausted, because of him, and he didn't want to wake her up.

The cries got louder as he made his way down the hall, and he walked into the room to see flailing movement coming from the crib. The baby was very unhappy, whatever the reason.

Joshua walked across the room and stood above the crib, looking down. If he was going to marry Danielle, then that meant Riley was his responsibility too.

Riley would be his son.

Something prickled at the back of his throat, making it tight. So much had happened after Shannon lost the baby that he didn't tend to think too much about what might have been. But it was impossible not to think about it right now.

His son would have been five.

He swallowed hard, trying to combat the rising tide of emotion in his chest. That emotion was why he avoided contact with Riley. Joshua wasn't so out of touch with his feelings that he didn't know that.

But his son wasn't here. He'd never had the chance to be born.

Riley was here.

And Joshua could be there for him.

He reached down, placing his hand on the baby's chest. His little body started, but he stopped crying.

Joshua didn't know the first thing about babies. He'd never had to learn. He'd never had the chance to hold his son. Never gone through a sleepless night because of crying.

He reached down, picking up the small boy from his crib, holding the baby close to his chest and supporting Riley's downy head.

There weren't very many situations in life that caused Joshua to doubt himself. Mostly because he took great care to ensure he was only ever in situations where he had the utmost control.

But holding this tiny creature in his arms made him feel at a loss. Made him feel like his strength might be a liability rather than an asset. Because at the moment, he felt like this little boy could be far too easily broken. Like he might crush the baby somehow.

Either with his hands or with his inadequacy.

Though, he supposed that was the good thing about babies. Right now, Riley didn't seem to need him to be perfect. He just needed Joshua to be there. Being there he could handle.

He made his way to the rocking chair in the corner and sat down, pressing Riley to his chest as he rocked back and forth.

"You might be hungry," Joshua said, keeping his voice soft. "I didn't ask."

Riley turned his head back and forth, leaving a small trail of drool behind on Joshua's skin. He had a feeling if his brother could see him now, he would mock him mercilessly. But then, he couldn't imagine Isaiah with a baby at all. Devlin, yes. But only since he had married Mia. She had changed Devlin completely. Made him more relaxed. Made him a better man.

Joshua thought of Danielle, sleeping soundly back in his room. Of just how insatiable he'd been for her earlier. Of how utterly trapped she was, and more or less at his mercy.

He had to wonder if there was any way she could make him a better man, all things considered.

Though, he supposed he'd kind of started to become a better man already. Since he had taken her on. And Riley.

He had to be the man who could take care of them, if he was so intent on fixing things.

Maybe they can fix you too.

Even though there was no one in the room but the baby, Joshua shook his head. That wasn't a fair thing to put on either of them.

"Joshua?"

He looked up and saw Danielle standing in the doorway. She was wearing one of his T-shirts, the hem falling to the top of her thighs. He couldn't see her expression in the darkened room.

"Over here."

"Are you holding Riley?" She moved deeper into the room and stopped in front of him, the moonlight streaming through the window shadowing one side of her face. With her long, dark hair hanging loose around her shoulders, and that silver light casting her in a glow, she looked ethereal. He wondered how he had ever thought she was pitiful. How he had ever imagined she wasn't beautiful.

"He was crying," he responded.

"I can take him."

He shook his head, for some reason reluctant to give him up. "That's okay."

A smile curved her lips. "Okay. I can make him a bottle."

He nodded, moving his hand up and down on the baby's back. "Okay."

Danielle rummaged around for a moment and then went across the room to the changing station, where he assumed she kept the bottle-making supplies. Warmers and filtered water and all of that. He didn't know much about it, only that he had arranged to have it all delivered to the house to make things easier for her.

She returned a moment later, bottle in hand. She tilted it upside down and tested it on the inside of her wrist. "It's all good. Do you want to give it to him?"

He nodded slowly and reached up. "Sure."

He shifted his hold on Riley, repositioning him in the crook of his arm so he could offer him the bottle.

"Do you have a lot of experience with babies?"

"None," he said.

"You could have fooled me. Although, I didn't really have any experience with babies until Riley was born. I didn't figure I would ever have experience with them."

"No?"

She shook her head. "No. I was never going to get married, Joshua. I knew all about men, you see. My mother got pregnant with me when she was fourteen. Needless to say, things didn't get off to the best start. I never knew my father. My upbringing was…unstable. My mother just wasn't ready to have a baby, and honestly, I don't know how she could have been. She didn't have a good home life, and she was so young. I think she wanted to keep me, wanted to do the right thing— it was just hard. She was always looking for something else. Looking for love."

"Not in the right places, I assume."

She bit her lip. "No. To say the least. She had a lot of boyfriends, and we lived with some of them. Sometimes that was better. Sometimes they were more established than us and had better homes. The older I got, the less like a mom my mom seemed. I started to really understand how young she was. When she would get her heart broken, I comforted her more like a friend than like a daughter. When she would go out and get drunk, I would put her to bed like I was the parent." Danielle took a deep breath. "I just didn't want that for myself. I didn't want to depend on anybody, or have anyone depend on me. I didn't want to pin my hopes on someone else. And I never saw a relationship that looked like anything else when I was growing up."

"But here you are," he said, his chest feeling tight. "And you're marrying me."

"I don't know if you can possibly understand what

this is like," she said, laughing, a kind of shaky nervous sound. "Having this idea of what your life will be and just…changing that. I was so certain about what I would have, and what I wouldn't have. I would never get married. I would never have children. I would never have…a beautiful house or a yard." Her words got thick, her throat sounding tight. "Then there was Riley. And then there was your ad. And then there was you. And suddenly everything I want is different, everything I expect is different. I actually hope for things. It's kind of a miracle."

He wanted to tell her that he wasn't a miracle. That whatever she expected from him, he was sure to disappoint her in some way. But what she was describing was too close to his own truth.

He had written off having a wife. He had written off having children. That was the whole part of being human he'd decided wasn't for him. And yet here he was, feeding a baby at three in the morning staring at a woman who had just come from his bed. A woman who was wearing his ring.

The way Joshua needed it, the way he wanted to cling to his new reality, to make sure that it was real and that it would last, shocked him with its ferocity.

A moment later, he heard a strange sucking sound and realized the bottle was empty.

"Am I supposed to burp him?"

Danielle laughed. "Yes. But I'll do that."

"I'm not helpless."

"He's probably going to spit up on your hot and sexy chest. Better to have him do it on your T-shirt." She reached out. "I got this."

She took Riley from him and he sat back and admired

the expert way she handled the little boy. She rocked him over her shoulder, patting his back lightly until he made a sound that most definitely suggested he had spit up on the T-shirt she was wearing.

Joshua had found her to be such a strange creature when he had first seen her. Brittle and pointed. Fragile.

But she was made of iron. He could see that now.

No one had been there to raise her, not really. And then she had stepped in to make sure that her half brother was taken care of. Had upended every plan she'd made for her life and decided to become a mother at twenty-two.

"What?" she asked, and he realized he had been sitting there staring at her.

"You're an amazing woman, Danielle Kelly. And if no one's ever told you that, it's about time someone did."

She was so bright, so beautiful, so fearless.

All this time she had been a burning flame no one had taken the time to look at. But she had come to him, answered his ad and started a wildfire in his life.

It didn't seem fair, the way the world saw each of them. He was a celebrated businessman, and she... Well, hadn't he chosen her because he knew his family would simply see her as a poor, unwed mother?

She was worth ten of him.

She blinked rapidly and wasn't quite able to stop a tear from tracking down her cheek. "Why...why do you think that?"

"Not very many people would have done what you did. Taking your brother. Not after everything your mother already put you through. Not after spending your whole life taking care of the one person who should have been taking care of you. And then you came here and answered my ad."

"Some people might argue that the last part was taking the easy way out."

"Right. Except that I could have been a serial killer."

"Or made me dress like a teddy bear," she said, keeping her tone completely serious. "I actually feel like that last one is more likely."

"Do you?"

"There are more furries than there are serial killers, thank God."

"I guess, lucky for you, I'm neither one." He wasn't sure he was the great hope she seemed to think he was. But right now, he wanted to be.

"Very lucky for me," she said. "Oh… Joshua, imagine if someone were both."

"I'd rather not."

She went to the changing table and quickly set about getting Riley a new diaper before placing him back in the crib. Then she straightened and hesitated. "I guess I could… I can just stay in here. Or…"

"Get the baby monitor," he said. "You're coming back to my bed."

She smiled, and she did just that.

The next day there were wedding dresses in Danielle's room. Not just a couple of wedding dresses. At least ten, all in her size.

She turned in a circle, looking at all of the garment bags with heavy white satin, beads and chiffon showing through.

Joshua walked into the room behind her, his arms

folded over his chest. She raised her eyebrows, gesturing wildly at the dresses. "What is this?"

"We are getting married in less than two weeks. You need a dress."

"A fancy dress to eat my Pop-Tart cake in," she said, moving to a joke because if she didn't she might cry. Because the man had ordered wedding dresses and brought them into the house.

And because if she were normal, she might have friends to share this occasion with her. Or her mother. Instead, she was standing in her bedroom, where her baby was napping, and her fiancé was the only potential spectator.

"You aren't supposed to see the dresses, though," she said.

"I promise you I cannot make any sense out of them based on how they look stuffed into those bags. I called the bridal store in town and described your figure and had her send dresses accordingly."

Her eyes flew wide, her mouth dropping open. "You described my figure?"

"To give her an idea of what would suit you."

"I'm going to need a play-by-play of this description. How did you describe my figure, Joshua? This is very important."

"Elfin," he said, surprising her because he didn't seem to be joking. And that was a downright fanciful description coming from him.

"Elfin?"

A smile tipped his lips upward. "Yes. You're like an elf. Or a nymph."

"Nympho, maybe. And I blame you for that."

He reached out then, hooking his arm around her

waist and drawing her toward him. "Danielle, I am serious."

She swallowed hard. "Okay," she said, because she didn't really know what else to say.

"You're beautiful."

Hearing him say that made her throat feel all dry and scratchy, made her eyes feel like they were burning. "You don't have to do that," she said.

"You think I'm lying? Why would I lie about that? Also, men can't fake this." He grabbed her hand and pressed it up against the front of his jeans, against the hardness there.

"You're asking me to believe your penis? Because penises are notoriously indiscriminate."

"You have a point. Plus, mine is pretty damn famously indiscriminate. By my own admission. But the one good thing about that is you can trust I know the difference between generalized lust and when a woman has reached down inside of me and grabbed hold of something I didn't even know was there. I told you, I like it easy. I told you… I don't deal with difficult situations or difficult people. That was my past failing. A huge failing, and I don't know if I'm ever going to forgive myself for it. But what we have here makes me feel like maybe I can make up for it."

There were a lot of nice words in there. A lot of beautiful sentiments tangled up in something that made her feel, well, kind of gross.

But he was looking at her with all that intensity, and there were wedding dresses hung up all around her, his ring glittering on her finger. And she just didn't want to examine the bad feelings. She was so tired of bad feelings.

Joshua—all of this—was like a fantasy. She wanted to live in the fantasy for as long as she could.

Was that wrong? After everything she had been through, she couldn't believe that it was.

"Well, get your penis out of here. The rest of you too. I'm going to try on dresses."

"I don't get to watch?"

"I grant you nothing about our relationship has been typical so far, but I would like to surprise you with my dress choice."

"That's fair. Why don't you let me take Riley for a while?"

"Janine is going to be here soon."

He shrugged. "I'll take him until then." He strode across the room and picked Riley up, and Riley flashed a small, gummy smile that might have been nothing more than a facial twitch but still made Danielle's heart do something fluttery and funny.

Joshua's confidence with Riley was increasing, and he made a massive effort to be proactive when it came to taking care of the baby.

Watching Joshua stand there with Riley banished any lingering gross feelings about being considered difficult, and when Joshua left the room and Danielle turned to face the array of gowns, she pushed every last one of her doubts to the side.

Maybe Joshua wasn't perfect. Maybe there were some issues. But all of this, with him, was a damn sight better than anything she'd had before.

And a girl like her couldn't afford to be too picky.

She took a deep breath and unzipped the first dress.

Chapter Ten

The day of the wedding was drawing closer and Danielle was drawing closer to a potential nervous breakdown. She was happy, in a way. When Joshua kissed her, when he took her to bed, when he spent the whole night holding her in his strong arms, everything felt great.

It was the in-between hours. The quiet moments she spent with herself, rocking Riley in that gray time before dawn. That was when she pulled those bad feelings out and began to examine them.

She had two days until the wedding, and her dress had been professionally altered to fit her—a glorious, heavy satin gown with a deep V in the back and buttons that ran down the full skirt—and if for no other reason than that, she couldn't back out.

The thought of backing out sent a burst of pain blooming through her chest. Unfurling, spreading, expanding. No. She didn't want to leave Joshua. No matter the strange, imbalanced feelings between them, she wanted to be with him. She felt almost desperate to be with him.

She looked over at him now, sitting in the driver's seat of what was still the nicest car she had ever touched, much less ridden in, as they pulled up to the front of his parents' house.

Sometimes looking at him hurt. And sometimes looking away from him hurt. Sometimes everything hurt. The need to be near him, the need for distance.

Maybe she really had lost her mind.

It took her a moment to realize she was still sitting motionless in the passenger seat, and Joshua had already put the car in Park and retrieved Riley from the back seat. He didn't bother to bring the car seat inside this time. Instead, he wrapped the baby in a blanket and cradled him in his arms.

Oh, that hurt her in a whole different way.

Joshua was sexy. All the time. There was no question about that. But the way he was with Riley... Well, she was surprised that any woman who walked by him when he was holding Riley didn't fall immediately at his feet.

She nearly did. Every damned time.

She followed him to the front door, looking down to focus on the way the gravel crunched beneath her boots—new boots courtesy of Joshua that didn't have holes in them, and didn't need three pairs of socks to keep her toes from turning into icicles—because otherwise she was going to get swallowed up by the nerves that were riding through her.

His mother had insisted on making a prewedding dinner for them, and this was Danielle's second chance to make a first impression. Now it was real and she felt an immense amount of pressure to be better than she was, rather than simply sliding into the lowest expectation people like his family had of someone like her, as she'd done before.

She looked over at him when she realized he was staring at her. "You're going to be fine," he said.

Then he bent down and kissed her. She closed her eyes, her breath rushing from her lungs as she gave herself over to his kiss.

That, of course, was when the front door opened.

"You're here!"

Nancy Grayson actually looked happy to see them both, and even happier that she had caught them making out on the front porch.

Danielle tucked a stray lock of hair behind her ear. "Thank you for doing this," she said, jarred by the change in her role, but desperate to do a good job.

"Of course," the older woman said. "Now, let me hold my grandbaby."

Those words made Danielle pause, made her freeze up. Made her want to cry. Actually, she *was* crying. Tears were rolling down her cheeks without even giving her a chance to hold them back.

Joshua's mother frowned. "What's wrong, honey?"

Danielle swallowed hard. "I didn't ever expect that he would have grandparents. That he would have a family." She took a deep breath. "I mean like this. It means a lot to me."

Nancy took Riley from Joshua's arms. But then she reached out and put her hand on Danielle's shoulder. "He's not the only one who has a family. You do too."

Throughout the evening Danielle was stunned by the warm acceptance of Joshua's entire family. By the way his sister-in-law, Mia, made an effort to get to know her, and by the complete absence of antagonism coming from his younger sister, Faith.

But what really surprised her was when Joshua's father came and sat next to her on the couch during dessert. Joshua was engaged in conversation with his brothers across the room while Mia, Faith and Joshua's mother were busy playing with Riley.

"I knew you would be good for him," Mr. Grayson said.

Danielle looked up at the older man. "A wife, you mean," she said, her voice soft. She didn't know why she had challenged his assertion, why she'd done anything but blandly agree. Except she knew she wasn't the woman he would have chosen for his son, and she didn't want him to pretend otherwise.

He shook his head. "I'm not talking about the ad. I know what he did. I know that he placed another ad looking for somebody he could use to get back at me. But the minute I met you, I knew you were exactly what he needed. Somebody unexpected. Somebody who would push him out of his comfort zone. It's real now, isn't it?"

It's real now.

Those words echoed inside of her. What did real mean? They were really getting married, but was their relationship real?

He didn't love her. He wanted to fix her. And somehow, through fixing her, he believed he would fix himself.

Maybe that wasn't any less real than what most people had. Maybe it was just more honest.

"Yes," she said, her voice a whisper. "It's real."

"I know that my meddling upset him. I'm not stupid.

And I know he felt like I wasn't listening to him. But he has been so lost in all that pain, and I knew… I knew he just needed to love somebody again. He thought everything I did, everything I said was because I don't understand a life that goes beyond what we have here." He gestured around the living room—small, cozy, essentially a stereotype of the happy, rural family. "But that's not it. Doesn't matter what a life looks like, a man needs love. And *that* man needs love more than most. He always was stubborn, difficult. Never could get him to talk about much of anything. He needs someone he can talk to. Someone who can see the good in him so he can start to see it too."

"Love," Danielle said softly, the word a revelation she had been trying to avoid.

That was why it hurt. When she looked at him. When she was with him. When she looked away from him. When he was gone.

That was the intense, building pressure inside her that felt almost too large for her body to contain.

It was every beautiful, hopeful feeling she'd had since meeting him.

She loved him.

And he didn't love her. That absence was the cause of the dark disquiet she'd felt sometimes. He wanted to use her as a substitute for his girlfriend, the one he thought he had failed.

"Every man needs love," Todd said. "Successful businessmen and humble farmers. Trust me. It's the thing that makes life run. The thing that keeps you going when crops don't grow and the weather doesn't cooperate. The thing that pulls you up from the dark pit when you can't find the light. I'm glad he found his light."

But he hadn't.

She had found hers.

For him, she was a Band-Aid he was trying to put over a wound that would end up being fatal if he didn't do something to treat it. If he didn't do something more than simply cover it up.

She took a deep breath. "I don't…"

"Are you ready to go home?"

Danielle looked up and saw Joshua standing in front of her. And those words…

Him asking if she wanted to go home, meaning to his house, with him, like that house belonged to her. Like he belonged to her…

Well, his question allowed her to erase all the doubts that had just washed through her. Allowed her to put herself back in the fantasy she'd been living in since she'd agreed to his proposal.

"Sure," she said, pushing herself up from the couch.

She watched as he said goodbye to his family, as he collected Riley and slung the diaper bag over his shoulder. Yes. She loved him.

She was an absolute and total lost cause for him. In love. Something she had thought she could never be.

The only problem was, she was in love alone.

It was his wedding day.

Thankfully, only his family would be in attendance. A small wedding in Copper Ridge's Baptist church, which was already decorated for Christmas and so saved everyone time and hassle.

Which was a good thing, since he had already harassed local baker Alison Donnelly to the point where she was ready to assault him with a spatula over his demands related to a Pop-Tart cake.

It was the one thing Danielle had said she wanted, and even if she had been joking, he wanted to make it happen for her.

He liked doing things for her. Whether it was teaching her how to ride horses, pleasuring her in the bedroom or fixing her nice meals, she always expressed a deep and sweet gratitude that transcended anything he had ever experienced before.

Her appreciation affected him. He couldn't pretend it didn't.

She affected him.

He walked into the empty church, looking up at the steeply pitched roof and the thick, curved beams of wood that ran the length of it, currently decked with actual boughs of holly.

Everything looked like it was set up and ready, all there was to do now was wait for the ceremony to start.

Suddenly, the doors that led to the fellowship hall opened wide and in burst Danielle. If he had thought she looked ethereal before, it was nothing compared to how she looked at this moment. Her dark hair was swept back in a loose bun, sprigs of baby's breath woven into it, some tendrils hanging around her face.

And the dress…

The bodice was fitted, showing off her slim figure, and the skirt billowed out around her, shimmering with each and every step. She was holding a bouquet of dark red roses, her lips painted a deep crimson to match.

"I didn't think I was supposed to see you until the wedding?" It was a stupid thing to say, but it was about the only thing he could think of.

"Yes. I know. I was here getting ready, and I was going to hide until everything started. Stay in the dressing room." She shook her head. "I need to talk to you, though. And I was already wearing this dress, and all of the layers of underwear that you have to wear underneath it to make it do this." She kicked her foot out, causing the skirt to flare.

"To make it do what?"

"You need a crinoline. Otherwise your skirt is like a wilted tulip. That's something I learned when the wedding store lady came this morning to help me get ready. But that's not what I wanted to talk to you about."

He wasn't sure if her clarification was a relief or not. He wasn't an expert on the subject of crinolines, but it seemed like an innocuous subject. Anything else that had drawn her out of hiding before the ceremony probably wasn't.

"Then talk."

She took a deep breath, wringing her hands around the stem of her bouquet. "Okay. I will talk. I'm going to. In just a second."

He shook his head. "Danielle Kelly, you stormed into my house with a baby and pretty much refused to leave until I agreed to give you what you wanted—don't act like you're afraid of me now."

"That was different. I wasn't afraid of losing you then." She looked up at him, her dark eyes liquid. "I'm afraid right now."

"You?" He couldn't imagine this brave, wonderfully strong woman being afraid of anything.

"I've never had anything that I wanted to keep. Or I guess, I never did before Riley. Once I had him, the thought of losing him was one of the things that scared me. It was the first time I'd ever felt anything like it. And now…it's the same with you. Do you know what you have in common with Riley?"

"The occasional tantrum?" His chest was tight. He knew that was the wrong thing to say, knew it was wrong to make light of the situation when she was so obviously serious and trembling.

"Fair enough," she said. Then she took a deep breath. "I love you. That's what you have in common with Riley. That's why I'm afraid of losing you. Because you matter. Because you more than matter. You're…everything."

Her words were like a sucker punch straight to the gut. "Danielle…"

He was such a jerk. Of course she thought she was in love with him. He was her first lover, the first man to ever give her an orgasm. He had offered her a place to live and he was promising a certain amount of financial security, the kind she'd never had before.

Of course such a vulnerable, lonely woman would confuse those feelings of gratitude with love.

She frowned. "Don't use that tone with me. I know you're about to act like you're the older and wiser of the two of us. You're about to explain why I don't understand what I'm talking about. Remember when you told me about your penis?"

He looked over his shoulder, then back at Danielle. "Okay, I'm not usually a prude, but we are in a church."

She let out an exasperated sound. "Sorry. But the thing is, remember when you told me that because you had been indiscriminate you knew the difference between common, garden-variety sex—"

"Danielle, Pastor John is around here somewhere."

She straightened her arms at her sides, the flowers

in her hand trembling with her unsuppressed irritation. "Who cares? This is our life. Anyway, what little I've read in the Bible was pretty honest about people. Everything I'm talking about—it's all part of being a person. I'm not embarrassed about any of it." She tilted her chin up, looking defiant. "My point is, I don't need you telling me what you think I feel. I have spent so much time alone, so much time without love, that I've had a lot of time to think about what it might feel like. About what it might mean."

He lowered his voice and took a step toward her. "Danielle, feeling cared for isn't the same as love. Pleasure isn't the same as love."

"I know that!" Her words echoed in the empty sanctuary. "Trust me. If I thought being taken care of was the same thing as love, I probably would have repeated my mother's pattern for my entire life. But I didn't. I waited. I waited until I found a man who was worth being an idiot over. Here I am in a wedding dress yelling at the man I'm supposed to marry in an hour, wanting him to understand that I love him. You can't be much more of an idiot than that, Joshua."

"It's okay if you love me," he said, even though it made his stomach feel tight. Even though it wasn't okay at all. "But I don't know what you expect me to do with that."

She stamped her foot, the sound ricocheting around them. "Love me back, dammit."

He felt like someone had grabbed hold of his heart and squeezed it hard. "Danielle, I can't do that. I can't. And honestly, it's better if you don't feel that way about me. I think we can have a partnership. I'm good with those. I'm good with making agreements, shaking hands, holding up my end of the deal. But feelings, all that stuff in between… I would tell you to call Shannon and ask her about that, but I don't think she has a phone right now, because I'm pretty sure she's homeless."

"You can't take the blame for that. You can't take the blame for her mistakes. I mean, I guess you can, you've been doing a great job of it for the past five years. And I get that. You lost a child. And then you lost your fiancée, the woman you loved. And you're holding on to that pain to try to insulate yourself from more."

He shook his head. "That's not it. It would be damned irresponsible of me not to pay attention to what I did to her. To what being with me can do to a woman." He cleared his throat. "She needed something that I couldn't give. I did love her—you're right. But it wasn't enough."

"You're wrong about that too," she said. "You loved her enough. But sometimes, Joshua, you can love somebody and love somebody, but unless they do something with that love it goes fallow. You can sow the seeds all you want, but if they don't water them, if they don't nurture them, you can't fix it for them."

"I didn't do enough," he said, tightening his jaw, hardening his heart.

"Maybe you were difficult. Maybe you did some wrong things. But at some point, she needed to reach out and tell you that. But she didn't. She shut down. Love can be everything, but it can't all be coming from one direction. The other person has to accept it. You can't love someone into being whole. They have to love themselves enough to want to be whole. And they have to love you enough to lay down their pain, to lay down their selfishness, and change—even when it's hard."

"I can't say she was selfish," he said, his voice rough. "I can't say she did anything wrong."

"What about my mother? God knows she had it hard, Joshua. I can't imagine having a baby at fourteen. It's hard enough having one at twenty-two. She has a lot of excuses. And they're valid. She went through hell, but the fact of the matter is she's choosing to go through it at this point. She has spent her whole life searching for the kind of love that either one of her children would have given her for nothing. I couldn't have loved her more. Riley is a baby, completely and totally dependent on whoever might take care of him. Could we have loved her more? Could we have made her stay?"

"That's different."

She stamped her foot again. "It is not!"

He didn't bother to yell at her about them being in a church again. "I understand that all of this is new to you," he said, fighting to keep his voice steady. "And honestly? It feels good, selfishly good, to know you see all this in me. It's tempting to lie to you, Danielle. But I can't do that. What I offered you is the beginning and end of what I have. Either you accept our partnership or you walk away."

She wouldn't.

She needed him too much. That was the part that made him a monster.

He knew he had all the power here, and he knew she would ultimately see things his way. She would have to.

And then what? Would she wither away living with him? Wanting something that he refused to give her?

The situation looked too familiar.

He tightened his jaw, steeling himself for her response.

What he didn't expect was to find a bouquet of flowers tossed at him. He caught them, and her petite shoulders lifted up, then lowered as she let out a shuddering breath. "I guess you're the next one to get married, then. Congratulations. You caught the flowers."

"Of course I damn well am," he said, tightening his fist around the roses, ignoring the thorn that bit into his palm. "Our wedding is in an hour."

Her eyes filled with tears, and she shook her head. Then she turned and ran out of the room, pausing only to kick her shoes off and leave them lying on the floor like she was Cinderella.

And he just stood there, holding on to the flowers, a trickle of blood from the thorn dripping down his wrist as he watched the first ray of light, the first bit of hope he'd had in years, disappear from his life.

Of course, her exit didn't stop him from standing at the altar and waiting. Didn't stop him from acting like the wedding would continue without a hitch.

He knew she hadn't gone far, mostly because Janine was still at the church with Riley, and while Danielle's actions were painful and mystifying at the moment, he knew her well enough to know she wasn't going to leave without Riley.

But the music began to play and no bride materialized.

There he was, a fool in a suit, waiting for a woman who wasn't going to come.

His family looked at each other, trading expressions filled with a mix of pity and anger. But it was his father who spoke up. "What in hell did you do, boy?"

A damned good question.

Unfortunately, he knew the answer to it.

"Why are you blaming him?" Faith asked, his younger sister defending him to the bitter end, even when he didn't deserve it.

"Because that girl loves him," his father said, his tone full of confidence, "and she wouldn't have left him standing there if he hadn't done something."

Pastor John raised his hands, the gesture clearly meant to placate. "If there are any doubts about a marriage, it's definitely best to stop and consider those doubts, as it is a union meant for life."

"And she was certain," Joshua's father said. "Which means he messed it up."

"When two people love each other…" The rest of Pastor John's words were swallowed up by Joshua's family, but those first six hit Joshua and pierced him right in the chest.

When two people love each other.

Two people. Loving each other.

Love going both ways. Giving and taking.

And he understood then. He really understood.

Why she couldn't submit to living in a relationship that she thought might be one-sided. Because she had already endured it once. Because she'd already lived it with her mother.

Danielle was willing to walk away from everything he'd offered her. From the house, from the money, from the security. Even from his family. Because for some reason his love meant that much to her.

That realization nearly brought him to his knees.

He had thought his love insufficient. Had thought it destructive. And as she had stood there, pleading with him to love her back, he had thought his love unimportant.

But to her, it was everything.

How dare he question her feelings for him? Love, to Danielle, was more than a ranch and good sex. And she had proved it, because she was clearly willing to sacrifice the ranch and the sex to have him return her love.

"It was my fault," he said, his voice sounding like a stranger's as it echoed through the room. "She said she loved me. And I told her I couldn't love her back."

"Well," Faith said, "not even I can defend you now."

His mother looked stricken, his father angry. His brothers seemed completely unsurprised.

"You do love her, though," his father said, his tone steady. "So why did you tell her you didn't?"

Of course, Joshua realized right then something else she'd been right about. He was afraid.

Afraid of wanting this life he really had always dreamed of but had written off because he messed up his first attempt so badly. Afraid because the first time had been so painful, had gone so horribly wrong.

"Because I'm a coward," he said. "But I'm not going to be one anymore."

He walked down off the stage and to the front pew, picking up the bouquet. "I'm going to go find her," he said. "I know she's not far, since Riley is here."

Suddenly, he knew exactly where she was.

"Do you have any other weddings today, Pastor?"

Pastor John shook his head. "No. This is the only thing I have on my schedule today. Not many people get married on a Thursday."

"Hopefully, if I don't mess this up, we'll need you."

Chapter Eleven

It was cold. And Danielle's bare feet were starting to ache. But there had been no way in hell she could run in those high heels. She would have broken her neck.

Of course, if she had broken her neck, she might have fully severed her spinal cord and then not been able to feel anything. A broken heart sadly didn't work that way. She felt everything. Pain, deep and unending. Pain that spread from her chest out to the tips of her fingers and toes.

She wiggled her toes. In fairness, they might just be frostbitten.

She knew she was being pathetic. Lying down on that Pendleton blanket in the loft. The place where Joshua had first made love to her. Hiding.

Facing everyone—facing Joshua again—was inevitable. She was going to have to get Riley. Pack up her things.

Figure out life without Joshua's money. Go back to working a cash register at a grocery store somewhere. Wrestling with childcare problems.

She expected terror to clutch her at the thought. Expected to feel deep sadness about her impending poverty. But those feelings didn't come.

She really didn't care about any of that.

Well, she probably would care once she was neck deep in it again, but right now all she cared about was that she wouldn't have Joshua.

If he had no money, if he was struggling just like her, she would have wanted to struggle right along with him.

But money or no money, struggle or no struggle, she needed him to love her. Otherwise…

She closed her eyes and took in a breath of sharp, cold air.

She had been bound and determined to ignore all of the little warnings she'd felt in her soul when she'd thought about their relationship. But in the end, she couldn't.

She knew far too well what it was like to pour love out and never get it back. And for a while it had been easy to pretend. That his support, and the sex, was the same as getting something back.

But they were temporary.

The kinds of things that would fade over the years.

If none of his choices were rooted in love, if none of it was founded in love, then what they had couldn't last.

She was saving herself hideous heartbreak down the road by stabbing herself in the chest now.

She snorted. Right now, she kind of wondered what the point was.

Pride?

"Screw pride," she croaked.

She heard the barn door open, heard footsteps down below, and she curled up into a ball, the crinoline under her dress scratching her legs. She buried her face in her arm, like a child. As if whoever had just walked into the barn wouldn't be able to see her as long as she couldn't see him.

Then she heard footsteps on the ladder rungs, the sound of calloused hands sliding over the metal. She knew who it was. Oh well. She had already embarrassed herself in front of him earlier. It was not like him seeing her sprawled in a tragic heap in a barn was any worse than her stamping her foot like a dramatic silent-film heroine.

"I thought I might find you here."

She didn't look up when she heard his voice. Instead, she curled into a tighter, even more resolute ball.

She felt him getting closer, which was ridiculous. She knew she couldn't actually feel the heat radiating from his body.

"I got you that Pop-Tart cake," he said. "I mean, I had Alison from Pie in the Sky make one. And I have to tell you, it looks disgusting. I mean, she did a great job, but I can't imagine that it's edible."

She uncurled as a sudden spout of rage flooded through her and she pushed herself into a sitting position. "Screw your Pop-Tart cake, Joshua."

"I thought we both liked Pop-Tarts."

"Yes. But I don't like lies. And your Pop-Tarts would taste like lies."

"Actually," he said slowly, "I think the Pop-Tart cake is closer to the truth than anything I said to you back in the church. You said a lot of things that were true. I'm a coward, Danielle. And guilt is a hell of a lot easier than grief."

"What the hell does that mean?" She drew her arm underneath her nose, wiping snot and tears away, tempted to ask him where his elfin princess was now. "Don't tease me. Don't talk in riddles. I'm ready to walk away from you if I need to, but I don't want to do it. So please, don't tempt me to hurt myself like that if you aren't…"

"I love you," he said, his voice rough. "And my saying so now isn't because I was afraid you were a gold digger and you proved you weren't by walking away. I realize what I'm about to say could be confused for that, but don't be confused. Because loving you has nothing to do with that. If you need my money… I've never blamed you for going after it. I've never blamed you for wanting to make your and Riley's lives easier. But the fact that you *were* willing to walk away from everything over three words… How can I pretend they aren't important? How can I pretend that I don't need your love when you demonstrated that you need my love more than financial security. More than sex. How can I doubt you and the strength of your feelings? How can I excuse my unwillingness to open myself up to you? My unwillingness to make myself bleed for you?"

He reached out, taking hold of her hands, down on his knees with her.

"You're going to get your suit dirty," she said inanely.

"Your dress is filthy," he returned.

She looked down at the dirt and smudges on the beautiful white satin. "Crap."

He took hold of her chin, tilting her face up to look at him. "I don't care. It doesn't matter. Because I would marry you in blue jeans, or I would marry you in this barn. I would sure as hell marry you in that dirty wedding dress. I… You are right about everything.

"It was easy to martyr myself over Shannon's pain. To blame myself so I didn't have to try again. So I didn't have to hurt again. Old pain is easier. The pain from that time in my life isn't gone, but it's dull. It throbs sometimes. It aches. When I look at Riley, he reminds me of my son, who never took a breath, and it hurts down deep. But I know that if I were to lose either of you now… That would be fresh pain. A fresh hell. And I have some idea of what that hell would be like because of what I've been through before.

"But it would be worse now. And… I was protecting myself from it. But now, I don't care about the pain, the fear. I want it all. I want you.

"I love you. Whatever might happen, whatever might come our way in the future… I love you. And I am going to do the hard yards for you, Danielle."

His expression was so fierce, his words so raw and real, all she could do was stare at him, listening as he said all the things she had never imagined she would hear.

"I was young and stupid the last time I tried love. Selfish. I made mistakes. I can't take credit for everything that went wrong. Some of it was fate. Some of it was her choices. But when things get hard this time, you have my word I won't pull away. I'm not going to let you shut me out. If you close the door on me, I'm going to kick it down. Because what we have is special. It's real. It's hope. And I will fight with everything I have to hold on to it."

She lurched forward, wrapping her arms around his neck, making them both fall backward. "I'll never shut you out." She squeezed her eyes closed, tears tracking down her cheeks. "Finding you has been the best thing that's ever happened to me. I don't feel alone, Joshua. Can you possibly understand what that means to me?"

He nodded gravely, kissing her lips. "I do understand," he said. "Because I've been alone in my own swamp for a long damned time. And you're the first person who made me feel like it was worth it to wade out."

"I love you," she said.

"I love you too. Do you still want to marry me?"

"Hell yeah."

"Good." He maneuvered them both so they were upright, taking her hand and leading her to the ladder. They climbed down, and she hopped from foot to foot on the cold cement floor. "Come on," he said, grabbing her hand and leading her through the open double doors.

She stopped when she saw that his whole family, Janine and Riley, and Pastor John were standing out there in the gravel.

Joshua's mother was holding the bouquet of roses, and she reached out, handing it back to Danielle. Then Joshua went to Janine and took Riley from her arms, holding the baby in the crook of his own. Then Joshua went back to Danielle, taking both of her hands with his free one.

"I look bedraggled," she said.

"You look perfect to me."

She smiled, gazing at everyone, at her new family. At this new life she was going to have.

And then she looked back at the man she loved with all her heart. "Well," she said, "okay, then. Marry me, cowboy."

Epilogue

December 5, 2017
FOUND A WIFE—

Local rancher Todd Grayson and his wife, Nancy, are pleased to announce the marriage of their son, a wealthy former bachelor, Joshua Grayson (no longer irritated with his father) to Danielle Kelly, formerly of Portland, now of Copper Ridge and the daughter of their hearts. Mr. Grayson knew his son would need a partner who was strong, determined and able to handle an extremely stubborn cuss, which she does beautifully. But best of all, she loves him with her whole heart, which is all his meddling parents ever wanted for him.

* * * * *

We hope you enjoyed reading

Enamored

by *New York Times* bestselling author

DIANA PALMER

and

Claim Me, Cowboy

by *New York Times* bestselling author

MAISEY YATES

Both were originally Harlequin® series stories!

From passionate, suspenseful and dramatic
love stories to inspirational or historical,
Harlequin offers different lines to
satisfy every romance reader.

New books in each line
are available every month.

BACHALO0319

*Unfairly labeled by his family's dark reputation,
brooding rancher Levi Tucker is done playing by the
rules. He demands a new mansion designed by famous
architect Faith Grayson, an innocent beauty he would
only corrupt...but he* must *have her.*

Read on for a sneak peek at
Need Me, Cowboy
by New York Times *bestselling author Maisey Yates!*

Faith had designed buildings that had changed skylines,
and she'd done homes for the rich and the famous.

Levi Tucker was something else. He was infamous.

The self-made millionaire who had spent the past five
years in prison and was now digging his way back...

He wanted her. And yeah, it interested her.

She let out a long, slow breath as she rounded the
final curve on the mountain driveway, the vacant lot
coming into view. But it wasn't the lot, or the scenery
surrounding it, that stood out in her vision first and
foremost. No, it was the man, with his hands shoved
into the pockets of his battered jeans, worn cowboy
boots on his feet. He had on a black T-shirt, in spite of
the morning chill, and a black cowboy hat was pressed
firmly on his head.

She had researched him, obviously. She knew what he looked like, but she supposed she hadn't had a sense of…the scale of him.

Strange, because she was usually pretty good at picking up on those kinds of things in photographs.

And yet, she had not been able to accurately form a picture of the man in her mind. And when she got out of the car, she was struck by the way he seemed to fill this vast, empty space.

That also didn't make any sense.

He was big. Over six feet and with broad shoulders, but he didn't fill this space. Not literally.

But she could feel his presence as soon as the cold air wrapped itself around her body upon exiting the car.

And when his ice-blue eyes connected with hers, she drew in a breath. She was certain he filled her lungs, too.

Because that air no longer felt cold. It felt hot. Impossibly so.

Because those blue eyes burned with something.

Rage. Anger.

Not at her—in fact, his expression seemed almost friendly.

But there was something simmering beneath the surface…and it had touched her already.

Don't miss what happens next!
Need Me, Cowboy
by New York Times *bestselling author Maisey Yates.*

Available April 2019 wherever
Harlequin® Desire books and ebooks are sold.

www.Harlequin.com

HARLEQUIN®
Desire

Family sagas...scandalous secrets...burning desires.

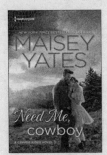

Save **$1.00**

on the purchase of ANY

Harlequin® Desire book.

Available wherever books are sold, including most bookstores, supermarkets, drugstores and discount stores.

Save $1.00

on the purchase of any Harlequin® Desire book.

Coupon valid until May 31, 2019.
Redeemable at participating outlets in the U.S. and Canada only.
Not redeemable at Barnes & Noble stores. Limit one coupon per customer.

52616352

5 65373 00076 2   (8100)0 12419

Love Harlequin romance?

DISCOVER.

Be the first to find out about promotions, news and exclusive content!

 Facebook.com/HarlequinBooks

 Twitter.com/HarlequinBooks

 Instagram.com/HarlequinBooks

 Pinterest.com/HarlequinBooks

ReaderService.com

EXPLORE.

Sign up for the Harlequin e-newsletter and download a free book from any series at **TryHarlequin.com.**

CONNECT.

Join our Harlequin community to share your thoughts and connect with other romance readers!
Facebook.com/groups/HarlequinConnection

HARLEQUIN®

ROMANCE WHEN YOU NEED IT

HSOCIAL2018

Reward the book lover in you!

Earn points on your purchase of new Harlequin books from participating retailers.

Turn your points into **FREE BOOKS** of your choice!

Join for FREE today at
www.HarlequinMyRewards.com.

Harlequin My Rewards is a free program (no fees) without any commitments or obligations.

MYR18